IMPRESSIONS OF AFRICA

IMPRESSIONS OF AFRICA

Raymond Roussel

In a new translation from the French
and with an introduction by
MARK POLIZZOTTI

Dalkey Archive Press
Champaign - Dublin - London

Originally published as *Impressions d'Afrique* by Alphonse Lemerre, Paris, in 1910
Republished in 1963 by Jean-Jacques Pauvert, Paris
Translation and introduction copyright © 2011 by Mark Polizzotti

Library of Congress Cataloging-in-Publication Data

Roussel, Raymond, 1877-1933.
[Impressions d'Afrique. English]
Impressions of Africa / Raymond Roussel ; translated [from the French] and with an introduction by Mark Polizzotti.
p. cm.
ISBN 978-1-56478-624-1 (pbk. : alk. paper)
1. Shipwreck victims--Fiction. 2. Captivity--Fiction. 3. Africa--Fiction. 4. Experimental
fiction. I. Polizzotti, Mark. II. Title.
PQ2635.O961681513 2011
843'.912--dc22
2011012937

Partially funded by a grant from the Illinois Arts Council, a state agency,
and by the University of Illinois at Urbana-Champaign

Cet ouvrage, publié dans le cadre du programme d'aide à la publication, bénéficie du soutien
du Ministère des Affaires Etrangères et du Service Culturel de l'Ambassade de France
représenté aux Etats-Unis.

This work, published as part of a program of aid for publication, received support from the
French Ministry of Foreign Affairs and the Cultural Services of the French Embassy in the
United States.

www.dalkeyarchive.com

Cover illustration: Trevor Winkfield, *Voyager IV*. Acrylic on linen, 45 ½ x 61 inches, 1997.
Courtesy Tibor de Nagy Gallery, New York. Book design by Mark Polizzotti.

INTRODUCTION:
A CHILD'S GARDEN OF ECCENTRICITIES

KNOWN — TO SOME — AS the Houdini of French literature, Raymond Roussel might also be its Peter Pan. The consummate verbal prestidigitator (André Breton dubbed him "the greatest mesmerizer of modern times") carried in his bag of tricks enough material for at least ten times his actual output, and devised the sort of technological novelties that invite comparison both with his idol Jules Verne and with another of the twentieth century's underrated oddballs, Nikola Tesla. In terms of compositional mechanics, his celebrated *procédé* (method), though its full implications remain largely unexplored, has resurfaced in the writings of the Surrealists, the New Novelists, the Oulipo, and the New York School. But in many ways, Roussel was also the boy who never grew up. In page after page, the reader of his novels finds himself seated before a seemingly endless spectacle, staged, it would appear, for Roussel's benefit alone. And as with many children of privilege—which Roussel was in spades— any discomfort or damage suffered by the performer takes a distant backseat to the demanding tot's enjoyment.

On the surface, in fact, *Impressions of Africa*, with its titular whiff of exoticism and H. Rider Haggard derring-do, would seem to appeal largely to an adolescent's sense of thrill. On the Ides of March, somewhere at the dawn of the twentieth century, European passengers bound for Argentina survive a shipwreck and wash up on the shores of a fictive African nation. There they are taken captive by the vainglorious local potentate and held for several months, until sufficient ransom can arrive from Europe. So far we have the makings of a relatively standard adventure tale set in a far-off latitude where curious things can, and often do, occur. But these are no ordinary passengers, and this is no pastiche of *King Solomon's Mines* (though Roussel, a fan of popular fiction, might well have read the book, judging by the similarity of the sovereign names Twala and Talou). In place of the intrepid Allan Quatermain, Roussel introduces a singularly gifted collection of castaways, ranging from circus freaks to inventors to scholars to theatrical prodigies, each, as luck would have it, a nonpareil in his or her specialty.

Indeed, very quickly the ostensible plot of African exile falls away, yielding to the author's real interest: a series of minutely described performances given by these castaways, as part of a gala they have devised to while away the time until deliverance. Theater—or, more precisely, theatrical effect, the sense of marvel produced by magical and well-disguised artifice—proves the most formidable protagonist of *Impressions of Africa*, and the novel's various characters merely its instruments. The human plight of these characters, the suspense surrounding their release from captivity, ultimately takes on far less importance than the question of whether their performance will come off without a hitch—and even that suspense is muted, for the true motor here is not *whether* the gimmick will work, but rather *that* it works and *how* it works. One can easily imagine Roussel, an avid theatergoer in real life, gaping with juvenile glee at the kaleidoscopic succession of wonders he has devised for his own amusement, each one following the last in a seamless and flawless procession, forming a world that is itself (as one critic put it) "a theater in which people go to the theater."

The matter of performance is no idle conceit. Obsessed with fame, Roussel spent his adult life haunted by the alluring, and ultimately elusive, specter of public adulation. He described for his doctor, the renowned psychiatrist Pierre Janet, the sensation of glorious bliss he had experienced at the age of nineteen while writing his first long poem, *La Doublure*:

> I was the equal of Dante and of Shakespeare, I was feeling what Victor Hugo had felt when he was seventy, what Napoleon had felt in 1811 and what Tannhäuser had felt whilee musing on

Venusberg: I experienced *la gloire* . . . Whatever I wrote was surrounded by rays of light; I used to close the curtains, for I was afraid that the shining rays emanating from my pen might escape into the outside world through even the smallest chink; I wanted suddenly to throw back the screen and light up the world. To leave these papers lying about would have sent out rays of light as far as China, and the desperate crowd would have flung themselves upon my house.

Needless to say, when *La Doublure* was finally published—at the author's expense, as its minute descriptions made it virtually unsalable, even for poetry—it occasioned no such desperate flings, and Roussel sank into a depression from which he never fully recovered. "Its lack of success shattered me," he wrote years later. "I felt as though I had plummeted to earth from the prodigious summits of glory."

He nonetheless continued to write, in an unceasing bid for public acclaim. First he composed several more, equally hermetic, epics in verse; then, deciding that fiction was a surer road to bestsellerdom, the two novels that form his literary apex, *Impressions of Africa* (published—again at his expense, as ultimately were all his works—in 1910) and *Locus Solus* (1914). Finding the response to these books still rather lukewarm, Roussel set his sights on the theater as a more reliable audience magnet. He hired playwrights to adapt his two novels for the stage, financing the productions with dogged persistence, spendthrift profligacy, and the obliviousness to ridicule of a Florence Foster Jenkins; but his preference for long, abstruse monologues over discernible action put the shows beyond the pale of audience tolerance, and they fizzled after only a few performances. Undaunted, Roussel then turned to composing original stage works, starting with *The Star on the Forehead* (1925)—its title a transparent metaphor for genius that figures in several of his writings, *Impressions of Africa* among them—followed by *The Dust of Suns* in 1927. Like their predecessors, both were costly flops.

Roussel saw one last work into print in his lifetime, the book-length poem *New Impressions of Africa* (1932)—a work so demanding, with its myriad extended similes, lengthy footnotes, and multiple layers of embedded parenthetical clauses, that not even its author can have expected much success for it. After this, as Roussel's biographer Mark Ford notes, he "started to experiment with other possible means of recovering the euphoria of *la gloire*," including alcohol and barbiturates. He also traveled in grand style, despite the vast depletion of his fortune largely due to his hefty self-publication bills.

In June 1933 Roussel and Charlotte Dufrène, his confidante, traveling companion, and "beard," checked into the Grande Albergo e delle Palme in Palermo, where he spent most of the day either cloistered in his rooms or being chauffeured randomly about the city; evenings were devoted to drug-induced transports. He suffered a first overdose two weeks after arriving, recovered, then was found in his bathroom two weeks after that, having clumsily opened his veins with a straight razor. From this too he recuperated, but soon after he tried unsuccessfully to bribe both Dufrène and the hotel valet into killing him. Finally, on the evening of July 13, he swallowed a handful of barbiturates and went to bed, while the sky outside his hotel window exploded in an ecstasy of fireworks and people flooded the streets—the combined results of a local festival and Mussolinian pomp that, as Mark Ford wrote, might well "have reminded him of the flames, the noise, and the turbulent crowds" of his dreams of glory.

Roussel died that night still seeking the "solace" of "a little posthumous recognition." In the decades following, his work was embraced by successive generations of French and American avant-gardists, and he attained, if not the household-name status he so envied in the likes of Verne and Victor Hugo, at least a solid reputation as one of the twentieth century's most original and influential littérateurs—a "writer's writer," to use the kiss-of-death phrase. Authors ranging from Edmond Rostand to André Gide, Alain Robbe-Grillet to John Ashbery, Italo Calvino to Georges Perec, Michel Foucault to Michel Leiris have dipped into the source he revealed; Dalí and Giacometti took visual cues from his works, while Duchamp acknowledged that *Impressions of Africa* "was fundamentally responsible" for the *Large Glass.* Yet, as Robbe-Grillet and others have pointed out, there remains an inexhaustible core of mystery in Roussel's work, an opaqueness within its own transparency, that holds us at a spectator's safe distance even as it keeps our gazes riveted, our minds constantly working at a puzzle we can barely conceive.

The Africa of these *Impressions* is not, to be sure, the Africa of geopolitical fact, but neither is it entirely a product of Roussel's fancy. The late nineteenth and early twentieth centuries witnessed an acceleration of European colonialist expansion throughout the Dark Continent, and reports in the press and travelers' tales, alongside the lurid imagery of popular adventure novels, helped foster the widespread Western notion of Africa as that alien place where weird practices, unspeakable horrors, and unheard-of flora and fauna lurked at every bend in the jungle path. The backdrop of Roussel's Ponukele in fact contains many of the by-then-standard attributes available in most basic accounts from his day, including many cribbed from his beloved Verne; as with the boulevard plays he adored, there is a stagy, conventional quality to the descriptions and sentiments that betrays the author's literary, rather than first-hand, experiences of the setting—and of life.

For all that, he manages to avoid many of his day's most prevalent stereotypes about race. And while *Impressions* does contain such markers of casual bigotry as frequent use of the word "Negro" (which I've retained, as true to the time and spirit in which the novel was written), or a certain bemusement at the Africans' demonstration of such "white" attributes as scientific curiosity, not to mention the requisite cannibals and human sacrifices, by and large both Ponukeleans and Europeans stand as fully fleshed characters, replete with the basic human virtues and failings—including a peculiarly Rousselian gung-ho adventurousness and willingness to oblige even the most extreme demands. As the original manuscripts tell us, this was both intentional and laboriously achieved: over various revisions, Roussel progressively smoothed out what was initially a much coarser and caricatured portrayal into something approaching a kind of verisimilitude. (In Louise Montalescot, moreover, he creates a much more independent, capable, and admirable female character than could be found in most "realist" fiction of the time.)

Roussel famously boasted that, although he had "traveled a great deal" (he listed "India, Australia, New Zealand, the Pacific archipelagos, China, Japan and America . . . Europe, Egypt and all of North Africa . . . Constantinople, Asia Minor, and Persia"), he "never took anything for [his] books" from these experiences. Rather than seeking to broaden the mind or discover new horizons, he often chose his destinations for their literary appeal: a trip to Tahiti, for instance, was determined by his admiration for the popular novelist Pierre Loti, who had set one of his best-known books there, while Baghdad was for him "the country of 1001 nights and Ali-Baba, which reminds me of [the operetta composer] Lecocq." The writer Michel Leiris, whose father was Roussel's financial adviser, later posited that "the outside world never broke through into the universe [Roussel] carried within him . . . In all the countries he visited, he saw only what he had put there in advance, elements which corresponded absolutely with that universe that was peculiar to him." Though he had visited Egypt in 1906, and even kept a diary ("Went to see the Valley of the Kings—Cold lunch—sun—heat"), there is no indication that any of his observations, such as they were, found their way into the book he would soon undertake: like Phileas Fogg, he had little interest in the surrounding countryside or populations. Later in life he took to voyaging in a specially built caravan (*roulotte*), a kind of proto-RV with only a few curtained windows behind which Roussel wrote in peace while the foreign landscapes paraded by unheeded; photos of the vehicle suggest nothing so much as a huge hearse.

Pierre Janet, in his 1926 study *De l'angoisse à l'extase*, which contains detailed notes on his sessions with Roussel (alias "Martial"), noted his patient's "very interesting conception of literary beauty. The work must contain nothing real, no observations on the world or the mind, nothing but completely imaginary combinations." Reading *Impressions of Africa*, one sees how far the author has drifted from the trade routes of reality in his descriptions of such "native" phenomena as moles that secrete an irresistible adhesive drool, or underwater sponges that spin like pinwheels under duress, or a giant zither-playing earthworm, or huge plants that (unlike their author) absorb and then project rigorously faithful images of their surroundings. Not to mention sci-fi inventions like a mechanical orchestra that runs on hot and cold fluids, grapes that contain entire miniature tableaux within their flesh, or metals so magnetic they could pull something halfway around the world. (As with any such inventions, what was once far-fetched eventually becomes commonplace: the automated loom to which Roussel lovingly devotes pages of explanation has been industry standard for some time; Louise Montalescot's "great experiment" sounds remarkably like the modern laser printer; and the battery-operated portable fan that Bex invents for young Fogar can now be bought for pocket change at the local hardware store. One wonders what Roussel would have made of such contemporary gewgaws as the iPad and streaming video.)

But the true originality of *Impressions of Africa*, as of most of Roussel's major works, lies not in its attempts to out-Verne Verne, but in an invention that its author kept scrupulously hidden from sight. For in virtually every case, the episodes, conceits, and details from which Roussel fashions his characters and their actions were determined not by authorial whimsy but by a highly regulated process in which language itself is the sole motor and guide. The genesis of *Impressions of Africa* lies in a short story written some ten years before, "Among the Blacks," in which the opening and closing sentences are virtually identical. Only one letter has changed in the passage from first to last, but on that small variant hangs the entire tale. As Roussel explained it:

> I chose two almost identical words . . . For example, *billard* [billiard table] and *pillard* [plunderer]. To these I added similar words capable of two different meanings, thus obtaining two almost identical phrases . . .
>
> 1. *Les lettres du blanc sur les bandes du vieux billard* . . . [The white letters on the cushions of the old billiard table]
>
> 2. *Les lettres du blanc sur les bandes du vieux pillard* . . . [The white man's letters on the hordes of the old plunderer]
>
> In the first, "lettres" was taken in the sense of lettering, "blanc" in the sense of a cube of chalk, and "bandes" as in cushions.
>
> In the second, "lettres" was taken in the sense of missives, "blanc" as in white man, and "bandes" as in hordes.
>
> The two phrases found, it was a case of writing a story which could begin with the first and end with the latter.

In *Impressions of Africa*, the game expands to include not merely one altered sentence but a vast proliferation, in which moment after moment hinges on similarly complex puns. The examples are too numerous to detail here, but to lift the curtain on just a few:

The Luenn'chetuz, the ritual dance performed by Talou's wives that results in copious belching, was generated by a dual interpretation of the phrase *théorie à renvois*: both a treatise with annotations (*renvois*)—in this case, Talou's proclamation of his own sovereignty—and a procession (*théorie*) involving burps (*renvois*).

Revers à marguerite (lapel with a daisy in the buttonhole) becomes *revers* (military defeat) *à Marguerite* (the French name for Gretchen in Goethe's *Faust*), hence the rival king Yaour's downfall while wearing Gretchen's dress.

Toupie à coup de fouet (a spinning top set in motion by a yank of the string) leads to the episode in which the old frump (*toupie*) Olga Chervonenkov is paralyzed by a muscle spasm (*coup de fouet*) while attempting a pirouette.

The talking horse Romulus, a true platinum standard (*étalon à platine*) among equines, is also an *étalon* (stallion) *à platine* (with a tongue, in slang).

Maison à espagnolettes (house with window latches) yields the *maison* (as in dynasty) of the descendants of Suann, founded when the patriarch simultaneously married the two *Espagnolettes*, or young Spanish twins. (*Deux amours de Suann?* Given the frequent comparisons made between Roussel and Proust and the two men's acquaintanceship, we can only wonder.)

None of this was apparent to the book's few French readers, any more than it would be to their English counterparts today. Roussel the master magician kept his tricks well concealed, and only stepped out from behind the curtain to tip his sleight of hand in a posthumously published manual-cum-apologia pro vita sua titled *How I Wrote Certain of My Books*. With a mix of unvarnished literary altruism ("It seems to me that it is my duty to reveal this method, since I have the feeling that future writers may perhaps be able to exploit it fruitfully"), his lifelong hunger for recognition, and an almost infantile inability to withhold a really good secret, Roussel trots out example after example of his derivations like an unusually clingy merchant intent on hawking his wares.

At the same time, the process by which Roussel gave away his creative method mirrors the dual movement already encoded in *Impressions of Africa*: first the magic, then the revelation of its workings. At the novel's halfway point, the author loops back to zero and starts his tale all over again, this time providing the missing back stories and justifications for the many curiosities we've just witnessed. Some editions even included an insert suggesting that "those who are not initiated into the art of Raymond Roussel" might wish to read the second half first. This would of course be to miss the point, for the first rule of magic is to keep your audience tantalized: dazzle before denouement.

The novelist Harry Mathews once remarked that Roussel's language taught him how "writing could provide me with the means of so radically outwitting myself that I could bring my hidden experiences, my unadmitted self into view." Hiding, concealment, non-admission are sewn into the fabric of *Impressions of Africa*—not just the behind-the-curtain mechanics of Roussel's compositional generator, but likely something deeper as well: an incursion, despite himself, of the author's personal reality into the "complete illusion of reality" he sought to achieve. It's no secret today that Roussel's proclivities ran to younger working-class males, but during his lifetime—and for decades afterward—it was cause for scandal and blackmail, and a source of mortification to his socially prominent family. We should therefore not be surprised at the role that secrecy and subterfuge play in the various plotlines of *Impressions of Africa*, nor, perhaps, in the fact that no adult sexual relationship in the book ends happily, and that they often have the dispassionate hue of a business transaction.

Indeed, virtually the only true love to be found here is that involving children—either the kind of substitute parent-child bond enjoyed by Velbar and Sirdah or, more often, between young quasi-siblings like Seil-kor and Nina or Meisdehl and Kalj. The painter and writer Trevor Winkfield notes that Roussel's own love for his sister "was one of the most formative influences of his life," and in that love seems to lie not only the kernel of the many idyllic brother-sister relationships in his work but an unhealed wound of nostalgia for the lost paradise of childhood itself. "Of my childhood I have preserved a delightful memory," he confided in *How I Wrote*. "I can claim to have known at that time many years of perfect bliss." So much so that he later said he'd felt no happiness since then, and that the memory of that former happiness was a source of torment. Just as

Seil-kor after Nina's untimely death rejects the places they had loved together, so, according to Leiris, Roussel refused to set foot in "certain towns which evoked particularly happy memories of his childhood ... for fear of spoiling his memories."

Instead, a spirit both childlike and childish infuses *Impressions of Africa*: marvelously, when it manifests as a constant openness to wonder, an ability to blur the lines of reality and fantasy without a grown-up's sense of restraint; naïvely, in its conception of a benign world in which the heroes all aim to please (I am constantly amazed at how eagerly characters accede to the most outrageous requests "without having to be asked twice"), and in which the cardinal threat is boredom; selfishly, when it treats the actors in the grand gala as mere instruments of juvenile pleasure, taking it for granted that each performance will run smoothly and that nothing will break the spell; horrifyingly, when it indulges in the kind of pull-off-the-wings cruelty evidenced in the tortures and gruesome deaths of the four convicts, a dark blood-spatter on the immaculate waves of Roussel's shifting, dazzling, treacherous, absorbing, blinding, engulfing African sands.

Every translation has its peculiar difficulties, and *Impressions of Africa*, with its special "method," might seem more arduous than most. John Ashbery once noted that even though Roussel's generative wordplay is buried well below the surface, its "presence imparts an undefinable, hypnotic quality to the text," to which he felt no translation could do justice; whether I've managed to convey at least a measure of this quality I leave to the reader's judgment. A further challenge lay in the compactness of the prose. Roussel prided himself on concision—"I forced myself to write each story with as few words as possible," he told Leiris—and much of my effort has gone into fashioning similarly compressed English. In other respects, the pitfalls of rendering this book proved not unlike those offered by any literary text: how to capture the author's signature style, in this case a peculiar mix of fluidity and flatness, invention and banality? how to preserve his turn-of-the-century phrasings and attitudes in a language that will speak to contemporary readers?

Then there are the author's various idiosyncrasies and lapses, such as his frequent use of the word "certain" (a veritable tic), some continuity issues (captions that appear both above and below the image; prison bars that change from thick to narrow), and plot points that beg herculean suspensions of disbelief (did Louise and her brother really lug that sack of machine parts across half a continent? would the cannibals have let the captured Velbar keep his rifle? would his watercolor sketches still be so pristine after eighteen years in the jungle?—and how fortunate that he thought to bring along his art supplies while fleeing for his life!). Chalk it up to the quirks of genius.

Readers wishing further insights into Roussel's life, work, and creative method are encouraged to explore Mark Ford's illuminating study, *Raymond Roussel and the Republic of Dreams* (2000), from which I've borrowed a number of biographical pointers. In the domain of English-language commentary, John Ashbery's essays "Reestablishing Raymond Roussel" (1962) and "In Darkest Language" (1967) remain the gold standard some fifty years after the fact, though they have since been seconded by essential writings from Harry Mathews and Trevor Winkfield. And of course, Roussel's own *How I Wrote Certain of My Books* (trans. Winkfield) is a must. The present translation of *Impressions of Africa* is based on the 2005 Flammarion edition, edited and annotated by Tiphaine Samoyault, which also provided some source material for this introduction. To all of the above, my gratitude.

—MP, December 2010

IMPRESSIONS OF AFRICA

I

At around four p.m. that June 25th, everything seemed ready for the coronation of Talou VII, Emperor of Ponukele and King of Drelchkaff.

Though the sun had passed its zenith, the heat remained stifling in that region of equatorial Africa, and we all sweltered in the sultry atmosphere that no breeze came to relieve.

Before me stretched vast Trophy Square, located in the very heart of Ejur, the imposing capital formed by countless huts and lapped by the Atlantic Ocean, whose distant roar I could hear to my left.

The perfect quadrangle of the esplanade was bordered on each side by a row of venerable sycamores. From spears planted deep into the bark of each trunk dangled severed heads, banners, and ornaments of every kind, which Talou VII or his ancestors had amassed there upon returning from many a victorious campaign.

To my right, before the midpoint of the row of trees, a red stage stood like a giant puppet theater; its pediment bore the words "The Incomparables Club" in silver letters forming three lines, around which broad golden strokes radiated like sun's rays.

On the visible stage, a table and chair appeared to be set for a lecturer. Several unframed portraits were pinned to the backdrop, underscored by an explanatory label that read "The Electors of Brandenburg."

Closer to me, in line with the red theater, rose a large wooden pedestal on which Nair, a young Negro of barely twenty, was standing doubled over, absorbed in an engrossing task. To his right, two stakes, each planted at a corner of the pedestal, were joined at their uppermost tips by a long, supple thread that sagged under the weight of three objects hanging in a row, displayed like fairground prizes. The first item was none other than a bowler hat, the black crown of which bore the word "PINCHED" written in dirty white capitals; then came a dark gray suede glove turned palm outward and decorated with a "C" lightly traced in chalk; and last hung a light sheet of parchment covered in obscure hieroglyphs, its header boasting a rather crude sketch of five caricatures made plainly ridiculous by their poses and exaggerated features.

Imprisoned on his pedestal, Nair's right foot was *collared* by a noose of thick rope firmly anchored to the solid platform; like a living statue, he performed a series of slow, regular movements while rapidly murmuring a string of words he'd committed to memory. In front of him, placed on a specially shaped stand, a fragile pyramid fashioned from three joined pieces of bark captured his full attention; the base, turned toward him and slightly raised, served as his weaving loom. Within reach, on an annex to the base, was a supply of fruit husks covered on the outside by a grayish vegetal substance much like the cocoon of a larva about to transform into a chrysalis. By pinching a fragment of these delicate envelopes with two fingers and slowly pulling back his hand, the youth created a flexible bond, reminiscent of the gossamer threads that stretch across the woods in springtime. These imperceptible strands helped him weave a subtle and complex embroidery, for his two hands worked with unparalleled agility, crossing, knotting, intermingling the fairylike ligatures into graceful patterns. The phrases he tonelessly recited served to regulate his perilous and precise maneuvers, for the smallest slip could have caused the whole structure irreparable damage. If not for the aid of a certain formula memorized word for word, Nair could never have reached his goal.

Lower down, to the right, other toppled pyramids at the edge of the pedestal—their tips facing away from the viewer—allowed one to appreciate the effect of these labors, once completed; each upright base was indicated by almost nonexistent tissue, more ephemeral than a spider's web. In each, a red flower held by its stem irresistibly drew the viewer's gaze through the imperceptible veil of the ethereal weave.

Not far from the Incomparables' stage, to the actor's right, two stakes set four to five feet apart supported a moving apparatus. A long pivot extended from the nearer of the two, around which a scroll of yellowed parchment was compressed into a thick roll; solidly nailed to the farther stake, a square board laid as a platform served as base for a vertical cylinder slowly made to revolve by clockwork.

The yellowish scroll, unspooling tautly over the entire length of the intervening gap, wrapped around the cylinder, which, turning on its axis, ceaselessly pulled it toward the other side, gradually depleting the pivot that was forced to spin along with it.

The parchment showed groups of savage warriors, rendered in broad strokes, parading by in highly varied poses. One cohort seemed to be in mad pursuit of the fleeing foe; another, crouching behind an embankment, awaited its moment to burst forth; here, two equally matched phalanxes engaged in fierce hand-to-hand combat; there, fresh troops surged bravely forward with grand gestures toward a distant melee. The continual procession offered endless surprises, owing to the infinite number of effects obtained.

Opposite, at the far end of the esplanade, rose a kind of altar preceded by several steps covered with a thick carpet. From a distance, a coat of white paint veined with bluish lines gave the whole the appearance of marble.

On the Communion table, represented by a long board placed halfway up the structure and covered with a cloth, one could see a rectangle of parchment dotted with hieroglyphics standing near a heavy cruet full of oil. Next to this, a large sheet of stiff luxurious paper bore the title, "Reigning House of Ponukele-Drelchkaff," written scrupulously in Gothic letters. Beneath this heading, a round portrait, a kind of delicately colored miniature, depicted two young Spanish girls aged thirteen or fourteen, coiffed in the national mantilla—twin sisters, judging by their perfect resemblance. At first glance, the image seemed part and parcel of the document; but upon closer inspection, one noticed a wide band of transparent muslin, glued onto both the circumference of the painted disk and the surface of the durable vellum, that melded the two objects seamlessly, though they were in fact separate. To the left of the dual effigy, the name "SUANN" paraded in large capitals; beneath it, a genealogical chart comprising two distinct branches, descended from the two lovely Iberians who formed the apex, occupied the rest of the sheet. One of these lineages ended with the word "Extinction," in letters almost as large as the title, clearly meant to catch the eye; by contrast, the other, stretching a bit lower than its neighbor, seemed to defy the future with the absence of any concluding sign.

Near the altar, to the right, a giant palm tree flourished, its admirable breadth attesting to its great age; a handwritten sign affixed to the trunk offered this commemorative phrase: "Restoration of the Emperor Talou IV to the throne of his forefathers." Off to one side and sheltered by the palms, a stake planted in the ground supported a soft-boiled egg on the square ledge of its upper tip.

To the left, at an equal distance from the altar, a tall plant, but old and pitiful, made a sorry complement to the resplendent palm; this was a rubber tree, its sap run dry and in a state of near rot. A litter of branches placed in its shade supported the recumbent corpse of the Negro king Yaour IX, classically costumed as Gretchen from *Faust* in a pink woolen dress with alms purse and thick blonde wig, its long yellow plaits, thrown over his shoulders, reaching almost to his legs.

*
* *

To my left, backed against the row of sycamores and facing the red theater, a stone-colored edifice looked like a miniature version of the Paris Stock Exchange.

Between this structure and the northwest corner of the esplanade stood a row of life-size statues.

The first showed a man mortally wounded by a spear plunged into his breast. Instinctively, his two hands clutched at the shaft; his body arched back on the verge of collapse as his legs buckled under the weight. The statue was black and at first appeared to be all of a piece; but gradually one's eye discovered a multitude of furrows running in all directions, forming clusters of parallel striations. In reality, the work was composed entirely of numerous whalebone corset stays cut and molded as the contours dictated. Flathead nails, their tips evidently bent beneath the surface, jointed these supple strips together so artfully that not the slightest gap remained between them. The face, its nose, lips, eyebrows, and eye sockets faithfully reproduced by minutely arranged little sections, bore a finely rendered expression of pain and anguish. The shaft of the weapon buried in the dying man's heart suggested some great difficulty overcome, thanks to the elegant handle that showed two or three stays cut into small rings. The muscular body, clenched arms, and nervous, crooked legs all seemed to tremble or suffer, due to the striking, flawless curves imposed on the invariable dark-colored strips.

The statue's feet rested on a simple vehicle, its low platform and four wheels composed of other black, ingeniously combined whalebone stays. Two narrow rails, made from some raw, reddish, gelatinous substance, which was none other than calves' lungs, ran along a dark wooden surface and, by their form if not their color, created the precise illusion of a section of railroad track. It was onto these tracks that the four immobile wheels fit, without crushing them.

The surface supporting the tracks formed the top of a jet black wooden plinth, the front of which bore a white inscription with these words: "The Death of the Helot Saridakis." Below it, also in milky letters, one saw this phrase, half-Greek and half-French, accompanied by a slim bracket:

$$\text{DUAL} \left\{ \begin{array}{l} \text{ἡστον.} \\ \text{ἡστην.} \end{array} \right.$$

Next to the helot, the bust of a thinker with knit brow wore an expression of intense and fruitful meditation. On the stand one could read the name:

IMMANUEL KANT

After this came a group of sculptures depicting a thrilling scene. A cavalry officer with the face of a thug seemed to be interrogating a nun flattened against the door of her convent. Behind them, in bas-relief, other men-at-arms mounted on fierce steeds awaited orders from their chief. On the base, in chiseled letters, the title *The Nun Perpetua's Lie* was followed by the question, "Is this where the fugitives are hiding?"

Farther on, a curious recreation, accompanied by the explanatory caption, "The Regent Bowing before Louis XV," showed Philippe d'Orléans paying his respects to the ten-year-old child king, who maintained a pose full of natural, unconscious majesty.

Unlike the helot, the bust and these two complex groupings were made of what looked like terracotta.

Calm and vigilant, Norbert Montalescot strolled among his works, watching especially over the helot, whose fragility made a careless jostle from some passerby a matter of special concern.

Past the final statue stood a small cabin with no doors, its four walls, of equal width, made of heavy black cloth that in all likelihood left the interior completely dark. The gently sloped roof was strangely composed of book pages, yellowed by time and trimmed into tiles; the text, fairly large and exclusively in English, was faded or completely erased, but the visible headers of certain pages still bore the clearly printed title *The Fair Maid of Perth*. The middle of the roof contained a hermetically sealed skylight, made not of glass but of similar pages, also discolored by wear and age. This delicate tiling no doubt filtered a diffuse, yellowish light, soft and restful.

A kind of chord, suggesting the timbre of brass instruments but much fainter, escaped at regular intervals from inside the cabin, like musical breaths.

*
* *

Just opposite Nair, a tombstone, in perfect alignment with the Stock Exchange, supported various elements of a Zouave's uniform. A rifle and cartridge pouches lay alongside these military effects, which to all appearances served as a pious memento of the departed.

Rising vertically behind the funerary slab, a panel draped in black fabric offered a series of twelve watercolors, arranged in threes over four even, symmetrically stacked rows. Given the similarity of the characters depicted, the suite of paintings seemed to relate some continuous dramatic narrative. Above each image one could read, like a title, several words traced with a brush.

On the first sheet, a noncommissioned officer and a flamboyantly attired blonde were camped in the back of a luxuriously appointed victoria; the words "Flora and Lieutenant Lécurou" summarily designated the couple.

Then came "The Performance of *Daedalus*," represented by a wide stage on which a figure in a Greek toga appeared to be singing lustily; in the front row of a box, one again found the lieutenant sitting beside Flora, who was training her opera glasses on the performer.

In "The Consultation," an old crone wearing an ample sleeve-less cloak drew Flora's attention to a celestial planisphere pinned to the wall, and leveled an authoritative finger at the constellation Cancer.

"The Secret Correspondence," inaugurating a second row of images, showed the woman in the cloak offering Flora one of those special *grilles* composed of a single sheet of cardboard with strange holes punched out, which are used in deciphering cryptograms.

"The Signal" took as its décor a nearly empty sidewalk café, at the front of which a tanned Zouave, sitting alone, indicated to the waiter a large bell tolling atop a neighboring church; below it, one could read this brief dialogue: "Waiter, what is that ringing?" "That's the Benediction." "In that case, bring me a *harlequin.*"

"The Lieutenant's Jealousy" showed a barracks courtyard in which Lécurou, raising four fingers of his right hand, seemed to be furiously upbraiding the Zouave from the preceding image; the scene was accompanied by this blunt phrase in military slang: "Four days in the cooler!"

At the head of the third row, "The *Bravo*'s Rebellion" introduced into the plot a very blond Zouave who, refusing to execute one of Lécurou's orders, answered with the single word "No!" inscribed under the watercolor.

"The Convict's Execution," underscored by the command "Aim!" depicted a firing squad that, at the lieutenant's orders, trained its rifles at the heart of the golden-haired Zouave.

In "The Usurious Loan," the crone in the cloak reappeared to hand Flora several banknotes; sitting at a desk, the latter seemed to be signing some kind of IOU.

The final row commenced with "The Police Raid the Gambling Den." This time, one saw a wide balcony and Flora hurling herself into the void, while through the open window, around a large gaming table, gamblers recoiled in horror at the unexpected arrival of several black-suited men.

The penultimate tableau, titled "The Morgue," showed a frontal view of a woman's corpse lying on a slab behind a pane of glass; plainly visible in the background, a silver chain sagged beneath the weight of a precious watch.

Finally, "The Fatal Blow" ended the series with a nocturnal landscape; in the half-light, one made out the tanned Zouave slapping Lieutenant Lécurou, while in the distance, standing out against a thicket of ship's masts, a placard lit by a bright lantern bore the three words, "Port of Bougie."

At my back, a dark rectangular structure of meager dimensions stood as a complement to the altar, a light grill with narrow bars of black-painted wood forming its façade. Four native detainees, two men and two women, paced quietly inside this exiguous prison. Above the grill, red letters spelled the word "Jail."

Next to me, the sizable group of passengers from the *Lynceus* stood waiting for the promised parade to begin.

II

Soon the shuffle of footsteps could be heard. All eyes turned to the left, and from the southwest corner of the esplanade we saw a strange and solemn cortege advancing.

At its head, the emperor's thirty-six sons, sorted by height into six rows, composed a dark phalanx ranging in age from three to fifteen. Fogar, the eldest, bringing up the rear with the taller boys, carried in his arms a huge wooden cube, transformed into a gaming die by a heavy coat of white paint dotted with circular black pips. At a sign from Rao, the native in charge of the parade's progress, the troop of children slowly moved forward along the edge of the esplanade occupied by the Stock Exchange.

After them, in a seductive single file, came the sovereign's ten wives, graceful Ponukeleans endowed with beauty and charm.

Finally, Emperor Talou VII himself appeared, curiously attired as a torch singer, his long blue gown with its plunging neckline dragging behind him in a long train, on which the number 472 stood out in black figures. His dark face, imbued with savage energy, was not lacking in character, and formed a sharp contrast with his luxuriant and scrupulously waved blond wig. With his hand he guided his daughter Sirdah, a slim child of eighteen, whose crossed eyes were veiled by opaque leucoma, and whose black forehead bore a red birthmark shaped like a minuscule corset from which yellow lines radiated.

Behind them marched the Ponukelean troops, superb ebony-hued warriors heavily armed beneath their ornamental finery of feathers and amulets.

The cortege slowly followed the same path as the group of children.

Passing in front of the Zouave's sepulcher, Sirdah, who had likely been counting her steps, suddenly veered off toward the tombstone, on which her lips gently placed a long kiss full of unadulterated tenderness. This pious duty fulfilled, the blind girl affectionately took her father's hand again.

As they reached the far end of the esplanade, the emperor's sons, under Rao's direction, turned right and skirted the north side of the vast quadrilateral; reaching the opposite corner, they turned a second time and headed back toward us, while the parade, still replenished at its source by numerous troops, precisely followed in their tracks.

Finally, the last of the black warriors having entered just as the advance guard of children touched the southernmost limit, Rao ordered the approach to the altar cleared, and all the newcomers crowded in orderly fashion along the two lateral areas, faces turned toward the center of the square.

On all sides, a black horde, comprising the population of Ejur, had assembled behind the sycamores to witness this tantalizing spectacle for themselves.

Still grouped into six rows, the emperor's sons reached the middle of the esplanade and halted opposite the altar.

Rao took the monstrous die from Fogar's arms, juggling it several times and then tossing it in the air with all his might. The twenty-inch cube spun as it rose, a black-speckled white mass; then, describing a very tight arc, it fell to earth and rolled on the ground before coming to rest. At a glance, Rao read the number two on the upper face and, walking toward the docile phalanx, pointed to the second row, which alone remained in place. The rest of the group, picking up the die, ran off to join the throng of warriors.

With majestic cadence, Talou marched to join the chosen ones whom fate had designated as his pages. Then, amid a profound silence, the emperor approached the altar, escorted by the six privileged children who each kept a firm hold on the train of his gown.

After climbing the few steps leading to the sparsely laid table, Talou bid Rao approach; the latter held in both hands a heavy sacramental cloak, presenting it inside out. Stooping, the emperor fit his head and arms into three openings cut in the middle of the garment; its large folds, as they fell, enveloped him to his feet.

Thus attired, the monarch turned proudly toward the assembly as if to offer his new costume to everyone's gaze.

The rich, silken fabric depicted a large map of Africa, with indications of the principal lakes, rivers, and mountains.

The pale yellow of landmasses sliced through the variegated blue of the sea, which stretched on all sides as far as required by the garment's overall shape.

Fine silver streaks covered the surface of the oceans with curved, harmonious zigzags, schematically representating the endless undulation of waves.

Only the southern half of the continent was visible between the emperor's neck and ankles.

On the western side, a black dot, accompanied by the name "Ejur," was situated near the mouth of a river whose source emerged from a mountain range a fair distance to the east.

Stretching from both banks of the wide waterway, a huge red area depicted the realm of the all-powerful Talou.

To flatter the emperor, the garment's designer had pushed back the limits—ill-defined as they were—of the imposing territory under Talou's scepter; dazzling carmine, heavily distributed to the north and east, stretched south all the way to land's end, across which the words "Cape of Good Hope" paraded in fat black letters.

After a while, Talou turned once more toward the altar; on his back, the other half of his robe showed the northern part of Africa, hanging upside-down in the same watery frame.

The solemn moment was upon us.

In a powerful voice, the monarch began intoning the native text traced in hieroglyphs on the sheet of parchment in the middle of the narrow table.

It was a kind of bull, through which Talou, already Emperor of Ponukele, now crowned himself King of Drelchkaff by virtue of his religious authority.

His proclamation over, the sovereign seized the cruet standing in for the Holy Ampulla and, turning his profile to us, poured oil over the tips of his fingers, with which he then anointed his brow.

He immediately replaced the flask and, descending the altar steps, strode briskly toward the litter of leaves shaded by the rubber tree. There, his foot resting on Yaour's corpse, he heaved a long sigh of joy, triumphantly raising his head as if to humiliate the late king's remains before one and all.

Returning after that prideful act, he handed the heavy cloak back to Rao, who promptly took it away.

Escorted by his six sons, who again carried his train, he walked slowly in our direction, then turned toward the Incomparables' theater, standing at the head of the crowd.

At that point, the emperor's wives advanced to the center of the esplanade. Rao joined them there, bearing a heavy tureen that he placed on the ground in their midst.

The ten young women fell upon the receptacle, which was full of a thick blackish porridge that they devoured greedily, lifting it to their lips with their hands.

After several minutes, Rao removed the now empty tureen, and the sated Negresses took their places for the *Luenn'chetuz*, a ritual dance, justly favored in that land, that was reserved for only the most solemn occasions.

They began with several slow gyrations mixed with supple and undulating movements.

Now and again they let escape from their gaping mouths formidable belches, which soon came faster and faster. Rather than trying to suppress these revolting noises, they did their best to expel them, trying to outdo each other in force and volume.

This widespread chorus, which accompanied the calm, graceful pavane like a musical score, revealed to us the peculiar properties of the unknown foodstuff they'd just ingested.

Little by little the dance became more frenetic and improvised, while their eructations, in a potent crescendo, grew increasingly frequent and intense.

There was an impressive moment of apogee, during which the sharp, deafening sound reached an infernal pandemonium; the feverish, disheveled dancers, shaken by their terrible burps as well as by their own fists, slammed into each other, pursued each other, gyrating in all directions as if in the grip of some vertiginous delirium.

Then, gradually, all grew calm, and after a long diminuendo the dance ended with the women grouped in a climactic display, underscored by a final chord that gradually faded to silence.

The young women, still wracked by some lingering hiccups, slowly resumed their original positions.

*
**

During the execution of the Luenn'chetuz, Rao had moved to the south side of the esplanade to open the prison, releasing a group of natives composed of one woman and two men.

Now only one detainee still paced behind the heavy bars.

Clearing a passage through us, Rao led the three newcomers to the spot the dancers had just trampled, their hands bound in front of them.

An anxious silence fell over the entire assembly, in anticipation of the tortures the fettered trio was about to endure.

Rao drew from his belt a mighty axe, its finely honed blade made of a strange wood that was hard as steel.

Several slaves had joined him to assist with the execution.

Held fast, the traitor Gaiz-duh was made to kneel, head bowed, while the two other convicts stood motionless.

With both hands Rao swung his axe and three times struck the traitor in the nape of the neck. With the third stroke Gaiz-duh's head rolled on the ground.

The area had remained unsoiled by red spatter, owing to the strange, sharp wood that, as it penetrated the flesh, produced an immediate clotting effect, meanwhile soaking up the initial drops that had unavoidably been shed.

The severed portions of the head and trunk had the solid, scarlet appearance of butcher's cuts.

We couldn't help thinking of those mannequins, cleverly substituted for stage actors through a false bottom in a cabinet, that are cleanly sliced into sections previously painted in a bloody trompe-l'oeil. In this case, the corpse's authenticity made that compact redness, usually a result of an artist's craft, more impressive still.

The slaves carried off Gaiz-duh's remains, along with the lightly soiled axe.

They soon returned and placed before Rao a fiery brazier in which rested two long iron pokers with coarse wooden handles, their tips glowing red.

Mossem, the second condemned man, was pushed to his knees facing the altar, the soles of his feet plainly exposed and his toenails to the ground.

Rao took from the hands of a slave a certain parchment that he unrolled at length: it was the fraudulent certificate of Sirdah's death, which Mossem had once issued.

Holding an immense palm, a Negro continually fanned the bright, raging hearth.

Resting one knee on the ground behind the condemned man and holding the parchment in his left hand, Rao took from the brazier a burning poker whose tip he pressed into one of the heels offered to him.

The flesh crackled, and Mossem, firmly gripped by the serfs, writhed in pain.

Inexorably Rao pursued his task; it was the text of the parchment itself that he copied slavishly onto the counterfeiter's foot.

At times he replaced the poker in the hearth, grasping its twin that glowed as it emerged from the coals.

When the left heel was entirely covered in hieroglyphs, Rao continued the operation on the right foot, still alternating between the two reddened iron tips as they cooled.

Mossem, choking on his own muffled roars, made monstrous efforts to escape his torture.

When finally the mendacious document had been copied down to the last character, Rao stood up and ordered the slaves to release Mossem, who, seized by horrible convulsions, expired before our eyes, overcome by his prolonged agony.

The body was taken away, along with the parchment and the brazier.

Back at their post, the slaves took hold of Rul, an oddly attractive Ponukelean, the only remaining member of the ill-fated trio. The condemned woman, whose hair sported long golden pins arranged in a crown, wore a frayed red velvet corset above her loincloth; the corset bore a striking similarity to the curious marking on Sirdah's brow.

Kneeling in the same direction as Mossem, the proud Rul vainly attempted a desperate resistance.

Rao removed from her hair one of the golden pins, then applied its tip perpendicularly to the woman's back, choosing the circle of skin visible behind the first eyelet to the right on the red corset with its frayed, knotted laces; then, with slow, even pressure, he buried the sharp spike, which penetrated the skin to the hilt.

At the scream provoked by this horrendous injection, Sirdah, recognizing her mother's voice, threw herself at Talou's feet to beg his sovereign mercy.

Immediately, as if to receive an unexpected change of orders, Rao turned toward the emperor, who, with an inflexible motion of his hand, commanded him to proceed with the torture.

A second pin, pulled from the woman's black locks, was planted in the second eyelet, and one by one the entire row bristled with shining golden studs. Repeated on the left, the operation finally stripped her hair of its ornamentation and successively filled all the eyelets.

It had been a while since the wretched creature had stopped screaming; one of the sharp points, penetrating her heart, had caused her death.

The corpse, quickly taken up, disappeared like the two others.

Lifting the mute, anguished Sirdah to her feet, Talou walked to the statues aligned near the Stock Exchange. The warriors parted to clear the way for his passage and, promptly joined by our group, the emperor made a sign to Norbert; the latter, approaching the small cabin, called out his sister's name.

After a moment the skylight in the paper roof slowly opened and flapped back, pushed from within by the slender hand of Louise Montalescot; gradually appearing through the wide aperture, she seemed to be climbing the rungs of a ladder.

Halfway out, she stopped and turned to face us. She was quite beautiful in her officer's uniform, her long blonde curls flowing freely from beneath a tight policeman's kepi tilted over one ear.

Her cavalryman's blue dolman, molding a superb waist, was decorated on the right with shining gold shoulder braids; from these emanated the discreet music we'd been hearing through the walls of the hut. The sound was generated by the woman's own breathing, thanks to a surgically established connection between the lobes of her lungs and the looped braids that concealed flexible, sonorous tubing. The gilded tips hanging from the ends of her aiguillettes like gracefully elongated counterweights were hollow and contained vibrating strips. At each contraction of her lungs, a portion of her exhaled breath passed through the multiple conduits and, activating the strips, triggered a harmonious tone.

A trained magpie perched motionless on the alluring captive's left shoulder.

Just then, Louise spotted Yaour's body, still laid out in Gretchen's costume in the shade of the withered rubber tree. Violent emotion played over her features and, clasping a hand to her eyes, she wept nervously, her breast wracked by terrible sobs that accentuated and quickened the chords from her shoulder braids.

Talou, losing patience, barked several unintelligible words that snapped the unhappy young woman back to attention.

Swallowing her grief, she reached her right hand toward the magpie, whose two claws hopped readily onto her proffered index finger.

With an expansive gesture, Louise stretched out her arm as if to launch the bird, which took wing, then landed in the sand before the statue of the helot.

Two barely perceptible openings, more than a yard apart, pierced the visible façade of the black plinth almost at ground level.

The magpie approached the farther opening and jabbed in its beak, activating some inner spring.

At once, the railway platform began to tilt, slowly sinking into the plinth on the left while rising above ground level on the right.

Its equilibrium broken, the vehicle bearing the tragic effigy trundled slowly over the gelatinous tracks, which now lay on a fairly pronounced slope. The four wheels, made of black strips, were kept from derailing by an inner lip that extended slightly beyond the rims and held them fast to the rails.

Reaching the bottom of its short descent, the small wagon was abruptly halted by the edge of the plinth.

During the several seconds the journey required, the magpie had hopped over to the other opening, into which its beak energetically poked.

Following a second activation, the movement occurred in reverse. The vehicle, gradually lifted, then pulled to the right by its own weight, rolled motorless over the silent rails and butted against the opposite edge of the plinth, which now stood as an obstacle to the lowered platform.

This seesaw motion was repeated several times, with the magpie constantly flitting between one opening and the other. The helot's statue remained fixed to the vehicle as it rode back and forth, and the whole was so light that the tracks, despite their lack of substance, showed not the slightest trace of flattening or damage.

Talou watched in awe the success of the perilous experiment that he himself had conceived, without thinking it possible.

The magpie stopped its maneuvers of its own accord and with a few flutters of its wings reached the bust of Immanuel Kant; from the top of the stand, at left, jutted a small perch on which the bird alighted.

No sooner had it done this than the inside of the skull shone brightly, its exceedingly thin walls perfectly translucent above the brow line.

One could divine the presence of many reflecting mirrors facing in all directions, judging from the dazzling rays, representing flames of genius, that burst violently from the incandescent light source.

Often the magpie flew up, only to land back on its perch again, alternately extinguishing and relighting the top of the skull, which alone shone brilliantly while the face, ears, and neck remained in darkness.

With each landing, it was as if a transcendent idea were hatching in the thinker's suddenly illumined brain.

Abandoning the bust, the bird alit on the wide stand featuring the band of thugs; once again its prying beak, this time thrusting into a narrow vertical pipe, activated a certain delicate concealed mechanism.

To the question "Is this where the fugitives are hiding?" the nun blocking entrance to her convent answered a persistent "No," shaking her head from side to side after each forceful jab of the bird's beak, as if it was pecking for grain.

Finally, the magpie arrived at the platform, smooth as a floor, on which the two last statues stood; the spot the intelligent creature chose to land on featured a delicate rosette, which sunk half an inch under this slight extra weight.

At that instant, the regent bowed even more deeply to Louis XV, whom this obeisance left unmoved.

The bird, hopping in place, provoked several more ceremonial greetings, then fluttered back to its mistress's shoulder.

After one last, long glance at Yaour, Louise descended back into her cabin and slammed the skylight shut, as if impatient to resume some mysterious task.

III

THE FIRST PORTION of the ceremony had ended and the Incomparables' gala could now get underway.

But first, there would be one final opportunity for trading shares.

The black warriors moved farther aside to clear the approach to the Stock Exchange, around which the passengers from the *Lynceus* gathered.

Five stockbrokers, played by the associated bankers Hounsfield and Cerjat and their three clerks, sat at five tables set up beneath the building's colonnade, and within moments they were calling out the rhymed orders that the passengers feverishly placed with them.

The stocks were named after the Incomparables themselves, each represented by one hundred shares that rose or fell in value depending on predictions regarding the players and the outcome of the contest. All transactions were handled in cash, in French or local currency.

For a quarter of an hour the five middlemen ceaselessly shouted execrable lines of verse, which the traders, following the fluctuations of the stock quotes, improvised hastily and with copious amounts of padding.

Finally, Hounsfield and Cerjat signaled the close of business by getting up from the table and walking down the stairs, trailed by their three clerks; they joined, as did I, the players crowding back into their former places, their backs to the prison.

The dark warriors again lined up in their original order, though at Rao's command they avoided the immediate vicinity of the Stock Exchange to allow free passage.

*
* *

The gala performance began.

First the four Boucharessas brothers made their appearance, each wearing the same acrobatic costume, which consisted of a pink leotard and black velvet trunks.

The two eldest, Hector and Tommy, lithe and vigorous adolescents, each carried in a solid tambourine six dark-colored rubber balls. They walked in opposite directions and soon turned to face each other, stopping at two very distant points.

Suddenly, at a softly called signal, Hector, who was standing near our group, vigorously launched his six balls one by one from his tambourine.

Meanwhile, Tommy, standing at the foot of the altar, successively projected from the musical disk in his left hand all his rubber projectiles, which crossed paths with his brother's.

This first feat accomplished, each juggler began bouncing individual balls back to his opposite number, effecting a constant exchange that now continued without interruption. The tambourines vibrated in unison, and the twelve projectiles formed a kind of elongated arc in perpetual motion.

Thanks to the perfect synchronicity of their movements, combined with a marked physical resemblance, the two brothers (one of whom was left-handed) gave the illusion of a single person reflected in a mirror. For several minutes the tour de force went on with mathematical precision. Finally, at a new signal, each player caught half the projectiles in the hollow of his upturned tambourine, abruptly ending the to and fro.

Immediately, Marius Boucharessas, a bright-looking ten-year-old, ran forward while his two older brothers cleared the area.

The child carried in his arms, on his shoulders, and even on top of his head a collection of young cats, each wearing a red or green ribbon around its neck.

With the edge of his heel, he drew two lines in the sand about forty to sixty feet apart, parallel to the side occupied by the Stock Exchange. The cats, jumping spontaneously to the ground, posted themselves in two equal camps behind these conventional boundaries and lined up facing each other, all the green ribbons on one side and all the red on the other.

At a sign from Marius, the graceful felines began a frolicsome game of Prisoner's Base.

To *begin*, one of the *greens* ran up to the *red* camp and three times, with the tips of its barely unsheathed claws, tapped the paw that one of its adversaries extended; at the last tap it swiftly ran away, chased close behind by the *red*, which tried to catch it.

At that moment, another *green* ran after the pursuer, which, forced to turn back, was soon aided by one of its partners; the latter lit upon the second *green*, which was forced to flee in turn.

The same maneuver was repeated several times, until the moment when a *red*, managing to tag a *green* with its paw, let out a victorious meow.

The match halted, and the *green* prisoner, entering enemy territory, took three steps toward its camp, then stood stock still. The cat that had earned the honor of the capture went to the *greens'* camp and *began* anew, by sharply rapping three times on a tendered paw, freely offered.

At that point, the alternating pursuits resumed with gusto, culminating in the capture of a *red*, which obediently stopped dead before the enemy camp.

Fast-paced and captivating, the game went on without any infractions of the rules. The prisoners, in two symmetrical and lengthening rows, sometimes saw their number decrease when a player's skillful tag was able to deliver one of its teammates. Such alert run-

ners, if they reached the opposing camp unhindered, became un-
touchable during their stay over the line they'd crossed in glory.

Finally, the group of *green* prisoners grew so large that Marius
imperiously decreed the *red* team the victors.

The cats, without a moment's delay, went back to the child and
scampered up his body, taking the places they'd had on arrival.

As he walked away, Marius was replaced by Bob, the last of the
brothers, a ravishing blond boy of four with big blue eyes and long
curly hair.

With incomparable mastery and miraculously precocious talent,
the charming lad began a series of impressions accompanied by elo-
quent gestures. The sounds of a train picking up speed, the cries of
various domestic animals, the shriek of a blade against a whetstone,
the sudden pop of a champagne cork, the gurgling of poured liquid,
fanfares of a hunting bugle, a violin solo, and the plaintive notes of
a cello formed a staggering repertoire that could give whoever momentarily shut his eyes the illusion of total reality.

The prodigy took his leave to rejoin Marius, Hector, and Tommy.

Soon the four brothers moved aside to let through their sister
Stella, a charming adolescent of fourteen, who, dressed as *Fortune*,
appeared balancing on the crest of a narrow wheel that she kept in
constant motion beneath her feet.

Rolling smoothly, the girl began turning the narrow rim in every
direction, pushing off with the tips of her heels in an uninterrupted
series of small hops.

In her hand she held a large, deep, convoluted horn of plenty,
from which money made of light, shining paper poured forth like a
shower of golden coins and floated slowly to the ground, producing
no metallic echo.

The louis, double louis, and large hundred-franc disks formed a
sparkling train behind the lovely traveler, who, maintaining a smile

on her lips and her place on the wheel, performed miracles of equilibrium and speed.

As with certain magician's cones that endlessly disgorge an infinite variety of flowers, the reservoir of coins seemed inexhaustible.
Stella had only to shake it gently to sow its riches, a thick, uneven
bed soon partially crushed by the circumnavigations of the errant
wheel.

After many twists and turns, the girl vanished like a sprite, sowing her pseudo-metallic currency to the last.

*
* *

All eyes now turned to the marksman Balbet, who had just taken
from the Zouave's tomb the cartridge pouches, which he fastened
to his flanks, as well as the weapon that was none other than a very
old-fashioned Gras rifle.

Walking quickly to the right, the illustrious champion, the focus
of everyone's attention, stopped before our group and carefully selected his spot, peering toward the north of the square.

Opposite him at a great distance, beneath the commemorative
palm, stood the square stake topped by a soft-boiled egg.

Further on, the gathered natives craning their necks behind the
row of sycamores moved aside at a sign from Rao to clear a wide
berth.

Balbet loaded his rifle; then, shouldering it with precision, he
aimed carefully and fired.

The bullet, skimming the upper portion of the egg, removed
part of the white, leaving the yolk exposed.

Several projectiles fired in succession continued the process; little
by little the albumen envelope disappeared to reveal the inner core,
which remained intact.

Sometimes, between two reports, Hector Boucharessas ran up to
turn the egg, gradually baring every point of its surface to the shots.

One of the sycamores acted as a backstop to halt the bullets that penetrated its trunk, part of which had been planed flat to prevent ricocheting.

The twenty-four cartridges in Balbet's provision were just enough to complete the experiment.

When the last of the smoke had poured from the weapon's barrel, Hector took the egg in the palm of his hand to show it around.

Not a trace of white remained on the delicate inner membrane, which, though entirely uncovered, still enveloped the yolk without showing a single scratch.

Then, at Balbet's request, to show that no excess boiling had eased his task, Hector closed his fist on the yellow orb and let the liquid ooze between his fingers.

The builder La Billaudière-Maisonnial appeared on schedule, carting before him, like a knife-grinder, a strangely complicated crank device.

Halting in the middle of the square, he set the voluminous machine down in the axis of the altar; two wheels and two legs kept it in perfect balance.

The entire mechanism consisted of a kind of millstone activated by a pedal, which could set in motion a whole system of cogs, levers, rods, and springs forming an inextricable tangle of metal; from one side emerged a jointed arm ending in a hand armed with a dueling foil.

After replacing the Gras rifle and cartridge pouches on the Zouave's tomb, Balbet took from a narrow bench that formed part of the new apparatus a handsome fencing outfit comprising a mask, plastron, glove, and foil.

At once, La Billaudière-Maisonnial, facing us, sat on the now empty bench and, his body hidden from sight by the astounding mechanism rising before him, rested his foot on the long pedal that turned the millstone.

Balbet, protected by his mask, glove, and plastron, energetically traced a straight line in the ground with the tip of his foil. Then, his left sole leaning on the fixed stroke, he elegantly took his guard before the articulated arm that emerged from the left, plainly standing out against the white background of the altar.

The two swords crossed, and La Billaudière-Maisonnial, with a movement of his foot, set the millstone turning at a certain speed.

The mechanical arm, after several expert and rapid feints, suddenly straightened and landed a direct hit on Balbet, who despite his widely celebrated agility had not managed to parry this infallible and marvelous thrust.

The artificial elbow had bent back, but the millstone kept turning, and soon a new deceptive evasion, completely different from the first, was followed by an abrupt jab that struck Balbet full in the chest.

The assault continued, thrust following upon thrust. The quarte, the sixte, and the tierce, as well as the prime, the quinte, and the octave, mixing with "disengages," "doubles," and "cuts," formed innumerable, unknown, and complex hits, each ending in an unexpected and lightning-quick thrust that always found its mark.

His left foot glued to the line that prevented his escape, Balbet sought only to parry, attempting to ward off the opposing foil and divert it to the side before it could touch him. But the millstone-driven mechanism was so perfect, the unfamiliar thrusts contained such distracting ruses, that at the last second the fencer's defensive maneuvers were regularly outwitted.

Now and again, La Billaudière-Maisonnial, with several pulls and pushes of a long toothed rod, completely varied the arrangement of the wheels, thereby creating a new cycle of feints unknown even to himself.

This process, capable of engendering an infinite number of fortuitous results, was not unlike the light taps that one applies to the tube of a kaleidoscope, which give rise, visually, to crystal mosaics with eternally new color combinations.

Balbet finally conceded the contest and stripped off his protective gear, delighted by his defeat, which had afforded him the chance to appreciate a mechanical masterpiece.

Lifting two short handles attached behind the bench he had just abandoned, La Billaudière-Maisonnial slowly departed, wheeling away his astonishing pedal device with great effort.

*
* *

After his departure, a black boy of twelve suddenly rushed forward with a mischievous grin, capering as he went.

This was Rhejed, one of the emperor's young sons.

He held under his left arm a kind of red-furred rodent that swiveled its thin, pointed ears in every direction.

In his right hand, the boy carried a light door painted white, which seemed to have been taken from a small armoire.

Setting this thin partition on the ground, Rhejed gripped the visible handle of a crudely made stylus slid vertically into his red loincloth.

Without missing a beat, he killed the rodent with a swift jab of the narrow blade, which sank into the furry neck and remained planted there.

The child grabbed the hind paws of the still-warm cadaver and placed it above the door.

Soon a sticky drool began flowing from its gaping mouth.

This phenomenon seemed to have been anticipated by Rhejed, who after a moment turned the door over and held it at a slant slightly above the ground.

The viscous flow, running down this second side of the partition, soon formed a circular layer of a certain width.

Finally, once the animal source had run dry, Rhejed laid the rodent at the very center of the fresh pool. Then he lifted the door upright without worrying about the cadaver, which remained stuck in place, held fast by the strange glue.

With a crisp movement, Rhejed loosened his loincloth and glued its end to the first side of the door, which was less coated than the second.

The red cloth adhered easily to the slobbery varnish, which it covered completely.

The door, again laid flat, hid part of his long wrap, leaving visible only the glued rodent.

Rhejed, spinning on his axis to unravel his loincloth, took several steps away and froze in an expectant posture.

For some time a peculiar odor, emanating from the flowing drool, had spread with remarkable pungency over Trophy Square.

Without appearing the least surprised by the potency of these effluvia, Rhejed raised his eyes skyward as if awaiting the appearance of an invited guest.

Several minutes passed in silence.

Suddenly Rhejed let out a cry of triumph, pointing south to a huge bird of prey drifting high above and approaching rapidly.

To the child's intense joy, the shiny black-plumed fowl swooped down upon the door, planting two tall, thin claws next to the rodent.

Above the hooked beak, its two quivering, nostril-like openings seemed to be endowed with a powerful sense of smell.

The revelatory odor had no doubt spread all the way to the bird's lair, and, first enticed and then guided by its keen olfactory organ, it had unfalteringly located the prey offered up to its voracity.

At the first greedy jab of its beak into the cadaver, Rhejed emitted a piercing shriek, waving his arms in wide, fierce movements.

Thus startled, the bird, unfolding its giant wings, again took flight.

But its claws, caught in the tenacious glue, took the door as well, lifting it horizontally in the air and with it the red cloth fused to its lower side.

Rhejed in turn left the ground, swinging at the end of his loincloth, much of which was still wrapped around his hips.

Despite this burden, the robust raptor soared quickly, egged on by the boy's shouts, his peals of laughter betraying his wild jubilation.

At the moment of liftoff Talou had rushed toward his son, an expression of violent terror on his face.

Arriving too late, the unhappy father could only follow with horrified eyes the swaying body of the mischievous boy, who flew ever higher without any fear of danger.

A profound stupor petrified those present, who anxiously awaited the outcome of this terrible incident.

Rhejed's preparations, the way he'd ensured that the area around the inert rodent was heavily coated with glue, proved the premeditation behind this aerial excursion, of which no one had had an inkling.

Meanwhile, the huge raptor, whose wingtips alone showed beyond the door, rose ever higher toward the upper reaches.

Growing smaller by the second, Rhejed swung furiously at the end of his loincloth; this increased tenfold his chances for a lethal fall, already made so great by the tenuousness of the bond joining the door to the red cloth and the two hidden claws.

Finally, no doubt tired by this unusual ballast, the bird began gliding closer to earth.

The descent soon accelerated, and Talou, filled with hope, stretched out his arms as if to draw the child toward him.

The nearly exhausted raptor plunged earthward with terrifying speed.

A few yards from the ground, Rhejed, ripping his loincloth, fell gracefully to his feet, while the unburdened fowl fled toward the south, still hauling the door garnished with a scrap of red cloth.

Too relieved to think about the scolding he deserved, Talou had rushed to his son, whom he hugged lengthily and in transports of joy.

*
* *

When the emotion had died down, the chemist Bex made his entrance, pushing an immense glass cage set on top of a mahogany platform furnished with four identical low wheels.

The care lavished on the manufacture of the simple yet luxurious vehicle proved the value of its fragile cargo, which it fitted precisely.

The rolling mechanism was perfectly smooth, thanks to thick tires lining the silent wheels, whose fine metal spokes seemed newly plated.

From the back extended two elegantly curved copper handles, attached at their upper ends by a mahogany grip that Bex pushed with both hands.

The whole thing looked like a more elegant version of those robust carts that ferry trunks and packages over train station platforms.

Bex stopped in the middle of the square, leaving everyone time to examine the apparatus.

The glass cage enclosed an immense musical instrument comprising brass horns, strings, circular bows, mechanical keyboards of every kind, and an extensive percussion section.

Against the cage, at the front of the platform, a large space was reserved for two huge cylinders, one red and one white; these communicated with the atmosphere sealed inside the transparent walls through a metal tube.

The fragile stem of an exceedingly tall thermometer, on which each degree was divided into tenths, rose from the cage, into which only its narrow reservoir dipped, filled with a sparkling purple liquid. No mounting held the thin diaphanous tube, placed a few centimeters from the edge that the two cylinders lightly touched.

With all eyes fixed on the curious machine, Bex offered a series of precise, lucid, and informed explanations.

We learned that the instrument before us would soon function thanks to an electric motor hidden in its sides.

Also powered by electricity, the cylinders pursued their two contrary objectives: the red one contained an infinitely powerful heat source, while the white constantly produced an intense cold capable of liquefying any gas.

It happened that the various components of the automated orchestra were made of *bexium*, a new metal that Bex had chemically endowed with phenomenal thermal sensitivity. Indeed, the entire musical apparatus was intended solely to highlight, in the most striking way possible, the properties of the strange substance that the able inventor had discovered.

A block of bexium subjected to various temperatures changed volume in proportions that could be quantified from one to ten.

The apparatus's entire mechanism was based on this single fact.

At the top of each cylinder, a smoothly turning knob regulated the opening of an inner spigot that communicated via the metal conduit with the glass cage; Bex could thus change the temperature of the interior atmosphere at will. As a result of these constant disturbances, the fragments of bexium, powerfully depressing certain springs, alternately activated or deactivated a given keyboard or group of pistons, which were moved at the correct moment by ordinary notched disks.

Despite these fluctuations in temperature, the strings invariably remained in tune, thanks to a certain preparation Bex had created to render them especially stiff.

The crystal used for the cage walls was at once marvelously thin and impenetrably resistant, and consequently the sound was scarcely muffled by this delicate, vibrating obstacle.

His demonstration complete, Bex took his place in front of the vehicle, eyes fixed on the thermometric column and each hand poised respectively above the two cylinders.

Turning the red knob first, he blasted a strong current of heat into the cage, then abruptly stopped the air jet when he saw the violet liquid reach the desired marking after a rapid climb.

With a quick movement, as if repairing a venial oversight, he pressed on a mobile pedal, much like the running board of a carriage, that had been concealed between the two cylinders, and that, when extended, reached to the ground.

Leaning his sole on this footrest with its supple spring, he activated the electric motor buried within the instrument, certain elements of which then set into motion.

First a slow, tenderly plaintive cantilena rose, accompanied by calm, regular arpeggios.

A wheel, resembling a miniature millstone, scraped like an endless bow against a long, cleanly resonant string stretched taut above a soundboard. On this string, automatically activated hammers fell like virtuoso's fingers, then lifted slightly, producing every note in the scale without a single gap.

By modifying its speed, the wheel produced a whole gamut of tonalities, and the resulting timbre sounded exactly like a violin melody.

Standing next to one of the crystal walls was a harp, each of its strings held by a slender wooden hook that plucked it, then curved back to regain its initial position; the hooks were attached at right angles to the tops of movable stems, whose supple and delicate motions produced languorous arpeggios.

As the chemist had predicted, the transparent envelope barely muffled the vibrations, whose penetrating resonance spread with charm and vigor.

Not waiting for this song without words to finish, Bex stopped the motor by releasing the pedal. Then, turning the red knob, he raised the internal temperature still further, keeping an eye on the thermometer. After a few seconds, he closed the heat tap and again pressed the pedal beneath his foot.

Immediately, a second wheel-bow, fatter than the first and rubbing a thicker string, gave off mellow and seductive cello sounds. At the same time, a mechanical keyboard, its keys dipping by themselves, began playing a rich, difficult accompaniment with perilously rapid passages.

After this sampling of a double sonata, Bex performed a new maneuver, this time raising the purple liquid a mere tenth of a degree.

The pseudo-violin joined the piano and cello to give the adagio the nuance of a classical trio.

Soon an additional section, playing in similar fashion, transformed the slow, serious piece almost into a lively scherzo, while maintaining the same combination of instruments.

Mechanically activating his pedal, Bex then turned the white knob, which lowered the violet column to around the zero mark midway up the glass tube.

A bright fanfare obediently burst forth from a cluster of horns of varying circumference, crowded into a compact ensemble. The entire brass family was represented in this particular corner, from the weighty bass to the pert, strident cornet. Reaching different subdivisions in the portion of the thermometer located below the glass, the white knob, moved several times, successively provoked a military march, a cornet solo, a waltz, a polka, and blaring clarion calls.

Suddenly, opening the cold tap full throttle, Bex rapidly obtained a frigid temperature drop, whose effects could be felt by the nearest spectators through the diaphanous partitions. All eyes turned to a gramophone with a large horn, which emitted a rich and powerful baritone voice. A huge box, perforated with air holes and placed beneath the device, apparently contained a series of records that caused the membrane to vibrate phonographically by means of a special wire; imperceptible fluctuations, carefully regulated by the chemist in the hyperborean atmosphere, offered us a host of recitativos and romances, sung by male or female voices in a wide range of timbres and registers. As a secondary function, the harp and keyboard took turns accompanying the sometimes lighthearted, sometimes tragic melodies in the seemingly inexhaustible repertoire.

Wishing to underscore the astounding flexibility of his extraordinary metal, not a fragment of which could be seen, Bex spun the red knob and waited a few seconds.

In no time the glacier changed into a furnace, and the thermometer shot up to its highest point. A group of flutes and fifes immediately punctuated a rousing march over sharp, regular drumbeats. Here again, different oscillations in temperature produced unexpected results. Several fife solos, discreetly supported by the brass fanfare, were followed by a graceful duet, based on the echo principle, that presented each scale twice in a row, performed first by a flute and then by a fluid soprano emanating from the phonograph.

Swelling anew, the purple liquid rose to the top of the tube, which seemed ready to burst. Several people stood back, discomfited by the torrid heat from the nearby cage, in which three hunting horns, set near the harp, lustily blew a deafening call. Minuscule dips in temperature then provided a sampling of the primary cynegetic fanfares, the last of which was a spirited *hallali*.

Having run through the main workings of his orchestra, Bex offered to take requests, and activate again any of the groups of instruments we'd already heard.

One by one, each of us expressed a wish that the chemist instantly gratified, with nothing more than his knobs. Demonstrating a second time and in random order his many polyphonic combinations, he slightly altered the character of the works by coquettishly introducing imperceptible thermal differences.

For his finale, Bex reached a special group of temperature markings, traced in red on the tube. Now practically every one of the instrument's components worked in concert, executing a grand, majestic symphony into which joined a choir clearly nuanced by the gramophone. The percussion, composed of a bass drum with cymbals, the drum played earlier, and several additional bells of various pitches, enlivened the piece with its plain, steady rhythm. The orchestral repertoire was infinitely rich, as Bex presented a panoply of dances, medleys, overtures, and variations, finishing with a furious gallopade that strained the bass drum to full capacity. He then lifted the pedal and again took his place at the rear of the vehicle, pushing it before him like a child's wagon.

As he turned to leave, everyone began talking excitedly about bexium and the marvelous results obtained with this astounding metal, whose stupefying qualities the instrument had just demonstrated so conclusively.

Bex, who had briefly vanished behind the Stock Exchange, soon returned, holding upright in both hands what looked like a giant button stick,[1] three feet wide and twice as high, made of a dull gray metal that suggested tarnished silver.

A narrow longitudinal slit like a buttonhole opened in the middle of the giant slab, except that the circular opening which would allow the buttons through was placed midway up the slit and not at its end.

With a glance, the chemist, keeping his distance, made sure he had our attention; he then designated ten large buttons aligned vertically one against the other near the bottom of the slit, naming the substance from which each was composed.

The whole thing formed a shiny, multicolored line giving off the most varied reflections.

At the top, the first button, of smooth, tawny gold, offered a sparkling surface. Below it, the second, of pure silver, barely stood

---

1. A small, flat guard that fits over and behind the button of a uniform, allowing one to polish the button without soiling the fabric around it. – Trans.

out from the similarly colored background of the button stick. The third, made of copper, fourth, of platinum, fifth, of pewter, and sixth, of nickel, were all of the same size and without ornamentation. The next four were made of various precious stones, delicately attached; one was composed solely of diamonds, the other of rubies, the third of sapphires, and the last of gleaming emeralds.

Bex spun the board around to show us its other side.

At the bottom hung a piece of blue cloth to which all the buttons were sewn.

Ten very thin strips of gray metal, attached to the fabric, lay one above the other along the slit, and were of exactly the same width. They occupied, on this side of the board, the places corresponding to each button, whose diameter was equal to their height. Ten lengths of metal thread, also gray, which anchored the precious disks solidly to the board, formed at the very center of each narrow rectangular strip a jumble of criss-crosses ending in a fat knot formed by the expert fingers of some able seamstress.

Bex dug the slightly sharpened base of the button stick into the sand; planted vertically against the Stock Exchange, it showed the back side of the buttons to the Incomparables' stage.

After stepping out of sight for a moment, he reappeared carrying under each arm ten long and cumbersome cylinders, made of the same gray metal already amply on display on the button stick.

He crossed the length of the esplanade and set down his heavy load before the red theater.

Each cylinder, a tight metal cap over one end, looked like a kind of huge pencil fitted with an ordinary lead protector.

Bex, piling his entire stock on the ground, composed an ingeniously regular geometric figure.

Four of the monstrous pencils, lying side-by-side flat on the sand, provided the base of the structure. A second row, set over the first, comprised three pencils laid in the shallow trenches formed by the rounded shape of their predecessors. The next, narrower level counted two pencils, themselves topped by the tenth and last, placed alone at the summit of the heap with its triangular façade.

Bex had first secured the whole thing with two heavy stones drawn from his pockets.

It was by following a scrupulously determined order and selection that the chemist had stacked his cylinders, taking care to identify each with a special marking engraved somewhere on their circumference.

The metal caps all aimed their tips at the distant button stick, which acted as a target to the ten giant pencils that were trained on it like cannon barrels.

Before pursuing the experiment, Bex removed his cufflinks, shaped like four golden olives; then, taking from his pockets his watch, money clip, and keys, he handed the lot to Balbet, who promised to look after the glittering deposit.

Back at his post, leaning over the pile of cylinders, Bex firmly gripped a large ring fastened to the tip of the highest lead protector.

The chemist needed only the slight traction of a few steps backward to slip off the metal cap, which fell like a pendulum against his legs.

Now uncovered, the formerly invisible portion of the uppermost cylinder became the focus of our attention. The silvery barrel, indeed looking like an actual and perfectly sharpened pencil, ended in a cone, from which emerged a fat, smooth, and rounded amber-colored lead.

Bex, repeating this same maneuver, successively uncapped the ten cylinders, of which all now showed the same yellowish and diaphanous lead sticking out of their regularly narrowed extremity.

This process finished, the chemist again crossed the esplanade, carrying under his arms the ten sheaths, which he dropped near the button stick.

An explanation was in order, and Bex took the floor to reveal the point of these various exercises.

The amber-colored leads enclosed in the giant pencils were made of a highly complex substance, which Bex had prepared and baptized *magnetine*.

Despite accumulated obstacles, magnetine was attracted from a distance by a specific metal or precious stone.

Owing to certain differences in composition, the ten leads before our eyes corresponded, in terms of attraction, to the ten buttons solidly held in the slots of the button stick.

To make possible and practicable the manipulation of the recently invented magnetine, it had become indispensable to discover an insulating compound. After extensive research, Bex had obtained *stanchium*, a dull gray metal produced through laborious efforts.

A thin sheet of stanchium, blocking the emanations from the magnetine, completely nullified its power of attraction, which not even the densest materials could themselves manage to dampen.

The pencils and lead-protectors were all made of stanchium, as were the button stick and the ten rectangular strips rising in tiers alongside the slit. The thread used to sew the buttons to the sheet was composed of the same metal, softened and braided.

By successively guiding the now-hidden disks into the circular opening in the slit, Bex, pushing against the button stick, would provoke the sudden displacement of the cylinders, each of which would rush forcefully toward the object placed in the vicinity of its amber-colored lead.

This last revelation caused the crowd to recoil in panic.

Indeed, many injuries were to be feared from the pencils, which, drawn by our jewelry, watches, coins, keys, or gold teeth, might suddenly come flying right at us.

The visible extremity of each lead, in short, eluded the protective power of the stanchium and fully justified these healthy apprehensions.

In a calm voice, Bex hastened to reassure his audience. To trigger the phenomenon of irresistible magnetism, a substance had to cause a strong reaction in the amber lead, which ran the entire length of each cylinder. The metals or precious stones placed in the axis of the bizarre stack were the only ones capable of such an effect. The button stick, by design, was wide enough to shield the entire threatened area; without it, the attraction would have been strong enough to pull in ships crossing the Atlantic, even as far away as the shores of America—if by some chance the earth's curvature didn't prevent this. As the operator, Bex would be very much exposed, and thus had apparently removed in advance any suspect element, including his vest and trouser buckles; his shirt and pants buttons were all made of bone, and a supple silk belt, encircling his waist, replaced his suspenders with their inevitable metal clips. He had definitively immunized himself at the final moment by entrusting Balbet with his most precious objects. By happy circumstance, his pure, excellent teeth were free of any foreign additions.

Just as the chemist was finishing his explanations, an unexpected phenomenon was signaled by a murmur from the crowd, which had slowly approached.

Everyone pointed in astonishment to the gold coins that had been scattered there by Stella Boucharessas.

For some time, the louis, double louis, and hundred-franc pieces had been trembling gently on the ground—to no one's surprise, as their light movement might have been caused by some capricious breeze.

In reality, the imponderable amount of currency was under the influence of the top cylinder and its powerful force; already several coins had flown straight toward its amber lead and attached themselves solidly. Others followed suit, sometimes round and intact, sometimes having been creased and trampled underfoot.

Soon the ground was completely bare along a strictly regular stripe, bordered on either side by the remainder of coinage located outside the zone of attraction.

The lead was now hidden beneath a veritable buffer of gilded paper, covered with dates and effigies.

Several infinitesimal atoms of real gold must have entered into the composition of those tinsel riches.

Indeed, by its position, the overlayered lead corresponded, without any doubt, to the gold button meant to fill the opening at the center of the button stick. Its very specific power could thus not have been exerted on an imitation that was completely devoid of auriferous elements.

The slowness of the coins, their initial hesitation, had been caused solely by an insufficiency of pure gold in their composition.

Paying little heed to the incident, which in no way disturbed his plans, Bex grasped the width of blue drapery by its upper end, pulling it smoothly toward the top of the button stick.

The easy and regular slide required almost no effort.

The cloth, climbing up the slit, gradually hid the circular opening, which, invisible but easily divined, soon framed the first strip of stanchium.

At that point, Bex, with his knees and left hand, had to restrain the button stick, which was being pulled mightily toward the group of cylinders.

Indeed, behind the cloth, the gold button corresponding to the first strip was now encircled by the round eyelet. Two fragments of its disk, deprived of their stanchium armor, now had no obstacle between them and the amber leads aimed their way.

Bex's resistance proved stronger than the first cylinder, which suddenly shot forward and flew like a rocket across the esplanade, slamming its tip into the button stick next to the thin protective strip.

Still leaning in mightily, the chemist had been careful to shift his body to the right, staying out of the path the monstrous pencil would take.

The force of the strike nearly toppled the button stick, but, in Bex's firm grip, it soon regained its balance.

Now immobile, the pencil hung in a gentle slope from its unsharpened end, dipping toward the ground, to the amber tip solidly adhered to the gold button despite the blue cloth between them.

The paper coins had in no way impeded the powerful attraction of the pure metal; flattened by the impact, they still decorated the lead with their artificial sparkle.

Through the cloth, Bex gently manipulated the gold button, which he labored to lift into the portion of the vertical slot above the eyelet.

The amber lead held fast, making the operation difficult.

The chemist persisted, for lack of a more practical method. Any attempt to pry the pencil loose would have proven fruitless. Only the slow, gradual interposition of a stanchium barrier could ultimately overcome the extraordinary attachment of the two bodies.

A series of laborious efforts eventually yielded the desired result.

At the very top of the slit, the gold button, still invisible, was once more completely sheltered behind the two panels of the button stick, rejoined at that spot by its faithful and rigid strip.

Bex stood the immense pencil upright.

With the sharp edge of a lead protector, he tried to scrape bare the amber tip that was still coated in gilded paper.

The thin, rounded blade, closely shaving the yellow surface, soon bested the light paper money, whose highly diluted alloy gave only feeble resistance.

When all the coins had drifted haphazardly to the ground, Bex fit the lead protector back onto the pencil, which he could now lay aside without fear of where it might point.

Then, returning to the button stick, he gently grasped the width of cloth and lifted it farther upward.

This second experiment, identical to the first, produced the flight of a second pencil, the lead of which rammed violently into the invisible silver button that had slipped into the gap.

After being liberated through the same painstaking process he'd previously employed, the pencil, now capped with a lead protector, was promptly set aside.

In its turn, the copper button, behind the blue cloth, attracted a third cylinder, which, briskly covered with stanchium, went to join the first and second.

The two top levels were now missing from the triangular façade initially formed by the stack of pencils.

Bex continued his unchanging maneuver. One by one, the buttons slid into the opening and drew the amber leads despite the distance; after this, Bex glided them into the upper part of the slot.

The pencils, having played their parts, were immediately capped and lined up on the ground one by one.

The last four disks, sumptuously composed of precious stones, corresponded to the lowest rung of cylinders, which alone remained facing the Incomparables' Theater.

Their power of attraction was in no way inferior to that of the metals, and the impact of the docile amber leads against them was extraordinarily violent.

The experiment completed, Bex, addressing us once more, told us of the exorbitant offers that certain banking houses, wishing to exploit his discovery, had thrown at him.

And indeed, his collection of cylinders, with their ability to locate ore and gem deposits, could have become the source of limitless wealth. Instead of relying on chance to prospect underground, miners, precisely guided by an instrument that could be easily built, would immediately find the richest veins, with no false starts or wasted efforts.

But famous scientists, motivated by their proverbial disinterest, had long observed a kind of professional tradition that Bex wished to perpetuate.

Therefore rebuffing the proffered millions and even billions, he had wisely contented himself with his giant button stick, which, in tandem with the cylinders, highlighted his discovery to no practical end.

As he spoke, Bex picked up his pencils, all ten of them secured by their lead protectors.

He then disappeared with his burden, preceding Rao, who carried off the promptly uprooted button stick.

* *
*

After a brief pause, we noticed the Hungarian Skariovszki in his tight-fitting red gypsy jacket, wearing a policeman's kepi of the same color.

His right sleeve, rolled up to the elbow, revealed a thick coral bracelet coiled six times around his bare forearm.

He carefully watched over three black porters bearing various objects, who halted with him in the middle of the esplanade.

The first Negro carried in his arms a zither and a folding stand.

Skariovszki opened the stand, planting its four feet solidly on the ground. Then, on a narrow hinged frame unfolded horizontally, he rested the zither, which resounded at this gentle impact.

To the left of the instrument, a metal stem attached to the frame of the stand rose vertically after a slight bend, then split at its end like two tines of a fork; to the right, another identical stem formed its companion piece.

The second Negro carried, with no great effort, a long, transparent receptacle that Skariovszki set like a bridge above the zither, fitting its two ends onto the metal forks.

The shape of the new object was ideally suited to this means of installation. Built like a trough, it was composed of four slabs of mica. Two main slabs, identically rectangular, formed a sharp-edged base by joining their two planes at an angle. In addition, two triangular pieces, facing each other and adhering to the narrow ends of the rectangles, completed the diaphanous apparatus, which looked like a yawning, oversized change purse. A gap the width of a pea ran along the entire bottom edge of the translucent trough.

The third Negro had just set down a large earthenware vessel brimming with clear water, the weight of which Skariovszki asked one of us to gauge.

La Billaudière-Maisonnial, skimming off a tiny portion in the hollow of his hand, showed the keenest surprise and exclaimed that the strange liquid felt heavy as mercury.

During this time, Skariovszki lifted his right forearm to his face, uttering several coaxing words with great tenderness.

We then saw the coral bracelet, which was none other than a giant earthworm as thick as the Hungarian's index finger, uncoil its two top rings and stretch slowly toward him.

La Billaudière-Maisonnial, straightening up again, now had to lend himself to another demonstration. At the gypsy's request, he received the worm, which crawled over his open hand; his wrist immediately dropped beneath the sudden weight of the intruder, which apparently was heavy as solid lead.

Skariovszki removed the worm, still coiled around his arm, and placed it on the lip of the mica trough.

The annelid crawled into the empty receptacle, pulling with it the rest of its body, which gradually slid from around the gypsy's flesh.

Soon the animal completely blocked the gap in the bottom edge, its horizontally stretched body supported by the two narrow inner ledges formed by the rectangular plates.

With great effort, the Hungarian hoisted the weighty vessel, the entire contents of which he poured into the trough, which was soon full to the brim.

Then, placing a knee on the ground and tilting his head to one side, he set the empty vessel beneath the zither, at a precisely determined point verified with a glance up and down the back of the instrument.

This last task accomplished, Skariovszki, standing nimbly upright, shoved his hands in his pockets, as if to limit himself from here on to a spectator's role.

The worm, left to its own devices, suddenly raised, then immediately let drop, a short segment of its body.

Having had time to slip into the gap, a drop of liquid fell heavily onto one of the zither strings, which on impact emitted a pure and ringing low *C*.

Farther on, another twitch in the obstructing body let through a second drop, which this time struck a bright *E*.

A *G*, then a high *C*, attacked in the same way, completed the perfect chord that the worm sounded again over an entire octave.

After the third and final *C*, the seven consonant notes, struck at the same time, provided a kind of conclusion to this trial prelude.

Thus warmed up, the worm launched into a slow Hungarian melody, tender and languorously sweet.

Each drop of liquid, released by an intentional spasm of its body, struck precisely the right string, which then split it into two equal globules.

A felt strip, glued into place on the wood of the zither, cushioned the fall of the heavy fluid, which otherwise would have produced a bothersome dripping noise.

The liquid, which accumulated in round puddles, penetrated inside the instrument via two circular openings drilled in the soundboard. Each of the two expected overspills rolled silently down a thin inner layer of felt specifically designed to absorb it.

A fine, limpid stream, emerging from some hidden egress, soon formed beneath the zither and ended precisely at the mouth of the earthenware vessel that Skariovszki had carefully set in place. The fluid, following the slope of the narrow and equally felt-lined channel, flowed noiselessly to the bottom of the enormous basin, which prevented any of it from inundating the grounds.

The worm continued its musical contortions, sometimes striking two notes at once, much like professional zither players who hold a hammer in each hand.

Several melodies, plaintive or lighthearted, succeeded the initial cantilena without a pause.

Then, moving beyond the scope of the instrument's habitual repertoire, the annelid launched into the polyphonic execution of a strangely danceable waltz.

Accompaniment and melody vibrated in harmony on the zither, which normally was limited to the production of a mere two simultaneous sounds.

To give some depth to the main theme, the worm raised itself a bit higher, thereby releasing a larger quantity of liquid onto the violently impacted strings.

The slightly hesitant rhythm discretely lent the whole the unique character typical of gypsy ensembles.

After the waltz, a panoply of dances gradually emptied the see-through trough.

Below, the vessel had refilled owing to the continuous flow that had now run dry. Skariovszki lifted it and for a second time decanted its contents into the lightweight receptacle before returning it to its proper place on the ground.

The worm, now completely resupplied, began playing a czardas punctuated by wild and abrupt shifts in tonality. Sometimes, huge tremors of its long reddish body produced clashing fortissimos; at others, imperceptible undulations, which let through only fine droplets, lowered the now tranquil zither to a bare murmur.

There was nothing mechanical about this performance, which radiated fire and conviction. The worm seemed to be like any virtuoso, who, following his spontaneous inspiration, ran through a series of variations, interpreting an ambiguous and delicate passage in new and controversial ways.

A long medley of light opera arias following the czardas again depleted the provision of liquid. Once more Skariovszki performed the rapid decanting while announcing the final piece.

This time, the worm energetically attacked a captivating Hungarian rhapsody, each measure of which seemed to bristle with the most harrowing difficulties.

The acts of agility followed one another seamlessly, spangled with trills and chromatic scales.

Soon, through a series of enormous jerks, the worm accentuated a certain canto of ample texture, each written note of which must have been part of a thick cluster. This theme, which formed the base, was embroidered with numerous light motifs produced by slight twitches of the supple body.

The animal was becoming intoxicated with music. Far from exhibiting the slightest weariness, it grew more animated with every harmonic wave it unleashed so relentlessly.

Its emotion was communicated to the audience, which was strangely moved by the expressive timbre of certain hauntingly plaintive sounds and by the incredible speed of the endless clusters of demisemiquavers.

A frenetic presto brought the annelid's enthusiastic delirium to a climax, and for several minutes it abandoned itself unreservedly to its chaotic gymnastics.

At the end, it prolonged the perfect cadence by a kind of expanding improvisation, reprising the final chords until the last of the percussive liquid had been entirely depleted.

Skariovszki extended his bare arm, around which the worm coiled itself anew after having scaled the mica slope.

The Negroes came to remove the various objects, including the earthenware vessel that was again as full as when it arrived.

Led by the Hungarian, they disappeared behind the Stock Exchange in single file.

IV

At rao's command, the entire portion of the black crowd assembled to the right made an about-face and took several steps back to contemplate the Incomparables' Theater before them.

Immediately, our group moved closer, the better to see Talou, who had just appeared onstage with Carmichael in tow; the young Marseillais's ordinary brown suit clashed with the extravagant imperial toilette.

Using a falsetto voice, an imitation of a woman's pitch that matched his dress and wig, Talou executed Dariccelli's *Aubade*, a piece requiring the most hazardous feats of vocalization.

Carmichael, score in hand, prompted the melody and its French text measure for measure, while the emperor, his guide's faithful echo, emitted numerous trills that, after several minutes of effort, ended on a pure and extremely high-pitched final note.

Once this romance was finished, singer and prompter again rejoined the audience, while the historian Julliard, succeeding them on the floorboards, sat to our left at his lecturer's desk, on which lay various notes that he began leafing through.

For twenty minutes, the marvelous orator enthralled us with his captivating elocution, delivering a brief exposé, filled with inspiring clarity of mind, concerning the history of the Electors of Brandenburg.

Sometimes he stretched a hand toward one of the effigies affixed to the backdrop, drawing our attention to a characteristic feature or a particular facial expression that his narrative had just evoked.

He concluded with a brilliant synthesis and, leaving the stage, left us dazzled by the vivid tints of his sparkling verve.

Immediately, the ichthyologist Martignon walked to the middle of the stage, holding in both hands a perfectly transparent aquarium, in which a certain whitish, oddly shaped fish slowly circled about.

In a few words, the learned naturalist introduced the Sturgeon Ray, an as yet unknown variety that had been procured for him the day before by a fortuitous deep-sea exploration.

The fish before our eyes was the product of a racial mixture; only the eggs of a ray fertilized by a sturgeon could engender the clearly articulated twin peculiarities that this single aquarium specimen brought together.

As Martignon slowly withdrew, watching carefully over the remarkable hybrid he had discovered, Tancrède Boucharessas, father of the five children whose skill we had earlier admired, made an impressive entrance by pushing a voluminous instrument on rollers to the front of the stage.

Though lacking both arms and legs, Tancrède, squeezed into a Bohemian costume, could still move swiftly by hopping on the stumps of his thighs. He clambered unaided onto a low platform situated at the middle of the unit he had just wheeled in and, turning his back to the public, found just at mouth level a large panpipe that, closely fitted to his chin, comprised an ensemble of pipes vertically tiered at regular intervals in descending order of size, from bottom to top. To the right was a hefty accordion, featuring a thick leather strap at the end of its bellows, its buckle fitted exactly to the incomplete bicep that extended barely four inches from the small man's shoulder. On the opposite side, a triangle hanging from a wire was ready to vibrate under the beats of a metal wand previously attached, with solid fasteners, to the performer's left stump.

After settling into the correct position, Tancrède, creating the illusion of a one-man orchestra, vigorously attacked a brilliant overture.

His head quickly and repeatedly spun back and forth, his lips finding the notes of the melody on the appropriate flute, while his two biceps worked simultaneously—one alternating between perfect and ninth chords by moving the accordion's bellows in both directions, the other striking the base of the triangle at the correct moment with the metal wand that was like the clapper of an alarm clock.

To the right, seen in profile and forming one of the lateral facades of the contraption, a bass drum with a mechanical drumstick was counterbalanced, on the left, by a pair of cymbals attached to the end of two solid copper supports. By means of a skillful twitch, confined only to his shoulders while his head remained still, Tancrède constantly shifted his weight up and down, causing the small board on springs on which he sat upright to activate the drumstick and the pair of cymbals simultaneously, their deafening clash blending with the loud thumping of the bass drum.

This masterful overture, with its fine and varied nuances, ended in a fast-paced *presto*, during which the little phenomenon's truncated thighs, bouncing with every beat on the board, punctuated a dizzying melody accompanied *fortissimo* by the vibrating bass notes of the accordion mixed with the multiple tings of the triangle.

After the final chord, the small man, lively as ever, left his place and disappeared into the wings, while his two sons Hector and Tommy came to clear the stage, promptly removing the instrument along with the lecturer's table and chair.

This task completed, an artist strode onto the boards, elegantly attired in a black suit and holding a top hat in his white-gloved hands. This was Ludovic, the famous singer with the quadruple voice, whose colossal mouth drew everyone's eyes.

With a lovely tenor's timbre, Ludovic softly began the famous canon "Frère Jacques"; but only the left corner of his mouth moved to utter the familiar words, while the rest of the huge abyss kept still and silent.

At the moment when, after the first notes, the words "*Dormez-vous*" sounded a third higher, a second buccal division attacked anew the words "*Frère Jacques*," starting at the tonic; Ludovic, through long years of practice, had managed to split his lips and tongue into independent portions and to articulate several intertwined parts effortlessly and simultaneously, differing in both tune and words. By now the entire left half of his mouth was moving, baring his teeth, while its undulations left the right side closed and motionless.

But a third labial fraction soon entered the chorus, precisely copying its predecessors. During this time the second voice intoned "*Dormez-vous*," enlivened by the first, which introduced a new element into the mix by singing "*Sonnez les matines*" on a silvery and spirited rhythm.

For a fourth time the words "*Frère Jacques*" were heard, this time pronounced by the right corner of his mouth, which had just ceased its inactivity to complete the quartet; meanwhile, the first voice completed the canon with the syllables "*Ding, ding, dong*," acting as bass to "*Sonnez les matines*" and "*Dormez-vous*" produced by the two intermediary voices.

Ludovic, his eyes glazed and dilated, needed a constant tension of mind to accomplish this inimitable tour de force without error. The first voice had picked up the song from the beginning, and the buccal compartments, each moving independently, parsed out the text of the round, whose four simultaneously performed fragments blended delightfully.

Little by little Ludovic accentuated his timbre, beginning a vigorous crescendo that sounded like a distant horde rapidly approaching.

There was a fortissimo of several measures during which, constantly evolving in a perpetual cycle from one labial compartment to the next, the four motifs, loud and resonant, burst forth powerfully in a slightly accelerated movement.

Then, calm having been restored, the imaginary troupe seemed to recede and fade out at a bend in the road; the concluding notes faded to a faint murmur, and Ludovic, exhausted by the terrible mental effort, left the stage mopping his brow.

*
* *

After a one-minute intermission, we saw Philippo appear, presented by Jenn, his inseparable impresario. The unattached head of a fifty-year-old, placed on a wide red disk with a metal collar that held it upright: this was Philippo. A short, thick beard added to the ugliness of his face, which was nonetheless made amusing and likeable by its intelligent wittiness.

Jenn, holding this solid disk—a kind of round table with no legs—in both hands, showed the public the bodiless head, which began to jabber gaily with the most inventive sort of volubility.

With every word his very prominent lower jaw emitted a spray of spittle that, spewing in a shower from his mouth, landed a certain distance in front of him.

We could find none of the customary subterfuges used in the classic *talking head* routine. There was no system of mirrors hidden under the disk, which Jenn manipulated freely and without any suspect precautions; moreover, the impresario walked to the edge of the stage and offered the round plate to whoever wanted it.

Skariovszki stepped forward to receive Philippo, who at that point, passing from hand to hand, carried on with each spectator a brief, impromptu, and droll conversation. Some held the platter at arm's length, trying to avoid the sprays of sputum flying from the prodigy's mouth, while his astounding repartee elicited continuous bursts of laughter from us all.

After making the rounds, Philippo returned to his point of origin and was handed back to Jenn, who had remained onstage.

Immediately the impresario pressed a hidden catch that opened the red platter as one unfolds an extraordinarily flat box, showing that it was actually composed of two parts held fast by a thin hinge.

The lower disk dropped in vertical profile, while, held up by Jenn, the circle that until then had acted as lid continued to support the bearded figure horizontally.

Below this, wearing the classic flesh-colored leotard, hung a minuscule human body that, through complete atrophy, had been able to fit in the narrow hiding place of the hollow plate, barely an inch thick.

This sudden vision completed the person of Philippo, a loquacious dwarf, who, displaying an outsized head, enjoyed perfect health despite the diminutiveness of his striking anatomy.

Still talking and spraying spittle, the astounding chatterbox gesticulated freely with his puppetlike limbs, as if to give full vent to his inexhaustible and exuberant gaiety.

Soon, gripping Philippo by the scruff of the neck, after releasing the metal collar that moved on several hinges with spring catches, the impresario, with his left hand, lowered the upper disk, its aperture allowing easy passage for the inconceivable body below, dressed in flesh tones.

The agile trinket, whose head, larger than Jenn's, was the same size as the entire rest of his person, abruptly took advantage of this new freedom of movement to scratch furiously at his beard, without missing a beat in his moist verbiage.

As Jenn carried him off into the wings, he gaily gripped a foot in each hand and disappeared wriggling, a final gibe sending copious droplets of his abundant saliva far afield.

Immediately the Breton Lelgoualch, dressed in the legendary costume of his region, rushed forward while doffing his round hat, the stage floorboards echoing under the shocks of his peg leg.

His left hand clutched a hollow bone, cleanly pierced with holes like a flute.

With a strong Brittany accent, the newcomer, reciting some prepared patter, gave us the following details about himself:

At age eighteen, Lelgoualch, a fisherman by trade, used to ply his skiff every day off the coast of Paimpol, his hometown.

The youth owned a bagpipe and was considered the best player in the county. Every Sunday people gathered in the public square to hear him perform, with a charm all his own, a host of Breton folk tunes, of which his memory kept an inexhaustible reserve.

One day, at the Paimpol town fair, Lelgoualch was scaling a greased pole when he fell and fractured his hip. Mortified by his clumsiness, which the whole village had witnessed, he got up and resumed his ascent, managing to complete it through sheer force of will. Then he limped home, still making it a point of honor to conceal his suffering.

When, after too long a delay, he finally sent for the doctor, the injury had developed into gangrene.

It was deemed necessary to amputate.

Lelgoualch, apprised of the situation, faced his trial with courage and, thinking only of how to make the best of it, asked the surgeon to save him his tibia, which he planned to put to some mysterious purpose.

They did as he requested, and on a certain day the poor amputee, sporting a brand-new wooden leg, went to see an instrument maker to whom he entrusted a carefully wrapped package, accompanied by precise instructions.

One month later, Lelgoualch received in a black, velvet-lined case the bone from his leg transformed into a strangely resonant flute.

The young Breton quickly learned the new fingerings and began a lucrative career playing the tunes of his region in music halls and circuses; the weirdness of the instrument, the provenance of which was explained at each performance, attracted crowds of curiosity seekers and increased his earnings far and wide.

The amputation was now twenty years in the past, and ever since then the flute's resonance had continued to improve, like a violin that mellows over time.

Finishing his story, Lelgoualch raised his tibia to his lips and played a Breton melody full of gentle melancholy. The pure, silken notes sounded like nothing we'd ever heard; the timbre, at once warm and crystalline, indescribably limpid, marvelously suited the particular charm of the calm, lilting tune, whose evocative contours transported our thoughts straight to Armorica.

Several refrains, by turns joyful or patriotic, amorous or stirring, succeeded this initial romance, each one retaining a distinct unity that emitted intense local color.

After a sweet final lament, Lelgoualch withdrew with an alert step, his wooden leg once more clattering over the boards.

The equestrian Urbain then made his appearance, in a blue jacket, calfskin jodhpurs, and turned-down boots, leading a magnificent black stallion full of fire and vigor. An elegant bridle was the only ornament on the animal's head; no bit fettered its mouth.

Urbain took several strides onto the stage and positioned the splendid steed to face us, introducing it by the name Romulus, which the circus folk jocularly nicknamed *tongue and hoove*.

At the equestrian's request to the audience to supply him a word at random, Juillard called out "equator."

Immediately, slowly repeating one by one the syllables that Urbain prompted aloud, the horse distinctly pronounced "*E . . . qua . . . tor . . .*"

The animal's *tongue*, instead of being square like those of its peers, had adopted the pointed form of the human organ. This peculiarity, noticed by chance, had convinced Urbain to attempt to educate Romulus, who, like a parrot, had learned over two years of work to clearly replicate any sound.

The equestrian resumed the experiment, now soliciting complete sentences from the audience that Romulus repeated after him. Soon, dispensing with its prompter, the horse volubly reeled off its entire repertoire, including a volley of proverbs, portions of fables, curses, and truisms, recited haphazardly and with no sign of intelligence or understanding.

At the end of this preposterous speech, Urbain led Romulus off-stage, the animal still muttering a few nonsensical observations.

Man and horse were replaced by Whirligig, slim and lithe in his clown costume and face powder. Using both hands and his teeth, he carried separately, by their edges, three deep, finely woven baskets, which he set down on the stage.

Ably mimicking a British accent, he introduced himself as a lucky devil who had just enjoyed huge winnings at two different casinos.

As he spoke he showed off his baskets, filled respectively with coins, dominoes, and dark blue playing cards.

First taking the basket of loose change, which he carried to the right, Whirligig, scooping out copper coins by the handful, erected on the edge of the platform a curious construction that rested against the partition.

Coins large and small swiftly piled up under the clown's nimble fingers, which were apparently quite used to the exercise. We soon made out the base of a feudal tower with a wide portal, its upper portion still missing.

Without pausing for breath, the agile worker pursued his task, accompanied by a metallic clinking full of resonant gaiety. Here and there, narrow loopholes dotted the vaulted walls that rose before our eyes.

Reaching the level marked by the top of the portal, Whirligig pulled from his sleeve a long, thin, flat rod, its brownish color easily confused with the grimy hue of common coinage. This rigid beam, placed like a bridge over the two jambs of the opening, allowed the clown to continue his task on a firm and ample support.

The coins continued to pile up and, when the basket was empty, Whirligig designated with a proud gesture a tall, artistically crenellated tower, which seemed to be part of some old façade of which only a single corner appeared, like a stage set.

With a pile of dominoes pulled in bunches from the second basket, the clown then went on to build, at the far right of the stage, a kind of wall balancing upright.

The uniform rectangles, placed in single file, were laid over each other symmetrically, showing many black backs with an occasional white front.

Soon a large section of wall, rising in a flawless vertical line, showed, against a white background, the black silhouette of a priest in a long cassock, wearing his traditional hat. Sometimes lying horizontally, sometimes upright, depending on the requirements of the priest's outline, the dominoes created their design by cleverly alternating their black or white faces; they looked as if they'd been glued together by their narrow edges, so precisely were they stacked.

In several minutes, Whirligig, working with neither mortar nor trowel, finished a wall a full ten feet long, which, stretching to the rear of the stage in a slightly oblique direction, formed a rigorously homogenous block. The original motif was repeated over the full

width of the mosaic, and we now saw what seemed like whole parade of vicars walking in small groups toward an unknown goal.

Approaching the third basket, the clown picked up and unfolded a
large black drape, which, by two corners, each fitted with a ring, was
easily suspended from two hooks attached before the performance
to the backdrop and to the left wall of the stage.

The black cloth, which hung to the floor, thus formed a wide
slanting corner; the axis of the domino wall stretching from the coin
tower abutted against it.

Freshly exposed to the air by Whirligig's action, the visible side
of the cloth was covered with a damp coating, a kind of shiny glue.

The clown gracefully positioned himself before this huge target,
against which, with remarkable skill, he began to toss the playing
cards that he pulled from his reserve by the fistful.

Each light projectile, spinning on its axis, infallibly landed with
its blue back against the cloth and remained prisoner of the tenacious
coating; the performer demonstrated great precision in symmetrically aligning his cards, which, black or red, high or low, lodged one
beside the other without regard for value or suit.

Before long, diamonds, clubs, spades, and hearts, succeeding
each other in narrow bands, sketched against the black background
the shape of a roof. Then came a complete façade pierced by several
windows and a wide door, on the threshold of which Whirligig, using an entire deck, carefully rendered the silhouette of a behatted
clergyman emerging from his home, who seemed to be greeting the
colleagues heading in his direction.

This tour de force completed, the clown turned to us to offer this
explanation of his triple masterpiece: "A fraternity of reverends leaving the tower of an old cloister to visit the parish priest in his rectory."

Then, still lithe and agile, he folded up the black cloth with all
the cards still attached and demolished in several seconds the evocative wall and brown tower.

Everything was soon returned to the solid baskets, with which Whirligig vanished like a sprite.

After a moment, the Belgian tenor Cuijper appeared onstage, squeezed into a tight frock coat.

He held between his fingers a fragile metal instrument, which he displayed to the audience as best he could by turning it slowly to alternately expose each of its sides.

It was a *squeaker*, similar, though slightly larger, to those little tin nasal attachments puppeteers use to imitate Punch's voice.

Cuijper briefly related the story of this trinket of his own invention, which, amplifying his voice a hundredfold, had shaken the Théâtre de la Monnaie in Brussels to its foundations.

We all remembered the fuss the newspapers had made about *Cuijper's Squeaker*, which no instrument-maker ever succeeded in replicating.

The tenor jealously guarded a certain secret regarding the composition of the metal and the shape of its many circumvolutions, which endowed the precious toy with fabulously resonant qualities.

Wary of providing opportunities for theft and indiscretion, Cuijper had manufactured only a single specimen, the object of his constant surveillance; we were therefore gaping at that moment at the very squeaker that, for an entire season, had allowed him to sing the lead roles on the stage of the Monnaie.

These preliminary explanations over, Cuijper announced the grand aria from *Gorlois* and placed the squeaker in his mouth.

Suddenly, a superhuman voice, which sounded as if it could be heard for miles around, burst from his throat, making every listener jump.

This colossal force in no way undermined the charm of its timbre, and the mysterious squeaker, the source of this incredible volume, clarified rather than garbled the elegant pronunciation of the lyrics.

Never straining for effect, Cuijper, seemingly without trying, stirred the air currents around him; yet no shrillness clouded the purity of his sound, which evoked both the delicacy of a harp and the loudness of an organ.

By himself he filled the space better than a huge choir could have done; his *fortes* would have covered the rumbling of thunder, and his *pianos* retained a formidable amplitude, while giving the impression of a light murmur.

The final note, begun softly, then artfully swelled and broken off at its apex, provoked a feeling of stupor in the crowd that lasted until Cuijper left the stage, his fingers once again twiddling the curious squeaker.

*
* *

A shiver of curiosity revived the audience as the great Italian trage-dienne Adinolfa came onstage, dressed in a simple black frock that heightened the fatal sadness of her physiognomy, itself darkened by her beautiful velvet eyes and opulent chestnut hair.

After a brief announcement, Adinolfa began declaiming in Ital-ian ample and mellifluous verses by Torquato Tasso. Her features expressed intense dolor, and certain vocal outbursts were nearly like sobs; she wrung her hands in distress while her entire person shook with pain, intoxicated by exaltation and despair.

Soon real tears sprung from her eyes, showing the devastating sincerity of her phenomenal emotion.

Sometimes she knelt, bowing her head beneath the weight of her grief, then again rose, fingers clasped and stretched to the heavens, to which she seemed to be fervently addressing her heartrending im-precations.

Her eyelashes dripped constantly, while, sustained by her strik-ing impressions, Tasso's stanzas echoed bitterly, spoken in a savage and gripping tone that evoked the cruelest emotional torments.

After a final, emphatic verse, each syllable of which was hammered out one by one in a voice made hoarse by the effort, the brilliant tragedienne slowly stepped offstage, holding her head in both hands, shedding her limpid and abundant tears until the end.

Immediately two red damask curtains, pulled by an unseen hand, emerged simultaneously from the wings of the empty stage, which they masked completely by joining together at the midpoint.

V

Two MINUTES PASSED, during which Carmichael went to stand at the front left of the theater, from which a bustling, unseen activity could be heard.

All at once the curtains opened onto a tableau vivant imbued with picturesque cheer.

In a rich timbre, Carmichael, designating the immobile apparition, pronounced this brief apostrophe:

"The Feast of the Olympian Gods."

In the middle of the stage, behind which hung black drapes, Jupiter, Juno, Mars, Diana, Apollo, Venus, Neptune, Vesta, Minerva, Ceres, and Vulcan, seated in full regalia at a sumptuously laid table, smilingly raised their brimming goblets. Ready to gaily toast the entire group, Mercury, played by the comic actor Soreau, appeared to be suspended in midair by the wings of his sandals and hovered above the banquet without any visible attachment to the flies.

Closing once more, the curtains blotted out the divine assembly, then parted anew after several moments' commotion to display a fairly complex scene in an entirely different setting.

The left half of the stage showed a tranquil waterway hidden behind a line of rosebushes.

A woman of color, who by her costume and finery seemed to belong to a savage tribe of North America, stood motionless in a light boat. Alone with her on the frail skiff, a little white girl held in both hands the handle of a fishing net; with a sharp jerk of her snare, she was yanking a pike from the waves. Lower down, one could see caught in the mesh the head of the fish trying to dive back into its element.

The other half of the stage depicted a grassy bank. In the foreground, a man who seemed to be running at breakneck speed wore on his shoulders a papier-mâché boar's head, which, completely obscuring his own, made him look like a wild pig with a human body. An iron wire forming a wide arc was attached by its two ends to the encircled wrists that the runner held out before him at different heights. A glove, an egg, and a wisp of straw, the spoils of a fictional theft, were strung on the metal wire at three different points of the graceful curve. The runaway's hands were open toward the sky, as if juggling the three objects frozen in their aerial path. The arc, inclined on a slant, gave the impression of rapid, irresistible momentum. Seen in rear three-quarters view and seemingly drawn by an invincible force, the juggler appeared to be rushing toward the rear of the stage.

Set back from him, a live goose held a pose as if taking wing, thanks to a kind of glue that attached its phenomenally widespread feet to the ground in mid-stride. The two white wings were extended broadly as if to power this headlong flight. Behind the bird, · Soreau, dressed in a flowing robe, represented wrathful Boreas; from his mouth escaped a long funnel of blue-gray cardboard that, striped with fine longitudinal lines copied from those great breaths that draftsmen put before the lips of swollen-cheeked zephyrs, artfully depicted a tempestuous wind. The flared end of the light cone was aimed at the goose, chased forward by the gust. In addition, Boreas, holding in his right hand a rose with a tall, thorny stem, coldly prepared to whip the fugitive to hasten its flight. Turned almost toward us, the bird was about to cross paths with the juggler, each one seeming to describe in opposite directions the sharp curve of the same parabola.

In the background rose a golden harrow; behind this, the ass Milenkaya stretched its closed jaw, through which a seton passed from top to bottom, toward a pail full of whole bran. Certain peculiarities hinted at the subterfuge used to simulate the painful and hunger-inducing obstacle. Only the two visible ends of the seton truly existed, glued to the ass's skin and respectively terminated by a transversal rod. At first glance, the effect obtained indeed suggested absolute closure, condemning the poor beast to the tortures of Tantalus in perpetuity.

Carmichael, indicating the girl, who, standing in the skiff, was none other than Stella Boucharessas, clearly uttered this brief explanation:

"Ursule, accompanied by the Huron Maffa, aids the bewitched of Lake Ontario."

The characters all maintained a sculptural stillness. Soreau, gripping between his teeth the end of his long, air-colored funnel, swelled his smooth, flushed cheeks, without letting the rose standing upright at the end of his outstretched arm tremble in the slightest.

The curtains came together, and immediately, behind this impenetrable obstacle, a prolonged din could be heard, caused by some new feverish and zealous activity.

Now the stage reappeared, completely transformed.

The center was occupied by a staircase, its contours disappearing into the flies.

Halfway up stood a blind old man dressed in Louis XV style, facing front on the landing. His left hand held a dark green bouquet composed of several branches of holly. Looking at the base of the spray, one gradually made out all the colors of the rainbow, represented by seven different ribbons knotted individually around the bundled stems.

His other hand armed with a hefty quill pen, the blind man wrote on the banister to his right, its flat shape and cream hue offering a convenient smooth surface.

Several background figures, crowded onto nearby steps, gravely followed the old man's movements. The closest one, holding a large inkwell, seemed to be awaiting the moment to moisten the quill anew.

His finger pointing to the scene, Carmichael spoke these words:

"Handel mechanically composing the theme of his oratorio *Vesper*."

Soreau, in the role of Handel, had created for himself a conventional blindness by painting his eyelids, which he kept almost entirely shut.

The scene vanished behind its veil of drapes, and a fairly long interval was marked only by the whispers of the audience.

"Czar Alexei unmasking Pleshcheyev's assassin."

This phrase, which Carmichael uttered at the moment the curtains next slid open on their rod, referred to a Russian scene from the seventeenth century.

At right, Soreau, playing the czar, held vertically at eye level a red glass disk that looked like the setting sun. His gaze, passing through that round window, rested on a group of servants at left flocking around a dying man, his face and hands completely blue, who had just fallen in convulsions into their arms.

The vision lasted but a short time and was followed by a fleeting intermission, which ended with this announcement from Carmichael:

"The echo in the Argyros woods sending Constantine Kanaris the scent of named flowers."

Soreau, playing the famous seaman, stood in profile in the foreground, his hands cupped like a megaphone around his mouth.

Nearby, several companions held a pose of awed surprise.

Without moving, Soreau distinctly pronounced the word "rose," which was soon repeated by a voice from the wings.

At the precise moment the echo sounded, an intense, penetrating smell of roses spread over Trophy Square, striking everyone's nostrils at the same time then fading almost immediately.

The word "carnation," which Soreau then uttered, yielded the same phonetic and olfactory response.

One by one, lilac, jasmine, lily of the valley, thyme, gardenia, and violet were named aloud, and each time the echo disseminated strong fragrances, in perfect accord with the obediently repeated word.

The curtains closed over this poetic scene, and the atmosphere promptly cleared itself of any intoxicating odors.

After a tedious wait, the next abruptly unveiled scene was indicated by Carmichael, who accompanied his gesture with this brief commentary:

"The fabulously wealthy prince Savellini, suffering from kleptomania, robs street hoodlums in the poor quarters of Rome."

For the first time Soreau appeared in modern dress, wrapped in an elegant fur coat and decked with precious stones that sparkled at his necktie and his fingers. In front of him a circle of sinister-looking advantage of the onlookers' concentration, who were too fully absorbed in the duel to notice his presence, the man in the fur coat furtively explored their repellent pockets from behind, emptying them of their sordid contents. His thrusting hands now clutched an old, dented watch, a grimy change purse, and a large, checkered handkerchief still partially buried in the depths of a much-patched jacket.

When the supple, habitual closure had covered over this antithetical *fait divers*, Carmichael left his post, thereby bringing to an end the series of frozen tableaux.

The stage was soon returned to view for the entrance of the aging ballerina Olga Chervonenkov, an obese, mustached Latvian who, dressed in a tutu ornamented with leafage, made her appearance on the back of the elk Sladki, which she crushed under her considerable weight. The good-natured beast trudged across the boards, then, relieved of its corpulent rider, plodded back toward the wings, while the performer assumed first position for *The Nymph's Dance*.

Her lips set in a smile, the former prima ballerina began a series of rapid turns, still showing certain vestiges of her past talent; beneath the stiff folds of her tulle skirt, her monstrous legs, squeezed into clinging pink tights, performed their practiced task with enough agility and remnants of grace to inspire justifiable surprise.

Suddenly, crossing the stage with tiny steps, both feet raised onto the point of their big toes, Olga fell heavily and cried out in anguish.

Doctor Leflaive left our group and, rushing onstage, diagnosed the lamentable condition of the patient, who had been immobilized by a *muscle cramp*.

Calling Hector and Tommy Boucharessas to assist him, the able doctor carefully lifted the unfortunate ballerina, who was carried offstage to receive the necessary care.

The moment the accident occurred, Talou, as if to prevent any interruption in the proceedings, had discretely given orders to Rao.

An immense choir suddenly rang out, composed of deep, vibrant male voices that buried poor Olga's distant wails.

At this sound, everyone turned toward the west side of the square, in front of which the black warriors, squatting near the weapons they'd laid on the ground, all sang the "Jeroukka," a kind of proud epic written by the emperor, who had taken as subject the detailed narrative of his own exploits.

The melody, with its bizarre rhythm and tone, was based on a single, fairly brief theme, repeated ad infinitum with new words each time.

The singers chanted each couplet, clapping their hands in unison as if they were a single man, and this glorious lament, executed with a certain opulence and character, produced a rather grandiose impression.

Nonetheless, the constant repetition of the single, eternally un-varied musical phrase gradually gave rise to an intense monotony, accentuated by the inevitable opportunities for prolongation offered by the "Jeroukka," a faithful and exhaustive record of the life of the emperor, whose notable deeds were many.

Completely inaccessible to European ears, the Ponukelean epic unfolded in garbled stanzas, no doubt relating many capital events, and night gradually fell without any indication that the tedious drone might be nearing an end.

Suddenly, just as we were despairing of ever reaching the final verse, the choir stopped short and was replaced by a lovely sopra-no—a marvelous, penetrating voice that echoed purely in the al-ready opaque twilight.

All eyes, seeking the spot from which this new performance originated, lit on Carmichael, who, standing at left before the front row of the chorus, thus completed the "Jeroukka" by phrasing solo, without changing a note of the musical motif, a supplemental canto devoted to the "Battle of the Tez."

His remarkable head-voice, which flawlessly reproduced a fe-male pitch, soared delightfully in the limitless acoustics of the open air, apparently unimpeded by the difficult pronunciation of the in-comprehensible sounds composing the song.

But after several moments, Carmichael, initially so self-assured, faltered in his recital, his memory refusing to recall one word in the series of unintelligible syllables that he'd conscientiously learned by heart.

From a distance, Talou loudly whispered the fragment forgotten by the young Marseillais, who, picking up the narrative thread, con-tinued without further hesitation to the end of the final couplet.

Immediately the emperor uttered several words to Sirdah, who, translating into excellent French the sentence her father had dic-tated, was forced to inflict three hours' detention on Carmichael as punishment for his slight lapse.

VI

THE BLACK WARRIORS, standing en masse, had just picked up their weapons.

Reassembled under Rao's direction, the original cortege, augmented by our group and most of the Incomparables, began filing quickly southward.

The southern part of Ejur was crossed at a brisk pace, and soon the plain appeared, bounded at left by the great trees of the Behuliphruen, a magnificent garden full of phenomenal unknown species.

Abruptly, Rao halted the immense column, having reached a great stretch of land whose very dimensions made it propitious for certain long-distance phonetic experiments.

Stéphane Alcott, husky and barrel-chested, stepped from the ranks with his six sons, young men aged fifteen to twenty-five, whose fabulous leanness showed starkly through their simple, skin-tight red leotards.

Their father, dressed like them, took a stance at a given point, his back to the setting sun; then, carefully making a half-quarter turn to the right, he stopped sharply, adopting the rigidity of a statue.

Starting at the exact point occupied by Stéphane, the eldest of the six brothers walked obliquely toward the Behuliphruen, scrupulously following the path forged by his father's line of sight and counting aloud along with his long, slow strides, making sure to give each a rigorously invariable length. He stopped at number one hundred seventeen and, turning around to face west, followed the paternal example by striking a studied pose. His youngest brother, who had accompanied him, made a similar trek toward the south-west and, after seventy-two mechanically identical steps, froze like a mannequin, his chest toward the sunrise. One by one, the four youngest performed the same movement, each time taking as departure point the conventional goal reached by the last measurer and bringing to the execution of this brief, marvelously regulated walk the mathematical precision normally reserved for geodesic surveys.

When the youngest was in place, the seven performers, placed at uneven distances, turned out to be staggered along a strange crooked line, each of its five whimsical angles formed by their two joined heels.

The seeming incoherence of the figure was intentional, due to the strict number of regular strides, the six respective totals of which varied between a minimum of seventy-two and a maximum of one hundred forty-nine.

Once standing in place, each of the six brothers, violently sucking in his chest and stomach with a painful muscular contraction, formed the boundaries of a wide, deep space, which the addition of his arms, rounded in a circle like supplementary edges, rendered deeper still. The leotards, thanks to a special coating, adhered tightly to every inch of the wearer's epidermis.

Cupping his hands in a megaphone, their father, in a deep and resonant timbre, shouted his own name toward the oldest.

Immediately, at irregular intervals, the four syllables *Sté-phane Al-cott* were repeated successively at the six points of the enormous zigzag, without the others' lips having moved in the slightest.

It was the family patriarch's actual voice that had just echoed off the thoracic antrum of the six young men, who, owing to their extraordinary thinness, scrupulously maintained by a draconian diet, offered the sound waves a sufficiently rigid and bony surface to deflect its every vibration.

This first attempt did not satisfy the performers, who modified ever so slightly their positions and postures.

The fine-tuning lasted several minutes, during which Stéphane often bellowed his name, monitoring the results. These were increasingly perfected by his sons, who sometimes shifted their feet a mere centimeter in a given direction, sometimes leaned slightly to better facilitate the rapid passage of sound.

The ensemble looked like some imaginary, difficultly tuned instrument whose proper adjustment required meticulous and patient care.

Finally, the last attempt having seemed correct, Stéphane, with a brief word that echoed six times in spite of him, ordered the emaciated sentinels to hold absolutely still.

At that point, the real performance began.

Stéphane, at the top of his voice, pronounced a wide variety of proper names, interjections, and everyday words, infinitely varying their register and intonation. And each time the sound, ricocheting from chest to chest, was reproduced with crystalline purity, hearty and strong at first, then gradually fading down to a final mumble no louder than a murmur.

No echo in forest, cave, or cathedral could have rivaled this artificial combination, which produced a true miracle of acoustics.

Obtained by the Alcott family at the cost of long months of study and trials, the geometric layout of the crooked line owed its artful irregularities to the particular form of each chest, whose anatomical structure offered a resonant power of greater or lesser range.

Several audience members, having approached each vibrating sentry, could verify the absence of trickery. The six mouths remained hermetically shut, the initial utterance alone causing the multiple repetitions.

Wishing to give the experiment the greatest possible breadth, Stéphane rapidly emitted short sentences, slavishly reiterated by the sextuple echo; certain iambic pentameters, recited one after the other, were perceived clearly without overlapping or muddle. Various bursts of laughter, deep for "ho," sharp for "ha," and shrill for "hee," created a sensation by evoking a lighthearted, mocking crowd. Cries of pain or alarm, sobs, pathetic exclamations, resounding coughs, and comic sneezes were registered one by one with the same perfection.

Moving from spoken word to song, Stéphane emitted strong baritone notes, which echoed beautifully at the different bends in the line and were followed by vocal exercises, trills, parts of tunes, and snatches of lively popular refrains.

As a finale, the soloist, taking a deep breath, continuously scaled a perfect chord in both directions, using the full breadth of his voice and giving the illusion of an impeccably attuned choir, thanks to the ample and lasting polyphony produced by all the echoes blending together.

Suddenly, deprived of the musical source that Stéphane, out of breath, had just cut short by falling silent, the false voices faded one by one, and the six brothers, resuming their natural pose with visible relief, could stretch voluptuously while heaving great sighs.

The parade, rapidly reassembled, headed south once more.

After a short, easy walk in the gathering darkness, the head of the line came to the edge of the Tez, a great, tranquil river whose right bank was soon crowded by the deployment of the column.

A dugout canoe carrying native oarsmen received onboard Talou and Sirdah, who were ferried over to the opposite shore.

Then, silently emerging from a bamboo hut, the black sorcerer Bashkou, an ivory goblet in hand, approached the blind girl, whom he guided by the shoulders toward the ocean.

Soon both entered the riverbed, progressively sinking as they moved away from shore.

After a few steps, immersed to his chest, Bashkou stopped, holding aloft in his left hand the goblet half full of a whitish liquid, while near him Sirdah disappeared almost completely into the dark, babbling waters.

With two fingers dipped in the milky balm, the sorcerer gently rubbed the girl's eyes, then patiently waited for the remedy to take effect; when enough time had elapsed he applied a thumb to each eyeball and with firm swipes cleanly detached the two blotches, which fell into the currents and were carried away to sea.

Sirdah emitted a cry of joy, proving the operation's complete success, which had indeed just given her back her sight.

Her father answered with a delirious shout, followed by an enthusiastic clamor from the entire crowd.

Rushing back to solid ground, the overjoyed child threw herself into the emperor's arms, while he held her in a long embrace of touching emotion.

Both again took their places in the dugout, which, crossing the river, let them off on the right bank, while Bashkou returned inside his hut.

Sirdah's skin retained the precious moisture from the sacred waters of the river that had witnessed her cure.

Guided by Rao, the column climbed back up the bank over a stretch of a hundred yards and stopped before a huge device that, set amid four posts, hovered above the water like the arch of a bridge.

Night had deepened little by little and, on the shore, an acetylene beacon affixed to the top of a stake lit up, by means of a powerful and carefully positioned reflector, every detail of the astounding machine toward which everyone's eyes now turned.

The contraption, made entirely of metal, immediately suggested a weaving loom.

In the middle, parallel to the river currents, stretched a horizontal *warp* composed of innumerable light blue threads, so remarkably fine that, placed side by side in a single thickness, they occupied a width of only six feet.

Several *heddles*, vertical strings each fitted with an eyelet, formed successive planes perpendicular to the warp, through which they crossed. Before them hung a *batten*, a kind of huge metal comb whose imperceptible and innumerable teeth smoothed the warp as if it were hair.

To the right along the edge of the warp, a large panel about three feet square was composed of numerous pigeonholes separated by wafer-thin partitions; each of these compartments housed a small fly-shuttle whose *quill*, a narrow bobbin attached at front and back, carried a supply of silk thread in a single color. The filaments inside the shuttles, numbering perhaps a thousand, represented every conceivable shade and variation of the seven colors of the prism. The threads, more or less unspooled depending on their position, converged at the first corner to the right of the warp, forming a strange and wonderfully multicolored network.

Underneath, almost at water level, many paddles of all sizes, arranged in a full square like a squadron, filled the entire base of the apparatus, supported on one side by the riverbank and on the other by two pilings sunk into its bed. Each paddle, suspended between two narrow rods, helped power a driving belt wrapped around an unoccupied portion of the thin hub to the left, its two parallel ribbons rising vertically.

Between the hydraulic paddles and the warp stretched a kind of long chest, no doubt containing the mysterious mechanism that drove the whole contraption.

The four posts supported at the top a thick rectangular ceiling from which hung the heddles and the battens.

Paddles, chest, ceiling, panel, shuttles, posts, and the ancillary parts—all, without exception, were made of fine steel of light gray hue.

After placing Sirdah in the front row so she could watch the automatic creation of a certain coat he wished to bestow on her, the inventor Bedu, the hero of the moment, pressed a switch on the chest to activate the precious machine born of his industrious perseverance.

Immediately various paddles plunged halfway into the river, exposing their blades to the powerful currents.

Invisibly moved by the driving belts, the upper portions of which disappeared into the shadows of the chest, the box of shuttles slid horizontally in the axis of the current. Despite their displacement, the countless threads attached to the corner of the warp remained taut, thanks to a system of retrograde tension with which all the shuttles were furnished; left to itself, each *spit*, or pin supporting the quill, turned in the direction opposite the unwinding, owing to a spring that offered a very slight resistance to the extraction of the silk. Some threads automatically contracted while others stretched; the weave preserved its original purity, becoming neither limp nor tangled.

The shuttle-box was held in place by a thick vertical shaft that, after a sharp bend, horizontally penetrated the chest; at that point, a long slot that couldn't be seen from the shore evidently permitted the silent horizontal adjustments that had begun only moments before.

Soon the shuttle-box stopped to change height. The vertical portion of the shaft extended slightly, revealing a system of collapsible sections like those of a telescope; a powerful corkscrew spring, triggered by the interaction of an inner rope and pulley, was the sole cause of this subtle ascent, which soon ended.

The movement of the shuttle-box had coincided with a slight shift in the heddles, certain strings of which had lowered while others rose. The work continued out of sight in the heights of the ceiling: only narrow slits were needed to allow passage of the immense fringes pulled earthward by a legion of thin lead weights, which reached nearly down to the chest. Each silken thread of the warp, individually crossing the eyelets of one of the heddle strings, was accordingly raised or lowered by a few centimeters.

Suddenly, quick as a flash, a shuttle launched by a spring in the shuttle-box passed through the open shed of the warp, flying across the entire width of silk threads to smack against a single compartment fixed at a predetermined and calculated spot. Unspooled from its fragile casing, a *shoot*, or weft thread, now stretched transversally across the warp and formed the beginning of the weave.

The batten, lowered by a movable shaft in one of the slots in the chest, struck against the shoot with its countless teeth, then immediately resumed its upright position.

The heddle strings, adjusting once more, provoked a complete change in the arrangement of the silks, which, moving swiftly back and forth, made a significant shift up or down.

Propelled by a spring in the left-hand compartment, the shuttle sped across the warp in the opposite direction and returned to its pigeonhole; a second shoot, unspooled from its bobbin, received a sharp chop from the batten.

While the heddles pursued this curious back-and-forth motion, the shuttle-box, keeping to a single plane, used its two means of displacement simultaneously to move on a diagonal; aimed at a predetermined spot, a second pigeonhole used a brief pause to expel a shuttle that, flying like a projectile into the collective corner of the silks, lodged itself in a compartment on the opposite side.

A blow from the batten onto the new shoot was followed by an ample movement of the heddles, which prepared the return path for the shuttle as it shot rapidly back to its socket.

The process continued, following an invariable path. Thanks to its marvelous mobility, the shuttle-box positioned shuttle after shuttle opposite the fixed compartments, their two-way voyage coinciding perfectly with the work of the batten and heddles.

Gradually the warp increased on one side, pulled by the slow rotation of the *warp beam*, a large transversal cylinder to which all the threads were attached. The weaving happened quickly, and soon a rich textile started appearing before our eyes, in the form of a thin, even band with finely gradated tonalities.

Down below, the paddles kept everything moving with their complex and precise operation—some remaining almost constantly immersed while others dipped for only a few moments in the current; the smallest paddles, for their part, merely brushed the waves with their blades for a second before rising again, only to lower in the same fleeting way after a short pause. Their number, the staggering of the various sizes, the disparity or simultaneity of the brief or lengthy dips, provided an infinite number of combinations, allowing for the creation of the boldest motifs. It was like some mute instrument plucking chords or arpeggios, sometimes slight and sometimes phenomenally lush, their rhythm and harmony constantly renewed. The driving belts, owing to their supple elasticity, lent themselves to these constant alternations between expansion and contraction. The entire apparatus, a wonder of design and lubrication, operated in silent perfection, suggesting a flawless mechanical marvel.

Bedu directed our attention to the heddles, activated solely by the paddles, which were themselves powered by an electromagnet that transmitted energy from the chest to the ceiling; the wires were hidden in one of the two rear supports, and this method dispensed with the use of punch cards as on Jacquard looms. There was no limit to the variations that could be obtained by the alternate raising and lowering of certain groups of threads. In combination with the parti-colored army of shuttles, this infinity of successive figures in the spacing of the warp allowed for the creation of fabulous textiles on a par with master paintings.

Manufactured in situ by an anomaly of this extraordinary machine, which was specially designed to perform for an attentive audience, the band of fabric grew rapidly, its details powerfully lit by the beacon. The tableau depicted a vast waterway, at the surface of which men, women, and children, eyes bulging in terror, clung desperately to bits of flotsam in a sea of wreckage; and so ingenious were the machine's fabulous gears that the result could have withstood comparison with the most artful watercolor. The fiercely expressive faces displayed admirable flesh tones, from the weathered brown of the old man and milky pallor of the young woman to the fresh pink of the child; the waves, running the gamut of blues, were covered in shimmering reflections, their degree of transparency varying with location.

Moved by a driving belt that rose from an opening in the huge chest, to which it was clinched by two supports, the warp beam pulled the textile that was already wrapping around it. The other end of the warp offered stiff resistance because of a steel rod that, acting as a selvage for the silk threads, was fixed between two parallel barriers attached to the chest by a series of vertical bars. Bolted to the left barrier was the immovable compartment in which each shuttle made a brief halt.

The textile motif gradually took shape, and we saw emerge a mountain toward which groups of humans and animals of all species swam for safety. A host of transparent, diagonal zigzags streaked the entire area and allowed us to grasp the subject, borrowed from the biblical description of the Flood. Calm and majestic at the surface of the waves, Noah's Ark soon lifted its regular, massive silhouette, embellished with finely wrought figures circulating amid a copious menagerie.

The shuttle-box drew our rapt attention by the marvelous steadiness of its alert, captivating gymnastics. One after another, the most varied hues were launched across the warp in the form of shoots, and all the threads together resembled some infinitely rich palette. Sometimes the shuttle-box made a wide movement so that two very distant shuttles could be used sequentially; at other times, several successive shoots belonging to the same area required only minimal shifts. The tip of the given shuttle always found its passage through the other threads, which, parting from nearby pigeonholes and stretched in a single direction, offered it a clear path with no possible obstacle.

On the textile, the half-submerged mountain was now visible to its peak. Everywhere, against its flanks, the condemned wretches, prostrate on this last refuge that would soon be taken from them, implored the heavens with great gestures of distress. The diluvial rain flowed in cataracts over every part of the image, littered with wreckage and islets where the same scenes of despair and supplication were being played out.

The sky progressively expanded toward the zenith, and huge clouds suddenly emerged, thanks to an amalgam of gray threads subtly assorted from the brightest to the murkiest shades. Thick curls of vapor unfurled majestically in the air, harboring inexhaustible reserves to endlessly replenish the horrific deluge.

At that moment, Bedu halted the apparatus by pressing another switch on the chest. Immediately the paddles fell silent, no longer transmitting life to the various components that now lay stiff and inert.

Turning the warp beam over, Bedu, with a finely honed blade, trimmed all the threads hanging loose from the soon detached cloth; then, with a needle previously threaded with silk, he made short work of gathering the upper portion with its border of streaming clouds. The fabric, wider than it was long, took the form of a simple, loose cloak.

Bedu approached Sirdah and draped the marvelous garment over her shoulders, its length enveloping the delighted and grateful girl to her feet.

The sculptor Fuxier had just approached the beacon, showing us in his open hand several lozenges of a uniform blue, which, as we knew, contained a host of potential images of his own devising. He took one and tossed it into the river, slightly downstream from the now inactive loom.

Soon, on the surface lit by the acetylene glow, swirls clearly took shape, tracing in relief a well determined silhouette, which each of us could recognize as Perseus holding the head of Medusa.

The lozenge alone, in melting, had briefly provoked this premeditated, artistic disturbance.

The apparition lasted for a few seconds, then the water, gradually growing calmer, regained its mirrorlike unity.

Skillfully thrown by Fuxier, a second lozenge sank into the current. The concentric circles engendered by its fall had barely dissipated when a new image emerged in fine, ample swirls. This time, dancers in mantillas, standing on a heavily laden table, performed amid the plates and tankards a rousing step punctuated by their castanets, to the cheers of the revelers. The liquid drawing was so detailed that in places one could make out the shadows of crumbs on the tablecloth.

When this convivial scene vanished, Fuxier continued the experiment by sinking a third lozenge, whose effect was not long in coming. The water, suddenly rippling, evoked—upon a rather large canvas—a certain dreamer who, sitting beside a stream, was jotting in a notebook the fruit of some inspiration; behind him, resting against the boulders of the nascent waterfall, an old man with long beard, like the personification of a river, leaned toward the fellow as if to read over his shoulder.

"The poet Giapalù allowing the old Var to rob him of the admirable verses his own genius had wrought," explained Fuxier, who soon tossed yet another lozenge into the newly calm waters.

The roiling settled to depict half a huge clock face with unusual markings. The word "NOON," clearly traced in relief by the water, occupied the place normally reserved for 3 o'clock; then came, on a single quarter-circle near the bottom, every division from 1 to 11 o'clock; at the lowest point, in place of the figure "VI," one could read "MIDNIGHT" spelled out in the diametrical axis; then, to the left, eleven more divisions ended with a second iteration of the word "NOON" replacing 9 o'clock. Acting as the clock's single hand, a long scrap of cloth, looking like the flame of a pennant, was attached to the point that would have been the exact center of the complete clock face; supposedly pushed by the wind, the supple banderole stretched rightward, marking 5 P.M. with its thin, streaming point. The clock, sitting at the top of a solidly planted pedestal, decorated an open landscape through which several people strolled, and the entire liquid tableau was astoundingly precise and accurate.

"The wind clock from the Land of Cockaigne," Fuxier resumed, amplifying his statement with the following commentary:

"In the blissful land in question, the perfectly regular wind took it upon itself to tell the time for the inhabitants. At high noon it blew violently from the west and gradually died down until midnight, a poetic moment when everything was utterly calm. Soon a light breeze from the east gradually rose and kept growing until the following noon, which marked its apogee. An abrupt shift then occurred, and once more the tempest rushed in from the west to resume its evolution of the day before. Remarkably adapted to these unvarying fluctuations, the clock here submitted in effigy for our appreciation fulfilled its functions far better than the ordinary sundial, its solely diurnal task further hampered no doubt by passing clouds."

The Land of Cockaigne had abandoned the watery surface, and the currents, smooth once again, swallowed a final lozenge immersed by Fuxier.

The surface, wrinkling artfully, sketched out a half-naked man holding a bird on his finger.

"The Prince of Conti and his jay," said Fuxier, showing us his empty hand.

When the undulations had flattened out one last time, the parade again took the path to Ejur, plunging into the pitch-blackness that the light from the beacon no longer dissipated, Rao having abruptly extinguished it.

*
* *

We had been walking for several minutes when suddenly, to our right, a bouquet of fireworks lit up the night sky, producing a host of detonations.

A spray of rockets climbed into the air, and soon, reaching the peak of their ascent, the incandescent nuclei exploded with a loud bang to form many luminous portraits of the young Baron Ballesteros, in place of the habitual and banal showers of fire and stars. Each image, bursting from its envelope, emerged independently then floated in the darkness with a gentle sway.

These remarkably executed drawings, sketched in fire, depicted the elegant bon vivant in the most varied poses, each one attributed a specific color.

Here the rich Argentine, in sapphire blue from head to foot, appeared in evening dress, gloves in his hand and a flower in his lapel; there a ruby-colored likeness showed him in his officer's uniform, ready to launch an attack; elsewhere a single bust of colossal dimensions, in frontal view and traced in lines of gold, appeared alongside a dazzling violet design in which the young noble, in top hat and buttoned frock coat, was captured in profile to mid-calf. Farther on, a diamond colored rendering evoked the brilliant sportsman in tennis garb, gracefully brandishing, at an angle, his racket. Other irradiant portraits blossomed on all sides, but the pièce de résistance was, without question, a certain large tableau in emerald green, in which the hero of this phantasmagoria, an impeccable horseman mounted on a trotting steed, gallantly greeted a passing female rider.

The cortege had stopped to ponder this attractive spectacle at its leisure.

The portraits, falling slowly and projecting their powerful polychromatic illumination over a vast expanse, hung in the air for some time without sacrificing any of their brilliance. Then they faded out noiselessly, one by one, and gradually the shadows spread once more over the plain.

Just as the last trace of fireworks vaporized in the night, the entrepreneur Luxo came to join us, proud of the superb effect produced by the pyrotechnical masterpiece he had personally engineered.

Suddenly a distant rumbling could be heard, long and dull; apparently the detonations of the fireworks had provoked a storm brewing in the muggy atmosphere. Immediately the same thought occurred in everyone's mind: "Jizme is about to die!"

At a sign from Talou, the cortege started up again and, swiftly crossing the southern part of Ejur, emerged once more onto Trophy Square.

The storm had already drawn near; bolts of lighting followed each other in quick succession, followed by increasingly loud bursts of thunder.

Rao, who had gone on ahead, soon reappeared with his men, who were straining under the weight of a curious litter that they set down in the middle of the esplanade. By the flashes of lightning, we could examine the strange composition of this object, which looked at once comfortable and terrifying.

A bed frame, raised off the ground by four wooden feet, supported a soft white mattress entirely covered in fine individuated designs, in shape and size not unlike the tailpieces that close the chapters of certain books. The most varied subjects were gathered in this collection of minuscule, independent, isolated images; landscapes, portraits, starstruck couples, groups dancing, ships in distress, and sunsets were treated with a naïve and conscientious art by no means lacking charm or interest. A cushion was slipped under one end of the mattress, raising it to support the sleeper's head; behind the place nominally reserved for the occiput stood a lightning rod, its shining stem rising high above the long berth. A metal skullcap, connected by a wire to the base of the tall vertical needle, was apparently intended to encircle the forehead of some convict sentenced to perish on the lethal couch; at the other end, two metal shoes, placed side by side, communicated with the earth by means of another wire, the tip of which had just been sunken into the ground by Rao himself.

Having reached its peak with the meteorological rapidity peculiar to equatorial regions, the storm now unfurled with extreme violence; a terrible wind shuttled fat black clouds, from which burst an incessant cataclysm.

Rao had opened the prison to release Jizme, the graceful and beautiful young native, who, since the triple execution earlier on, had remained alone behind the dark bars.

Offering no resistance, Jizme lay down on the white mattress, placing her own head in the iron skullcap and her feet in the stiff shoes.

Prudently, Rao and his aides edged away from the dangerous contraption, which then stood completely isolated.

Jizme grasped with both hands a parchment chart hanging by a thin cord from her neck and stared at it at length, taking advantage of the occasional flash of lightning to exhibit it to everyone with a defiantly joyous expression; a name in hieroglyphics, inscribed in the middle of the supple rectangle, was underscored at a distance, to the right, by a small triple drawing depicting three phases of the moon.

Soon, Jizme let go the chart and shifted her look away from the front of the red theater, settling her gaze on Nair; the latter, still imprisoned on his pedestal, had abandoned his delicate labors since the appearance of the beautiful convict, whom he devoured with his eyes.

By then the thunder was rumbling continually, and lighting flashed often enough to give the illusion of false daylight.

Then, with a horrible roar, a blinding zigzag of fire jolted across the sky and struck the tip of the lightning rod. Jizme, whose arms had begun stretching toward Nair, was unable to complete her gesture; the electricity coursed through her body, and the white litter soon supported nothing more than a cadaver with staring eyes and inert limbs.

During the brief silence the storm observed after the next deafening clap of thunder, heartrending sobs drew our attention to Nair, who shed tears of anguish while keeping his eyes fixed on the deceased.

The porters removed the apparatus without disturbing Jizme's corpse, and we waited in pained stupor while the elements gradually receded.

The wind continued chasing the clouds southward and the thunder moved swiftly away, losing more of its force and duration with each passing minute. Little by little the sky cleared and the moon shone brightly over Ejur.

VII

TEN SLAVES APPEARED in the wan light, carrying a heavy burden that they set down in the very place where Jizme had just expired.

The new object was composed mainly of a white wall, facing us, which was propped up by two long iron beams planted in the ground on one side.

From the top of the wall jutted a large awning, its two forward corners six feet exactly above the ends of the beams.

The porters left the area as the hypnotist Darriand slowly came forward, leading by the hand the Negro Seil-kor, a poor lunatic in his twenties who walked while uttering soft, incoherent words in perfect French.

Darriand abandoned his patient momentarily to inspect the white wall, especially the awning, which seemed to absorb all his attention.

During this time, Seil-kor, left to his own devices, calmly gesticulated, displaying in the moonlight an oddly carnival-like outfit comprising a pillbox cap, a mask, and a ruff, all three cut out of paper.

The ruff was pieced together entirely from blue covers of the magazine *La Nature*, whose title stood out in various places; the surface of the mask was tightly veined with numerous and varied signatures printed in facsimile; and the word "Tremble" paraded in bold letters across the crest of the cap, visible during certain movements of the young man's head, who in this get-up looked like a make-believe noble from the court of the last Valois.

Too small for Seil-kor, the three objects seemed better suited to the measurements of a twelve-year-old boy.

Darriand, reclaiming everyone's attention with a few words, had just tilted the white wall back to show us the underside of the over-hanging canopy: entirely covered in reddish plants, it looked like an inverted window box.

Restoring the object to its upright position, the hypnotist offered us several details about a certain experiment he intended to try.

The plants we'd just seen, rare and precious specimens whose seeds he'd gathered during his travels in distant Oceania, possessed extremely potent hypnotic properties.

A subject placed beneath the fragrant canopy was permeated by this unsettling fragrance, which immediately plunged him into a veritable hypnotic ecstasy; at that point, the patient, facing the wall, saw a host of colored images parade across the white surface thanks to a system of electric projection, which the temporary overstimulation of his senses made him take for reality. The sight of a hyper-borean landscape, for instance, would immediately chill him to the bone, making his limbs shiver and his teeth chatter; conversely, a scene simulating a white-hot hearth provoked abundant perspiration and could ultimately cause serious burns to his skin. By show-ing Seil-kor a striking episode from his own past, Darriand hoped to revive the memory and sanity that the young Negro had recently lost to a head injury.

His preamble finished, Darriand again took Seil-kor by the hand and led him beneath the awning, positioning his face to receive the reflections from the white wall. The poor imbecile was immediately overcome by violent spasms; his breathing sped up and his fingertips ran over the ruff, cap, and mask, seeming to find at the unexpected contact of these three objects some private and painful memory.

All at once an electric lamp, set at midpoint on the lower lip run-ning along the awning's wide border and powered by a concealed battery, lit the wall with a large bright square due to the combined action of a lens and a reflector. The actual light source remained hidden, but we could clearly see the beam as it projected downward, widening until it met the screen, its path partly blocked by Seil-kor's head.

Darriand, who had himself activated this light, now slowly turned a silent crank, set at hand height in the left end of the wall. Soon, produced by a colored slide placed before the projector, an image appeared on the white screen, showing Seil-kor a ravishing blonde child of about twelve, full of charm and grace; above the portrait we could read the words "The Young Candiote."

At this sight, Seil-kor fell deliriously to his knees as if before a goddess, crying, "Nina . . . Nina . . ." in a voice trembling with joy and emotion. Everything in his posture showed that his senses, heightened by the intense emanations from the Oceanic plants, made him believe that the adorable girl he'd named so rapturously was an actual, living presence.

After a moment's pause, Darriand turned the crank again, setting in motion, by means of a hidden diaphanous strip on a system of sprockets, a series of views appearing one after another before the bright lens.

The portrait slid left and disappeared from the screen. On the brilliant surface we now saw a region on the map of France marked with the word "Corrèze"; the capital of this region, a large black dot, carried a simple question mark in place of the word "Tulle." Before this sudden question, Seil-kor nervously shook his head as if seeking some elusive reply.

Under the title "Fishing for Electric Rays," a moving scene replaced the geographic map. Here, wearing a navy-blue dress and sturdily armed with a long, flexible pole, the young girl Seil-kor had called Nina fell in a faint, gripping a white fish that flopped at the end of her line.

Darriand continued his operation and the captioned views followed each other without interruption, profoundly afflicting Seil-kor, who, still on his knees, heaved sighs and whimpers that betrayed his growing excitement.

After "Fishing for Electric Rays" came "The Martingale": on the steps of an imposing building, a very young Negro, bouncing several silver coins in his hand, headed toward an entrance surmounted by the three words "Casino of Tripoli."

"The Fable" showed a page of a book propped against a huge Savoy cake.

"The Ball" consisted of a merry party in which children moved by twos through a vast salon. In the foreground, Nina and the young Negro with the silver coins rushed toward each other, arms outstretched, while a woman with a benevolent smile seemed to be encouraging their tender embrace.

Soon "The Valley of Oo," a deep, green landscape, was followed by "The Bolero in the Shed," in which we saw Nina and her friend dancing feverishly in the middle of an unadorned interior littered with carriages and harnesses.

"The Guiding Path" depicted a tangled forest in which Nina advanced courageously. Next to her, as if to mark his retreat like Tom Thumb, the young Negro tossed a white morsel on the ground from the tip of his knife, having no doubt just cut it from a heavy Swiss cheese wilting in his left hand.

Nina, after sleeping on a bed of moss in "The First Night of Advent," reappeared standing in "Orientation," her finger raised toward the stars. Finally, "The Coughing Fit" depicted the young heroine wracked by a horrible cough and sitting, penholder in hand, before an almost completely filled sheet of paper. In a corner of the scene, a page shown in cutaway was apparently an enlargement of the document under the girl's hand: beneath a series of scarcely legible lines, the title "Resolution," followed by an unfinished sentence, suggested the conclusion of a catechism exercise.

Throughout this series of images, Seil-kor, in the grip of incredible agitation, had never stopped his violent thrashing, stretching his arms to Nina and tenderly moaning her name.

Letting go of the crank, Darriand abruptly turned off the lamp, lifted Seil-kor to his feet, and pulled him outside, for the young Negro's turmoil, having reached paroxysm, made one fear the deleterious effects of too prolonged a stay beneath the bewitching vegetation.

Seil-kor soon came to his senses. Darriand having removed his paper trappings, he looked around him like a slowly awakening sleeper, then murmured softly, "Oh! I remember, I remember now ... Nina ... Tripoli ... the Valley of Oo ..."

Darriand observed him intently, happily noting these first signs of a cure. Soon the hypnotist's triumph was plain to all, for Seil-kor, recognizing everyone's face, began replying rationally to a host of questions. The marvelously triumphant experiment had restored the poor lunatic to reason, leaving him full of gratitude for his savior.

Darriand was roundly congratulated, while the porters removed the admirable projection device whose effectiveness had just been demonstrated so successfully.

After a moment we saw appear at left, effortlessly dragged by a serf, a certain Roman chariot whose two wheels produced as they turned a constant and fairly high C note, sounding true and pure in the night.

On the vehicle's narrow platform, a wicker armchair supported the frail and puny body of young Kalj, one of the emperor's sons. Next to the axle walked Meisdehl, a graceful, charming black girl who was conversing gaily with the impassive boy.

Both children, aged seven or eight, wore red headpieces that stood out against their ebony faces. Kalj's, a kind of simple dust-cap cut from the pages of some illustrated newspaper, displayed on its circumference in the lunar light a richly colored picture of cavalrymen charging, underscored by the name "Reichshoffen," the incomplete remnant of an explanatory caption. Meisdehl wore a narrow bonnet of similar provenance, its red hues, due to abundantly depicted house fires, were elucidated by the word "Commune" legible on one of its edges.

The chariot crossed the square, still emitting its shrill C, then halted next to the Incomparables' stage.

Kalj climbed down and disappeared to the right, taking Meisdehl with him, while the crowd gathered in front of the small theater to watch the final scene of *Romeo and Juliet*, performed with many new additions taken from Shakespeare's authentic manuscript.

Soon the curtains parted to reveal Meisdehl, lying on a raised bed in profile, as Juliet in the depths of her narcotic slumber.

Behind the deathbed, greenish flames, colored with mineral salts, escaped from a powerful brazier hidden at the bottom of a dark metal container, of which only the edges were visible.

After several moments, Romeo, played by Kalj, appeared to contemplate in grieving silence the corpse of his adored companion.

Though they were lacking traditional costumes, the actors' red bonnets, with their characteristic shape, would identify the Shakespearean couple.

In the flush of a final kiss placed on the dead girl's forehead, Romeo brought a thin flask to his lips, then flung it away after having downed its poisonous contents.

Suddenly Juliet opened her eyes, rose slowly, and descended from her bed before Romeo's frantic gaze. The two lovers fell into each other's arms and exchanged many caresses, abandoning themselves to their trembling joy.

Then Romeo, running to the brazier, pulled from the flames an asbestos thread, the end of which hung over the lip of the metal container. This incombustible wick bore fiery coals over its entire length, which, cut like precious stones and glowing red from the heat, looked like shining rubies.

Returning center stage, Romeo clasped the curious ornament about Juliet's neck, her skin enduring without a tremor the burning contact of those terrible jewels.

But the lover beaming with hope and confidence was suddenly seized in mid-joy by the first throes of agony. With a desperate gesture he showed the poison to Juliet, who, contrary to events in the familiar version, discovered at the bottom of the flask a remnant of the liquid, which she greedily swallowed as well.

Half-collapsed on the risers leading to the bed, Romeo, under the spell of the fatal potion, was on the verge of gripping hallucinations.

Everyone had been waiting for this moment to gauge the effect of certain red lozenges: fashioned by Fluxier and thrown into the brazier one by one by Adinolfa, who was concealed behind the deathbed, they were designed to release clouds of smoke in various meaningful shapes.

The first apparition soon emerged from the flames, in the form of an intense and precisely formed vapor that depicted the Temptation of Eve.

In the middle of this vision, the serpent coiled around a tree trunk reached its head toward a graceful, relaxed Eve, whose conspicuously raised hand seemed to rebuff the evil tempter.

The contours, at first very sharp, thickened as the cloud rose into the air; soon the details blurred into a shifting, chaotic mass, which promptly vanished into the flies.

A second puff of smoke reproduced the same scene; but this time Eve eagerly stretched her fingers toward the apple, about to pluck it.

Romeo turned his distraught eyes toward the hearth, its green flames infusing the stage with a tragic glow.

Another thick, meticulously sculpted billow of smoke, escaping from the brazier, created before the dying youth a joyous bacchanal; women performed a feverish dance for a group of debauchees with jaded smiles; in the background lay the remains of a feast, while in the foreground the presumed host directed his guests' admiration toward the lithe, lascivious dancers.

Romeo, as if recognizing the vision, murmured these words: "Thisias ... the orgy in Zion ... !"

Already the vaporous scene was rising and beginning to dissipate. After it had drifted away, a new cloud of smoke, originating in the usual place, reprised the same figures in different postures; this time joy gave way to terror, and dancers and libertines, jumbled together on their knees, bowed their heads before the apparition of God the Father, whose infuriated face hovered in mid-air above them all, motionless and terrible.

A new emergence of sculpted fog, succeeding the interrupted gyrations, was greeted by this cry from Romeo: "Saint Ignatius!"

Now the smoke formed two superimposed subjects, to be viewed individually. On the bottom, Saint Ignatius, thrown to the beasts in the Roman circus, was but an inert, mutilated corpse; on the top, a little to the rear, Heaven, populated with haloed figures and depicted as an enchanted isle surrounded by calm waters, welcomed a second image of the saint, more transparent than the first, which represented his soul separated from his body.

"Pheor of Alexandria!"

This exclamation of Romeo's was directed toward a phantom that, in its sculpted nebulosity, had just emerged from the brazier following Saint Ignatius. The new figure, standing amid an attentive crowd, looked like some illuminatus preaching the good word; his simple robe flapped around his ascetic body, apparently wasted by fasting, and his emaciated face contrasted sharply with his voluminous temples.

This presentation inaugurated a storyline rapidly continued by a second emission of purely delineated smoke. There, in the middle of a public marketplace, two groups formed two perfectly regular squares, one made up solely of old men, the other solely of youths.

Pheor, following a violent harangue, found himself facing the anger of the young men, who had thrown him to the ground without pity for the feebleness of his scrawny limbs.

A third aerial episode showed Pheor on his knees, in an ecstatic pose provoked by the passage of a courtesan surrounded by an entourage of slaves.

Little by little the smoke that composed these human groupings spread a drifting, impalpable veil over the stage.

"Jeremiah . . . the stoning . . . !"

After these words, inspired by a dull, fleeting eruption above the hearth showing Jeremiah stoned by a massive crowd, the exhausted Romeo fell dead before the horrified eyes of Juliet, who, still wearing the necklace that already glowed less brightly, succumbed in turn to the potion's hallucinatory power.

A light suddenly shone at left, behind the backdrop, illuminating an apparition visible through a fine painted grille, which until then had seemed as opaque and homogenous as the fragile wall surrounding it.

Juliet turned toward the flood of light, crying, "Father . . . !"

Capulet, played by Soreau, stood in a long golden robe, silky and floating; his outstretched arm pointed at Juliet in a gesture of hatred and reproach, clearly related to her guilty elopement.

Then darkness fell anew, and the vision disappeared behind the again unremarkable wall.

Juliet, kneeling in a supplicant posture, stood up, wracked by sobs, to remain for a few moments with her face buried in her hands.

A second luminous image made her raise her head and drew it to the right, toward an evocation of Christ, who, mounted on the legendary donkey, was only slightly concealed by a second painted grille, forming a pendant to the first.

It was again Soreau, having rapidly changed, who played the role of Jesus, his presence seeming to admonish Juliet for having betrayed her faith by voluntarily summoning death.

The divine, immobile specter, suddenly growing dim, vanished behind the wall, and Juliet, as if stricken by madness, smiled softly at some enchanting new dream beginning to form.

At that moment a bust of a woman's head appeared onstage, mounted on a small trolley that an unknown hand pushed laterally from stage left using a stiff rod hidden at floor level.

The pink and white bust, much like a barber's dummy, had wide blue eyes with long lashes and a magnificent head of blonde hair separated into thin braids that hung naturally on all sides. Certain of her braids, which we could see because chance had placed them over her chest or against her shoulders, bore numerous gold coins up and down their outer surface.

Enchanted, Juliet moved toward the visitor murmuring the name "Urgela . . . !"

Then the stand, shaken side to side by the rod, communicated its jolts to the bust, whose hair violently swung about. The poorly attached gold coins fell in an abundant shower, proving that the unseen plaits in back were no less festooned than the others.

For a moment the fairy spread her dazzling riches without measure, until, presumably pulled back by the same hand, she silently disappeared.

Juliet, as if pained by this abandonment, looked about aimlessly, her eyes coming to rest on the still glowing brazier.

Once more, a torrent of smoke rose above the flames.

Juliet recoiled, crying out in stark terror: "Pergovedula . . . the two heifers . . . !"

The intangible and fugitive shape evoked a woman with frizzy hair, seated before a monstrous repast composed of two heifers cut into large quarters and avidly brandishing an immense fork.

The vapor, in dissipating, revealed behind the hearth a fearsome apparition, which Juliet designated by the same name, "Pergovedula," spoken with heightened anxiety.

It was the tragedienne Adinolfa, who had quickly stood up in a peculiar guise. Her face, thickly coated in ochre greasepaint, clashed with her mildew-green lips, which parted in a wide and horrifying rictus; her bushy hair made her look precisely like the vision that had just emerged from the brazier, and her eyes stared insistently at the terror-stricken Juliet.

Billows of smoke, now in no specific shape, were still pouring from the brazier, masking Adinolfa's face; by the time this ephemeral veil dispersed, she had vanished.

Less brilliantly adorned by the necklace that was gradually fading, Juliet in her final agony collapsed onto the steps leading to the bed, arms hanging limp, head thrown back. Her eyes, now devoid of expression, ended by staring into space at a second Romeo who slowly descended toward her.

This new supernumerary, played by one of Kalj's brothers, personified the light and lively soul of the inert corpse stretched out near Juliet. A red headpiece, like that of his model, decorated the brow of this perfect double, who, with outstretched arms, came smiling to claim the dying girl and lead her to her immortal repose.

But Juliet, seemingly deprived of sanity, turned indifferently away, while the ghost, contrite and dismissed, rose noiselessly back into the wings.

After a few last weak and automatic movements, Juliet fell dead next to Romeo, just as the two stage curtains closed rapidly.

Kalj and Meisdehl had astonished us all with their marvelously tragic pantomime and by the few French phrases they had uttered without a trace of error or accent.

Returning to the esplanade, the two children made a prompt departure.

Pulled by the serf and faithfully escorted by Meisdehl, the chariot, once more emitting its shrill, continuous note, carried to the left the sickly Romeo, visibly exhausted by the strain of his lengthy performance.

The high C was still ringing in the distance when Fuxier came toward us, his spread right hand holding against his chest an earthen pot from which a vine-stock jutted.

His left hand carried a transparent cylindrical jar, which, furnished with a large cork stopper pierced by a metal tube, displayed in its lower portion a volume of chemical salts that had burgeoned into graceful crystals.

Setting his two burdens on the ground, Fuxier took from his pocket a small covered lantern, which he lay flat on the potting soil brushing against the inner edges of the stoneware vessel. An electrical current, switched on within this portable beacon, suddenly projected a dazzling shaft of white light, which a powerful lens pointed toward the zenith.

At that point, lifting the jar and holding it horizontally, Fuxier turned a key at the end of the metal tube, whose opening, carefully aimed at a predetermined portion of the stock, released a violently compressed gas. A brief explanation taught us that this element, when allowed contact with the atmosphere, provoked an intense heat, which, combined with certain very specific chemical properties, would cause a bunch of grapes to ripen before our eyes.

He had barely finished his commentary when already the promised phenomenon occurred in the form of an imperceptibly small cluster. Possessing the power that legend ascribes to certain Indian fakirs, Fuxier performed for us the miracle of instant blossoming.

Under the action of the chemical flow, the fruit buds developed rapidly, and soon a cluster of green grapes, heavy and ripe, hung alone on one side of the vine-stock.

Fuxier set the jar back down on the ground, having sealed the tube with another twist of the key. Then, drawing our attention to the cluster, he showed us minuscule human figures imprisoned at the center of the diaphanous globes.

Through a process of modeling and coloration even more meticulous than the labor required to prepare his blue or red lozenges, Fuxier had deposited in each bud the seed of an elegant tableau, which had reached fruition in tandem with the grape's accelerated maturity.

Looking closely, we could easily make out, through the grapes' unusually delicate and transparent skins, the various scenes that the lantern's electric beam lit from below.

The operations on the grape buds had entailed the suppression of pips, and so nothing disturbed the purity of the translucent and colored Lilliputian statues, whose matter was furnished by the pulp itself.

"A glimpse of ancient Gaul," said Fuxier, his finger touching a first grape in which we saw several Celtic warriors readying for battle.

Each of us admired the subtlety of contour and richness of tone that the lamp highlighted so beautifully.

"Eudes sawed in two by a demon in Count Valtguire's dream," Fuxier resumed, indicating a second grape.

This time we distinguished, behind the sheer envelope, a sleeper in armor stretched out at the foot of a tree; a puff of smoke, seemingly escaping from his forehead to depict some dream, contained, in its tenuous clouds, a demon armed with a long saw whose sharp teeth sliced into the flesh of one of the damned, writhing in pain.

A third grape, summarily explained, showed the Roman circus teeming with a throng enflamed by a gladiator fight.

"Napoleon in Spain."

These words applied to a fourth grape, in which the emperor, attired in green, passed victoriously on horseback amid the citizens, their hatred visible in their silently hostile manner.

"A gospel of Saint Luke," continued Fuxier, lightly touching a triplet of grapes side by side on a single stem with three branches, in which the following three scenes contained the same characters:

In the first, one saw Jesus holding out his hand to a small girl, who, lips open and eyes fixed, seemed to be singing some fine and prolonged trill. Next to her, on a pallet, a young boy immobilized in the sleep of death still clutched in his fingers a long wicker strand; near the deathbed, his grief-stricken father and mother wept silently. In a corner, a skinny, hunchbacked girl child kept humbly to the side.

In the middle grape, Jesus, turned toward the pallet, looked at the dead boy, who, miraculously restored to life, braided the light and flexible wicker strand like a practiced basket weaver. The wonder-struck family expressed its joyous stupefaction with ecstatic gestures.

The final tableau, containing the same décor and characters, glorified Jesus touching the young invalid, who had become tall and beautiful.

Leaving this trilogy aside, Fuxier lifted the bottom of the cluster and showed us a superb grape with this commentary:

"Hans the woodsman and his six sons."

Here, a strangely robust old man carried on his shoulder a formidable load of wood, made of entire tree trunks mixed with bundles of logs held together by shoots. Behind him, six young men each strained beneath a burden of the same type, though infinitely lighter. The old man, half turning his head, seemed to be mocking the slow-pokes who were less hardy and energetic than he.

In the penultimate grape, an adolescent wearing Louis XV garb looked on with emotion as he passed by a young woman in a poppy-colored dress sitting in her doorway.

"The first stirrings of love felt by Jean-Jacques Rousseau's Emile," explained Fuxier, who, moving his fingers, made the electric rays play over the bright red glimmers of the woman's dazzling dress.

The tenth and final grape contained a superhuman duel that Fuxier told us was a reproduction of a canvas by Raphael. An angel, hovering several feet above ground, was aiming his lance at Satan's chest, while the latter faltered and dropped his own weapon.

Having presented the entire cluster, Fuxier extinguished his covered lantern, which he put back in his pocket; he then walked away as he'd come, again carrying the earthen pot and cylindrical container.

VIII

WE WERE STILL GAZING after the evocative grape vine when Rao appeared leading his slaves, who were groaning beneath a voluminous and rather elongated object.

Next to the group, Fogar, the emperor's eldest son, walked in silence, holding in his right hand a magnificent purple flower whose stem bristled with thorns.

The new burden was set in the usual place, and Fogar remained alone to watch over it as the others quickly retreated.

The object, freely exposed to the moonlight, was none other than a very rudimentary bed, an uncomfortable-looking box frame decorated with many diverse attributes.

To the right, attached behind the raised portion intended to support the sleeper's torso, a pot of dirt held the root of a huge, whitish plant that rose into the air, then curved to form a kind of bed canopy.

Above this graceful baldachin, a spotlight, unlit at the moment, hung from a metal pole bent at the top.

The farthest side of the bed frame bore numerous ornaments, arranged with care.

Just before the right-hand corner, a long triangular surface, suggesting a pennant, unfurled to the side at the top of a narrow raised stake made of blue-painted wood. The whole thing looked like the flag of some unknown country, given the colors on the muslin: a cream-colored background shot through with asymmetrical red streaks and two close-set black dots stacked one above the other near the vertical base of the triangle.

A little to the left rose a minuscule portico, barely an inch wide.

Hanging from the lintel at top, the fringe from a dress or costume swayed its many white, even strands at the slightest disturbance; each of these strands ended in a bright red tip.

Pursuing our examination in the same direction, we found a shallow receptacle from which emerged white soap covered with thick foam.

Then came a metal recess containing a large, thin sponge.

Next to the recess, a fragile platform supported an amphora with strange contours, against which leaned a cylindrical object fitted with a propeller.

Finally, concluding this incomprehensible series of ornaments on the left side, a round zinc plate balanced horizontally on a narrow pillar.

The side of the bed frame facing the plant and the spotlight was no less crowded.

Against the corner next to the zinc plate one first saw a kind of gelatinous block, yellow and motionless.

Next, along the same plane, was a piece of carpet, on which a thin layer of dry cement was spread; in the cement, one hundred thin, sharp jade needles were vertically embedded in ten even rows.

The block and carpet rested alongside each other on a short board barely large enough for them.

Three gold ingots, whose perfect spacing seemed to prolong the median line of the frame, rose from three iron supports that held them solidly in their claws. One could not differentiate among them, as their cylindrical shape and rounded ends were identical.

Closer to us, next to the narrow space occupied by the three precious ingots, a second board mirrored the first.

On it, we first saw a basket containing three cats: lent by Marius Boucharessas, they were none other than three of the *greens* from the game of prisoner's base, still sporting their ribbons.

Next to this, a delicate object, which looked like the door to a cage, was composed of two thin slats that, laid horizontally a few centimeters apart from each other, pressed between their four inner extremities two fragile vertical risers. In the rectangle thus formed, taut black horsehairs stretched top to bottom between the two wooden slats, passing through imperceptible holes and knotted at both ends. Nearby lay a very straight twig, sliced in half lengthwise, that displayed a slightly resinous inner surface.

Finally, placed directly on the board against the near corner of the bed frame, a fat candle stood next to two dark-colored pebbles.

From almost halfway down the bed, at what would be the sleeper's left, rose a metal rod; upright at first, it then bent sharply to the right and ended in a kind of curved handle like the armpiece of a crutch.

Fogar carefully inspected the various components of the cot. His ebony face shone with precocious intelligence, to a degree astonishing in a boy who had just reached adolescence.

Using the only side that remained free of clutter, he climbed onto the bed and slowly stretched out, bringing his left armpit in line with the curved handle that fit it perfectly.

His arms and legs completely rigid, he froze in a corpselike pose, after having placed the purple flower within reach of his right hand.

His lids ceased blinking over his staring, vacant eyes, and the rhythm of his breathing gradually decreased under the influence of the powerful lethargic slumber that soon overcame him.

A few moments later, his prostration was absolute. The adolescent's chest remained as motionless as if he were dead, and his half-open mouth seemed to exhale no breath.

Bex, walking up, pulled an oval mirror from his pocket and placed it before the young Negro's lips; no fog tarnished the brilliant surface, and its shine remained intact.

Then, laying his hand over the patient's heart, Bex shook his head to indicate the lack of a pulse.

Several seconds passed in silence. Bex had quietly retreated, leaving the area around the bed unencumbered.

Suddenly, as if he'd found some scrap of consciousness in the depths of his torpor, Fogar's body gave an imperceptible twitch, which activated the handle under his armpit.

Immediately the spotlight lit up, projecting downward a dazzlingly white electric beam, its brightness increased tenfold by a freshly polished reflector.

The white plant that formed the bed canopy received the full force of that intense light, which seemed to be aimed specifically at it. Through the transparent overhang, we could see a delicate, clear, and vivid image, of a piece with the plant's very fibers, which we now saw were tinted through and through.

The whole thing was oddly reminiscent of a stained-glass window, admirably unified and blended due to the absence of any seam or harsh glare.

The diaphanous image evoked some Oriental site. Under a cloudless sky stretched a splendid garden filled with alluring flowers. In the center of a marble basin, a fountain spurting from a jade tube gracefully described its slender arc.

To one side rose the façade of a sumptuous palace, in which one open window framed a couple locked in an embrace. The man, a fat, bearded individual dressed like a wealthy merchant from the *Arabian Nights*, wore on his beaming face an expression of expansive and inalterable joy. The woman, a full-blooded Moor judging by her dress and features, remained languid and melancholy despite her companion's good humor.

Beneath the window, not far from the marble fountain, stood a young man with curly locks, whose outfit was consonant in time and place with the merchant's. Lifting his face in inspiration toward the couple, he sang some elegy of his own composition through a megaphone made of dull, silvery metal.

The Moorish eyes avidly sought out the poet, who, for his part, was intoxicated by the young woman's striking beauty.

Suddenly, a shift of molecules occurred in the fibers of the luminous plant. The image lost its clarity and contour. The atoms all vibrated at once, as if trying to settle into a new, predetermined arrangement.

Soon a second tableau formed, as resplendent as the first and similarly of a piece with the fine, translucent vegetal fibers.

In this scene, a large dune in golden hues retained several footprints on its arid flanks. The poet from the first image, bent toward the friable sand, gently placed his lips on the deep trace of a slim, graceful foot.

After several moments' immobility, the atoms, again unsettled, recommenced their turbulent maneuver, yielding a third brightly colored view.

This time the poet was not alone: next to him a Chinaman in a purple robe pointed at a large bird of prey, whose majestic flight doubtless had some prophetic import.

A new reshuffling in the sensitive plant depicted, in a curious laboratory, the same Chinaman receiving several gold coins from the poet in exchange for a manuscript tendered and accepted.

Each bizarre image from the plant lasted the same amount of time; one by one the following scenes succeeded each other on the canopy screen:

The laboratory yielded to a richly appointed banquet hall. Sitting at the fully laid table, the fat, bearded merchant breathed in the aroma of a dish he held in both hands. His eyelids were growing heavy under the spell of the appetizing steam, which bore some treacherous substance. Opposite him the poet and the Mooress eagerly awaited the onset of this deep slumber.

Then we saw a marvelous Eden on which the burning rays of the noonday sun beat down. In the background flowed a graceful waterfall, tinted with green glimmers. The poet and the Moorish woman slept side by side, in the shade of a fabulous flower like some giant anemone. To the left, a Negro entered at a run, as if to warn the two lovers of some impending danger.

The same setting, evoked a second time, framed the amorous couple mounted on a spirited zebra that took off at breakneck speed. Sitting on its rump behind the solidly straddling poet, the Mooress laughingly brandished a purse containing a few gold coins. The Negro followed their departure with a respectful gesture of farewell.

The enchanting site eclipsed definitively to give way to a sunbaked road, at the edge of which rose a stall filled with various foodstuffs. Lying in the middle of the road and cradled by the anxious poet, the Moorish woman, pale and exhausted, received some nourishment provided by the attentive and zealous shopkeeper.

In the following apparition, the recovered Mooress wandered with the poet. Near her, a strange-looking man seemed to be making dire predictions that she took in with alarm and distress.

A final image, evidently containing the tragic denouement of the idyll, showed a terrible abyss whose walls bristled with sharp protuberances. The Mooress, her body smashing against these countless spikes, was in the midst of a horrifying fall, having succumbed to the dizzying pull of many bodiless, faceless eyes, their harsh expression fraught with menace. At the top of the precipice, the desperate poet was throwing himself after his lover.

This dramatic scene was replaced by the unexpected picture of a wolf with glowing eyes. The animal's body alone took up as much space as each of the preceding views; beneath it one could read, in fat capitals, the Latin designation "LUPUS." No similarity of color or proportion seemed to link this giant portrait to the Oriental scenes, whose own unity was evident.

The wolf soon vanished and the initial image reappeared, with its garden and marble fountain, singing poet, and couple posted at the window. All the tableaux paraded by a second time in the exact same order, separated by pauses of the same length. The wolf again concluded the series, which was followed by a third cycle, rigorously identical to the first two. Indefinitely the plant repeated its curious molecular revolutions, which seemed an integral part of its own existence.

When the initial garden and its fountain appeared for the fourth time, everyone's gaze, weary of following this now-monotonous spectacle, lowered onto the still inanimate Fogar.

The young Negro's body and the objects placed on the edges of his bed were covered in multicolored reflections coming from the strange bed canopy.

Like the floor slabs of a church on which sunlight reproduces the smallest subtleties of stained glass, the entire area of the bed frame slavishly plagiarized the shapes and hues fixed on the screen.

One could recognize the protagonists, water fountain, and palace façade, all enlarged by projection, as they sumptuously tinted the different lumps or objects they happened to fall on, espousing their infinitely varied forms.

The polychromatic waves overflowed extensively onto the ground, causing a scattering of fantastic colored shapes on either side.

Even without raising our eyes toward the plant canopy, we could still witness each pictorial change, the reflections echoing the now familiar and anticipated scenes.

Soon afterward Fogar's prostration came to an end. His chest rose slightly, marking the resumption of his breathing. Bex rested his hand on the heart that had been stilled for so long, then returned to his place, notifying us of the timid, barely perceptible pulse.

Suddenly a blink of the boy's eyelids indicated his complete return to life. His eyes lost their abnormal stare, and Fogar, with a sudden movement, grasped the purple flower lying limp near his right hand.

With a thorn on its stem, he made a longitudinal gash in his left wrist, then opened a bulging, swollen vein and pulled out a huge blood clot, greenish in color and completely coagulated, which he laid on the bed. Then, with a petal of the flower nimbly plucked and squeezed between his fingers, he created a few drops of an effective serum that, dripping onto his vein, swiftly sealed the two separated edges.

At that point his circulation, cleared of all obstacles, could resume easily.

The identical operation, which Fogar himself performed on his chest and near the inner bend of his right knee, procured two more blood clots like the first. Two more petals, needed to seal the blood vessels, were now missing from the purple flower.

The three clots, which Fogar now held side by side in his left hand, looked like three sticks of gummy, translucent angelica.

The young Negro had obtained the desired effect by his voluntary catalepsy, whose only purpose, indeed, was to entail a partial condensation of his blood and thus provide the solidified fragments full of delicate hues.

Turning to the right toward the red-streaked pennant, Fogar took one of the blood clots, which he raised gently to the blue flagpole.

Suddenly the whitish muslin, bathed in reflections from above, started quivering. Immobile until then, the triangle began to descend, clinging to its stem; rather than a simple rag, we saw before us some strange animal endowed with instinct and movement. The reddish streaks were actually powerful blood vessels, and the two symmetrical black dots a monitory, unblinking pair of eyes. The vertical base of the triangle adhered to the pole via numerous suction cups, which a series of contortions had now begun moving in a constant direction.

Fogar, still lifting his green clot, soon reached the animal, which regularly pursued its descent.

Only the upper suction cups remained affixed, while the lower ones, detaching themselves from the pole, avidly seized upon the clot that the adolescent abandoned to it.

With a greedy sucking action, the animal's ingesting mouths, working in concert, quickly devoured the sanguine treat of which it seemed inordinately fond.

The meal over, the suction cups adhered once more to the pole, and the creature, immobile once more, resumed its initial appearance as a stiff flag sporting unfamiliar colors.

Fogar put his second clot near the fragile portico rising to the left of the blue flagpole on the edge of the bed.

Immediately, the fringe hanging from the horizontal lintel began to stir feverishly, as if attracted by a powerful lure.

Its upper spine was composed of a system of suction cups similar to the ones on the triangular animal.

Various acrobatics allowed it to reach one of the stiles and descend along it toward the proferred delicacy.

Floating tentacles, possessing life and strength, delicately gripped the clot and carried it to some of the suction cups, which, detached from the stile, feasted on it without further ado.

When the prey had been entirely absorbed, the fringe hoisted itself by the same path back to the upper lintel, where it regained its customary position.

The last clot Fogar placed in the container occupied by the white cake of soap.

At once, we saw movement in the thick foam spread over the top of the solid, slippery block.

A third animal had just revealed its presence, heretofore concealed by absolute stillness joined with its misleading appearance.

A certain snowlike carapace covered the body of the strange creature, which, crawling slowly, let out at regular intervals a dry, plaintive hiccup.

The reflections from the bed canopy took on particular vigor as they hit the immaculate tegument, giving it especially bright hues.

Having reached the edge of the soap, the animal descended the sheer vertical slope to reach the flat base of the container; there, filled with impatient gluttony, it gobbled down the blood clot, then settled in heavy silence to begin its calm, leisurely digestion.

Fogar knelt on his cot to more easily reach the objects placed farther from him.

With his fingertips, he moved a thin lever attached outside the metal recess that immediately followed the cake of soap.

At that very instant, a brilliant burst of light inflamed the sponge before everyone's eyes. Several glass tubes, shot through by a luminous current, were aligned horizontally along the inner walls of the recess, which was suddenly inundated with brightness.

Made translucent in the glare, the sponge revealed, in the middle of its quasi-diaphanous tissue, a veritable miniature human heart attached to a highly complex circulatory system. The well-defined aorta transported a host of red globules, which, through a series of infinitely ramified branch arteries, distributed life even to the farthest reaches of the organism.

Fogar took up the amphora standing beside the recess and slowly poured several pints of pure, fresh water on the sponge.

This sudden shower seemed to displease the astounding specimen, which contracted vigorously to expel the unwelcome liquid.

A central opening, cut in the floor of the recess, provided drainage for the rejected water, which leaked onto the ground in a thin trickle.

Several times the adolescent repeated the same exercise. Amid the electric irradiation, the droplets sometimes harbored glints like diamonds, owing to the perpetually renewed multicolored projections.

Fogar replaced the amphora and picked up the cylinder with propeller lying next to it.

This new object, entirely made of metal and of very small dimensions, contained a powerful battery that the young man activated by pressing a switch.

As if obeying an order, the propeller, attached to the end of the cylinder as if to the stern of a ship, began spinning rapidly with a light whirring sound.

Soon the instrument in Fogar's hand hovered over the horizontal zinc plate, which was still balancing at the top of its column.

Held downward, the propeller constantly fanned the grayish surface, whose appearance gradually began to change; the zephyr, successively caressing all points of the circumference, caused the strange disk to shrink in diameter and bulge like a dome; it was like the membrane of a giant oyster contracting under the effects of something acidic.

Fogar, without prolonging the experiment, shut off the fan, which he put back next to the amphora.

Deprived of wind, the edges of the dome slowly relaxed, and in just a few moments the disk regained its former rigidity, losing, through its deceptive appearance, all traces of the animal life it had just manifested.

Turning to the left toward the other side of his bed, Fogar lifted the gelatinous block and placed it carefully onto the hundred jade needles planted vertically in the layer of cement; released by the young Negro, the inert mass of flesh sank slowly under its own weight.

Suddenly, owing to the sharp pains caused by pricks from a hundred dark-colored points, a tentacle, placed toward the rear of the block, stood erect in a sign of distress, unfurling at its tip three divergent branches, each of which ended in a narrow suction cup facing frontward.

Fogar took from the basket the three sleepy cats. As he moved, the shadow of his body no longer fell upon the block, which now showed part of the enormous silhouette of the wolf, appearing for at least the tenth time in the fibers of the vegetable screen.

One by one the cats were attached by their backs to the three suction cups that held their prey with irresistible force, like the arms of an octopus.

Meanwhile, the hundred jade tips were sinking ever deeper into the flesh of the amorphous animal, whose increased suffering was expressed in a rotation of the three branches, which began spinning like a pinwheel.

Slow at first, the spinning accelerated feverishly, to the great distress of the cats that struggled helplessly with claws bared.

Soon everything blended into a frantic whirl punctuated by a furious chorus of yowls.

The phenomenon caused no movement in the ever-stable tentacle, which acted as support. Thanks to some subtle and mysterious hub, this sight was more powerful and interesting than the illusory spectacle offered by the Rotifera.

The speed of the gyrations accentuated still further under the influence of the hundred jabs, more and more painful as they sank deeper; the violently fanned air produced a constant hum of continually rising pitch; the cats, blending into each other, formed an uninterrupted disk streaked with green, from which escaped their fierce complaints.

Fogar lifted the block again and put it back in its original place.

With the suppression of the pain, the remarkable spinning quickly slowed, then stopped altogether.

With three violent shakes, Fogar liberated the cats, which he placed dizzy and moaning in their basket, while the tentacle with its three branches again fell inert amid the constantly varying reflections.

Shifting to the right, the adolescent picked up the amphora again and poured on the white soap a certain quantity of water, which soon dripped in a shower from beneath via small openings drilled in the bottom of the container.

Completely empty, the amphora was put back next to the cylinder with its propeller, and the young Negro firmly gripped the wet soap by the six flat surfaces of the slightly flattened cube.

Then, backing as far as possible toward the head of the bed, Fogar, his left eye shut, carefully took aim at the three gold ingots, which he saw one behind the other in perfect alignment between the basket of cats and the carpet with its hundred dark points.

At once, the young man's arm uncoiled fluidly.

The soap, seeming to execute a complete series of perilous jumps, described a slender arc, then fell onto the first ingot; from there it rebounded, still doing cartwheels, to the second gold ingot, which it skimmed for but an instant; a third trajectory, accompanied only by two much slower somersaults, made it land on the third massive cylinder, on which it remained balanced, upright and immobile.

The viscosity of the object, added to the upper roundness of the three ingots, made the success of this feat of dexterity even more remarkable.

After replacing the soap in its special container, Fogar continued his exploration and carefully picked up the delicate object built like a cage door in his left hand.

Then, with three fingers of his right hand first wiped on his loincloth, he lifted the half-twig cut lengthwise.

This latter object, used as a bow, allowed him to stroke, as if it were a violin string, one of the black horsehairs stretched between the two pillars of the small rectangular harp.

The twig rubbed the string with its inner surface, on which a resistant coating, due to some natural secretion, made an excellent substitute for rosin.

The horsehair vibrated powerfully, simultaneously producing, thanks to the effect of certain very curious nodes along its length, two perfectly distinct notes separated by an interval of a fifth; looking up and down the hair, we could see two well defined and clearly uneven zones of vibration.

Fogar, changing place, ran his bow over another horsehair, which entirely unaccompanied produced a pitch-perfect major third.

One by one, each resonant string, tested independently with the bowing twig, simultaneously rendered two sounds of the same amplitude. Harmonious or dissonant, the intervals all differed, giving the experiment an entertaining variety.

The adolescent, putting away the harp and bow, grabbed up the two dark pebbles, which he struck forcefully against each other above the fat candle placed against the corner of the bed; some of the sparks generated by that initial friction fell onto the highly combustible wick, which caught immediately.

The substance of the candle, its peculiarity suddenly revealed by the light near the calm, upright flame, looked like the porous and appetizing pulp of some delicately veined fruit.

Within seconds, the atmosphere was rent by a formidable clamor coming from the candle itself, which, as it melted, imitated the sound of thunder.

A short silence separated this first roar from a second, even more violent noise, itself followed by several low rumbles marking a moment of calm.

The candle burned down fairly quickly, and soon the evocation of the storm acquired a marvelous perfection. Certain terribly loud claps of thunder alternated with the distant voice of the dying, prolonged echoes.

The full moonlight contrasted with this convincing racket, which needed only howling wind and flashes of lightning to complete the illusion.

When the candle, growing shorter and shorter, had almost entirely disappeared, Fogar blew out the wick, and peaceful silence was immediately restored.

At once, the black porters, who had returned several instants earlier, lifted the narrow cot, on which the adolescent reclined nonchalantly.

The group moved away noiselessly to the still changing lights emitted by the polychromatic projections.

Now came the solemn moment to award the prizes.

Juillard removed from his pocket a pendant cut from a thin sheet of tin, in the shape of an equilateral triangle representing a capital Greek *delta*; one of its angles bore a small ring, carefully twisted to sit perpendicular to the ornament.

This trinket, apparently nickel-plated and hanging from a wide, circular blue ribbon slipped through the ring, constituted the *Great Sash of the Order of the Delta*, whose wearer would enrich the wise investors who had put their faith in him.

Choosing as sole criterion the reactions of the Negro public to each of the exhibitions, Juillard unhesitatingly called on Marius Boucharessas, whose young cats, with their game of prisoner's base, had consistently earned the Ponukeleans' enthusiasm.

Promptly decorated with the supreme insignia, the child came back to us proud and delighted, admiring the effect of the blue ribbon as it crossed his chest diagonally over his pale pink leotard, while at his left hip the gleaming pendant, catching the moon's rays, shone brightly against the black background of his velvet shorts.

Within the group of speculators, several cries of joy had burst forth from those who held shares in Marius, among whom a prize of ten thousand francs would soon be split.

After awarding the Great Sash, Juillard had produced six other *deltas*, smaller than the first but identical in shape and cut from the same metal. This time, each attached ring, parallel to the ornament itself, was threaded with a narrow blue ribbon several inches long, the two ends of which bore slightly bent pins.

Still impartially guided by the amount of native approval bestowed on the various candidates, Juillard called forward Skario-vszki, Tancrède Boucharessas, Urbain, Lelgoualch, Ludovic, and La Billaudière-Maisonnial, to affix to each man's chest, without speeches or congratulations, one of the six new decorations symbolizing the rank of *Chevalier of the Delta*.

The rest hour had sounded.

On the orders of Talou, who, approaching with great strides, personally gave us the signal to retire, the natives scattered into Ejur.

Our entire group returned to the special quarters reserved for us in the heart of the strange capital, and soon we were all asleep in the shelter of our primitive huts.

IX

THE NEXT MORNING, Norbert Montalescot woke us at daybreak.

Our compact group hastily assembled and followed the path to Trophy Square, sensuously relishing the relative coolness of the morning air.

Also alerted by Norbert, the emperor and Sirdah arrived at the esplanade at the same time as we. Abandoning his costume from the day before, Talou had donned his habitual chieftain's garb.

Norbert summoned us to the cabin where Louise had been up all night working. Awake with the dawn, he had come for his sister's orders; the latter, calling from inside without showing herself, had commanded him to fetch us immediately.

Suddenly, with a sharp tearing sound, a certain gleaming blade, partially visible to us, seemed to slice through one of the cabin's black walls of its own accord.

The edge, forcefully sawing the thick fabric, ultimately traced a large rectangular path; it was Louise herself who manipulated the knife from within, and it was she who, ripping away the cut portion of cloth, soon leapt outside, carrying a large and tightly packed travel bag.

"Everything is ready for the experiment!" she cried with a smile of joyful triumph.

She was tall and charming, looking like a soldier in her baggy breeches tucked into tight riding boots.

Through the gaping hole she'd recently made we could see, scattered on a table, a panoply of beakers, retorts, and shallow basins, which made the cabin seem an odd laboratory.

The magpie had just escaped and flitted from one sycamore to another, giddy with freedom and fresh air.

Norbert took the heavy bag from his sister's hands and began walking beside her toward the south of Ejur.

The entire retinue, Talou and Sirdah at its head, followed the siblings, who moved forward quickly in the ever-increasing daylight.

After leaving the village limits, Louise continued on a moment, then, seduced by certain combinations of hues, she halted at the exact place from which we had contemplated the fireworks the evening before.

Dawn, illuminating the magnificent trees of the Behuliphruen from behind, produced curious and unexpected light effects.

Talou chose a suitable spot from which to view the tantalizing experiment, and Louise, opening the bag her brother had brought, unpacked a folded object, which once set in its correct position formed a rigorously vertical easel.

A fresh canvas, tautly mounted on its stretcher, was placed halfway up the easel and held firmly in place by a screw clamp that Louise lowered to the desired level. Then, with great care, the young woman took from a lightproof box a previously prepared palette, which fit snugly in a certain metal frame attached to the right side of the easel. The paints, in carefully separated dollops, were arranged in a semicircle of geometric precision on the upper half of the wooden slab; like the empty canvas, it faced the Behuliphruen.

In addition, the bag contained a folding stand similar to a photographer's tripod. Louise grabbed hold of it and unfolded its three extensible legs, then set it on the ground near the easel, scrupulously adjusting its height and stability.

At that moment, obeying his sister's command, Norbert took from the travel bag a heavy case and placed it behind the easel; its glass lid revealed that it contained several batteries placed side by side.

Meanwhile, Louise, slowly and with infinite precaution, unpacked what was clearly a very fragile item, which looked to us like a thick, massive plate, protected by a metal lid that fit its rectangular shape tightly.

Reminiscent of the stiff arms of a scale, the upper part of the tripod was composed of a kind of widely spread fork, abruptly terminating in two vertical tines between which Louise could cautiously fit her plate lengthwise, setting it into two deep grooves intended to take a pair of carefully placed knobs, the whole designed to allow for easy removal of the lid.

Wishing to check the arrangement of the various items, the young woman, blinking one eye, backed toward the Behuliphruen the better to gauge their respective distances. To her right she saw the tripod, to her left the easel in front of the heavy case, and between them the palette with its supply of paints.

The smooth lid of the rectangular plate, which could be grasped by a ring in its center, directly faced the glare of dawn; the plate's unprotected verso disgorged a mass of remarkably thin metal wires, like an overly straight head of hair, which served to connect each infinitesimal area of the surface to a kind of device furnished with an electrical energy source. The wires were gathered in a thick coil under an insulating sleeve, ending in a long ingot, which Louise, kneeling back at her post, plugged into a socket on the side of the battery case.

Now the bag provided a rigid vertical tube, somewhat like a photographer's headrest, which, firmly set on a heavy circular base, was flanked at its summit by an easily turned screw that adjusted an inner metal shaft to the desired height.

Setting the device before the easel, Louise raised the adjustable shaft out of the tube and tightened the screw after scrupulously verifying the level reached by its uppermost tip, which was placed exactly opposite the still virgin canvas.

On the stable, isolated tip, the young woman solidly embedded, like a ball in a cup, a certain large metal sphere bearing a kind of horizontal, pivoting, articulated arm whose extremity, aimed at the palette, held about ten brushes arranged like the spokes of a wheel laid flat on the ground.

Soon the operator had connected a double wire between the sphere and the electrical case.

Before launching the experiment, Louise, unstopping a small burette, poured a drop of oil on the bristles of each brush. Norbert set aside the cumbersome bag, almost empty now that the young woman had removed the metal sphere.

During these preparations, daylight had gradually risen and the Behuliphruen was now resplendent with dazzling lights, forming a magical and multicolored tableau.

Louise could not suppress a cry of wonder when she turned toward the splendid park that gave off such an enchanted glow. Deeming the moment unsurpassable and miraculously propitious to the success of her project, the young woman approached the tripod and gripped the ring on the lid covering the plate.

All the spectators huddled around the easel, so as not to block the sun's rays.

Louise, on the verge of attempting her great experiment, was visibly moved. Her orchestral breathing quickened, giving greater frequency and vigor to the monotonous chords continually exhaled by the aiguillettes. With a sudden pull, she yanked off the lid, and then, slipping behind the easel stand, came to join us to keep watch over the movements of the apparatus.

Deprived of the shutter that the young woman still held in her hand, the plate now lay exposed, showing a surface that was smooth, brown, and shiny. All eyes latched onto that mysterious substance, endowed by Louise with strange photomechanical properties. Suddenly a slight tremor shook the automatic arm facing the easel, a single, glossy, horizontal rod bent in the middle. The flexible angle of the elbow tended to open fully under the action of a powerful spring, which a single metal wire, running from the sphere and attached to the arm's extremity, counteracted by regulating its spread; at the moment, the lengthening wire was letting the angle progressively widen.

This first movement provoked a slight stir in the anxious, uncertain audience.

The arm stretched slowly toward the palette, while the horizontal, rimless wheel created at its extremity by the star of brushes gradually rose to the top of a vertical axle, itself moved upward by a toothed gear directly linked to the sphere by an elastic transmission belt.

The two combined movements guided the tip of one brush toward a plentiful supply of the color blue, amassed near the top of the palette. The bristles rapidly coated themselves, then, after a short descent, spread their purloined particles over an uncovered area of the wooden surface. Several iotas of white pigment, picked up the same way, were deposited on the spot recently daubed with blue, and the two colors, which some prolonged rubbing had left perfectly blended, yielded a very attenuated pale cerulean.

Retracted slightly by the metal wire, the arm then pivoted gently and stopped by the upper left-hand corner of the canvas mounted on the easel. Immediately the brush, impregnated as it was with delicate hues, automatically traced on the edge of the future painting a narrow, vertical strip of sky.

A murmur of admiration greeted this first sketch, and Louise, now sure of her success, breathed a huge sigh of satisfaction accompanied by a noisy fanfare from her aiguillettes.

The wheel of brushes, once more at the palette, abruptly rotated on itself, moved by a second transmission belt that, made like the first of stretchable material, led inside the sphere. A sharp click was heard, produced by a ratchet that firmly set a new brush with clean bristles in the place of honor. Soon several additional unadulterated paints, blended on another area of the palette, composed a vivid yellowish tint, which, transposed onto the canvas, extended the vertical ribbon begun moments earlier.

Turning toward the Behuliphruen, we could verify the absolute accuracy of this sudden juxtaposition of two tones, which formed a clearly defined line in the sky.

The work continued with speed and precision. At this point, during each visit to the palette, several brushes effected by turns their different blends of colors; brought before the painting, they deployed again in the same order, each one applying to the canvas, sometimes in infinitesimal amounts, its particular new pigment. This process allowed for the subtlest gradations of hues, and little by little a section of landscape full of realistic splendor spread before our eyes.

While watching over the machine, Louise supplied helpful explanations.

The brown plate alone set everything in motion, through a system based on the principle of electromagnetism. Despite the absence of an actual lens, the polished surface, owing to its extreme sensitivity, received extremely powerful impressions of light, which, transmitted by the countless wires in back, activated an entire mechanism inside the sphere, which measured more than a yard in circumference.

As we had witnessed with our own eyes, the two vertical arms ending the fork on the supporting tripod were made of the same brown material as the plate itself; thanks to their perfect fit, they and it formed a single, homogenous block and now contributed, in their particular area, to the continual progress of the photomechanical communication.

Louise revealed that the sphere contained a second rectangular plate. Provided with another network of wires that transmitted to it the polychromatic impressions received by the first, this second plate was criss-crossed from edge to edge by a metal wheel that, through the electrical current it produced, could power a complex assortment of rods, pistons, and cylinders.

The image spread progressively toward the right, always in vertical strips painted one after another from top to bottom. Each time the rimless wheel turned in front of the palette or the canvas, we heard the high-pitched squeal of the fastening clip holding a given brush in place for the length of its brief task. This monotonous sound reproduced, albeit much slower, the prolonged screech of fairground turnstiles.

The entire surface of the palette was now sullied or blemished; the most heterogeneous blends lay side by side, constantly modified by some new addition of unadulterated paint. Despite the disconcerting riot of tones, no confusion ensued, each brush remaining devoted to a certain category of hues that conferred on it a given, loosely defined specialty.

Soon the entire left half of the painting was complete.

Louise watched joyfully over the operation of her machine, which so far had functioned without accident or error.

This success did not falter for a moment during the completion of the landscape, whose second half was painted with marvelous sureness.

A few seconds before the end of the experiment, Louis had again positioned herself behind the easel, then behind the tripod, in order to stand once more near the photosensitive plate. By then, all that remained was a narrow strip of white at the far right edge of the canvas, promptly filled.

After these final brushstrokes, Louise vigorously clapped the obturating lid over the brown plate, and by this act alone immobilized the articulated arm. Freed from any further concern over the machine's workings, the young woman could appreciate at leisure the painting that had been executed so curiously.

The great trees of the Behuliphruen were faithfully reproduced with their magnificent limbs, whose leaves, of strange hue and shape, were covered with a host of intense reflections. On the ground, large flowers in blue, yellow, or crimson sparkled amid the mosses. Farther up, the sky peeked through the trunks and branches: at bottom, a first horizontal area in blood red faded to make way, a bit higher up, for an orange strip, which itself lightened and yielded to a vibrant yellow-gold; then came a pale, scarcely tinted blue, in which a final, tardy star shone to the right. The work, in its entirety, gave a singularly powerful impression of color and remained rigorously faithful to the model, as everyone could verify with a single glance at the park itself.

Aided by her brother, Louise, loosening the clamp on the easel, replaced the canvas with a drawing pad of equal dimensions, formed by a thick accumulation of white sheets bound at the edges; then, removing the last brush used, she put in its place a carefully sharpened pencil.

A few words revealed to us the ambitious young woman's plan: wishing now to show us a simple drawing, necessarily more precise than the painting in the subtlety of its outlines, she had only to activate a certain switch placed at the top of the sphere to slightly modify the internal mechanism.

In order to furnish a dense and animated subject, fifteen or twenty spectators, at Louise's request, went to stand together a short distance away, in the plate's visual field. Seeking to obtain a brisk, lively effect, they posed as pedestrians on a busy street; several, their postures evoking a rapid gait, lowered their foreheads with a look of deep preoccupation; others, more relaxed, conversed in strolling couples, while two friends crossing paths exchanged a familiar greeting.

Urging her figures to hold absolutely still, like a photographer, Louise, posted near the plate, removed the lid with a sudden movement; then she again made her habitual detour to come oversee the pencil's maneuvers from closer up.

The mechanism, renewed as well as modified by the action of the switch pushed on the sphere, gently moved the articulated arm to the left. The pencil began running from top to bottom over the white paper, following the same vertical paths previously forged by the brushes.

This time there was no detour toward the palette, no change of brush, and no mixing of pigments to complicate the task, which progressed rapidly. The same landscape appeared in the background, but its interest, now secondary, was eclipsed by the figures in the foreground. Their movements sketched from life, the well-defined *habitus*, the curiously amusing silhouettes, the strikingly lifelike faces—all had the desired expression, be it grave or joyful. One body, leaning slightly toward the ground, seemed endowed with great forward momentum; a beaming countenance expressed the pleasant surprise of a chance encounter.

The pencil, though often pulling away from the surface, glided nimbly over the sheet, which was filled in a matter of minutes. Louise, who had returned to her post in time, replaced the shutter on the plate, then called to her actors, who, glad to stretch their limbs after their prolonged immobility, came running to admire the new opus.

Despite the conflicting décor, the drawing gave the precise impression of a bustling city street. Everyone easily recognized himself amid the compact group, and the heartiest congratulations were showered on a moved and radiant Louise.

Norbert took charge of disassembling all the utensils and putting them back in the bag.

During this time, Sirdah notified Louise of the emperor's complete satisfaction, the latter marveling at the perfect way the young woman had fulfilled all the conditions he had strictly imposed.

*
* *

Ten minutes later we had all returned to Ejur.

Talou brought us to Trophy Square, where we saw Rao accompanied by a native warrior.

Before everyone, the emperor pointed at Carmichael, accompanying his gesture with a few words of commentary.

Immediately Rao went up to the young Marseillais, whom he led toward one of the sycamores near the red theater.

The warrior was posted as a sentry to watch over the poor detainee, who, standing face to the tree trunk, began the three hours of punishment during which he was to rehearse continually the same "Battle of the Tez" that he had misremembered the day before.

Taking the chair Juillard had used from the empty wings, I went to sit beneath the branches of the sycamore, offering to help Carmichael with his task. He immediately handed me a large sheet on which the barbarous pronunciation of the Ponukelean text was meticulously transcribed into French characters. Stimulated by the dread of another failure, he began reciting his bizarre lesson with full concentration, murmuring the song in a low voice, while I followed each line syllable by syllable, ready to point out the slightest error or prompt a forgotten word.

The crowd, deserting Trophy Square, had slowly spread into Ejur, and, hardly distracted by my purely mechanical chore, I could not help reflecting in the great morning silence on the many adventures that had occupied my life for the past three months.

X

The previous march 15th, planning a certain long-term journey through the curious regions of South America, I had embarked in Marseille aboard the *Lynceus,* a huge, fast vessel setting sail for Buenos Aires.

The first days of the crossing were lovely and calm. With the familiarity born of shared meals, I lost no time in getting acquainted with a certain number of passengers, of whom I give here a brief annotated list:

1. The historian Juillard, a man of independent means who frequently took pleasure cruises, occasionally stopping to deliver scholarly lectures renowned for their witty and engaging lucidity.

2. The aging Livonian Olga Chervonenkhov, formerly a prima ballerina in Saint Petersburg, now obese and mustached. For the past fifteen years, having retired from the theater in her prime, Olga, surrounded by an abundance of animals that she cared for lovingly, lived a quiet, secluded life on a small property she had bought in Livonia, not far from her native village. Her two favorite charges were the elk Sladki and the she-ass Milenkaya, who both came at her slightest call and often followed her into her private suite. Not long before, one of the ex-dancer's cousins, residing since childhood in the Republic of Argentina, had died and left behind a small fortune amassed by way of his coffee plantations. Olga was sole heir; notified of her good luck by the deceased's lawyer, she resolved to go look after her interests personally. She left without delay, entrusting her menagerie to her neighbor, a zealously devoted woman; but at the last minute, unable to bear the painful separation, Olga bought two

openwork crates for the elk and donkey, who were carefully settled among the cargo. At every stopover, this tenderhearted traveler visited the two prisoners with a solicitude that, as time passed on board, only increased.

3. Carmichael, a twenty-year-old native of Marseilles, already renowned for his prodigious falsetto that gave the perfect illusion of a woman's voice. For the past two years, Carmichael had triumphed on cabaret stages throughout France, dressed in female attire and singing, with infinite suppleness and virtuosity, and in the appropriate tessitura, the most trying passages in the soprano repertoire. He had booked passage on the *Lynceus* after having accepted a splendid engagement in the new world.

4. Balbet, French sharpshooting and fencing champion, the popular favorite in an international marksmanship contest to be held in Buenos Aires.

5. La Billaudière-Maisonnial, maker of precision objects, looking to present at the same competition a mechanical foil capable of multiple transcendent feints.

6. Luxo, a pyrotechnics entrepreneur, who owned a huge plant in Courbevoie where all the great fireworks of Paris were manufactured. Three months before embarking, Luxo had received a visit from the young Baron Ballesteros, an inordinately wealthy Argentine, who for several years had been leading in France a wildly dissolute life of unbridled ostentation. Now ready to return home and be married, Ballesteros wanted, on the occasion of his nuptials, to set off a fireworks display worthy of royalty in the vast park of his castle near Buenos Aires; in addition to the agreed price, Luxo would receive a handsome bonus if he came to oversee the operation himself. The entrepreneur accepted the commission, which he promised to deliver personally to its destination. Before taking his leave, the young baron, whose reputation for his looks, while justified, had gone to his head, formulated a certain thought that betrayed a rather extravagant frame of mind, though not lacking in surprise or origi-

nality. For the grand finale, he wanted rockets that, upon exploding, would spread over the skies different aspects of his own image, in place of the traditional but hopelessly ordinary caterpillars and multicolored stars. Luxo deemed the project feasible and the next day received a voluminous packet of photographs, which, perfectly suited as models, depicted his improvident client in the most varied guises. One month before the wedding was to be celebrated, Luxo had departed with his entire cargo, not forgetting the famous finale wrapped separately with special care.

7. The great architect Chènevillot, summoned by the same Baron Ballesteros, who, wishing to effect some major renovations in his castle while he was on his honeymoon, had decided that only a French builder could do a satisfactory job. Chènevillot brought with him several of his best workmen to keep careful watch over the chores assigned to the local laborers.

8. The hypnotist Darriand, wishing to introduce to the new world certain mysterious plants whose hallucinatory properties he'd been able to fathom, and whose scent could enflame a subject's faculties to the point of making him take for reality what were merely projections of finely colored film.

9. The chemist Bex, who for the past year had traveled through many lands with the sole, selfless aim of popularizing two marvelous scientific discoveries, the fruits of his ingenious and patient efforts.

10. The inventor Bedu, bringing to America a perfected loom that, placed over the currents of a river, could weave the richest fabrics automatically, thanks to a curious system of paddles. By installing the device built from his blueprints on the Rio de la Plata, the inventor expected to receive lucrative orders for similar looms from manufacturers throughout the country. Bedu personally drew and colored the various models of silkwear, damask, or Persian that he wished to obtain; once the movement of the countless paddles had been regulated to follow a master pattern, the machine could reproduce the same design indefinitely, without aid or supervision.

11. The sculptor Fuxier, who with great subtlety modeled numerous seductive images, which he placed in embryo in certain red lozenges of his own creation, so that they might blossom into smoke on contact with an open flame. Other lozenges, of a uniform bright blue, instantly dissolved in water to produce veritable bas-reliefs on the surface, resulting from the same interior preparation. Hoping to distribute his invention, Fuxier was bringing to Buenos Aires an ample provision of the two substances he'd concocted, so as to produce, on site and upon request, an evanescent tableau encased in a red lozenge, or else a liquid bas-relief contained in a blue lozenge. In a third variation, he used his process of instantaneously blooming sculptures to create delicate subjects inside grapes that could ripen in just minutes. For his experiments, Fuxier had taken along several vine-stocks in voluminous earthenware pots, scrupulously overseeing their watering and ventilation.

12. The associated bankers Hounsfield and Cerjat, whom various important matters called to the Argentine Republic, along with three of their clerks.

13. A large theatrical company heading for Buenos Aires to act in a series of operettas, among them the comic actor Soreau and the diva Jeanne Souze.

14. The ichthyologist Martignon, off to join a scientific expedition that, embarking in Montevideo on a small steam yacht, was going to conduct soundings in the southern oceans.

15. Leflaive, the ship's doctor.

16. Adinolfa, the great Italian tragedienne, about to appear for the first time before an Argentine audience.

17. The Hungarian Skariovszki, a highly talented zither player, who performed prodigious feats on his instrument in gypsy garb, for which concert promoters on both sides of the ocean paid handsomely.

18. The Belgian Cuijper, who justifiably expected to earn astronomical fees with his beautiful tenor voice, which the use of a

squeaker made of some mysterious metal rendered magical and remarkable.

19. A strange assortment of curiosities, trainers, and acrobats heading for a brilliant three-month engagement in a Buenos Aires circus. This odd assortment of personnel included the clown Whirligig; the equestrian Urbain, owner of the steed Romulus; Tancrède Boucharessas, an individual without arms or legs, accompanied by his five children, Hector, Tommy, Marius, Bob, and Stella; the singer Ludovic; the Breton Lelgoualch; Stéphane Alcott and his six sons; and the impresario Jenn with the dwarf Philippo.

For an entire week the journey remained peaceful and pleasant. But in the middle of the eighth night, a terrible hurricane broke out in mid-Atlantic. The propeller and rudder were snapped off by the violence of the waves, and after two days of aimless drifting, the *Lynceus*, shoved around like dead wreckage, ran aground on the coast of Africa.

No one was missing from roll call, but, examining the mangled ship, now carrying nothing more than staved-in lifeboats, we had to abandon all hope of heading back to sea.

Scarcely off the ship, we saw rushing toward us, with supple leaps, several hundred Negroes who surrounded us gaily, manifesting their joy with loud shouts. They were led by a young chief with an open, intelligent face, who, introducing himself by the name Seil-kor, surprised us profoundly by answering our initial questions in correct, fluent French.

In just a few words Seil-kor apprised us of his mission, which was to lead us to Ejur, capital of the emperor Talou VII, his master, who'd been awaiting for hours the inevitable wreck of our vessel that a native fisherman had alerted him to; Talou intended to keep us in his power until he was paid a sufficient ransom.

We had to bow before the strength of their numbers.

While the Negroes busied themselves with unloading the ship, Seil-kor, yielding to our entreaties, good-naturedly provided various details about our future residence.

Sitting on a narrow boulder in the shade of a tall cliff, the young orator began by recounting his own story to our attentive group, stretched out here and there in the soft sand.

At the age of ten, wandering about the same region where fate had just cast us, Seil-kor had met a French explorer named Laubé, who, no doubt seduced by the child's bright expression, had decided to take him under his wing and bring this living souvenir of his journey back among his people.

Laubé, who had disembarked on the western coast of Africa, had sworn never to retrace his steps; accompanied by a valiant entourage, he forged onward far to the east, then, turning north, crossed the desert on camelback and finally reached Tripoli, his predetermined destination.

During the two years devoted to this voyage, Seil-kor had learned French by listening to his companions; struck by his facility with language, the explorer had pushed solicitude to the point of giving the child many fruitful lessons in reading, history, and geography.

In Tripoli, Laubé expected to rejoin his wife and daughter, who, following certain arrangements made at the time of their separation, should already have been at the Hôtel d'Angleterre for the past two months.

The explorer experienced a sweet delight on learning from the hotel porter that the two loved ones he'd left behind were indeed waiting for him, after such a long absence from his tender affections.

Seil-kor slipped out to explore the city, not wishing to intrude on those first joyful moments his protector had awaited so impatiently.

Returning after an hour, he saw Laubé in the vast main lobby; the explorer showed Seil-kor his room, located on the ground floor and brightly lit by a large open window looking out onto the hotel gardens.

Having already vaunted Seil-kor's extraordinary learning, the explorer thought it best to run the child through a brief practice quiz before introducing him to his two new life companions.

A few questions about key historical events obtained satisfactory replies.

Next, broaching French geography, Laubé asked for the capitals of various regions cited at random.

Sitting opposite the window, Seil-kor had not made a single mistake in his almost mechanical recitation, when suddenly, as he was about to name the capital of La Corrèze, he felt faint; his eyes clouded up and his legs began to shake, while his heart thudded rapidly in his chest.

This disturbance was caused by the sight of a ravishing blonde child of about twelve, who had just entered the garden, and whose marvelous, deep blue gaze had for an instant met Seil-kor's bedazzled eyes.

Meanwhile, Laubé, having noticed none of this, repeated impatiently: "The capital of La Corrèze . . . ?"

The apparition had vanished, and Seil-kor regained his wits enough to murmur, "Tulle."

For all eternity, the name of this town would remain linked in Seil-kor's memory with the unsettling vision.

The quiz over, Laubé brought Seil-kor to meet his wife and daughter, Nina, in whom the ecstatic young Negro, with heavenly joy, recognized the blonde girl from the garden.

From that moment on, Seil-kor's life was illuminated by Nina's presence, for the two children, being of the same age, were constantly together for both play and study.

At the time of Nina's birth, Laubé had been living in Crete with his wife, working on a voluminous tome called *Candia and Its Inhabitants*. It was thus on foreign soil that the girl had spent her first years, and there she was raised by a tenderhearted Candiote nurse who had imparted to her the soft, charming trace of an accent.

This accent delighted Seil-kor, whose love and devotion grew with each passing hour.

He dreamed of holding Nina in his arms for just a moment; in the depths of his imagination he envisioned her beset by a thousand dangers, from which he saved her with heroic ardor before the eyes of her anxious and grateful parents.

These fantasies would soon turn into a sudden reality.

One day, standing on a terrace of the hotel lapped by the sea, Seil-kor was fishing with his sweetheart, who looked ravishing in a navy blue dress that he adored.

Suddenly Nina shouted with joy upon seeing, at the end of her hook, which she had just lifted out of the water, a heavy, wiggling fish. Pulling the end of her line toward her, she gripped her catch forcefully in order to unhook it. But at the first touch she received a violent shock and collapsed in a dead faint. The fish, which looked like an inoffensive ray, was actually a *torpedo fish*, whose electric charge had caused this unexpected outcome.

Seil-kor gathered Nina in his arms and carried her inside the hotel, where, before her father and mother, who had immediately rushed in, she soon came to her senses after her harmless fainting spell.

His initial fears allayed, Seil-kor blessed the perilous adventure that, making his dream come true, had allowed him to hold his beloved companion for an instant.

Nina's birthday fell a few days after this event. For the occasion, Laubé decided to throw a small children's party, to which he invited the several European families living in the city.

Having resolved to celebrate the great day by reciting a fable for the girl, Seil-kor spent part of his nights secretly memorizing and practicing his delivery.

Wishing to give his dear friend a present as well, he decided to risk at gambling the few silver coins he owed to Laubé's generosity.

A certain accessible casino in Tripoli featured a game of Parcheesi whose stake could accommodate even the most modest purse.

Favored by what is commonly called beginner's luck, Seil-kor, using a martingale, promptly won enough to order a monstrous Savoy cake from the best pastry shop in town, to be served at the height of the party.

The festivities, which began in daytime, filled the grand ball-room of the hotel with joyful commotion. At around five o'clock, the children, passing into the next room, sat down at an immense table laden with fruits and sweets. At that moment they brought in Seil-kor's famous cake, which was greeted with cheers and shouts. All eyes turned to the gift-giver, who, standing up without a hint of shyness, recited his fable in a clear, assured voice. At the final verses applause burst out from all sides, and Nina, standing in turn, pro-posed a toast in honor of Seil-kor, who for a moment became king of the banquet.

After the snack, the ball continued. Seil-kor and Nina waltzed together, then, tired out from having covered the entire floor sev-eral times, they broke off near Mme Laubé, who, standing calmly, watched with delight the beautiful childish merriment all around her.

Seeing her daughter approach with her companion, the excel-lent woman, grateful for all of Seil-kor's attentions, turned smiling to the young Negro and said in a gentle voice, pointing at Nina, "Give her a kiss!"

Seil-kor, his head spinning, wrapped his arms around his friend and deposited on her fresh cheeks two chaste kisses that left him giddy and unsteady on his feet.

Not long after this grand yet somehow intimate occasion, Laubé, whose energies had been revived by the stay in Tripoli, decided to return to France. The explorer owned a small family château, near a village called Port d'Oo in the Pyrenees, whose calm and isolation he prized highly. It would be the ideal place for him to turn his notes into a detailed account of his voyage.

The departure was set without delay. After a pleasant crossing,

Laubé and his family disembarked in Marseille, where they took a train for Port d'Oo.

Seil-kor was very happy in his new residence; the château was located in the breathtaking Valley of Oo, and every day the young African and Nina went on long adventures in the forest, enjoying the last rays of a warm, clement autumn.

One evening, their aimless stroll having led them to the village, the two children happened upon a traveling circus troupe squeezed into a cart that slowly cruised the streets; they distributed leaflets to the curious onlookers and drew the crowd's attention with sales patter and thumps of the bass drum.

Seil-kor, who had been handed two leaflets, read them with Nina. The first, laid out like a broadside, began with a long sentence in large letters announcing the sensational arrival of the Ferréol troupe, comprising acrobats, dancers, and tightrope walkers. The second half emphatically urged all Frenchmen to beware, given the presence on their territory of the ringleader, the famous wrestler Ferréol, who could singlehandedly demolish armies and topple ramparts. The exhortation began, "Tremble, people of France! . . ." with the word "Tremble" splashing across the page in huge, eye-catching letters that formed a kind of headline.

The other leaflet, smaller in size, carried this simple testimonial: "We were bested by Ferréol," followed by countless signatures, reproduced in facsimile, from fearsome professionals whom the illustrious champion had laid flat.

The next day, Seil-kor and Nina returned to the village square to see the announced performance. A large dais stretched high into the air, and the two children had a great time watching the jugglers, clowns, magicians, and trained animals that paraded before their eyes for two hours.

At a certain moment, three men appeared and set up on the right, at the edge of the dais, a section of Renaissance façade, its upper floor pierced by a large balcony window.

Soon, a second, similar stage set stood on the left, at the other end of the floorboards, and one of the stagehands carefully hung an iron wire between the two balconies, which were positioned exactly opposite each other.

Scarcely were these preparations completed when the right-hand window quietly opened to let through a young woman dressed like a princess from the time of Charles IX. The stranger made a sign with her hand, and immediately the other window yielded to a richly adorned nobleman who appeared at his own balcony. The newcomer, in a brocaded doublet, short breeches, and velvet pillbox cap, wore a stiffly encasing ruff and a mysterious mask appropriate to the clandestine expedition he seemed to be planning.

After an exchange of signals full of admonitions and promises, the lover, straddling his balustrade, posed his foot on the tightwire; then, arms outstretched like a balancing pole, he endeavored to cross, via the aerial route he had, in his daring, chosen, the distance separating him from his lovely neighbor.

But suddenly, cocking her ear toward the inside of the house as if listening for the step of a jealous rival, the woman rushed back to her room, warning the bold lover with a hand signal; the latter, retreating with great strides, regained his point of departure and hid behind the curtains.

Several moments later, the two windows opened almost simultaneously, and the hazardous voyage began again with renewed hope. This time the crossing continued to the very end without false alarms, and the two lovers fell into each other's arms amid prolonged applause.

The tightwire and twin stage sets were hastily removed, and a young Spanish couple, rushing onstage, immediately began dancing a frenetic bolero, accompanied by shouts and stamping feet. Both the woman, in a mantilla, and the man, in a waist-length jacket and sombrero, held in their right hands Basque tambourines with jingles, on which they beat vigorously in time. After ten minutes of continual pirouettes and hip thrusts, the two dancers ended by freezing in a smiling, graceful pose, while the electrified crowd applauded wildly.

The performance ended with several stunning victories by the famous Ferréol, and night was already falling when Seil-kor and Nina, delighted by their afternoon, headed arm in arm back to the château.

The next day, kept indoors by a fine, persistent drizzle, the two children had to forgo their daily walk. Happily, the château grounds contained a huge shed with a vast space suitable for even the most rambunctious games; it was under this shelter that the two scamps went to spend their playtime.

Haunted by the previous day's show, Nina had taken along her sewing basket, intending to make Seil-kor an outfit like the one the tightrope walker had worn. In the back of the shed, two horse carriages facing each other, their harnessing shafts placed end to end, offered a convenient and easy testing ground for a first attempt by the still novice funambulist.

Armed with a pair of scissors, a needle and thread, and the two leaflets Seil-kor had kept, Nina set to work; from the first sheet she cut a pillbox cap, and from the second a mask decorated with two strings to go around the back of the ears.

The ruff required a larger supply of paper; in a corner of the shed, thrown on a scrap heap, lay a pile of back issues of *La Nature*, a magazine Laubé received regularly and for which he wrote all his travel narratives. Ripping the blue covers from numerous copies, Nina was able to fashion an elegant collar of uniform hue, and soon, adorned with the three items carefully confected by the adroit craftswoman, Seil-kor made his debut in the tightrope walker's trade, crossing the narrow, unsteady path provided by the two shafts from one end to the other.

Encouraged by this initial success, the children then decided to copy the Spanish couple's bolero.

Seil-kor removed his paper disguise and the dance began, soon turning chaotic and feverish. Nina in particular put a strange ardor into her gesticulations, clapping her hands sharply to replace the rhythmic resonance of the Basque tambourine and continuing her giddy frolics without a thought for fatigue or shortness of breath. Suddenly, halted in full frenzy by the bell for afternoon tea, the two dancers left the shed to return to the château.

The temperature had dropped with the early twilight, and a kind of melted snow, penetrating and frigid, fell slowly from the opaque sky.

Bathed in sweat from the mad, prolonged dance, Nina was overcome by terrible shivers, which stopped in the dining room, where the first fire of the season blazed in the hearth.

The next day the shining sun had returned, lighting one of the last pure, translucent days that every year precede the coming of winter. Wanting to take advantage of the calm afternoon that perhaps marked the last fine weather of the year, Seil-kor gaily suggested to Nina a long walk in the forest.

The girl, burning with fever but convinced she was suffering only from a passing cold, accepted her friend's offer and set off at his side. Seil-kor carried a copious snack in a large basket dangling from his arm.

After an hour's walk in the deep woods, the two children found themselves before an inextricable tangle of trees, marking the beginning of a vast, unexplored thicket that the locals called "the Maze." The name was justified by an extraordinary mesh of branches and vines; no one could venture into the Maze without the risk of becoming lost forever.

Until that day, during their escapades, Seil-kor and the girl had wisely skirted around the fearsome border. But, enticed by the unknown, they'd promised each other to someday attempt a bold expedition to the heart of that mysterious region. This seemed a good opportunity for them to accomplish their project.

Seil-kor, with foresight, decided to mark the return path in the manner of Tom Thumb. He opened his basket of provisions, but, recalling the famous hero's misadventure, did not tear his bread into crumbs. Instead he chose a Swiss cheese of dazzling whiteness, whose particles, undigestible to bird's stomachs, would stand out clearly against the dark background of moss and briar.

The reconnaissance began; every five steps, Seil-kor poked the cheese with the tip of his knife and tossed a small fragment to the ground.

For half an hour, the two heedless children plunged into the Maze without finding the other end; daylight began to wane, and Seil-kor, suddenly worried, gave the signal for retreat.

For a while, the boy found his way, which he had marked continually. But soon the trail ended; some famished animal, fox or wolf, sniffing out the appetizing markers, had licked up the particles of cheese, severing the two wanderers' lifeline.

Little by little the sky had darkened and the night grew opaque.

Terror-stricken, Seil-kor persisted for a long time in trying to find a way out of the Maze, but in vain. Nina, exhausted and shivering with fever, followed him with great difficulty, at every moment feeling her strength about to fail her. Finally, the poor child, faltering despite herself and letting out a cry of distress, lay down on a bed of moss at her feet; Seil-kor approached, anxious and discouraged.

Nina fell into a morbid sleep; it was now dark night and the cold was bitter. Advent had just begun, and a feeling of winter floated in the damp, glacial atmosphere. Seil-kor, frantic, removed his jacket to cover the girl, whom he didn't dare wake from a rest she so desperately needed.

After a long doze fraught with restless dreams, Nina awoke and stood up, ready to resume her walk.

The stars shone with their brightest light in the clear sky. Nina, who knew how to orient herself, pointed to the North Star, and the two children, now following an invariable direction, reached the

edge of the Maze after an hour. A final leg brought them to the château, where the girl fell into the arms of her parents, who were ashen
with fright and anxiety.

The next day, still wishing to deny the illness that was now pro-
gressing rapidly, Nina awoke as usual and went to the study room,
where Seil-kor was writing some French composition that Laubé
had assigned.

Since returning from Africa, the young girl had been taking catechism at the village church; that morning, she was to finish her own
composition, due to be handed in the next day.

A half hour of concentrated work was all she needed to finish
her task and reach her final resolution.

Having written these first words: "I resolve . . ." she turned to
Seil-kor to ask his advice about the rest, when a terrible coughing fit
shook her entire body, provoking deep, painful rattles in her chest.

Horrified, Seil-kor approached the sick girl, who between two
spasms told him everything: the shivers she'd felt when coming out
of the shed—and the fever that, not having lowered since the day
before, had certainly grown worse during her dangerous nap on the
bed of moss.

Nina's parents were immediately notified, and the girl was put
back to bed without further ado.

Alas! Neither the resources of science nor the many attentions
of a passionately devoted entourage could triumph over this terrible
malady, which in less than a week removed the poor child from the
worshipful affection of her kin.

After this sudden demise, Seil-kor, driven mad with despair,
came to loathe the places until then divinely illuminated by his
friend's presence. Sites he'd visited so many times with Nina were
made odious by the horrible contrast between his present grief and
his lost happiness. On top of which, the cold season horrified the
young Negro, who in his heart of hearts felt nostalgic for the African
sun. One day, setting on the table a letter for his beloved protector,

full of affection, gratitude, and regrets, he fled from the château, taking with him like holy relics the pillbox cap, ruff, and mask that Nina had made.

Working odd jobs at various farms he found along the way, he managed to save up enough to buy passage to Marseille. There, he signed on as stoker on a ship scheduled to skirt the western coast of Africa. During a stopover in Porto Novo, he deserted his post and returned to his native land, where before long his education and intelligence earned him a prominent position beside the emperor.

We had listened in silence to the story told by Seil-kor, who, pausing a moment from the emotions roused by so many poignant memories, soon resumed to tell us about the master he served.

Talou VII, of illustrious ancestry, boasted of having European blood in his veins. At an already distant epoch, his forebear Suann had conquered the throne by sheer force of daring, then had sworn to establish a dynasty. And this is what tradition held on the subject:

A few weeks after Suann's coronation, a great sailing vessel, driven forward by a storm, had run aground near the shores of Ejur. Two young girls of fifteen, the sole survivors of the catastrophe, clutching onto a loose piece of flotsam, had managed to reach dry land after braving a thousand perils.

The castaways, ravishing twin sisters of Spanish nationality, had such identical faces that no one could tell them apart.

Suann fell in love with the charming adolescents, and, in his impetuous desire for progeny, married both of them that very day, pleased to affirm the supremacy of his race by the admixture of European blood that could strike the fetishistic imagination of his subjects, both then and in times to come.

It was not long afterward, again on the same day and at the same hour, that the two sisters each gave birth to a male child.

Talou and Yaour—for so the infants were named—later caused their father grave concern: caught short by the unexpected advent of two simultaneous births, he did not know which to choose as heir to his throne.

The perfect resemblance of his spouses prevented Suann from decreeing which one had conceived first, the only way to establish one brother's rights over the other's.

They tried in vain to elucidate this latter point by questioning the two mothers; using the few native words they had painstakingly learned, each testified firmly on behalf of her own son.

Suann decided he would defer to the Great Spirit.

Under the name "Trophy Square," he had just built in Ejur a vast quadrilateral esplanade, so as to hang on the trunks of the sycamores planted around its border the spoils won from the enemies who, with fierce determination, had tried to block his path to power. He went to the northern end of the new site and had planted at the same time, in suitably prepared ground, the seed of a palm tree on one side and the seed of a rubber tree on the other. Each tree was associated with one of his sons, previously designated before witnesses; in accordance with divine will, the first tree to sprout from the earth would determine the future sovereign.

Care and watering were impartially lavished on both fecundated spots.

It was the palm tree, planted at right, that first peeked through the surface of the earth, thus proclaiming Talou's rights over those of Yaour, whose rubber tree was a full day late.

Scarcely four years after their arrival in Ejur, the twins, overcome by fever, perished at almost the same time, felled by the terrible ordeal of a particularly torrid season. During the shipwreck they had managed to save a certain miniature portrait depicting both of them side by side, coiffed in the national mantilla; Suann preserved this image, a precious document that proved the superior vintage of his race.

Talou and Yaour grew and, with them, so did the two trees planted at their births. The influence of Spanish blood was manifested in the two young brothers only by the slightly lighter complexion of their black skin and a slightly less accentuated thickness of the lips.

Watching as they grew, Suann sometimes worried about the murderous quarrels that might one day break out between them over his succession. Fortunately a new conquest helped allay his fears, by giving him the chance to create a kingdom for Yaour.

The empire of Ponukele, founded by Suann, was bordered to the south by the river named the Tez, the mouth of which was located not far from Ejur.

Beyond the Tez stretched Drelchkaff, a fertile region that Suann, after a successful campaign, managed to place under his dominion.

From the start, Yaour was designated by his father to sit one day upon the throne of Drelchkaff. Compared with the neighboring empire, the privilege seemed rather modest; Suann nonetheless hoped this compensation would calm the jealousy of his disinherited son.

The two brothers were twenty when their father passed away. Things followed their intended course: Talou become emperor of Ponukele, and Yaour king of Drelchkaff.

Talou I and Yaour I—for so they were designated—took many wives and founded two rival houses, always on the verge of entering into war. The house of Yaour demanded the empire, contesting the rights of the house of Talou; and the latter, for its part, emboldened by the divine intervention that had granted it the supreme rank, demanded the crown of Drelchkaff, of which it had been deprived through a mere whim of Suann's.

One night, Yaour V, king of Drelchkaff, direct and legitimate descendant of Yaour I, crossed the Tez with his army and entered Ejur by surprise.

The emperor Talou IV, Talou I's great-grandson, had to flee to avoid certain death, and Yaour V, realizing the dream of his ancestors, gathered under a single scepter both Ponukele and Drelchkaff.

By that time, the palm and rubber trees in Trophy Square had reached full maturity.

Yaour V's first action after claiming the title of emperor was to burn down the palm associated with the abhorred race of Talou and to pull out every root of the cursed tree, whose early emergence from the soil had dispossessed his family.

Yaour V reigned for thirty years and died at the height of his power.

His successor, the cowardly and inept Yaour VI, made himself unpopular by his constant gaffes and his cruelty. Talou IV, leaving the distant exile where he had languished for so long, was then able to surround himself with numerous partisans, who fomented revolt by rousing the discontented populace to their cause.

Terrified, Yaour VI fled before the battle could start and took refuge in his kingdom of Drelchkaff, where he managed to preserve his crown.

Emperor of Ponukele once more, Talou IV planted a new palm seed in the spot Yaour V had desecrated; soon a tree emerged, identical to the first, whose significance it recalled while evoking, like an emblem, the restoration of the legitimate branch.

Since then, everything had proceeded normally, without violent overthrows or problems of succession. It was now Talou VII who reigned over Ponukele, and Yaour IX over Drelchkaff, both perpetuating the traditions of hatred and jealousy that, from time immemorial, had divided their forebears. The mark of European blood, long erased by many purely native unions, no longer left any trace on the persons of the two sovereigns, who resembled their subjects in the shape of their faces and the color of their skin.

On Trophy Square, the palm planted by Talou IV now magnificently outshone the rubber tree, half dead with age, that served as its counterpart.

XI

AT THAT POINT IN his narration, Seil-kor stopped to catch his breath, then broached certain more intimate details concerning the emperor's private life.

At the beginning of his reign, Talou VII had married a young, ideally beautiful Ponukelean named Rul.

Utterly smitten, the emperor refused to choose other brides, despite the customs of his land where polygamy was the norm.

One stormy day, Talou and Rul, then three months pregnant, were walking arm in arm along the beach of Ejur to admire the sublime spectacle of the furious waves, when they saw out at sea a ship in distress that, after smashing against a reef, foundered straight to the bottom before their eyes.

Speechless with horror, the couple stood there for a long time, watching the fatal area where bits of wreckage had started bobbing to the surface.

Soon the corpse of a young white woman, evidently from the sunken ship, floated toward the strand, tossed about by the waves. The passenger, lying flat with her face to the sky, wore a Swiss costume composed of a dark-colored skirt, an apron with multicolored embroidery, and a red velvet corset that, stretching only down to her waist, encased an unbuttoned white blouse with wide, puffy sleeves. Through the transparent waters, they could see behind her head the glint of long golden hairpins, arranged in a star around a solidly braided chignon.

Rul, who was mad about finery, immediately became entranced by that red corset and those golden pins, and dreamed only of how they would look on her. Yielding to her pleas, the emperor sent a slave who climbed into a dugout canoe and headed out with orders to retrieve the drowned woman's body.

But the foul weather made the task difficult, and Rul, whose morbid desire was only whetted further by the obstacles in its path, anxiously followed, with a mix of hope and discouragement, the perilous maneuvers of the slave whose prey kept eluding him.

After an hour of unrelieved battle against the elements, the slave finally reached the cadaver, which he managed to hoist into his boat; it was then that they discovered the corpse of a two-year-old child strapped to the dead woman's back, her neck convulsively encircled by two feeble arms still clinging tight. The poor toddler was probably the drowned woman's nursling, whom she had tried to save at the last instant by swimming for safety with her precious burden.

The nurse and child were carried to Ejur, and soon Rul took possession of the gold pins, which she arranged in a circle in her hair, and of the red corset, which she coquettishly fastened above the loincloth encircling her hips. From that moment on those adornments became her pride and joy and never left her body; as her pregnancy advanced she simply loosened the laces, which slid easily through the fine metal grommets of the eyelets.

For a long time following the disaster, the sea continued to toss ashore wreckage of all kinds, including numerous chests filled with a wide variety of items that were carefully gathered. Amid the debris, they found a sailor's cap bearing the word *Sylvander*, the name of the ill-fated vessel.

Six months after the storm, Rul gave birth to a daughter whom they named Sirdah.

The hour of anxiety that the young mother had spent before the Swiss woman's body was brought ashore had left its mark: the child, in all other respects healthy and well formed, bore on her forehead a peculiarly shaped red birthmark, from which radiated long yellow lines arranged like the famous golden pins.

The first time Sirdah opened her eyes, they noticed that she was severely wall-eyed; her mother, very proud of her own beauty, was humiliated at having produced an ugly duckling and developed an aversion to this child who offended her vanity. On the other hand, the emperor, who had so keenly desired a daughter, felt only deep love for the poor innocent, whom he showered with care and tenderness.

At that time, Talou's adviser was a certain Mossem, a Negro tall of stature, at once a sorcerer, medicine man, and scholar, who served as the emperor's prime minister.

Mossem had fallen for the alluring Rul, who for her part fell under the sway of the seductive adviser, admiring his majestic bearing and great learning.

The affair followed its inevitable course, and Rul, one year after Sirdah's birth, delivered a son who was the spit and image of Mossem.

Fortunately, Talou did not notice the fatal resemblance. Still, this son never quite entered his heart, where Sirdah still had pride of place.

Following a law Suann had instituted, each deceased sovereign was succeeded by the firstborn child, no matter the sex. Twice already, in each of the rival branches, girls had been called to rule; but in every case their premature deaths had transmitted to their brothers the right of supreme leadership.

Mossem and Rul hatched a despicable plot to do away with Sirdah so that one day their son could become emperor.

While this was happening, Talou, prey to his bellicose impulses, left for a long campaign and entrusted the throne to Mossem, who during the monarch's absence would exert absolute authority.

The two accomplices seized upon the opportunity, so favorable to the realization of their plan.

To the northeast of Ejur stretched the Vorrh, an immense forest primeval where none dared venture because of a certain legend that the shade of its trees was populated with evil spirits. All they had to do was abandon Sirdah there, where her body, protected by superstition, would not be found by any search parties.

One night, Mossem went off carrying Sirdah in his arms; the following evening, after a long day's walk, he reached the edge of the Vorrh and, too intelligent to believe in wives' tales, fearlessly penetrated among the haunted trees before him. Reaching a wide clearing, he laid the sleeping infant Sirdah on the moss, then headed back to the plain by the same path he had just forged through the thick branches and vines.

Twenty-four hours later, he entered Ejur under cover of night; no one had witnessed his departure or his return.

During his absence, Rul had posted herself at the door of the imperial hut to forbid all access. Sirdah was dangerously ill, she said, and Mossem was remaining at the child's side to treat her. After her accomplice's return, she announced that poor Sirdah had succumbed, and the next day they simulated a ceremonious funeral.

Tradition demanded that a death certificate be drawn up for every deceased member of the ruling family, detailing the circumstances of the demise. Mossem, who had an in-depth knowledge of Ponukelean writing, assumed the chore and drafted on parchment an invented account of Sirdah's last days.

Great was the emperor's grief upon his return, when he learned of his daughter's passing.

But nothing could make him suspect the plot against Sirdah; the two accomplices, giddy with joy, thus saw their odious machinations to bring their son to the throne succeed just as they had wished.

Two years passed during which Rul did not conceive another child. Annoyed by this sterility, Talou, without renouncing the woman whom he still believed faithful, finally decided to take other wives, in hopes of having a second daughter whose features would remind him of his beloved Sirdah. But his hopes were disappointed: he sired only sons, none of whom could make him forget the dear departed.

Only warfare distracted him from his sorrows; he launched new campaigns constantly, pushing ever farther the boundaries of his vast realm and attaching numerous spoils to the sycamores around Trophy Square.

Endowed with a poet's sensitivity, he had begun a vast epic, each verse of which celebrated one of his great military exploits. The work was called the "Jeroukka," a Ponukelean word that evoked triumphant heroism. Filled with ambition and pride, the emperor had vowed to eclipse in personality all other princes of his race and to transmit to future generations a poetic narrative of his reign, which he wished to portray as dominant and glorious.

Every time he finished a section of the "Jeroukka," he taught it to his warriors, who, in unison, sang it in chorus on a kind of slow, monotonous recitative.

The years passed without bringing the slightest cloud between Mossem and Rul, who continued their love affair in secret.

One day, however, the emperor was informed of their relations by one of his younger wives.

Unable to lend credence to what he took for bald-faced slander, Talou gleefully recounted the gossip to Rul, recommending she beware the jealous hatred that her superior beauty inspired in her rivals.

Although reassured by the emperor's jovial tone, Rul sensed danger and vowed to double her precautions.

She pleaded with Mossem to publicly take a mistress, whom he would conspicuously lavish with honors and gifts to allay whatever suspicions the monarch may have had.

Mossem agreed to the plan, which seemed to him, as to Rul, of the utmost urgency. He set his sights on a young beauty named

Jizme, whose intoxicating smile revealed dazzlingly white teeth in an ebony countenance.

Jizme soon grew accustomed to the privileges of her elevated status; Mossem, intent on playing his part well, satisfied her every whim, and with a word the young woman obtained the most undeserved favors for her own sycophants.

This credit soon earned the minister's favorite a swarm of solicitors who hastened to beg an audience. Jizme, pleased and flattered, was soon forced to regulate this onrush.

At her request, Mossem cut from several sheets of parchment a certain number of thin, supple rectangles, on each of which he finely traced the name "Jizme," then depicted in one corner, with a rudimentary sketch, three different phases of the moon.

These were, in short, visiting cards, which, distributed in great number, indicated to interested parties the three days in each four-week period in which the all-powerful intermediary was available to receive visitors.

Jizme took great enjoyment in playing queen. Whenever one of the appointed dates occurred, she adorned herself magnificently and received the crowd of petitioners, granting her support to some and refusing it to others, confident that her decisions would be completely ratified by Mossem.

Still, there was one thing missing from Rul's happiness. Beautiful, passionate, and full of youthful exuberance, she burned with feverish desire.

But Mossem, faithful to Rul, had never given even the slightest kiss to she who passed in everyone's eyes for his idolized lover.

Aware of her role as front, Jizme resolved to give herself entirely and without reservations to whoever could understand and appreciate her.

During each of her audiences, she had noticed, in the front row of petitioners, a young black named Nair, who seemed never to speak to her without emotion or shyness.

Several times she thought she saw Nair hiding behind some bush, spying on her during her daily walk in hopes of catching a momentary glimpse.

Soon she had no doubts about the passion she had inspired in the young man. She took Nair into her personal service and abandoned herself unrestrainedly to her gentle suitor, whose ardent feelings she soon came to share.

A perfectly plausible pretext explained in Mossem's mind the new page's assiduousness vis-à-vis his favorite.

At that time, Ejur was infested by a legion of mosquitoes whose bite carried fever. As it happened, Nair knew how to make little traps that caught the dangerous insects without fail.

He had discovered a red flower he used as bait, its very sharp scent attracting the creatures from a great distance. Certain fruit husks provided him with extremely delicate filaments, with which he himself wove a tissue finer than spiders' webs, but sufficiently resistant to stop mosquitoes cold. This latter task required great precision, and Nair could accomplish it only with the help of a long recipe that, recited by heart, reminded him step by step of each movement to make and each knot to form.

Like a child, Jizme derived an endlessly renewed pleasure from watching her lover's fingers as they industriously wove together the strands.

Nair's presence could thus be explained by the powerful entertainment that this highly inventive and subtle talent procured for Jizme.

An artist in several respects, Nair knew how to draw, and would relax from the painstaking production of his traps by sketching portraits and landscapes of a strange and primitive character. One day, he gave Jizme a curious white mattress, which he had patiently decorated with a quantity of small sketches depicting a wide variety of subjects. With this gift, he meant to watch over his beloved's sleep, who from then on rested each night on the soft bedding, a constant reminder of her lover's tender and attentive solicitude.

The young couple thus lived in peace and contentment, when an imprudence on Nair's part suddenly lifted the scales from Mossem's eyes.

Some of the chests the sea had washed up after the wreck of the *Sylvander* contained articles of clothing that had so far gone unclaimed. Jizme, with Mossem's authorization, drew from that reserve an abundance of baubles that perfectly suited her light, insouciant frivolity.

A pair of long suede gloves in particular amused the gleeful child, who, at every slightly formal occasion, enjoyed imprisoning her hands and arms in these supple sheaths.

During her explorations of this plentiful, heterogeneous inventory, Jizme had discovered a bowler hat that Nair had put on with intense pleasure. From then on, the young Negro went nowhere without the stiff headgear, which made him easily recognizable from a distance.

To the southeast of Ejur, not far from the right bank of the Tez, was an immense and magnificent park called the Behuliphruen, which a host of slaves maintained in a state of unparalleled luxuriousness. Talou, like a true poet, adored flowers and composed the stanzas of his epic beneath the delightful shade trees of this grandiose garden.

In the center of the Behuliphruen stretched a kind of elevated plateau, painstakingly arranged as a terrace, which was covered in admirable vegetation. From there, one could look down on the entire vast garden, and the emperor loved spending long hours of leisure sitting near the balustrade of branches and foliage that bordered this delightfully cool spot. Often, in the evening, he went to dream alongside Rul in a certain corner of the plateau, from where the view was particularly splendid.

Unable to appreciate this serene contemplation, which to her seemed rather tedious, Rul one day invited Mossem to come enliven the imperial tête-à-tête. Blind and trusting as ever, Talou had no objections to granting this whim; the presence of Jizme, moreover, would remove any unwelcome suspicions from his mind.

Nair, who every evening had a rendezvous with his love, was vexed to hear of the event that would keep them from enjoying each other's company. Resolved to be near Jizme all the same, he conceived a bold exploit that would make him the unseen fifth member of the Behuliphruen party.

But since Jizme was granting audience to the usual flood of solicitors that day, and had already begun receiving, Nair could not have with her the long private conversation needed in order to explain his complicated plan.

A writer as well as an artist, Nair knew Ponukelean script, which he had taught to Jizme during their long and frequent hours together. He decided to set down for his paramour all the urgent recommendations he could not detail for her face to face.

The letter was written out on parchment, then, in the midst of the tumult, handed nimbly from Nair to Jizme, who slid it deftly into her wrap.

But Mossem, who was wandering among the crowd, had noticed the clandestine maneuver. Moments later, putting his arm around Jizme, who was used to receiving such displays of affection from him in public, he made away with the epistle, which he went off to decipher in private.

As a header, Nair had drawn the five principal actors in that evening's scenario arranged in single file: to the right, Talou walked alone; behind him, making mocking gestures, were Mossem and Rul, themselves ridiculed by Nair and Jizme who were next in line.

The text contained the following instructions:

Once she was sitting in the corner of the cool terrace, Jizme would look out for Nair, who would come up silently by a certain predetermined path. In the shadows, the young Negro's silhouette would be easily recognizable thanks to the bowler hat he'd be sure to wear. The spot Talou chose for his absorbing reveries was surrounded by almost sheer drops; nonetheless, by clinging to the roots and shrubs with all his might, Nair could hoist himself cautiously to the level of the casual group. Jizme would let her hand dangle over the flowered balustrade; then, having ascertained the visitor's identity by carefully touching his hat, she would extend this hand for a kiss from her lover, who could remain suspended for a moment by the strength of his arms.

After committing to memory all the details he'd just intercepted, Mossem went back to Jizme and, under pretext of more caresses, slipped the note back into the favorite's wrap.

Wounded in his pride and furious at the thought of having long become a public laughingstock, Mossem sought a way to obtain flagrant proof against the two accomplices, whom he vowed to punish severely.

He devised a plan and went to see Seil-kor, who at that time had already been serving the emperor for several years and could, at night, look like Nair thanks to their similar age and bearing.

This was Mossem's plan:

Wearing the bowler hat that was meant to allay suspicion, Seil-kor would go to Jizme along the path clearly designated in the note. Before starting his ascent, the false Nair would inscribe on the hat, with a fresh, sticky substance, certain predetermined letters. Jizme, following her compulsive habit, would surely be wearing her gloves for an evening with the emperor; by making the prudent gesture that, as the letter instructed, should precede the kiss, the favorite would give herself away by imprinting on the suede one of the revelatory characters.

Seil-kor accepted the mission. In any case, it was impossible to refuse, for the all-powerful Mossem could have made this request into an order.

The first crucial step was to intercept Nair on his nocturnal expedition. Fearing an indiscretion that could spell the failure of his plot, Mossem wished to avoid using any outside help.

Forced to act alone, Seil-kor remembered the nooselike collars with which hunters captured game animals in the forests of the Pyrenees. Using ropes gathered from the distant wreck of the *Sylvander*, he went to set his snare in the middle of Nair's intended path. With this ruse, Seil-kor was sure to overcome an adversary half paralyzed by insidious fetters.

This task accomplished, Seil-kor placed at the foot of the cliff he was later to scale a certain mixture, rapidly composed, of chalkstones and water.

When evening fell, he went to hide not far from the snare he'd set.

Nair appeared and his foot was soon caught in the adroitly placed trap. A moment later, the imprudent one was bound and gagged by Seil-kor, who had leapt upon him in one bound.

Pleased with his discreet and silent victory, Seil-kor donned the victim's hat and headed to the rendezvous.

From afar he spied Jizme, who was furtively watching for him while making conversation with the royal couple and Mossem.

Fooled by the newcomer's silhouette and especially his hat, Jizme thought she recognized Nair and draped her arm beyond the balustrade in anticipation.

Reaching the foot of the slope, Seil-kor dipped his finger into the chalky mix and, in a mischievous spirit, traced in capital letters on the black hat the word "PINCHED," which he already imagined the unfortunate Jizme to be. After this, he began hauling himself up the cliff, grasping laboriously at any branch that might bear his weight.

Reaching the level of the plateau, he stopped and touched the overhanging hand, which, after having brushed the stiff felt hat, dropped lower to receive the promised kiss.

Seil-kor silently pressed his lips against the suede glove that Jizme, on Mossem's recommendation, had been all too happy to put on.

His task completed, he clambered back to earth without a sound.

On the plateau, Mossem had kept a constant eye on Jizme's movements. He saw her pull her arm back and discovered at the same time as she a *C* clearly imprinted on the gray glove, which stretched from the roots of her fingers to the heel of her palm.

Jizme quickly hid her hand, while Mossem inwardly rejoiced at the success of his ruse.

One hour later, Mossem, now alone with Jizme, ripped the stained glove from her and took from the unfortunate's wrap the damning letter, which he shoved before her eyes.

The next day, Nair and Jizme were arrested and kept under guard by fierce sentinels.

Talou having demanded an explanation for this harsh measure, Mossem seized the occasion to buttress the emperor's trust, as he still feared suspicions about Rul and himself. He presented as a jealous lover's vengeance what was really mere anger, due to a ruffling of his pride. He intentionally exaggerated the depth of his resentment and lengthily recounted to the sovereign every detail of the adventure, including specifics regarding the noose, the hat, and the glove. Meanwhile, he was able to keep secret his own affair with Rul by avoiding any mention of the compromising portraits that Nair had drawn at the top of his letter.

Talou approved the punishment that Mossem meted on the guilty pair, who remained in captivity.

Seventeen years had elapsed since Sirdah's disappearance, and Talou still pined for his daughter as if it were yesterday.

Having kept in memory a very precise image of the child he so faithfully mourned, he tried to recreate in his imagination the young woman she would now have been had death not taken her away.

The features she'd had as a barely weaned girl-child, deeply etched in his mind, served as his basis. He accentuated them while changing nothing of their shape, tending to their gradual development year after year, and thus managed to create for himself alone an eighteen-year-old Sirdah whose clearly delineated ghost accompanied him at all times.

One day, during one of his customary campaigns, Talou came upon an enchanting child named Meisdehl, the sight of whom left him dumbstruck: before him was the living portrait of Sirdah as he pictured her at the age of seven, in the uninterrupted suite of images in his mind.

It was while passing in review several families of prisoners, who had escaped from the flames of a village he'd just put to the torch, that the emperor noticed Meisdehl. He took the girl under his wing and treated her as his own daughter after his return to Ejur.

Among her adoptive brothers, Meisdehl soon noticed a certain Kalj, seven years old like her, who seemed the ideal playmate to share her games.

Kalj was in such delicate health that everyone feared for his life; he lived almost entirely in his head. Advanced for his age, he surpassed most of his brothers in intelligence and sensitivity, but his body was pitiably frail. Aware of his condition, too often he let himself wallow in a deep melancholy that Meisdehl made it her mission to overcome. Filled with mutual tenderness, the two children formed an inseparable couple; seeing the newcomer constantly at his son's side, Talou, from the abyss of his grief, could sometimes enjoy the illusion that he really had a daughter again.

Not long after the adoption of Meisdehl, several natives arrived from Mihu, a village located near the Vorrh, to tell the citizens of Ejur that a lightning fire had been raging in the southern part of the vast primeval forest since the previous evening.

Talou, riding in a kind of palanquin borne by ten stout runners, traveled to the edge of the Vorrh to witness the dazzling spectacle, which appealed to his poetic soul.

He stepped onto the ground just as night was falling. A strong wind from the northeast scattered the flames nearest him, and he stood motionless, watching as the fire quickly spread.

The entire population of Mihu had gathered so as not to miss this grandiose spectacle.

Two hours after the emperor's arrival, only about a dozen intact trees remained, forming a thick clump at which the flames began lapping.

Then they saw a young native of eighteen fleeing the thicket, accompanied by a French soldier wearing a Zouave's uniform and armed with his rifle and cartridge belts.

By the light of the forest fire, Talou distinguished on the young woman's brow a red birthmark with radiating yellow lines. There could be no mistake: it was his beloved Sirdah who stood before his eyes. She was very different from the imaginary portrait he'd so painstakingly crafted and that Meisdehl so perfectly incarnated, but this mattered little to the emperor who, mad with joy, ran up to his daughter to embrace her.

He then tried to talk to her, but Sirdah, recoiling in fear, did not understand his language.

During the happy father's effusions, a tree consumed at the base suddenly toppled, violently striking the head of the Zouave, who fell unconscious. Sirdah immediately rushed to the soldier's aid, her face contorted with anxiety.

Talou didn't wish to abandon the injured stranger who seemed to inspire such pure affection in his daughter; plus, he was counting on the man's eyewitness revelations to illuminate the longstanding mystery of Sirdah's disappearance.

Several moments later, the palanquin, lifted by the runners, headed back to Ejur, carrying the emperor, Sirdah, and the unconscious Zouave.

Talou entered the capital the next day.

Brought before her daughter, Rul, terror-stricken and under

threat of torture, made a complete confession to the emperor, who immediately ordered Mossem's arrest.

While searching his minister's hut for some proof of the abject felony, Talou discovered the love letter that Nair had written to Jizme several months before. Seeing himself ridiculed on the drawing that headed the sheet, the monarch flew into a rage, resolving to torture both Nair, for his brazenness, and Jizme, for the duplicity she'd committed by accepting such a document and not denouncing its author.

Lavished with care in a hut where they had laid him down, the Zouave came to his senses and recounted his odyssey to Seil-kor, who had been charged with learning his story.

Velbar—for so the patient was named—came from Marseille. His father, a decorative painter, had taught him his own trade early on, and the admirably talented youngster had improved his craft by taking free local classes in which he learned drawing and watercolor. At eighteen, Velbar had discovered he had a strong baritone; for days on end, while on his scaffolding painting some shop sign, he lustily belted out many fashionable romances, and passersby stopped to listen, marveling at the charm and purity of his generous voice.

When he reached the age for military service, Velbar was sent to Bougie to join the Fifth Zouaves. After a smooth crossing, the young man, delighted to see new lands, disembarked on African soil one beautiful November morning and was pointed to the military barracks amid a large detachment of conscripts.

The rookie Zouave's beginnings were difficult and marked by a thousand daily vexations. Rotten luck had placed him under the command of one Lieutenant Lécurou, a ruthless and fastidious martinet who made a boast of his legendary harshness.

At the time, to satisfy the demands of a certain Flora Crinis, a demanding and profligate young woman who was his lover, Lécurou spent long hours in a secret gambling club where a tempting roulette wheel spun continually. As luck had so far smiled on the impetuous gambler, the richly kept Flora appeared in public dripping with jewels and strutted about in a carriage beside the lieutenant down the city's elegant promenade.

Meanwhile, Velbar pursued his arduous apprenticeship as a soldier.

One day, as the regiment, returning to Bougie after a long march, still found itself in the middle of the countryside, the Zouaves were ordered to strike up a spirited tune to help them forget their road-weariness.

Velbar, who by now was known for his splendid voice, was assigned to sing solo the verses of an interminable lament, to which the entire regiment answered in chorus with an eternally unvarying refrain.

At dusk they crossed through a small wood, in which a lone dreamer, sitting beneath a tree, was jotting onto music paper some melody born of his solitude and reflection.

Hearing Velbar's voice, which alone carried more loudly than the huge chorus that periodically answered him, the inspired stroller suddenly jumped to his feet and followed the regiment back to town.

The stranger was none other than the composer Faucillon, whose celebrated opera *Daedalus*, after a brilliant run in France, had just been staged throughout the major cities of Algeria. Accompanied by the performers, Faucillon had only recently arrived in Bougie, the next stop in their triumphant tour.

But since the last performance, the baritone Ardonceau, overwhelmed by the difficult title role and suffering from a tenacious sore throat, had become unable to go on; Faucillon, completely at a loss, had nearly given up finding a replacement for his leading man, when his ear had been struck by the young Zouave singing on the road.

The next day, having made his inquiries, Faucillon went to find Velbar, who jumped at the chance to perform onstage. They easily obtained the colonel's authorization and, after several days of intense rehearsal under the composer's direction, the young debutant felt prepared.

The performance was held before a packed house; in the front row of a box, Flora Crinis sat enthroned with Lieutenant Lécurou.

Velbar, magnificent in the role of Daedalus, conveyed like a consummate actor the anxieties and hopes of an artist obsessed with the grandiose designs of his genius. The Greek toga flattered his superb physique, and the ideal timbre of his powerful voice ended each phrase with an abrupt surge of vigor.

Flora could not keep her eyes off of Velbar, training the lenses of her opera glasses on him and feeling within her an irresistible sensation that had begun the moment the young singer had appeared onstage.

In the third act, Velbar triumphed with the principal aria, a kind of hymn to joy and pride in which Daedalus, having completed the construction of the labyrinth and profoundly moved by the sight of his masterpiece, rapturously greeted the realization of his dream.

The admirable interpretation of this rousing passage made the turmoil in Flora's heart overflow, and the very next day she hatched a subtle plan to get close to Velbar.

Before undertaking any project, the superstitious Flora always consulted Old Angélique, an overfamiliar and talkative busybody who read cards, palms, and horoscopes, loaned money, and, for the right fee, handled all sorts of dubious errands.

Summoned by an urgent missive, Angélique went to see Flora. The old crone looked every bit the fortuneteller, with her filthy gunnysack and large, shapeless cloak that for the past ten years had protected her against the often harsh Algerian winters.

Flora confessed her secret and asked, first and foremost, if her desire had been conceived under an auspicious sign. Angélique immediately took from her gunnysack a celestial planisphere that she pinned to the wall; then, using the previous day's date as starting point for her horoscope, she sank into a deep meditation, seemingly absorbed in active and complex mental calculations. In the end, she pointed to the constellation Cancer, whose benign influence should preserve Flora's future love affairs from misfortune.

Once that matter was settled, the main thing was to conduct the affair as secretly as possible, as the lieutenant, a suspicious and jealous man, kept a watchful eye over his mistress's every movement.

Angélique put the planisphere back in her sack, then pulled from its depths a sheet of cardboard perforated by a certain number of irregularly spaced holes. This device, which cryptographers call a *grille cipher*, would permit the two lovers to communicate without fear of discovery. A sentence, written in the holes placed over a sheet of blank paper, could then be made unintelligible by filling in the spaces between them with random letters. Only Velbar could reconstruct the meaning of the billet-doux by positioning an identical grille over the coded text.

But this subterfuge required some explanation: Velbar and Angélique needed to talk privately. The crone couldn't go to the barracks without risking a dangerous encounter with the lieutenant, who was fully aware of her close relationship with Flora; on the other hand, summoning Velbar to her home would awaken the young Zouave's suspicions, as he would see in it only a self-interested bid for a paid consultation. Angélique therefore decided to arrange a rendezvous in a public place, predetermining a sign by which to assure identification, to prevent any mishaps.

In Flora's presence, the old woman composed an anonymous letter full of seductive promises: Velbar should sit the following evening at a sidewalk table of the Café Leopold and order a mixed plate, called a "Harlequin," at the precise moment when the Benediction rang in the church of Saint-Jacques; immediately a confidant would approach the young soldier bearing the most gratifying revelations.

The following day at the appointed hour, Angélique was at her post in front of the Café Leopold, not far from a Zouave who was calmly and silently smoking his pipe. The crone, not knowing Velbar and not wishing to commit a faux pas, prudently awaited the agreed signal to deliver her message.

When the sound of church bells suddenly began pealing in the tower of nearby Saint-Jacques, the Zouave asked the waiter a question and then ordered a Harlequin.

Angélique went up and introduced herself, referring to the anonymous letter, just as the waiter placed before Velbar the requested Harlequin, a kind of multicolored assemblage of assorted meats and vegetables piled on the same dish.

The old woman briefly explained the situation, and Velbar, enchanted, received an absolutely perfect double of the grille that Angélique had given Flora.

The two lovers lost no time in beginning a secret, torrid correspondence. Velbar, having received a hefty fee for his performance in *Daedalus*, devoted a portion of his earnings to renting and furnishing a seductive retreat, where he could receive his mistress without fear of discovery. With the rest of the money he bought Flora a present, choosing, at the finest jeweler in town, a silver chatelaine from which hung a magnificent, finely wrought watch.

Flora let out a squeal of joy as she accepted this charming souvenir, which she immediately pinned to her belt; they agreed that, as far as Lécurou was concerned, she had purchased this extravagance for herself.

Still, in spite of the constellation Cancer, the affair would come to a tragic end.

Lécurou, finding that Flora had begun acting strangely, followed her one day to the apartment Velbar had rented. Hidden around the corner, he waited two long hours and finally saw the lovers emerge, tenderly parting after a few steps.

As of the very next day, Lécurou ceased all relations with Flora and conceived a mortal hatred of Velbar, whom he began persecuting cruelly.

He constantly watched his rival, waiting to catch him out on the slightest pretext and persistently inflicting on him the harshest and most unjust punishments. Folding in the thumb of his raised right hand, he had a way of announcing confinement to the brig with the words "Four days in the cooler!" that made Velbar flush hot with rage and nearly drove him to talk back to his superior officer.

But a terrible example brought home to the young Zouave that he needed to rein in his dangerous rebellious impulses.

One of his comrades, a fellow named Suire, was said to have lived a rather turbulent life between the ages of eighteen and twenty. Frequenting the seediest quarters of Bougie and living among pimps and prostitutes, Suire, before joining the regiment, was a kind of *bravo* who, gossips said, had committed two as yet unpunished murders for hire.

Fierce and violent by nature, Suire had difficulty bending to the demands of discipline and chafed under Lécurou's continual reproofs.

One day, the lieutenant, inspecting the barracks, ordered Suire to remake his pack, which was uneven.

Suire, already in a foul mood, didn't budge.

The lieutenant repeated his order, to which Suire replied with the single word, "No!"

Furious, Lécurou screamed abuse at Suire in his shrill voice, detailing with acrid joy the thirty days of prison that would quite certainly follow this insubordonation; then, before turning to leave, as a final insult he spat in Suire's face.

Suire lost his head at that moment, and snatching up his bayonet, shoved it full into the chest of the despicable lieutenant, whom they immediately carried off.

Although unconscious and bloody, Lécurou was only slightly wounded by the weapon, which had glanced off a rib.

Suire was nonetheless court-martialed and sentenced to death.

Lécurou, soon recovered, commanded the firing squad, which included Velbar.

When the lieutenant shouted, "Aim!" Velbar, realizing he was about to kill someone, was overcome by uncontrollable trembling.

Suddenly he heard the word "Fire!" and Suire collapsed, struck by twelve rounds.

Velbar would never forget that horrible moment.

Flora now conducted her affair with Velbar openly; but, since Lécurou had abandoned her, the poor girl was racking up debt after debt. Knowing the gambling den that, for a time, had procured the lieutenant his resources, she decided to tempt fate in turn and sat day by day at the roulette table.

But persistent bad luck caused her to lose even her last louis.

She then resorted to Angélique, and the crone, sensing an advantageous prospect, immediately loaned Flora a fairly sizeable sum at usurious rates, using the borrower's jewelry and furniture—her sole remaining assets—as collateral.

Alas, the wheel soon made away with this new capital as well.

One day, sitting before the green baize, the nervous and agitated Flora risked her very last gold coins. A few throws of the dice were enough to complete her ruin. The wretched woman, seeing in a flash her jewelry sold off and furniture repossessed, was suddenly haunted by thoughts of suicide.

At that moment, a loud bang was heard at the door of the clandestine establishment, and someone rushed in crying, "It's the police!"

Panic gripped those present, some of whom threw open the windows as if to find an escape route. But four stories separated the balcony from the street, making flight impossible.

Soon the door burst open and a dozen plainclothesmen rushed into the foyer, then into the gaming parlor.

The hysteria around Flora had brought her anxiety to a climax. The prospect of a scandal, added to the specter of indigence, hastened the accomplishment of her fatal plan. In a bound she ran to the balcony and hurled herself to the pavement below.

The next day, learning simultaneously of the drama at the gambling den and his mistress's disappearance, Velbar felt a sinister foreboding. He went straight to the morgue, where he saw, hanging above the corpse of a woman with a mangled and unrecognizable face, the famous silver chain that he himself had given poor Flora. This clue left no doubt as to the dead woman's identity, whose funeral service the young Zouave paid for by selling off at rock-bottom prices the furniture he had recently bought with his stage earnings.

Flora's death did nothing to lessen Lécurou's hatred, and he abused his rival more than ever with insults and punishments.

One moonless night in May, at a certain halt in a nocturnal march lit only by the stars, Lécurou went up to Velbar, on whom he inflicted a week under police guard for a supposed violation of the dress code. After which the lieutenant began coldly insulting the young Zouave, who, pale with anger, clenched every muscle to remain in control.

In the end, Lécurou reprised the conclusion of his scene with Suire by spitting in Velbar's face; the latter saw red and, acting purely on instinct, roundly slapped the lieutenant across the face before he knew what he was doing.

Immediately, the terrible consequences of this quasi-involuntary action appeared to him with terrifying clarity, and in a flash he saw the horrible vision of Suire crumbling beneath a hail of bullets. Shoving past the lieutenant and the several officers running up to lend their chief a hand, he plunged straight ahead through the countryside, soon protected from pursuit by the nighttime darkness.

He reached the port of Bougie and hid out in the cargo hold of the *Saint Irenaeus*, a large packet boat bound for South Africa.

The next day, the *Saint Irenaeus* lifted anchor; but five days later, disoriented after a storm, it ran aground within sight of Mihu. Counting the *Sylvander* and the vessel carrying the Spanish twins, it was the third time such a thing had occurred in the region since the long-distant coronation of Suann.

Hastening from his hiding place, Velbar, still in uniform and carrying his rifle and full cartridge belts, went to blend in with the crowd of passengers.

The inhabitants of Mihu, fearsome cannibals, placed the castaways under heavy guard to gorge on their flesh; every day one of the prisoners, after a summary execution, was devoured then and there in the others' presence. Soon only Velbar remained, having seen his ill-fated companions disappear to the last man.

When the time came for his own agony, he decided to attempt an impossible escape from his killers. As they reached for him, he suddenly began swinging his rifle butt, clearing himself a passage through the crowd, then began fleeing blindly, chased by some twenty natives who bolted after him in hot pursuit.

After an hour of solid running, as his strength was beginning to flag, he saw the edge of the Vorrh and made one last dash in hopes of finding a thicket in the huge forest to hide him.

The flesh-eaters, urging each other on with frantic shouts, managed to close in on the captive, and it was just as they were about to grab him that Velbar dove into the outermost foliage. The chase ended then and there, as the natives dared not follow him into the dark lair of the evil spirits.

Velbar lived peacefully in the safe haven of the Vorrh, never venturing out for fear of being recaptured by the fierce anthropophagi. He fashioned a small hut from branches and lived on fruits and roots, preciously guarding his rifle and cartridges in case of attack by wild beasts.

When he'd given the lieutenant the fatal slap, Velbar had had on his person his box of watercolors and sketchbook. Using water from a stream transported in a concave stone, he managed to dilute his paints and fill his long, solitary days with work. He wanted to summarize in images the somber drama of Bougie, and he marshaled all his talents to accomplish this absorbing task.

Long months passed without bringing any variation to the poor recluse's routine.

One day, Velbar heard some distant wails cutting through the normally still silence of his vast domain. Nearing the spot from where the noise originated, he discovered Sirdah, whom Mossem had recently abandoned there; he scooped the poor child up in his arms, at which her crying immediately ceased. A few days earlier, he had trapped a pair of wild buffalo, keeping them tethered with strong vines wrapped around their horns and attached to a tree trunk. With the milk from the female he was able to feed his adoptive daughter, and his life, so solitary until then, was now imbued with interest and purpose.

As she grew up, Sirdah, full of grace and charm despite her wall-eye, repaid in affection all the kindnesses her protector showered on her daily. Velbar taught her French and urged her never to set foot outside the Vorrh, fearing she would fall back into the clutches of the fiendish enemies who had so cruelly exposed her to certain death, and who would surely recognize her by the mark on her forehead.

The years passed, and the child was already becoming a woman when a violent forest fire, decimating the Vorrh, expelled the two recluses who, up to the last moment, had hidden under the ever-shrinking canopy of tall trees.

Once outside the retreat where he had hidden for so long, Velbar expected to fall prey once again to the cannibals of Mihu. Fortunately, the emperor's presence preserved him from that horrible fate.

Talou, when Seil-kor had translated Velbar's tale for him, promised to richly reward the man who had saved his daughter's life.

But alas, there was no time to put his generous plan into action, for Velbar did not survive the terrible blow he'd received from the fallen tree. One week after his arrival in Ejur, he breathed his last in the arms of his adoptive daughter, who until the end had bravely and lovingly attended to her devoted benefactor, the only mainstay of her childhood.

Talou, wishing to render supreme homage to Velbar, told Seil-kor to bury the Zouave's body with full honors in the middle of the west side of Trophy Square.

Copying the model of French sepulchers, Seil-kor, with the help of several slaves, laid the body to rest in the designated spot, then covered him with a large funeral slab on which he placed his uniform, rifle, and cartridge belts, symmetrically arranged. The autobiographical watercolors found in one of the Zouave's pockets served to decorate a kind of vertical panel erected behind the tomb and wrapped in dark cloth.

After this loss, which left her in a grief-stricken stupor, Sirdah, a gentle, loving soul, transferred all her affection onto the emperor. Seil-kor had revealed to her in French the secret of her birth, and she wished, through constant attentions, to compensate her father for the long years of separation that an unjust fate had imposed on the two of them.

With Seil-kor's help, she studied the language of her ancestors, so as to speak fluently with her future subjects.

Each time her steps led her near Velbar's grave, she piously pressed her lips on the stone slab commemorating the dear departed.

Sirdah's return did not upset Meisdehl; she still enjoyed the love of the emperor, who, despite recent events, continued to see in her the living image of the unreal phantom he so often used to evoke.

In honor of his old love, Talou decided to spare Rul's life, and the woman, now numbering among the slaves assigned to cultivate the Behuliphruen, had to spend her days bent low to the ground, hoeing or weeding without respite. The monarch's vengeance did not extend to her adulterine son, whose likeness to Mossem had only increased with the years. Devastated by Sirdah's arrival and by the discovery of the distant conspiracy perpetrated for his sake, the unfortunate young man, who had thought himself destined to reign one day under the name Talou VIII, was stricken by a languishing illness and expired after only a few weeks.

Mossem, Nair, and Jizme were slated for grisly tortures, deferred from one day to the next by the emperor, who enjoyed imposing on the guilty trio as further atonement the anguish of a cruel, prolonged wait.

A Negro named Rao, Mossem's pupil, who had been schooled in his master's complex knowledge, was appointed to succeed the disgraced minister in the important functions of adviser and overseer.

Meanwhile, Rul, who'd suffered all the humiliation she could stand, had sworn to take her vengeance. Especially furious with Sirdah, whose return had been the cause of these misfortunes, she sought a means to assuage her hatred of the daughter whose very birth she now cursed.

After much reflection, this is what the perfidious mother devised:

A certain illness was ravaging the land in epidemic proportions, manifested by the occurrence of two white and highly contagious blotches that spread over the eyes and grew thicker by the day.

Only the sorcerer Bashkou, a taciturn, solitary old man, knew how to cure the dangerous infection by means of a secret unguent. But the rapid cure could only be effected at a sacred spot in the very bed of the Tez. Immersed with the patient in a certain specific eddy, Bashkou, applying his balm, could then detach the two stigmata, which would immediately follow the current out to sea where their terrible contamination was no longer a threat. Many sufferers immediately recovered their sight after this operation; others, less fortunate, remained forever blind, because the illness, spreading too far, had gradually covered the entire eyeball.

Rul knew how contagious these blotches were. One evening, slipping past the guards dotted throughout the Behuliphruen, she reached the seashore and sailed a dugout to the mouth of the Tez. She knew that Bashkou always worked at nightfall, to offer his newly cured patients a soft and restful twilight. Protected by the crepuscular veil, Rul awaited unseen the arrival of the blotches the sorcerer had removed; she caught one in passing as it drifted by on the current, then regained the shore at her departure point.

In the middle of the night, she stole into Sirdah's hut, which juxtaposed the emperor's. Creeping forward cautiously, guided by the light of a single moonbeam, she softly rubbed her sleeping daughter's eyelids with the hazardous blotches squeezed between her fingers.

But Talou, awakened by Rul's furtive footfalls, rushed into Sirdah's hut just in time to witness the heinous act. He immediately grasped the intent of the unnatural mother, whom he brutally dragged outside and put in the hands of three slaves ordered to keep watch over her.

The emperor then returned to Sirdah, who had been wrested from her deep sleep by the noise. The evil was already taking effect, and a veil began spreading over the poor child's eyes.

By order of Talou, drunk with rage, Rul, condemned to an excruciating death, was imprisoned alongside Mossem, Nair, and Jizme.

By the next day, Sirdah's illness had made stunning progress; two opaque leucoma, which had formed in mere hours, had left her completely blind.

Wishing to operate immediately, the emperor crossed the Tez with his daughter that very evening and approached the large hut where Bashkou lived.

But the eddy devoted to the magic treatment was located on the right bank of the river, and because of this fact belonged to Drelchkaff.

Now, King Yaour IX, having learned of Rul's crime and predicting the father's and daughter's next move, had hastened to give Bashkou hard and fast instructions.

Accordingly, the sorcerer refused to treat Sirdah by order of Yaour, who, he added, demanded the young girl's hand in exchange for a cure only he could authorize.

Were there to be such a marriage, Yaour would then be in line to share Talou's succession with Sirdah, and therefore would one day reunite Ponukele and Drelchkaff under his sole dominion.

Revolted by these terms and by the idea of seeing his estates pass to the enemy bloodline, Talou brought his daughter back to Ejur without deigning to answer.

Since that event, which had occurred only several weeks earlier, the situation remained unchanged and Sirdah was still blind.

XII

STILL LYING IN THE FINE SAND in the shade of the tall cliff, we had
followed the ins and outs of Seil-kor's long, dramatic tale without a
single interruption.

Meanwhile, the Negroes had extracted from the bowels of the
Lynceus a mass of objects and crates, which at an order from Seil-kor
they suddenly hoisted onto their shoulders; his clear voice, after the
end of his story, had just sounded the signal for departure. Several
more trips would complete the unloading of the vessel, whose entire
cargo would gradually be transported to Ejur.

Several instants later, forming a column amid the Negroes bent
under their various burdens, our group, led by Seil-kor, headed in
a straight line toward the announced capital. The midget Philippo
was carried like an infant by his impresario Jenn, while Tancrède
Boucharessas, with a family of trained cats, rode on a small cripple's
trolley pushed by his son Hector. At the head, Olga Chervonenkhov,
followed by Sladki and Milenkaya, walked near the equestrian Urbain, who proudly dominated the group on his horse Romulus.

It took us only half an hour to reach Ejur, where we soon met
the emperor, who received us on Trophy Square surrounded by his
daughter, his ten wives, and all his sons, of whom he had thirty-six.

Seil-kor exchanged a few words with Talou and immediately
translated for us his sovereign decree: each of us was to write a letter
to a friend or family member, with the goal of obtaining a ransom
whose amount would vary depending on the signatory's outward
appearance; once this was done, Seil-kor, walking north with a large

detachment of natives, would go to Porto Novo and mail the precious correspondence to Europe; once he was in possession of the requisite amounts, the faithful envoy would purchase various supplies that his men, still led by him, would carry to Ejur. Following this, the same Seil-kor would act as our guide back to Porto Novo, from where we would have no trouble obtaining passage home.

Each letter was to contain a special codicil to the effect that any attempt to rescue us would bring about our immediate deaths. Regardless, those who could not buy their freedom would meet with swift capital punishment.

By a strange scruple, Talou, not wishing to look like a common thief, let us keep what money we had on us. In any case, the cash gathered from relieving us of it would have added only a pittance to the huge combined bounty of the anticipated ransoms.

A hoard of stationery supplies was unpacked and everyone hastened to write his letter, indicating the emancipating sum, whose amount was fixed by Seil-kor at the emperor's instigation.

Eight days later Seil-kor headed out for Porto Novo, accompanied by the same Negroes who had appeared before us when we ran aground, and who in less than a week, through continual return trips, had transported to Ejur the entire contents of our ill-fated ship, which the passengers often revisited.

For us this departure marked the beginning of a monotonous and tedious existence. We yearned for the hour of deliverance, sleeping at night in the huts reserved for our use and spending our days reading or speaking French with Sirdah, who was delighted to know compatriots of Velbar's.

To help keep us occupied and entertained, Juillard proposed the foundation of a kind of elite association or unusual club, in which each member would have to distinguish himself through either an original work or a fabulous demonstration.

Applications immediately poured in, and Juillard, who had the credit of coming up with the idea, was drafted president of the new association, which adopted the pretentious appellation "The Incomparables Club." Each charter member would have to rehearse for a grand gala performance intended to celebrate Seil-kor's return and our liberation.

As no club could do without a headquarters, Chènevillot offered to build a small structure that would also serve as the group's emblem. Juillard agreed and, with the future exhibitions in mind, asked him to design the monument in the form of a slightly raised stage.

But to use a plot of ground on Trophy Square required the emperor's authorization.

Sirdah, who entirely supported our cause, volunteered to intervene with Talou; the latter, enchanted to learn that we wished to beautify his capital, welcomed our request but nonetheless asked the purpose of this planned new building. Sirdah briefly explained about the gala, and the emperor, delighted at the prospect of this unexpected celebration, spontaneously granted us full latitude to take from the spoils of the *Lynceus* whatever we needed to organize our show.

When the girl had told us the happy result of her mission, Chènevillot, aided by his workmen, who had no shortage of tools, cut down a certain number of trees in the Behuliphruen. The trunks were sliced into planks, and construction got underway on Trophy Square, at the midpoint of the side farthest from the sea.

Wishing to inspire a sense of competition among the club members, Juillard decided to invent a new decoration, to be conferred on the most deserving of them. After a long search for a motif both original and easy to make, he settled on the Greek capital *delta*, which seemed to satisfy both necessary conditions. Taking apart a certain old container found among the *Lynceus*'s supplies gave him a sheet of tin from which he cut six triangles, each topped with a ring; each *delta* thus fashioned was hung from a short length of blue ribbon, destined for the chest of a *chevalier* of the order.

Wishing in addition to establish a supreme and unique distinction, Juillard, without altering his model, cut a large *delta* made to be worn over the left hip.

These decorations would be awarded at the conclusion of the gala performance.

*
* *

Meanwhile, everyone began preparing for the big day.

Olga Chervonenkhov, planning to perform *The Nymph's Dance*, her greatest triumph from the olden days, often exercised out of everyone's sight in hopes of regaining her former limberness.

Juillard outlined a brilliant lecture on the Electors of Brandenburg, with illustrative portraits.

After agreeing to appear on the program, Balbet, whose luggage contained arms and munitions, found all his cartridges soaked by the sea, which in high tide had partially invaded the hold of the *Lynceus* through a wide breach opened by the wreck. Sirdah, apprised of this calamity, generously donated Velbar's weapon and cartridge belts. The offer was accepted, and Balbet entered into possession of an excellent Gras rifle, along with twenty-four cartridges that had remained in perfect condition thanks to the arid African climate. Leaving everything in its place on the Zouave's tomb, the illustrious champion announced for the day of the gala a prestigious exercise in marksmanship, to be followed by a sensational duel with La Billaudière-Maisonnial's fencing machine.

Luxo's packages had suffered even more water damage than Balbet's, and all of his fireworks, though fortunately insured, were irrevocably ruined. Only the final flourish, packed separately with great care, had escaped the disaster; Luxo decided to embellish our complex spectacle by shooting off this group of dazzling portraits, which at this point would not arrive in time for the wedding of Baron Ballesteros.

The ichthyologist Martignon spent his time on the waves in a dugout that Sirdah had procured him. Armed with an immense net with long ropes retrieved from one of his trunks, he performed countless soundings, hoping to make some interesting discovery that he could display to enrich the gala's program.

All the other members of the club, inventors, artists, trainers, curiosities, or acrobats, rehearsed their different specialties, wishing to be at their best on the day of the grand occasion.

In a certain part of the *Lynceus* especially damaged by the wreck, we had discovered twelve two-wheeled vehicles, like Roman chariots decorated with vivid paintings. During their tours, the Boucharessas and Alcott families, joining forces, used these vehicles to perform a curious musical exercise.

Each of the chariots, once set in motion, sounded a pure, vibrant note produced by the rotation of the wheels.

When it was showtime, Stéphane Alcott and his six sons, plus the four Boucharessas brothers and their sister, would suddenly appear in the circus and climb separately into the dozen chariots, each harnessed to a single horse that had been given some cursory training.

Together, the music-making devices, aligned side by side at a given point on the circular track, produced the diatonic scale of C, from the low tonic up to high G.

At a sign from Stéphane Alcott, a slow, melodious parade began. The chariots, advancing one by one following a determined order and rhythm, executed a host of popular tunes, carefully chosen from among refrains or choruses that didn't have too much modulation. The alignment was soon broken by the length and frequency of the notes; a given chariot, emitting a full note, went forward four or five yards, while the neighboring vehicle, meant to emit only a sixteenth note, advanced barely a few steps. Soon dispersed over the entire stretch of track, the horses, whipped with precision, always started walking at just the right moment.

Eleven of the chariots had been smashed when we ran aground. Talou confiscated the one intact specimen for young Kalj, who, growing weaker by the day, needed to take long and restorative outings that wouldn't tire him out.

A wicker armchair retrieved from the *Lynceus* was attached by its four feet to the floor of the vehicle, whose wheels as they turned emitted a high C.

A slave between the two harness shafts completed the rig, which clearly enchanted Kalj. From then on we often saw the sickly boy installed in his wicker chair, the valiant Meisdehl walking beside him.

XIII

IN THREE WEEKS, CHÈNEVILLOT completed a small and utterly charming stage. Among his workmen, all of whom had demonstrated un-
flagging zeal, the house painter Toresse and the upholsterer Beaucreau deserved special praise. Toresse, highly dubious of the supplies
he'd find in South America, had stocked a provision of barrels filled
with various paints, and he covered the entire structure in brilliant
red; on the pediment, the words "The Incomparables Club" were
haloed by a cluster of rays symbolizing the glory of the brilliant association. And Beaucreau, having brought along a stock of fabrics
intended for Ballesteros, employed a supple scarlet damask to hang
two wide curtains that met at the middle of the platform or opened
into the wings. A white Persian with fine gold arabesques served to
mask the wall of planks raised as a backdrop.

Chènevillot's creation met with great success, and Carmichael
was chosen to inaugurate the new stage by singing several romances
from his repertoire in his marvelous soprano.

That very day, at around four in the afternoon, Carmichael, having laid out his feminine attire, retired to his hut and reappeared an
hour later utterly transformed.

He wore a blue silk gown decorated with an opulent train on
which we could read the number 472 in black. A woman's wig with
thick golden curls, perfectly suited to his still beardless face, completed the curious metamorphosis. Asked about the meaning of the
strange figure inscribed on his skirt, Carmichael told us the following story:

Toward the end of winter, eager to leave for America where a brilliant engagement awaited him but kept in Marseille until March 14, the date of his military draft lottery, Carmichael had selected from among the available steamers the *Lynceus*, which lifted anchor on the 15th of that month.

At the time, the young man sang every night to phenomenal acclaim at the Folies Marseillaises. When he appeared at town hall on the morning of March 14, the assembled conscripts easily recognized their famous compatriot and, after the lottery, they all cheered him spontaneously at the exit.

Carmichael, following their example, had to pin a flexible, brightly spangled number to his hat, and for the next hour the streets of the city witnessed a joyous and fraternal parade bursting with songs and merriment.

When the time came for good-byes, Carmichael handed out complimentary tickets to his new friends, who that evening burst drunkenly into the backstage of the Folies Marseillaises, brandishing their hats still decorated with dazzling figures. The most inebriated of the lot, the son of one of the city's leading tailors, seeing Carmichael in full regalia and about to go onstage, yanked from his pocket a pair of scissors and a threaded needle wrapped in a large swatch of black silk; then, with a drunkard's insistence, he began sewing onto the elegant blue gown the number 472, which his illustrious comrade had drawn that morning.

Carmichael, laughing, gladly lent himself to this strange whim and, after ten minutes' work, three artfully cut and sewn figures spread in black over his long train.

Several moments later, the conscripts, seated in the hall, noisily cheered Carmichael, calling for encores of all his romances and shouting out, "Long live number 472!" to the great joy of the spectators, who stared in amazement at the number inscribed on the young singer's train.

Leaving the next day, Carmichael hadn't had time to remove

the extravagant decoration, which he now wanted to preserve as a precious memento of his native city, from which a simple whim of Talou's might keep him forever.

His story over, Carmichael climbed onto the Incomparables' stage and gave a dazzling rendition of Dariccelli's *Aubade*. His falsetto, rising with unparalleled elasticity to the extreme heights of the soprano's range, effortlessly performed the most tortuous vocalizations; chromatic scales shot off like rockets, and the breathtakingly rapid trills stretched to infinity.

A prolonged ovation underscored the final cadence, soon followed by five new romances, each as stupefying as the first. The entire audience, full of emotion and gratitude, warmly greeted Carmichael as he left the stage.

Talou and Sirdah, present since the beginning of the performance, visibly shared our enthusiasm. The stupefied emperor prowled around Carmichael, whose eccentric get-up seemed to fascinate him.

Soon, a few imperious words, promptly translated by Sirdah, told us that Talou, wishing to sing like Carmichael, demanded that the young artist give him a certain number of lessons, the first of which would begin right away.

Sirdah had not yet finished her sentence when the emperor was already mounting the stage, with Carmichael obediently in tow.

There, for half an hour, Talou, emitting a rather pure headvoice, endeavored to copy slavishly the examples furnished by his instructor, who, amazed at the monarch's unusual skill, brought to the task a tireless and genuine zeal.

At the end of this impromptu session, the tragedienne Adinolfa wanted to try out the acoustics of Trophy Square from a declamatory perspective. Dressed in a magnificent jade gown quickly donned for the occasion, she took the stage and recited some Italian verses accompanied by striking postures and expressions.

Meisdehl, the emperor's adoptive daughter, had just joined us and appeared mesmerized by the brilliant poses the famous artist adopted.

The next day, Adinolfa was in for a great surprise while strolling beneath the fragrant vaults of the Behuliphruen, whose blazing vegetation daily attracted her vibrant soul, which always sought out natural or artistic splendors.

For a while the tragedienne had been crossing a heavily wooded area carpeted with brilliant flowers. She soon came across a clearing, in the middle of which Meisdehl, improvising words in her jargon full of lyrical eloquence, was reproducing for Kalj the captivating gestures that had drawn everyone's attention to the Incomparables' stage the day before, after Talou's lesson.

The chariot, parked twenty paces away, was guarded by a slave reclining on a bed of moss.

Adinolfa silently watched Meisdehl for some time, astonished by the graceful aptness of her gestures. Wishing to encourage this theatrical instinct, she approached the girl to teach her the fundamentals of stagecraft.

Their first attempts yielded fabulous results. Meisdehl easily understood the subtlest indications and spontaneously devised tragic facial expressions of her own.

Over the following days, several new sessions were devoted to the same subject, and Meisdehl quickly became a veritable artist.

Encouraged by this marvelous progress, Adinolfa thought to teach her pupil an entire scene, to be acted on the day of the gala.

Seeking to give her protégé's debut a powerful boost, the tragedienne conceived an ingenious idea that required telling us a little of her past.

Adinolfa was celebrated the world over, but the English in particular professed an ardent and fanatical cult for her. The ovations the London public showered upon her were like no other, and it was by the thousands that they sold her photograph in every corner of Great Britain, which had become like her second home.

Wanting a fixed residence for her prolonged stays in the City of Fog, the tragedienne bought a sumptuous and very old castle on the banks of the Thames; the owner, a certain Lord Dewsbury, ruined by unsound investments, sold her in a package deal, and at rock-bottom price, the building and all its contents.

From this residence one could easily reach London, while preserving the advantages of wide-open spaces and fresh air.

Among the various ground-floor rooms used for entertaining, the tragedienne was particularly fond of the huge library, its walls garnished top to bottom with old volumes in precious bindings. A wide shelf filled with theatrical works attracted the great artist's attention most often, and, well versed in the English language, she spent long hours browsing through the national masterworks of her adoptive country.

One day, Adinolfa had taken down ten volumes of Shakespeare and set them on her desk, looking for a certain scholarly note she recalled, without remembering exactly which drama it referred to.

Having found and transcribed the note, the tragedienne went to return the books to their place; but, back in front of the library, she noticed a thick layer of dust lying on the empty section of shelf. Temporarily setting her burden on an armchair, she dusted off the smooth, powdered surface with her handkerchief, taking care as well to run the improvised dustcloth over the back wall of the cabinet, the vertical portion of which also required some cleaning.

Suddenly, a sharp click was heard, produced by a secret catch that Adinolfa had just activated by inadvertently pressing on a certain spot.

A thin, narrow board snapped back, revealing a secret compartment from which the tragedienne, with pounding heart, carefully withdrew a very old and scarcely legible manuscript.

She immediately brought her discovery to London, to the great expert Creighton, who, after a rapid examination under a loupe, let out a cry of stupefaction.

There could be no doubt that they had before them the original manuscript of *Romeo and Juliet*, written in Shakespeare's own hand!

Thunderstruck by this revelation, Adinolfa commissioned Creighton to make her a clean, faithful copy of the precious document, which might contain some unknown scene of incalculable interest. Then, having determined the value of the weighty manuscript, which the expert put at an astronomical sum, she rode back to her new abode, lost in thought.

According to the precise and irrevocable sales contract, the entire contents of the castle belonged by rights to the tragedienne. But Adinolfa was far too principled to take advantage of a fortuitous circumstance that skewed the deal so shamefully in her favor. She therefore wrote to Lord Dewsbury to tell him of her adventure, enclosing a check for the amount at which, in the expert's opinion, the impressive relic was valued.

Lord Dewsbury expressed his warmest gratitude in a long letter of thanks, in which he furnished the probable explanation for the mysterious discovery. Only one of his ancestors, Albert of Dewsbury, a major collector of autographs and rare books, could have conceived such a hiding place to preserve a manuscript of that magnitude from theft. Now, Albert of Dewsbury, who died suddenly while in excellent health, his skull fractured in a terrible riding accident, had no time to reveal to his son, as he'd no doubt intended to do on his deathbed, the existence of the treasure he'd so carefully cloistered, which since then had remained undisturbed.

Two weeks later, Creighton personally delivered the manuscript to the tragedienne, along with two copies: the first scrupulously faithful to the text, its archaisms and obscurities intact; the second clear and comprehensible, a veritable translation with modernized language and usage. After the expert's departure, Adinolfa took up the second copy and began reading attentively.

Each page filled her with profound stupefaction.

Many times had she played the part of Juliet, and she knew the entire drama by heart. But in the course of her reading, she continually came across lines of dialogue, stage directions, and details of expression or costuming that were entirely new and unfamiliar.

From start to finish, the play proved to be adorned with a host of enrichments that, without altering the substance, studded it with many picturesque and unexpected scenes.

Certain of having in hand the true version of the celebrated drama of Verona, the tragedienne hastened to announce her discovery in the *Times*, an entire page of which was devoted to quotations taken from the manuscript itself.

The article had enormous repercussions. Artists and scholars flocked to the former residence of the Dewsburys to see the extraordinary document, which Adinolfa let them browse through while discreetly keeping a careful watch.

Two camps immediately formed, a violent polemic breaking out between the partisans of the famous document and its adversaries who declared it apocryphal. Newspaper columns were filled with heated editorials, their contradictory proofs and other details soon dominating conversations throughout England and the entire world.

Adinolfa thought she'd take advantage of this hubbub to stage the play in its new version, reserving for herself the role of Juliet, the sensational debut of which could crown her name with imperishable brilliance.

But no director would touch the project. The outsized staging costs required by each page of the manuscript dissuaded even the hardiest souls, and it was in vain that the great actress knocked at door after door.

Demoralized, Adinolfa lost interest in the matter and soon the debate subsided, unseated by a sensational crime that captured the public's attention overnight.

It was the final scene of Shakespeare's tragedy that Adinolfa wanted Meisdehl to play, in the version from the celebrated auto-graph. The tragedienne had brought with her the modernized copy, just in case arrangements panned out with some American direc-tors. The delicate and talented Kalj would make a charming Romeo, and the many subtle gestures and expressions could easily replace the dialogue, which was beyond the children's grasp; besides, words were hardly needed to convey such a popular subject.

Lacking a number of props, they had to come up with some scrap of costume or personal item that would identify the two char-acters. Hats seemed the simplest and most expedient solution. But according to the manuscript, the two lovers were dressed in fabrics with red decorations and *richly embroidered* matching headwear.

This latter requisite was weighing on Adinolfa's mind one day, as she took her usual stroll through the thickets of the Behuliphruen. Suddenly, while walking with eyes on the ground, absorbed in her thoughts, she stopped short at what sounded like a slow, interrupted monologue. She turned and spotted Juillard seated cross-legged on the grass, holding a notebook and drafting his notes, which he then repeated aloud. A large illustrated volume lying open on the ground drew the tragedienne's attention because of certain reddish hues that happened to match her innermost thoughts perfectly. She ap-proached Juillard, who vaunted the powerful charms of his chosen retreat. It was to this place of meditation and silence that he came each day, since the recent completion of his lecture for the gala, to draft a long article on the Franco-Prussian War. With a sweep of his arm he showed, spread around him, several works that had been published during the terrible conflict of 1870, among them the large volume in which the two pages the actress had spotted depicted with great verve, respectively, the battle of Reichshoffen and an episode from the Commune; the red tones, used at left for the uniforms and plumes, at right for a blazing building, could from a distance give the illusion of embroidery as specified in the Shakespearean manuscript. Hoping to use this ideally colored paper in lieu of fabric, Adinolfa made her request of Juillard, who tore out the coveted pages without having to be asked twice.

With scissors and pins, the tragedienne fashioned for Kalj and Meisdehl the two classic headpieces worn by the lovers from Verona.

That first matter settled, Adinolfa returned to Shakespeare's text, carefully studying the stage directions in every detail.

Certain episodes of the final portion were explained in a fairly lengthy prologue, comprising two scenes devoted to Romeo and Juliet's childhoods, before they'd met.

It was this prologue that absorbed Adinolfa's particular attention.

In the first scene, young Romeo listened to the teachings of his preceptor, Father Valdivieso, a learned monk who inculcated in his pupil the purest and most devout moral principles.

For a number of years, Valdivieso had burned the midnight oil, surrounded by the folios that were his joy and the ancient parchments whose secrets unfailingly yielded to his wisdom. Gifted with phenomenal memory and inspiring elocution, he charmed his disciple with highly imagistic stories, whose meanings nearly always contained some worthy moral. The initial scene was almost entirely composed of his monologues, which were only occasionally interrupted by little Romeo's naïve interjections.

Bible stories flowed from the monk's lips. He evoked in minute detail the temptations of Eve, then recounted the adventures of the debauched Thisias, who, in the middle of an orgy in Zion, saw before him the fearsome and livid specter of God the Father.

Then came the following details on the legend of Pheor of Alexandria, a young libertine and Thisias's contemporary:

Devastated at being left by a beloved mistress, who had let him know of their breakup by not bothering to arrive for a rendezvous, Pheor, renouncing his life of pleasures and seeking consolation in faith, had retreated to the desert to live as an anchorite, sometimes returning to spread the good word in the same places where he had committed his past errors.

Following long privations, Pheor had grown alarmingly thin; his unusually large head seemed immense compared to his frail body, and his salient temples protruded from both sides of his gaunt face.

One day, Pheor appeared in the public square just when the citizens had gathered to discuss matters of state. At the time, two distinct assemblies, one for the young and one for the elderly, met on an appointed day at this forum, the former proposing bold initiatives that the latter tempered with moderation. Each group was arranged in a perfect square that might cover as much as an acre.

The arrival of Pheor, famous for his sudden conversion, momentarily suspended the debates.

Immediately the neophyte, as was his habit, began preaching his fervent disdain of wealth and pleasures, especially aiming his remarks at the younger group, to which he seemed to impute every vice and turpitude.

Incensed by this provocative stance, the targets of his harangue leapt onto him and knocked him down in a rage. Too weak to defend himself, Pheor painfully stood and hobbled away covered in bruises, cursing his attackers. Then, at a bend in the road, he fell to his knees in ecstasy at the sight of his former lover, who passed by without a hint of recognition, richly adorned and trailing a crowd of slaves. For a moment, Pheor felt his old passion well up inside him; but, once the vision had passed, he regained control of himself and returned to the desert, where after years of constant penitence he died free of his obsessions and forgiven of his sins.

After the legend of Pheor, the monk Valdivieso described two famous martyrdoms, that of Jeremiah whom his countrymen stoned with many sharp, pointed flints, then that of Saint Ignatius thrust among wild beasts, which lacerated his body while his soul, in a contrary movement, rose to heaven, fancifully portrayed as an enchanted isle.

As a whole, these lessons had great coherence. Their striking subjects were clearly intended to guide Romeo's spirit toward good, which also explained how Juliet, the very image of pure, conjugal love, could so easily conquer a young man who had initially given in to frivolous, debasing affairs.

The second scene of the prologue, a touching counterpart to the first, showed little Juliet sitting with her nurse, who kept her spellbound with tales both delightful and terrifying; among other fabulous characters, the storyteller depicted the good fairy Urgela, who shook out her tresses to spread countless gold coins along her path, and the ogress Pergovedula, she of the hideous yellow face and green lips, who wolfed down two heifers for supper when she had no children to sate her.

In the play's final scene, the one Adinolfa intended to stage, numerous images borrowed from the prologue reappeared before the eyes of the two lovers, who, having downed a lethal potion, were subject to constant hallucinations.

Following the manuscript's indications, all these phantoms composed a series of tableaux vivants in rapid succession, which would no doubt prove hugely difficult to produce in Ejur.

Adinolfa immediately thought of Fuxier, whose picturesque lozenges might stand in for costumes and stage props.

Acquiescing to the actress's wishes and promising to perfect all the requested visions, Fuxier, who was quite conversant with the subtleties of the English language, familiarized himself with the prologue and the final scene; these gave him ample material on which to exercise his talents.

One direction in the manuscript called for a greenish hearth next to Juliet's tomb, which might cast a tragic light over the poignant scene the two lovers played. This brazier, whose flames could be colored with sea salts, seemed the perfect vehicle for burning the evocative lozenges. Adinolfa, made up so she could appear toward the end as the ogress Pergovedula, would lie down behind the tomb and, thus hidden from sight, toss into the coals, at the opportune moment, the lozenge needed to produce a given image.

Even so, they could not dispense entirely with cameo roles. Two apparitions, Capulet dressed in a shining gold robe and Christ seated on the famous donkey, had to be acted by Soreau, who had in his costume chest all the necessary components to fashion what he needed. It would take him only a few seconds to change from one costume to the other offstage, and the docile ass Milenkaya could be pressed into service. Chènevillot agreed to fit into the backdrop two fine grilles, cleverly painted, which the light from a reflector lamp would make transparent at the appropriate moment; behind them, two niches of sufficient size would be installed at the requisite height.

As Romeo's ghost was supposed to descend from heaven at the end above Romeo's own corpse, one of Kalj's brothers, who bore a striking likeness in age and features, was designated as his double. From the rest of the page illustrating the cavalrymen at Reichshoffen they cut a second cap identical to the first, and Chènevillot easily devised a hand-operated suspension system with some rope and a pulley from the *Lynccus*.

For Urgela, they took from the ship's hold a certain mannequin head that had remained intact at the bottom of a trunk addressed to a barber in Buenos Aires. A rolling pedestal was quickly fashioned to support the white-and-pink bust with wide blue eyes. Not far from the trunk, a cascade of gilded tokens, like twenty-franc louis, had spilled from a crushed package filled with various games. Using a tiny dab of glue, they attached them tentatively to the bust's magnificent blonde hair, which fell in loose braids over both shoulders; the slightest jostle would dislodge these dazzling coins, which the generous fairy could thus sow in profusion.

The rest of the staging, including the tomb and the brazier, they left entirely to Chènevillot.

According to a brief indication in the manuscript, Romeo placed on Juliet, who had just awoken from her lethargic slumber, a rich necklace of rubies, which the groom at first thought would adorn only his beloved's cold corpse.

This detail gave Bex the chance to use a balm of his own devising, with which he'd always had success when handling materials for his experiments.

This was an anesthetic strong enough to make the skin insensitive to burns; by applying this protective coating to his hands, Bex could manipulate at any temperature a certain metal he'd invented called *bexium*. Had he not discovered this precious element beforehand, the chemist could never have brought forth bexium, whose special properties were triggered by extremes of heat or cold.

To replace the rubies, which were unavailable in Ejur, even in imitation, Bex suggested several glowing coals strung onto asbestos, which he'd supply. Kalj would have only to take from the brazier the strange, sparkling red jewel and put it on Meisdehl, whose chest and shoulders would be immunized in advance with the infallible balm.

The tragedienne accepted Bex's offer, having first made sure that the trusting, brave Meisdehl would consent.

The entire scene was to be played without dialogue. But, in rehearsing their gestures, Kalj and Meisdehl demonstrated so much intelligence and good will that Adinolfa, encouraged by this success, also tried to teach her pupils a few phrases translated into French, which would help explain the various apparitions. The attempt yielded rapid results, and at that point all that remained was to finetune, until the day of the gala, the touching pantomime that the two children had understood so completely.

XIV

INSPIRED BY THE SUCCESS of the Incomparables' Theater, Juillard suggested another innovation that would generate excitement over the big day and afford Chènevillot a new opportunity to use his building skills. The plan was to offer shares in each member of the club and create a game of chance, for which the grand prize would hinge on whoever won the grand ribbon of the new order. Once this proposal was ratified, they immediately set about putting it into action.

Fifty passengers began by contributing two hundred francs each to create a kitty of ten thousand francs; then each member of the club was represented by one hundred shares, small squares of paper endorsed with his or her signature.

All the shares, gathered together, were lightly shuffled like playing cards, then split into fifty equal packets, fairly distributed one each to the fifty contributing passengers.

At the conclusion of the gala, the ten thousand francs would be divvied up among those who held shares in the lucky wearer of the supreme *delta* insignia; until that time, the shares might undergo all sorts of fluctuations, depending on each contestant's perceived chances of winning.

The club members were prohibited from partaking in the lottery, for the same reason that jockeys are not allowed to place bets.

Intermediaries were needed to handle the trading of shares. Hounsfield, Cerjat, and their three clerks, all five having accepted the role of stockbrokers, took in the jackpot for safekeeping, and Chènevillot was asked to create a new edifice for these transactions.

Two weeks later, a miniature Stock Exchange, an exact reduction of the one in Paris, rose opposite the Incomparables' stage; though made of wood, the monument gave the perfect illusion of stone, owing to a coat of white paint that Toresse had applied.

To provide clear access to the much-used structure, they had moved the mortal remains of the Zouave a few yards to the south, along with his tombstone still accompanied by its black slab and brilliant watercolors.

The originality of investing in the Incomparables themselves demanded a language of its own, and it was decided that only orders written in alexandrines would be honored.

At six o'clock on the very day of its completion, the Stock Exchange opened for the first time, and the five stockbrokers sat at five tables set up for them behind the diminutive colonnade. Soon they were reading aloud a host of slips that, thrust into their hands by the players thronging around them, contained buy and sell orders written in mediocre twelve-syllable lines rife with padding and false enjambments. Stock quotes were established based on the size of the offer or demand, and the shares, immediately paid for and delivered, passed from hand to hand. New slips of paper constantly flowed onto the tables, and for one hour there was a bustle of hectic activity. Each name preceded by a definite article served to indicate one of the stocks. At the close of business, *the Carmichael* was worth fifty-two francs and *the Tancrède Boucharessas* two louis, whereas *the Martignon* paid twenty-eight sous and *the Olga Chervonenkhov* sixty centimes. *The Balbet*, on the promise of his demonstration of marksmanship, found a buyer at fourteen francs, and *the Luxo* was at eighteen francs ninety, counting on stupendous results from his fireworks display.

The exchange closed at seven o'clock sharp, but from then on it opened for twenty minutes each day, to the intense delight of the investors. A large number of them, uninterested in the final outcome, tried instead to make a killing on rising and falling stock prices, and toward this end spread all kinds of rumors. One day, the Carmichael dropped nine points because the young singer was supposedly suffering from a hoarse voice; the next day, after the news was proven false, the stock rebounded twelve francs. The Balbet also underwent strong fluctuations, due to endlessly conflicting reports on the working order of the Gras rifle and the condition of its cartridges.

Thanks to daily lessons, Talou had learned to sing Dariccelli's *Aubade*, repeating the measures that Carmichael whispered in his ear one after another. The emperor now wanted to don the female attire that had aroused his envy from first glance, so as to endow his performance with the proper theatrical gestures and costuming. Sirdah translated her father's wishes and, helped by the young Marseillais, he adorned himself carefully, with childish glee, in the blue gown and blonde wig; the double strangeness of it delighted his poet-monarch's soul, usually so little prone to exhibitionism.

Thus costumed as a soprano, the emperor mounted the stage, and this time Carmichael, as he gave his lesson, slowly deconstructed the various arm movements that were so familiar to him, and trained his pupil to walk naturally while adroitly kicking the long, cumbersome train out of the way. From then on, Talou always practiced in full regalia and ultimately acquitted himself honorably of the task he'd taken on.

On the day of the gala, a series of tableaux vivants was to be staged by the troupe of operetta singers, who were hardly lacking for costumes and accessories.

Soreau, who had taken initiative and leadership of the project, decided to begin with a *Feast of the Olympian Gods*, easily staged with props left over from *Orpheus in Hell*.

For the other groupings, Soreau took inspiration from five anec-
dotes he'd recently heard during his tours of North America, England, Russia, Greece, and Italy.

First came a Canadian tale heard in Quebec, a kind of children's
legend that goes like this:

On the banks of Lake Ontario lived a rich planter of French
origin named Jouandon. Recently widowed, Jouandon transferred
all his love onto his daughter Ursule, a charming girl of eight in the
care of the devoted Maffa, a kind and considerate Huron who had
nursed the child at her own breast.

Jouandon at the time was prey to the scheming of a busybody
named Gervaise, whose ugliness and poverty had left her an old
maid, and who was determined to marry the well-to-do planter.

Weak by nature, Jouandon let himself be snared by the shrew's
adroit semblance of love, and she soon became his second wife.

From that moment, life in the planter's house, once so peaceful and radiant, became intolerable. Gervaise had invited her sister
Agatha and her two brothers Claude and Justin to move into the
house, all three as greedy as she was; this infernal clique set the rules,
shouting and waving their arms from morning until night. Ursule
became the chief target of mocking comments from Gervaise and
her acolytes, and only with great difficulty was Maffa able to save the
girl from the ill treatment they threatened.

After two years Jouandon died of consumption, worn down by
sorrow and remorse, wracked with guilt over the unhappiness he
had visited on his daughter and himself by the deplorable union that
he hadn't had the strength to terminate.

Gervaise and her three accomplices set more fiercely than ever
on the unhappy Ursule, whom they hoped to kill off like her father
in order to lay their hands on her wealth.

Outraged, Maffa went one day to visit the warriors of her tribe
and described the situation to the old sorcerer No, famous for his
great powers.

No pledged to punish the guilty parties and followed Maffa to the cursed abode.

Skirting Lake Ontario, they spotted from afar Gervaise and Agatha heading to the banks, escorted by their two brothers carrying a still, silent Ursule.

The four miscreants, taking advantage of the nurse's absence, had bound and gagged the child, whom they planned to drown in the deep waters of the lake.

Maffa and No hid behind a clump of trees, and the group arrived at the bank without seeing them.

Just as the two brothers were swinging Ursule's body to toss it into the currents, No pronounced a magic and resonant incantation that immediately caused four sudden metamorphoses.

Gervaise was changed into a she-donkey and placed before a pail full of appetizing bran; but, the moment she approached the abundant sustenance, a kind of seton suddenly passed through her jaws and kept her from satisfying her ravenous hunger. When, weary of this torture, she tried to flee the frustrating temptation, a golden harrow rose in front of her, blocking her passage and unpredictably springing up at any given point of a strictly defined enclosure.

Agatha, transformed into a goose, ran about in a frenzy, chased by Boreas who blew on her with all his might and whipped her with a thorny rose.

Claude retained his human body but his head turned into a wild boar's. Three objects of different weights, an egg, a glove, and a wisp of straw, began jumping from his hands, which uncontrollably and continually tossed them in the air and caught them again. Like a juggler who, instead of commanding his knickknacks, was at their mercy, the wretched fellow ran in a straight line, prey to a kind of dizzying magnetic pull.

Justin metamorphosed into a pike and went flying into the lake, which he had to swim around indefinitely at great speed, like a horse let loose in a giant hippodrome.

Maffa and No rushed to Ursule to rid her of her gag.

Filled with compassion and not one to hold a grudge, the girl, who had seen the quadruple miracle occur, tried to intercede on her torturers' behalf.

She asked the sorcerer if there was a way to break the spell, passionately pleading the guilty quartet's cause, who according to her did not deserve eternal punishment.

Touched by such goodness, No gave her this precious information: once a year, on the anniversary and at the precise hour of the incantation, the four bewitched were fated to reunite on the bank at the exact spot occupied by the donkey, who would alone remain sedentary while the three wanderers rushed crazily onward; this reunion would last only a second, as the unlucky runaways were granted no rest. If, during that barely perceptible instant, a generous hand armed with some device managed to fish out the pike and throw it onto the bank, the charm would immediately end, and the four condemned souls would regain their human form; but even a minor slip in the liberating gesture would delay any chance at a new attempt for another year.

Ursule memorized every detail of this revelation and thanked No, who returned alone to his tribe of savages.

One year later, a few minutes before the prescribed hour, Ursule climbed into a skiff with Maffa and waited for the pike near the place where the she-donkey continued to sniff uselessly at her ever-full bucket.

Suddenly the girl saw in the distance, in the transparent waters, the swift-moving fish she awaited; just then, from two opposite points on the horizon, the boar-headed juggler and the wind-whipped goose came running toward the same goal.

Ursule vertically dipped a large fishing net, blocking the path of the pike, which dove like an arrow into the floating device.

With a sudden jerk, the young fisherwoman tried to flip the fish onto the bank. But no doubt their atonement wasn't yet sufficient, for the netting, although fine and solid, let the captive through; the pike fell back into the water and resumed its mad race.

The juggler and the goose, for a moment reunited near the donkey, crossed paths without slowing down and soon disappeared in opposite directions.

Evidently Ursule's mishap was due to supernatural intervention, for after that event the meshes of the net remained intact.

Three new attempts, each one year apart, yielded the same negative results. Finally, on the fifth year, Ursule made a movement so skillful and quick that the pike landed on the outer edge of the bank, without having time to slip through the imprisoning weave.

Instantly the four siblings regained human form and, terrified by the prospect of another spell, immediately fled the area and were never heard from again.

In England, Soreau had learned the following information, related in *Handel as I Knew Him* by Count Corfield, a close friend of the great composer.

By 1756, Handel, already old and deprived of sight for more than four years, hardly ever left his London home, where his admirers flocked to see him.

One evening, the famous musician was in his upstairs study, a huge, sumptuously appointed room that he preferred to his ground-floor salons because of a magnificent organ leaning against the paneling of one wall.

Amid the bright lights, several guests conversed noisily, made merry by a copious dinner supplied by the maestro, a great lover of fine foods and good wines.

Count Corfield, who was present, steered the conversation to the genius of their gracious host, whose masterworks he praised with the most sincere enthusiasm. The others chorused their agreement, and each admired his innate creativity, which the hoi polloi could not acquire through even the most intense efforts.

According to Corfield, a musical phrase hatched by a brow endowed with such a divine spark could enliven many pages of score with its breath, even when banally developed by a mere technician. On the other hand, the speaker added, an ordinary theme, treated by even the most inspired mind, would necessarily preserve its heaviness and awkwardness, never managing to conceal the indelible stamp of its undistinguished origins.

At these words Handel let out a bellow of protest, claiming that, even on a mechanically devised motif furnished solely by chance, he was quite sure he could write an entire oratorio worthy of inclusion among his works.

This assertion having provoked certain murmurs of doubt, Handel, stimulated by the libations of the feast, stood abruptly, declaring that he wanted, then and there and before witnesses, to establish honestly the skeleton of such a work.

Feeling his way, the illustrious composer headed toward the fireplace and plucked from a vase several branches of holly left over from the previous Christmas. He lined them up on the marble mantelpiece, drawing everyone's attention to their number, which rose to seven; each branch was to represent one note of the scale and carry some kind of sign that would make it identifiable as such.

The maestro's elderly housekeeper, Madge, an expert seamstress, was immediately sent for and ordered to provide—that very instant—seven thin ribbons of different hues.

The ingenious woman, hardly put out by such a trifle, returned after a brief moment with seven ribbons, each partaking of one color of the prism.

Corfield, at the great composer's request, knotted a ribbon around each stem without disturbing the regularity of the alignment.

This done, Handel invited his guests to contemplate for a moment the gamut spread before their eyes, each attendee attempting to keep in memory the correspondence of colors to notes.

Then the maestro himself, his sense of touch prodigiously refined by blindness, proceeded to a minute examination of the clusters, scrupulously registering in his memory a given particularity created by the arrangement of leaves or the spread between their thorny points.

Once he was sure, Handel gathered the seven branches of holly in his left hand and pointed toward his worktable, bidding Corfield bring his pen and inkwell.

Guided out of the room by one of his faithful devotees, the blind maestro had himself led to the stairway, whose flat, white banister lent itself perfectly to his designs.

At length, after shuffling the branches of holly, which no longer retained a trace of their initial order, Handel called for Corfield, who handed him the plume dipped in ink.

Brushing haphazardly, with the free fingers of his right hand, one of the spiky clusters, which for him had individual personalities recognizable to the touch, the blind man approached the handrail, on which he easily wrote, in ordinary letters, the note indicated by the rapid contact.

Descending one step and again shuffling the thick bouquet, Handel, by the same purely random process of touch, gathered a second note, which he inscribed a bit lower on the rail.

And so his descent continued, slow and regular. At each step, the maestro conscientiously rearranged the sheaf in every direction before seeking, with his fingertips, the designation of some unpremeditated sound immediately inscribed in sufficiently legible letters.

The guests followed their host step by step, easily verifying the rectitude of the process by checking the variously colored ribbons. Sometimes, Corfield took the plume and dipped it in ink before handing it back to the blind man.

After ten minutes, Handel wrote the twenty-third note and descended the last step, which left him back at the ground floor. Reaching a bench, he rested a moment from his labors, telling his friends his main reason for choosing such an unorthodox form of notation.

Sensing his end was near, Handel had bequeathed his entire

house to the City of London, which planned to turn it into a museum. A large quantity of manuscripts, curios, and memorabilia of all sorts already promised to make any visit to the illustrious home highly worthwhile. Still, the maestro remained haunted by the constant desire to augment the attraction of the future pilgrimage site. This was why, seizing the propitious opportunity, he had that very evening made of the handrail in question an imperishable monument, by autographing onto it the odd and incoherent theme whose length was alone determined by the previously unspecified number of steps, which thereby added a supplemental peculiarity to the mechanical and deliberate aspect of the composition.

Restored by these few moments of rest, Handel, accompanied by his friends, went back up to his study, where the evening ended on a gay note. Corfield volunteered to transcribe the musical phrase spawned by the whims of chance, and the maestro promised to follow its parameters strictly, reserving only two liberties for himself: the duration of the notes and the pitch, which could move unrestrictedly from one octave to the next.

The very next day, Handel set to work with the help of a secretary accustomed to taking his dictation.

Blindness had in no way lessened the famous musician's intellectual faculties.

In his hands, the theme with its bizarre contours acquired an engaging and beautiful grace, through ingenious combinations of rhythm and harmony.

The same twenty-three-note phrase, repeated over and over but each time presented in different form, alone constituted the famous oratorio *Vesper*, a powerful and serene work whose success continues to this day.

Soreau, traveling through Russia, had taken these historical notes on Czar Alexei Mikhailovich:

Toward the end of 1648, Alexei, barely out of childhood and already emperor for the past three years, allowed his two favorites, Pleshcheyev and Morozov, to govern as they liked, though their injustice and cruelty were creating widespread discontent.

Pleshcheyev in particular, hated by all who knew him, left a trail of implacable resentments.

One December morning, news spread throughout the palace: Pleshcheyev, howling in pain on the floor of his suite, was writhing in horrible convulsions, eyes bloodshot and frothing at the mouth.

When the czar, his doctor in tow, entered the favorite's rooms, a horrifying spectacle greeted him. Lying on the carpet, Pleshcheyev, his limbs contorted, face and hands completely blue, had just breathed his last.

On the table were the remains of the breakfast the dead man had just eaten. The doctor approached and, in a leftover bit of liquid at the bottom of a cup, recognized the peculiar smell of a very virulent poison.

The czar, launching an immediate investigation, summoned all of Pleshcheyev's servants; but no confession could be obtained, and in the days following the most thorough search yielded no results.

Alexei then devised a method that would lead the guilty party to incriminate himself. Very conspicuously, he retired alone to his chapel to pray God for inspiration. He emerged an hour later and sent for the suspected servants, who soon made their silent entrance into the holy place.

Facing one of the walls, Alexei showed the newcomers a precious stained-glass window whose transparent mosaic depicted Christ in agony on the cross at nightfall. Almost at the horizon, the sun, about to disappear, was represented by a perfectly regular red circle.

On Alexei's orders, two servants unattached to the group climbed to the window by scaling the sufficiently protuberant stone border. Using their knives, they pried off the lead strips soldered to the circumference of the radiant star, then managed to grasp the glass disk with their fingertips, bringing it gleaming and intact back to the czar.

Before employing this bizarre object, Alexei recounted a dream he'd just had in that very place during his meditation and solitude: he was praying God to reveal the name of the murderer when a sudden light made him raise his eyes. He then saw, on the now incomplete window, the image of Jesus come to life. Christ's eyes stared ardently at him, and soon his supple, living lips articulated this sentence: "Detach from the window this sun that lights my torture. Crossing through this prism sanctified by my agony, your gaze will strike down the guilty man, who for his punishment will suffer the tortures of the poison poured by his own hand." After these words, Christ's image regained its initial immobility, and the czar, dazzled by this miracle, prayed for a long time afterward to give thanks to the Lord.

The group of servants had listened to this story without moving a muscle.

Alexei, now silent, slowly brought the red sun up to his eyes and looked one by one, through the diaphanous disk, at the expectants lined up before him.

It was with good reason that the czar had counted on the effects of religious exaltation to accomplish his goal, for his words had profoundly affected his audience. Suddenly, stricken by the accusatory gaze that shone behind the colored glass, a man faltered with a cry and collapsed into the arms of his comrades, his limbs contorted, face and hands turning blue, just like the dying Pleshcheyev. The czar approached the unfortunate, who confessed his crime before expiring in horrible agony.

Greece had furnished Soreau with a poetic anecdote during his stay in Athens, where he spent his free time on a guided tour of the beauties of the city and surrounding countryside.

One day, deep in the Argyros woods, the guide led Soreau to a shady crossroads, asking him to try out the echo there, celebrated for its astonishing purity.

Soreau obeyed and called out a series of words or sounds that were immediately reproduced with perfect exactitude.

The guide then told him the following tale, which suddenly endowed the place with unexpected interest:

In 1827, Kanaris, the idol of all Greece and the author of its independence, had recently taken his place in the Hellenic parliament.

One certain summer evening, the famous mariner, in the company of a few close friends, was walking slowly through the Argyros woods, enjoying the charm of a renowned dusk and discoursing on the future of the country, the happiness of which was his sole concern.

Reaching the echoing crossroads, Kanaris, who had come to this place for the first time, received from one of his companions the standard revelation about the acoustic phenomenon tested out by every passerby.

Wishing to hear the mysterious voice for himself, the hero stood in the designated spot and called out at random the word "rose."

The echo repeated the sound faithfully, but, to everyone's astonishment, an exquisite and penetrating smell of roses spread through the air at that same instant.

Kanaris renewed the experiment, successively naming the most aromatic flowers; each time the clear and sudden response arrived wrapped in an intoxicating breath of the corresponding scent.

The next day the news spread from mouth to mouth, and only enhanced the Greeks' enthusiasm for their savior. As they saw it, nature itself had seen fit to honor the victor by sowing on his path the delicate and subtle essence of its most marvelous petals.

A more modern episode reminded Soreau of his time in Italy.

This one concerned Prince Savellini, an incorrigible kleptomaniac who, despite his vast wealth, prowled around train stations and any other populous area; each day, his phenomenal skill yielded an abundant harvest of watches and purses.

The prince's folly led him especially to rob the poor. Dressed with supreme elegance and adorned with priceless jewels, he would venture into the impoverished neighborhoods of Rome, seeking with discernment the grimiest pockets in which to plunge his ring-laden hands.

Arriving one day in a street of ill repute, a refuge for prostitutes and pimps, he spotted from afar a crowd that immediately made him quicken his steps.

Coming closer, he noticed thirty or forty sinister-looking hood-lums bunched around two of their own, who were lunging at each other with flashing knives.

For an instant the prince felt faint; never had he been offered such an opportunity to satisfy his vice.

Drunk with joy, clenching his jaw to keep his teeth from chattering, he took several wobbling steps on his trembling legs, his chest hammered by the dull pounding of his heart, his breathing labored.

Aided by the bloody spectacle that gripped everyone's attention, the kleptomaniac could practice his art uninhibited, rifling through the blue canvas or corduroy pockets with unparalleled dexterity.

Small change, cheap watches, tobacco pouches, and trinkets of all sorts poured in an unending stream into the deep inner cavities with which the prince had lined his luxurious fur coat.

But then, several policemen, attracted by the ruckus, descended on the group and seized the two combatants, whom they hauled off to the police station along with the prince, whose own maneuvers had not escaped their notice.

A search of the Savellini palace brought to light the countless robberies the poor lunatic had committed.

The next day the horrible scandal broke in the newspapers, and the noble kleptomaniac became a legend throughout Italy.

Aided by Chènevillot, who promised to handle the artificial construction of all the props, Soreau threw himself into the task of realizing the six promised tableaux.

For the Feast of the Gods, a black cord, indistinguishable against a similarly colored backdrop, would suspend Mercury in mid-air; the ship's steward would take charge of setting a richly laid table.

The legend of Lake Ontario required more complicated efforts. Lent by Olga Chervonenkhov, the she-ass Milenkaya, wearing in her jaw the two end bits of an illusory seton, would play her part before fake bran; made from small shreds of yellow paper, it would not risk tempting the beast and revealing the falseness of the restraint. Soreau had chosen to depict one of the fruitless attempts to deliver the bewitched. Stella Boucharessas would play the charitable Ursule trying in vain to catch the fleeting pike; next to her, Jeanne Souze, face and hands darkened, would assume the role of the faithful Maffa. In front of the donkey, Soreau as Boreas would chase forward a goose taken from the steward's hen yard; the creature's wings would be held apart by an invisible armature, and its feet, adhered to the floor by a tenacious glue, would hold a pose of rapid flight. Among the troupe's accoutrements, they found for the juggler a perfectly executed papier-mâché boar's head; this ornament normally served as a prop in the third act of a certain operetta, in which all the characters attended the masked ball of a rich, flamboyant foreigner.

For the scene of Handel composing, Chènevillot received very precise instructions from Soreau, who had seen in London, with his own eyes, the famous handrail piously conserved in the South Kensington museum.

The apparition of Czar Alexei was easy to recreate; so was that of Kanaris, the only complication being the requisite addition of strong and varied perfumes.

This latter problem could only be solved by Darriand, who, pursuing his discovery of ocean vegetation, had conducted numerous studies of plant scents.

The able scientist, planning new projects to occupy his time while traveling, had equipped himself with essences of all kinds, which, artfully blended, could provide the most diverse aromas.

Hidden in the wings, Darriand would himself repeat, as the echo, the names of the flowers called out, uncorking a few seconds in advance a given vial filled with an extremely volatile compound, whose emanations would suddenly strike the spectators' sense of smell from all sides.

For the kleptomania scene, Soreau, as Prince Savellini, would don an ample fur coat, which during the crossing had allowed him to brave on deck the ever-sharp winds of the high seas.

Carmichael, assigned the role of narrator, would briefly explain the subject being depicted by each of the six groups.

XV

THERE WAS IN EJUR a captivatingly original phenomenon known as Fogar, the emperor's oldest son.

Barely fifteen years old, this adolescent astounded us all with his sometimes terrifying strangeness.

Fogar, who was drawn to all things supernatural, had received from the sorcerer Bashkou various magic formulas that he had then adapted in his own way.

An instinctive poet like his father, the young man was a fanatical water-lover; the ocean in particular exerted an irresistible charm on his young mind. He would spend hours sitting on the beach, contemplating the shifting currents and dreaming of the secret marvels buried in their liquid depths. An excellent swimmer, he took sensuous delight from bathing in the element that so fascinated him, diving below for as long as he could so as to furtively experience the mysterious sites that occupied his precocious fancy.

Among other obscure practices, Bashkou had taught Fogar a way to put himself, with no outside help, into a lethargic near-death state.

Lying on the primitive cot that served as his bed, the young man, frozen in a kind of hypnotic ecstasy, could gradually suspend the beating of his heart by completely stopping the respiratory rhythm of his chest.

Sometimes, when the experiment ended, Fogar felt certain areas of his veins obstructed by his coagulated blood.

But this effect was predictable, and to remedy it the adolescent always kept within reach a certain flower that Bashkou had pointed out to him.

With a thorn from its stem, he opened the engorged vein and withdrew a compact clot. Then a single petal, crushed between his fingers, yielded a purple liquid, a few drops of which would seal the potentially lethal gash.

Haunted by his obsessive desire to visit underwater realms, which he couldn't help imagining populated by dazzling phantasmagoria, Fogar resolved to cultivate the mysterious art that allowed him to suspend his vital functions.

His glorious intent was to dive protractedly beneath the surface, benefiting from the state of hypnosis that so perfectly annulled the workings of his lungs.

Through progressive training, he could remain for half an hour in that state of artificial death that served his designs so well.

He began by stretching out on his bed to impose a beneficial calm on his circulation, which eased his task.

After several minutes his heart and chest were immobile, but Fogar still retained a dreamlike half-consciousness accompanied by a kind of almost mechanical activity.

He tried to stand up, but after only a few, automaton-like steps, he fell to the ground for lack of balance.

Heedless of obstacles or dangers, Fogar wanted to try right away the aquatic expedition he'd dreamed of for so long.

He went to the shore, armed with a thorny purple flower that he set aside in a rocky recess. Then, lying on the sand, he delivered himself up to the hypnotic slumber.

Soon his breathing ceased and his heart stopped pumping. Then, like a sleepwalker, Fogar rose and entered the sea.

Supported by the dense salt water, he easily kept his balance and steadily negotiated the sudden descents that formed the continuation of the bank.

A gap in the rocks offered him unexpected access to a kind of long and winding labyrinth that he explored at random, going ever deeper.

Unencumbered and buoyant, he passed through narrowly sinuous galleries, where no diver would ever have risked his breathing tube.

After many detours, he emerged into a wide cavern, whose walls, coated in some kind of phosphorescent substance, shone with sumptuous brilliance.

Strange sea creatures abounded on every side of this enchanted lair, which was even more magnificent than the visions the adolescent had imagined.

He had only to stretch out his hand to grab hold of the most stupefying marvels.

Fogar took several steps toward a live sponge that sat immobile on a protruding ledge of one of the cavern walls. The phosphorescent effluvia, passing through the animal's body, revealed inside the saturated tissue a miniature human heart connected to a circulatory system.

With infinite precaution, Fogar gathered the curious specimen, which, not being part of the plant kingdom, had no roots to keep it attached.

A bit higher up, three equally bizarre samples were affixed to the wall.

The first, of very elongated shape, bore a row of five tentacles that looked like the fringe on a chair or article of clothing.

The second, flat and flaccid like supple fabric, looked like a thin triangle adhered to the wall by its base; everywhere, powerful arteries formed red striations which, along with two round eyes as fixed as black dots, gave the floating ensemble the appearance of a pennant representing some unknown nation.

The last sample, smaller than its two neighbors, carried on its back a kind of very white carapace, which, similar to solidified soap foam, was notable for its fine, light quality.

Adding this triple booty to the original sponge, Fogar turned to head back.

At that moment, he picked up a large, gelatinous block in a corner of the grotto. Finding nothing particularly interesting about the object, he put it down haphazardly on a nearby rock whose surface bristled with jagged edges and spears.

Seeming to awaken on contact with these excruciating darts, the block quivered and, as a sign of distress, raised a tentacle like an elephant's trunk, divided at its extremity into three divergent branches.

Each of these branches ended in a suction cup like those on the terrible arms of an octopus.

The deeper the spears sank into the animal's flesh, the more it suffered.

Its exasperation soon produced an unexpected display. The suction-cupped branches began spinning like the spokes of a wheel, their initially reasonable momentum steadily increasing.

Changing his mind at the sight of this strange appendage, Fogar retrieved the block, now judged worthy of attention. Free of the darts that tormented it, the animal abruptly stopped its maneuvers and fell back into its original inertia.

The young man reached the exit of the grotto.

There, an object floating at eye level blocked his path.

It was like a metal plate, round and lightweight, held in suspension by the density of the water as it slowly descended.

Sweeping his arm, Fogar tried to brush the obstacle aside.

But hardly had he touched it when the fearful, hypersensitive plate folded in on itself, changing shape and even color.

Eagerly grasping this new specimen, to which he had originally attached no value, Fogar began ascending by way of the tortuous corridor he'd taken earlier.

Supported by the water pressure, he rose with minimal effort to the beach, where he took a few steps before collapsing to the ground.

Little by little his heart and lungs resumed their functions, and his lethargic slumber gave way to complete lucidity.

Fogar looked around, only dimly recalling the details of his solitary voyage.

The experiment, more prolonged than usual, had increased the number of coagulated blood clots in his veins.

Moving swiftly, he went to fetch the purple flower that he'd brought in anticipation.

The usual operation, followed by immediate suture, saved him from the elongated clots, which he carelessly tossed on the sand.

Immediately a shudder ran through the group of sea creatures, which had remained scattered and immobile on the beach since the adolescent's collapse.

No doubt used to feeding on the blood of their prey, the three samples from the vertical wall, obeying some terrible instinct, seized greedily upon the dull, petrified, compact rolls and devoured them.

The impromptu meal was accompanied by a soft, gluttonous burp emitted by the strange mollusk with the white carapace.

Meanwhile, the block with three rotary branches, the sponge, and the flat grayish disk lay unmoving on the smooth sand.

Now completely revived, Fogar ran back to Ejur, then returned to the beach with a container that he filled with sea water before tossing in his guests from the undersea grotto.

In the days following, Fogar, thrilled with the yield from his dive, planned a curious exhibit of his discoveries at the gala.

He had closely studied the six specimens, which remained alive even out of their element but stayed completely inert.

This inertia annoyed Fogar, who, rejecting the more commonplace idea of presenting his subjects immersed in the sea, wanted to show them off on dry land, like some carnival lion tamer.

Remembering the enthusiastic way half his troupe had wolfed down the blood clots he'd thrown on the sand, he decided to repeat the same method of overstimulating them.

His demonstration would therefore have to include a lethargic slumber, in which the young Negro would recline lazily on his cot before everyone, amid his various, symmetrically arranged animals.

For the sponge, an easy solution was provided by chance.

In his first attempts to accustom his charges to fresh air, Fogar, proceeding gradually, would occasionally pour a certain quantity of seawater on the living tissues, which otherwise would have perished from dehydration.

One day, not having enough ocean liquid on hand, the young man made do with fresh water and began by sprinkling the sponge, which immediately contracted in horror to expel this fluid so inimical to its bodily functions.

An identical shower, administered on the day of the gala, would surely produce the same effect and stimulate the same response.

The gelatinous block proved particularly apathetic.

Luckily, Fogar, thinking back to the grotto, remembered the rocky protrusions that, as they painfully entered the animal's flesh, had provoked the pinwheel movement of the three divergent stems.

He looked for an elegant way to imitate those jagged and irregular stone spikes.

A certain rustle then flooded his mind, and he recalled the gown Adinolfa had worn to inaugurate the Incomparables' stage.

He charged Sirdah to ask the tragedienne for a few of the thickest jade needles that were sewn to the silk.

Adinolfa generously put the entire gown at his disposal, and it was an easy task to harvest what he needed from the abundantly garnished skirt and corsage.

A small amount of cement, borrowed from one of Chènevillot's workmen, was spread in a thin, even layer over a swatch of carpet. Soon a hundred jade needles, planted in ten equal rows before the substance had a chance to set, raised their narrow, threatening points.

To make his display of the gelatinous block more interesting, Fogar thought to attach a captive to each of the suction cups at the

tips of the three spinning stems, whose muscle strength and gyra-
tional speed would be displayed more effectively.

At his request, the Boucharessas family vouchsafed the partici-
pation of three trained cats, who would suffer only a passing dizzi-
ness from the exercise.

The grayish plate, once out of the water, turned stiff as zinc.

But Fogar, blowing on it from various angles, caused many
graceful and subtle ripple patterns that he planned to use on the day
of the gala.

Wishing to obtain continual and prolonged transformations
without tiring his lungs, the young man, as always through his sister's translation, turned to Bex himself; the scientist, with a spare
battery he'd reserved for a certain thermomechanical orchestra produced during his long working nights, fashioned a practical and
lightweight propeller fan.

The advantage this device had over human lungs was the perfect
regularity of its gentle, uninterrupted breath.

Fogar, constantly at Bex's side, had watched intently as the
inventor fit the various components into the clever breeze-making
instrument.

With his curious talent for assimilation, he had grasped all the
subtleties of the mechanism, and expressed in sign language his admiration for an especially delicate gear or cleverly placed ratchet.

Intrigued by this strange personality, which he'd hardly expected
to encounter in a country such as this, Bex initiated Fogar into certain of his chemical secrets, pushing indulgence to the point of giving the young man a preview of his automatic orchestra.

Fogar remained petrified before the many organs, which under
Bex's manipulations produced long and varied flows of harmony.

Nevertheless, the relative poverty of one detail surprised him,
and through Sirdah, who was also present, he asked Bex for certain
explanations.

He was particularly amazed that each string could produce only one sound at a time. According to him, certain rodents, endemic to a specific part of the Behuliphruen, had a kind of mane, each hair of which, if stretched taut enough, would produce two simultaneous, distinct notes when bowed.

Bex refused to believe such nonsense and, with a shrug, let himself be led by Fogar, who, sure of his facts, wanted to show him the lair of the rodents in question.

With his guide, the chemist penetrated into the depths of the Behuliphruen and came to an area riddled with holes that looked like burrows.

Fogar stopped, then performed an astounding pantomime for Bex, tracing several zigzags of lightning with his finger and imitating with his throat the rumble of thunder.

Bex nodded in approving comprehension: the young man had just explained to him, perfectly clearly, that the rodents, now scattered about the thickets, were terrified of storms and would scamper in panic back to their burrows at the first threat of lightning.

Gazing upward, Bex noted the immutable purity of the sky and wondered what Fogar was hoping to prove; but the latter guessed his thoughts and signaled him to be patient.

The dappled clearing was shaded by tall, oddly shaped trees, whose fruits, which looked like giant bananas, littered the ground about them.

With his fingers, Fogar peeled one of the fruits, whose whitish and malleable pulp he kneaded until it lost its gently curved shape.

He thus obtained a perfectly regular cylinder, which he perforated lengthwise with a thin, straight twig.

In the resulting gap, he slipped a certain vine gathered from a tree trunk, then consolidated it all with some more rapid kneading.

Little by little, the fruit had been transformed into a veritable candle, whose highly flammable wick quickly caught fire from the caress of a few sparks that Fogar drew from two carefully chosen flints.

Bex soon understood the reason for this complicated procedure.

The candle, set upright on a flat stone, gave off as it burned a loud, prolonged sputtering that sounded exactly like booming thunder.

The chemist approached, intrigued by the strange properties of the combustible fruit, which flawlessly parodied the fury of a violent storm.

Suddenly a stampede echoed under the trees, and Bex saw a band of black animals, fooled by the mendacious thunder, rushing back to their burrows as fast as their legs would carry them.

When the herd was within reach, Fogar, flicking a stone randomly, struck one of the rodents dead, which remained inert on the ground while its fellows dove into their countless holes.

After putting out the vegetable wick, whose noisy carbonization was no longer needed, the adolescent picked up the rodent, which he held up to Bex.

The animal, vaguely resembling a squirrel, bore a thick, coarse black mane over nearly the entire length of its spine.

Examining the hairs, the chemist noted certain strange nodes, which could no doubt produce the dual sounds that so piqued his curiosity.

As they were leaving, Fogar, heeding his companion's advice, picked up the snuffed-out candle, only a small portion of which had been consumed.

Back in Ejur, Bex wished to verify his young guide's claim then and there.

He chose several hairs with different-looking nodes from the rodent's back.

Then, needing some kind of support, he sliced off two thin wooden slats, which he clamped together and drilled simultaneously to create minuscule, evenly spaced holes.

That done, each solid hair was easily guided through the double surface, then amply knotted at both ends so as to hold it firmly.

The boards, spread as far apart as they would go, were kept in place by two vertical risers, which, pulling the hairs taut, transformed them into musical strings.

Fogar himself provided a certain thin, flexible branch that, plucked in the heart of the Behuliphruen and sliced lengthwise, offered a perfectly smooth and slightly viscous inner surface.

Bex carefully trimmed one section of the twig into a fragile bow, which silkily attacked the strings of the minuscule lute he had so rapidly created.

As Fogar had predicted, all the hairs, vibrating separately, simultaneously produced two distinct and equally resonant notes.

Enthused, Bex convinced the young man to exhibit the inconceivable instrument at the gala, along with the vegetal candle he could so easily relight.

Encouraged by his successes, Fogar sought out new marvels that might further enhance the appeal of his demonstration.

One evening, seeing a sailor from the *Lynceus* washing his laundry in the currents of the Tez, he was surprised by the resemblance between one of his sea creatures and the soapsuds floating on the water.

His laundry finished, the sailor, for a laugh, gave his soap to Fogar, accompanying the jocular gift with a friendly jape regarding the young Negro's skin color.

Clumsily, the adolescent dropped the wet cake, which slipped through his fingers, but which, carefully retrieved, inspired him with a double plan for the gala.

First, Fogar intended to place on the soap itself the white-shelled animal, which, mistaken for an inert block of lather, would impress the audience by suddenly revealing its status as a living being.

Then, wishing to exploit the strangely slippery properties of this previously unknown substance, Fogar thought to toss the cake of soap at a given target after he made it unstable with a little water.

In this connection, the young man recalled a gold ingot that Bashkou had found at the bottom of the Tez, one day when the river was more limpid than usual. Diving quickly, the sorcerer had latched onto the shining object, which since then he guarded with jealous solicitude.

Given its cylindrical form and rounded ends, the ingot would be ideal for the meticulous experiment Fogar had in mind.

But the sorcerer was too attached to his discovery to let it go for even a moment.

Figuring the Tez must surely harbor other ingots identical to the first, Fogar planned his own dive into the fresh water, from which he confidently expected a fruitful yield. Like a gambler on a lucky streak, he envisioned only success and already imagined himself in possession of several precious cylinders, their brilliant shine and unusual provenance inspiring lively commentary and further embellishing his cot, which was already richly decorated with odd creatures.

Gathering another purple flower, Fogar lay down on the banks of the Tez and waited for the lethargic sleep.

Attaining the curious state of semi-consciousness favorable to his designs, he rolled toward water's edge and disappeared in the depths of the river at the very spot where Bashkou had spotted his ingot.

Kneeling on the riverbed, Fogar sifted through the sand with his fingers and, after patient searching, came upon three glinting golden cylinders that, no doubt washed along from distant regions, had been buffed into a clear, perfect patina.

The young man had just stood up and was about to rise back to the surface when suddenly he froze in surprise.

Right near him, an enormous plant, off-white in color and fully mature from top to bottom, rose vertically like a giant reed.

Now, on the screen formed by this plant, Fogar saw his own image kneeling in the sand, his body arched forward.

Soon the image altered, showing the same figure in a slightly different pose.

Then other changes occurred, and the stupefied adolescent saw his principal movements reproduced by the strange photosensitive plate, which had been functioning unbeknownst to him since his slow descent to the bottom of the river.

One by one the three ingots extracted from the sands appeared on the living screen, which faithfully recorded all the colors, although slightly attenuated due to the opacity of the liquid environment.

Scarcely had the group of scenes ended than they started over, unaltered and in identical order.

Without waiting for the end of this new cycle, Fogar dug into the silt around the huge white reed, which he was able to detach from the ground with its roots intact.

Several plants of the same type, but younger, were growing around the same area. The able diver uprooted a few of them, then finally swam up to the surface with his harvest and his ingots.

Revived and fully conscious, rid of his blood clots with the help of the purple flower, Fogar ran to shut himself in his hut so as to study his precious plants at leisure.

The first plant ceaselessly repeated the same series of images set in an unvarying order.

But the others, though rigorously similar in detail, appeared unable to capture light impressions.

Apparently it was only in a certain phase of their gigantic growth cycle that the snowy reeds retained the colored impressions that struck their tissues.

The young man resolved to watch for the right moment and put it to good use.

Indeed, the views fixed in the original plant, too murky in appearance, did not satisfy him.

He wanted to create clear, sharp images, worthy of being placed before his audience's eyes.

Alone, Fogar gathered from the Behuliphruen a provision of humus that he massed in a thick layer against one wall of his hut.

It was there that he transplanted his monstrous reeds, which, like certain amphibious algae, easily adapted to this new, purely terrestrial soil.

From then on, the young Negro remained confined to his hut, jealously watching over his flowerbed, which he tended with unwavering care.

One day, cultivating his narrow clump, he was looking at one of the plants, which, already tall and slender, seemed to have attained a certain degree of maturity.

Suddenly something occurred within the plant fibers, which Fogar studied more closely still.

The white, vertical surface renewed itself at regular intervals following a strange molecular movement.

A series of transformations then took place over a fairly prolonged period of time, after which the phenomenon changed its nature, and Fogar, who expected it this time, saw his own features vibrantly reproduced by the picture-hungry plant.

Various poses and expressions from its sole model paraded by on the screen, which was continually shaken by an inner shuffling, and the adolescent was able to confirm the enigma that he had more or less divined: his arrival at the bottom of the Tez had coincided with the recording phase in the evolution of the first plant, which had greedily soaked up the images placed before it.

Sadly, the new series of views, though perfectly clear, was absolutely devoid of aesthetic interest. Fogar, ill prepared, had merely struck a number of strange poses, and his comic grimaces filed past with tedious monotony.

Noticing that another plant seemed close to entering its period of light receptivity, the young man resolved to prepare in advance a series of images worthy of the public's attention.

A few days earlier, crossing back through the Behuliphruen with his provision of humus, Fogar had come across Juillard sitting under the dense shade.

The scholar was in his favorite place, the same one where Adinolfa had already discovered him absorbed in his old illustrated periodicals.

This time, pursuing research of a different kind, Juillard was leafing through a precious folio embellished with sumptuously colored engravings of Oriental subjects.

After taking a few moments to enjoy the dazzling illustrations, Fogar, without even attracting the thinker's notice, had continued on his way.

Now that book drummed on his mind, as it seemed ideal for his plan.

Unbeknownst to Juillard, he absconded with the luxurious tome. A long look at the illuminations piqued his curiosity, and he went to find Sirdah to learn the meaning of the story they told.

The young girl had Carmichael read her the fairly basic text, then gave her brother the following synopsis of an Arabic tale called "The Poet and the Beautiful Mooress."

In Baghdad there once lived a rich merchant named Shahnidjar.

Cultivating life's pleasures with the utmost refinement, Shahnidjar passionately loved art, women, and fine foods.

The poet Ghiriz, a member of the merchant's staff, was charged with composing many gay or plaintive stanzas and then singing them winsomely on cleverly improvised melodies.

Determined to see life through rose-colored glasses from the moment he awoke, Shahnidjar demanded from Ghiriz a daily serenade, which would gently clear from his brain its wan procession of pleasant dreams.

Precise and obedient, the poet went every morning at daybreak to the magnificent garden that surrounded his master's palace. Arriving beneath the wealthy sleeper's windows, he halted near a marble basin in which a slender jet of water rose through a jade tube.

Then, raising to his lips a kind of megaphone made of dull, delicate metal, Ghiriz began singing some new elegy that had blossomed in his fertile imagination. Because of a strange echo, his lightweight trumpet doubled each note with another one third lower, and so the poet performed a veritable one-man duet that heightened still further the charm of his renowned diction.

Soon Shahnidjar, now completely awake, appeared at the window with his favorite mistress, Neddu, the beautiful Mooress he loved so well.

At that very instant, Ghiriz felt his agitated heart pound violently. In a state of intoxication he looked at the divine Neddu, who for her part cast him long looks filled with burning desire.

When the serenade was over, the window pulled shut, and the poet, wandering beneath the azure sky, carried in his heart the dazzling vision—too fleeting, alas! Ghiriz passionately loved Neddu and knew he was loved by her.

Every evening, Shahnidjar, earnest admirer that he was, climbed a certain sandy monticule with his favorite to view the sunset, at a place where the vista stretched endlessly toward the west.

Reaching the crest of the arid outcropping, the good-natured merchant reveled joyfully in the magical spectacle offered by the bloodstained horizon.

Once the opulent fireball had completely disappeared, Shahnidjar climbed back down arm-in-arm with his companion, already dreaming of the delectable foodstuffs and choice wines that very soon would procure his well-being and jubilation.

Ghiriz watched for the moment of this retreat when, finding himself alone, he ran to kiss ardently the traces freshly embossed in the soft sand by Neddu's diminutive feet.

These were the poet's most intense joys, as he had no means of communicating with the Mooress whom Shahnidjar so jealously guarded.

One day, weary of pining from afar without the hope of approaching his beloved, Ghiriz went to consult the Chinaman Keou-

Ngan, who practiced in Baghdad the dual trade of fortune teller and sorcerer.

Asked what the future could be of so star-crossed an intrigue, Keou-Ngan led Ghiriz into his garden, then released a large bird of prey that began describing majestic and widening curves in the skies above them.

Studying the paths of the powerful creature, the Chinaman predicted the forthcoming realization of the poet's desires.

The bird came back to rest on the shoulder of its master, who returned to his laboratory with Ghiriz in tow.

Inspired by numerous documents spread before him, the Chinaman wrote certain instructions on parchment that the poet had to follow in order to reach his goal.

Taking the instructions, Ghiriz handed Keou-Ngan several gold coins in recompense for the consultation.

Once outside, the hopeful poet hastened to decipher the precious grimoire.

He found the recipe for a very complex culinary dish, the mere steam from which would plunge Shahnidjar into a deep and lasting sleep.

In addition, a magic formula was clearly inscribed at the bottom of the sheet.

Pronounced three times aloud, this incoherent string of syllables would give the dish laden with soporific ingredients a crystalline hum in harmony with the importunate chaperone's drowsiness.

As long as the sound remained strong and quick, the two lovers could freely revel in their intoxication, without fear of discovery by the benighted sleeper.

A progressive decrescendo would warn them of impending danger well in advance of his awakening.

Ghiriz prepared the dish in question for that very evening and set it on a silver plate-warmer in the middle of the table copiously laid for his master.

At the sight of this new and unfamiliar delicacy, the charmed Shahnidjar lifted the serving dish in both hands and voluptuously inhaled its strange emanations.

Immediately overcome by a leaden torpor, he sank back into his chair, eyes closed and head slumped to one side.

Ghiriz uttered the triple incantation, and the serving dish, clattering back onto the table, emitted a loud and rapidly oscillating ring.

When her poet told her of the Chinaman's efficacious ministrations, the beautiful Neddu trembled with joy and proposed a nocturnal escape into Shahnidjar's vast gardens.

The Negro Stingo, the Mooress's faithful serf, was placed on guard next to the merchant, with orders to warn the two lovers the moment the telltale ring gave signs of faltering.

Protected by their sentinel's absolute devotion, Ghiriz and Neddu ran outside without a second thought.

A long night of ecstasy was theirs to enjoy, in an enchanted Eden amid the rarest of flowers; then they peacefully drifted to sleep in the rising dawn, rocked by the murmur of a waterfall.

The sun had already followed half its course when Stingo ran up to sound the alarm, warning that the magic jingling had begun slowing down and would soon stop.

Jolted awake, the two lovers, filled with voluptuous memories, envisioned in horror the prospect of a new separation.

Neddu could think only of slipping Shahnidjar's yoke and fleeing with Ghiriz.

Suddenly a zebra appeared, having wandered there by chance.

Startled by the presence of these unexpected humans in its path, the animal tried to turn back.

But at his mistress's order, the Negro leapt forward and seized the charger by the nostrils, quickly dominating it.

Ghiriz had understood what Neddu was thinking; lithe and light, he leapt onto the zebra, then helped his companion up behind him.

The next moment, the two fugitives, with a wave of farewell to Stingo, galloped away on their swift mount. The Mooress, laughing at her newfound poverty, brandished a purse containing a few gold pieces, the only fortune left them to meet the costs of this perilous journey. Ghiriz, having given all his savings to Keou-Ngan the day before, could add nothing to their modest nest egg.

That evening, after a mad, headlong dash, the exhausted zebra collapsed in the thick of a gloomy forest.

Convinced they had outwitted any pursuers, at least momentarily, Ghiriz and Neddu sought to appease their hunger, whetted by fatigue and the whipping wind.

The two lovers divided up the chores. Ghiriz was to gather a provision of succulent fruits, while Neddu would look for a fresh-water spring where they could slake their thirst.

A certain hundred-year-old tree, its giant trunk easily recognizable, was chosen as meeting point, and each one set off in the gathering dusk.

After many twists and turns, Neddu came across the desired spring.

The young woman wanted to return right away, but in the rapidly fallen darkness she became increasingly lost and anxiously wandered for hours without managing to find the huge tree they'd designated.

Frantic with distress, Neddu began to pray, vowing to fast for ten days running if she could only get back to Ghiriz.

Comforted by this appeal to the supreme power, she resumed her walk with renewed courage.

Soon afterward, without quite knowing by what mysterious path, she suddenly found herself beside Ghiriz, who, bleary-eyed and not daring leave their appointed rendezvous, had been waiting for her while calling out her name.

Neddu fell into the poet's arms, thanking Allah for his prompt intervention.

Ghiriz displayed his harvest of fruits, but Neddu refused to eat her portion, relating the details of her successful vow.

The next day, the two fugitives continued their path on foot, for in the night the zebra had broken its bonds and escaped.

For several days, the couple went from village to village, wandering haphazardly.

Neddu began to feel the tortures of hunger. Though desperate, Ghiriz didn't dare urge her to break her promise for fear of calling divine fury down upon her.

By the tenth day, the young woman was so weak that she could barely walk, even when leaning on her lover's arm.

Suddenly she stumbled and fell prostrate onto the ground.

Ghiriz, shouting for help, saw a shopkeeper come running from her grocery stand at the side of the road.

Sensing that death was about to steal his mistress, the poet made a quick decision.

At his request, the shopkeeper rushed back with various foods, and Neddu, opening her eyes, feasted with delight on this restorative nourishment.

Her strength replenished, the young woman resumed her walk, hoping to elude the many agents that the wealthy Shahnidjar, whose ardent passion she knew all too well, had surely sent after them.

But one thing gnawed at her without respite: remorse over having broken her fast before the promised time.

An encounter the very next day only heightened her anxieties, which suddenly gained terrible precision.

In the middle of the countryside, an apparent lunatic accosted her, flailing his arms and sowing panic in her heart with his predictions of a dizzying fall, punishment for her betrayal.

The next several hours Ghiriz and Neddu passed in silence, stricken by the singular prophecy.

That evening, at a bend in the road, the young woman let out a cry of terror and began flailing her arms, as if trying to ward off some horrible vision.

Before her, countless eyes without bodies or faces appeared two by two, staring harshly in anger and reproach.

Little by little, these spellbinding gazes drew her toward the edge of the road, which bordered a bottomless abyss bristling with rocky protuberances.

Unaware of this sudden hallucination, Ghiriz could not understand his beloved's horror.

All at once, without even having time to hold her back, he saw Neddu pulled toward the precipice by an irresistible force.

The poor unfortunate plummeted over the edge, her body crashing against rock after rock, pursued in her fall by the ominous eyes that seemed to blame her for her offense against the Divinity.

Ghiriz, leaning over the chasm, wanted only to share his lover's fate, and he leapt after her into the void.

Their two bodies came to rest side by side, united for all eternity in those unfathomable depths.

Fogar had listened attentively to Sirdah's narration.

The illustrations now took on a clear and fully coherent meaning, which confirmed his plan to use them.

At the time of his misdemeanor, the adolescent had stolen not only the folio but also, as a precaution, a school primer in which every page contained the portrait of an animal captioned by its Latin name.

As the colored scenes of the Arabic tale might prove too few in number, this second volume, in which each picture stood alone, provided a copious supplement that would fully satisfy the plant's demand for visuals.

Armed with the folio and the back-up primer, Fogar, now a conscious and informed observer, awaited the opportune moment.

When the time came, he placed successively before the enormous white reed, whose atomic transformations he'd been awaiting, all the Oriental engravings spread out in correct order.

When this series was finished, he opened the primer just in time to record one page.

The receptive phase having come to an end, the young man could verify the complete success of his operation, watching the images parade by sharply on the delicately impressed plant screen.

All that remained was to tend the plant, which from now on would reproduce ad infinitum the delicate images that were now an integral part of it.

Fogar surreptitiously returned the two volumes to their rightful place; Juillard, absorbed in some new study, had not even noticed their temporary absence.

Now possessing all the elements of his exhibition, the adolescent found an ingenious way to coordinate them.

He decided to group everything along his bed frame, which was a convenient place to obtain the lethargic, clot-generating slumber.

Chènevillot fitted the cot with the desired attachments, each one scrupulously adapted to the particular shape of a given animal or object.

The automatic colorations of the giant reed seemed ideal for distracting the audience during the boy's voluntary syncope, which would necessarily last a wearisome amount of time.

Since, on the other hand, the first phase of the fainting spell held some real interest due to the gradual weakening of vital signs, it was best to let Fogar be the sole attraction until his absolute prostration made him a virtual corpse.

Toward that end, Chènevillot arranged the plant like a bed canopy and placed above it a bright electric spotlight.

By choosing a sufficiently dark time of day for the experiment, they could make the changing views bright or dim, depending on the malleable strength of the adjustable current.

Fogar, who wanted to do everything himself, insisted on controlling the lights. But in order for his blood to congeal, his lethargic slumber required complete rigidity of the arms and legs. Chènevillot therefore set the electrical current to be regulated by a horizontal wand, ending in a kind of crutch designed to fit under the sleeper's left armpit. As such, the adolescent, still lucid enough when the first image came on, could, with an imperceptible movement of his body, brighten the beacon at the desired moment.

A small recess with a special light would serve to display in all its detail the inner structure of the strange, living sponge.

When Chènevillot had finished his labors, Fogar patiently practiced bouncing his wet soap off the three gold ingots attached to the foot of his bed, held in place by three solid supports with claws.

He quickly acquired remarkable skill at this difficult sport, performing true marvels of precision and balance.

Meanwhile, he tended his plant with utmost care.

The scrupulously preserved root now rested in an earthenware pot attached to the bed frame. Regular watering maintained the vitality of the tissues, whose endlessly repeated imprints retained all their clarity.

XVI

EVER SINCE OUR ARRIVAL in Ejur, the Hungarian Skariovszki had practiced daily on his zither, with its pure and unsettling sounds.

Squeezed into the gypsy costume he never changed, the able virtuoso executed head-spinning compositions, which had the ability to astonish the natives.

An attentive and populous group of Ponukeleans followed all his performances.

Annoyed by this distracting audience, the great artiste looked for a solitary, welcoming retreat in which to practice, safe from unwelcome eavesdroppers.

Carrying his zither and the foldable stand designed to hold it, he reached the Behuliphruen and marched swiftly forward beneath its tall trees, with no apparent hesitation about which direction to follow.

After a fairly long walk, he halted at the edge of a spring in a charming, picturesque spot.

Skariovszki already knew of this isolated, mysterious place; once he had even tried to bathe in the limpid stream, which flowed with a million glints over shimmering mica rocks. But to his great surprise, he could not overcome the surface tension of the water, whose remarkable density prevented him from penetrating to any appreciable depth. Dropping to his hands and knees, he had managed to cross the heavy stream in both directions without wetting his body, which remained on the surface.

Ignoring the strange waterway this time, Skariovszki quickly set up his zither and stand before a low rock that could serve as his bench.

Soon, seated before the instrument, the virtuoso began playing a slow Hungarian melody full of tender yearning.

After several measures, although fully absorbed in the rise and fall of his hammers, Skariovszki intuited a slight movement coming from near the river.

A rapid glance revealed a giant earthworm, which, emerging from the water, began crawling onto the bank.

Without breaking his rhythm, the gypsy, with a series of furtive glances, watched the newcomer as it gently approached the zither.

Stopping beneath the stand, the worm curled up unafraid between the Hungarian's feet, who, gazing down, saw it lying still on the ground.

Soon putting the incident out of his mind, Skariovszki continued his labors, and for three long hours waves of harmony flowed continuously from his poetic instrument.

When evening fell, the performer finally stood up; looking at the clear sky harboring no threat of rain, he decided to leave the zither in situ for his next session.

As he was leaving his retreat, he noticed the worm, which, heading back the way it came, slid toward the bank and soon disappeared into the depths of the river.

The next day, Skariovszki again settled next to the bizarre stream and began practicing a difficult slow waltz.

During the first refrain, the virtuoso was somewhat distracted by the colossal worm, which, rising from the currents, returned directly to its place from the day before, where it remained gracefully coiled until the end of the performance.

Once more, before leaving, Skariovszki watched the inoffensive, melody-sated annelid as it noiselessly slid back into the calm brook.

The same thing happened for several days running. Like a snake charmer, the Hungarian, by his talent, infallibly attracted the music-loving worm, which once captured could not tear itself away from its ecstasy.

The gypsy grew keenly interested in the creature, whose trusting nature astounded him. One evening, his day's work over, he blocked its path with his hand in an attempt to tame it.

The worm, with no apprehension whatsoever, scaled the fingers offered to him, then wrapped itself several times around the Hungarian's wrist as he progressively rolled up his sleeve.

The formidable load Skariovszki felt on his arm amazed him. Adapted to the dense environment provided by the water of the stream, the worm, despite its suppleness, was of considerable weight.

This first experiment was followed by many others. The worm soon recognized its master and could obey the slightest command from his voice.

Such docility inspired in the gypsy's mind a plan that might yield valuable results.

The trick was to train the worm to produce sounds from the zither on its own, by patiently cultivating its mysterious passion for the sonorous disturbance of air currents.

After lengthy deliberation, Skariovszki imagined a device that could exploit the peculiar weight of the special waters the creature inhabited.

The rocks in the stream provided him with four solid, transparent slabs of mica, which, when sliced thin and sealed with clay, formed a receptacle well suited to certain goals. Two sturdy branches with forked ends, planted vertically in the ground on either side of the zither, supported the device that was built like a trough with a long, tapering base.

Skariovszki trained the worm to slide into the mica receptacle and stretch out, thereby stopping up a gap in the bottom edge.

Using a large fruit husk, he soon drew from the river several pints of water, which he poured into the transparent trough.

After this, with the end of a twig, he lifted, for a fraction of a second, an infinitesimal fragment of the worm's recumbent body.

A drop of water slipped through and fell onto a zither string, which vibrated quite clearly.

The experiment, renewed several times in neighboring areas, produced a series of notes that formed a ritornello.

Suddenly the same musical formation was repeated by the worm, which all by itself created paths for the liquid through a series of tremors accomplished flawlessly in all the correct places.

Never would Skariovszki have dared count on such rapid comprehension. At this point his task struck him as simple and infallible.

Measure by measure, he taught the worm several lively or wistful Hungarian melodies.

The gypsy began by using the twig to educate the animal, which then reproduced the given fragment on its own.

Seeing that water was dripping inside the zither through its two sound holes, Skariovszki, with a pin, bored an imperceptible drain in the bottom of the instrument that allowed the excess liquid to escape in a fine stream.

Occasionally more water was collected from the nearby river, and the work continued without interruption.

Soon, driven by his growing ambition, the Hungarian, a twig in each hand, tried to obtain two notes simultaneously.

As the worm lent itself at once to this new demand, every zither composition, invariably based on the sometimes coincident strike of two hammers, was now within their reach.

Deciding to perform at the gala as a trainer rather than a performer, for the next several days the gypsy applied himself fanatically to his pedagogic task.

In the end, raising the difficulty level, he tied a long twig to each of his ten fingers and could thereby teach the worm many polyphonic acrobatics generally excluded from his repertoire.

Now certain of being able to exhibit the astonishing creature, Skariovszki thought up various refinements to improve the overall apparatus.

At his request, Chènevillot replaced the two forked branches that had until then supported the mica trough with a twin metallic mount, attached directly to the zither's stand.

In addition, a partial felt lining was added to the instrument to gently absorb the echoing drip of the heavy water droplets.

To avoid drenching Trophy Square, an earthenware vessel with felt-lined channel would receive the thin stream escaping from the zither.

These preparations finished, Skariovszki completed the education of his worm, which every day, at the first sounds of the zither, emerged promptly from the dense river, into which the Hungarian personally hastened to plunge it again at the end of their lessons.

XVII

OF ALL THE EMPEROR'S sons, the twelve-year-old Rhejed was the most mischievous and rambunctious.

He spent his days inventing odd and rather outlandish games whose seeming intent was to put his life in danger.

The Behuliphruen, the usual scene of his hijinks, provided ample opportunity to give his impetuosity free rein. Sometimes the agile black child scaled a tall tree to pluck nests from the highest branches; sometimes he threw stones to chase away birds or quadrupeds, which he also knew how to catch with ingenious traps.

One day, emerging into a narrow clearing, Rhejed noticed a red-furred rodent that seemed to be sniffing the ground to find its way.

The child was holding a heavy stick he'd recently torn from a bush. With a sharp throw of the primitive weapon he slaughtered the rodent, which fell to its side on the bare ground.

Moving closer, Rhejed noticed an abundant puddle of drool leaking from the corpse's mouth that gave off a remarkably strong and peculiar odor; disgusted by the sight, he crossed the clearing and continued on his way.

Suddenly he heard a violent beating of wings; turning around, he saw a formidable bird of prey with long waderlike claws, which, after describing several concentric circles, alit next to the rodent.

Rhejed retraced his steps, thinking he might also kill the bird, which was already attacking the carcass with its beak.

Wanting to get a bead on the especially vulnerable head, he softly approached from the front while the bird's neck was lowered.

The boy was then surprised to see two olfactory openings above the beak that, no doubt picking up the smell of the strange drool from a distance, had alerted and then guided the bird in its rush to taste the promised feast.

Still armed with his stick, Rhejed ran up and struck the bird full in the occiput; it dropped without a sound.

But when he went to examine his new victim more closely, he felt himself held fast to the ground by a powerful magnetic force.

His right foot was resting on a heavy flat stone covered in the rodent's drool.

Already half dry, this substance formed an irresistibly powerful glue, and Rhejed was able to dislodge his bare foot only at the price of violent efforts that left deep, painful abrasions on his sole.

When he was finally free, the little scamp, fearing he'd be trapped a second time, thought only of getting away from that dangerous place as fast as possible.

But a moment later, a distant shuddering of wings made him turn his head, and he saw in the sky a second raptor of the same race, which, attracted by the ever more pungent odor, was speeding toward the enticing bait.

Rhejed then conceived a bold plan, based on the adhesive properties of the astonishing drool and on the effect its smell clearly had on certain kinds of birds with mighty wingspans.

Some freshly trampled herbs showed him the path the rodent had recently taken.

At one point along these tracks, which another animal of the same species would likely soon follow, Rhejed dug a small hole that he concealed with delicate branches.

The next day, delighted by the success of his trap, the boy pulled from the tight excavation a red-furred rodent identical to the first, which he brought back alive to his hut.

Inspired by Fogar's project and wishing to do something similar, the adventurous Rhejed planned to enliven the gala by having one of the nostril-birds that nested throughout the Behuliphruen lift him into the air.

The rodent, killed at the last moment, would furnish abundant drool that would both attract the required raptor and help quickly fashion an aerial harness.

This latter condition required a flat object that could hold the animal adhesive, which if simply spread on the ground would have been useless.

Exploring the wreckage of the *Lynceus*, Rhejed discovered a lightweight cabinet door perfectly suited to his purposes.

The boy revealed only a portion of his plan; fearing the inevitable paternal veto, he kept to himself anything related to his voyage into the wild blue yonder.

XVIII

IT HAD BEEN TWO MONTHS since Seil-kor's departure and we were impatiently awaiting his return: with preparations for the gala now complete, we feared that boredom, thus far kept at bay by rehearsals or playing our stock market, would soon regain its hold.

Fortunately, a wholly unexpected event provided a powerful distraction.

One evening, Sirdah came to tell us of a serious incident that had occurred earlier that day.

At around three o'clock, an ambassador from King Yaour, crossing the Tez in a dugout, had been admitted to Talou's hut, where he relayed some glad tidings: the sovereign of Drelchkaff, having got wind of events in Ejur, keenly desired to hear the emperor sing in falsetto, dressed in his fabulous attire. He would unconditionally grant Sirdah's cure if the blind girl's father consented to get up on the Incomparables' stage for him and sing Dariccelli's *Aubade* in his female voice.

Flattered by the request and delighted at the prospect of restoring his daughter's sight so cheaply, Talou was already formulating an affirmative reply when Gaiz-duh—for such was the Negro ambassador's name—came forward and whispered some secret revelations. The supposed desire so ardently expressed was merely a ruse to allow Yaour to freely enter Ejur at the head of a sizeable entourage. Aware of Talou's pride and predicting that his fearsome neighbor, wishing to dazzle his guest, would receive him surrounded by his entire army, the king planned to catch the enemy forces in a trap in the relatively confined space of Trophy Square. While the populace of Ejur would be drawn to the esplanade by the performance, the Drelchkaffian army would cross the Tez on a makeshift bridge of dugout canoes, then spread around the capital like a human cincture and invade the square from all sides at once. Just then, Yaour would give his entourage the signal to attack, and the Ponukelean warriors, squeezed as if in a vise, would be massacred by their fierce aggressors, who among many advantages would have that of surprise. As clear victor, Yaour would proclaim himself emperor, reducing Talou and all his lineage to slavery.

Gaiz-duh thus remorselessly betrayed his master, who had been rewarding him poorly for his services and often treated him cruelly. As to the price for this information, he deferred to Talou's generosity.

Taking advantage of this forewarning, the emperor sent Gaiz-duh back with the mission to summon King Yaour the next day at sunset. Scenting in advance a magnificent recompense, the ambassador went off filled with hope, while Talou was already formulating in his head an entire plan of defense and attack.

The next day, on the emperor's orders, half the Ponukelean troops hid in the vegetation of the Behuliphruen, while the rest took shelter in small groups in the huts of Ejur's southernmost quarter.

At the appointed hour, Yaour and his entourage, led by Gaiz-duh, stood in a dozen dugouts and crossed the Tez.

Posted on the right bank, Rao, Mossem's successor, awaited their landing; he led the king to Trophy Square, where Talou was waiting for him unarmed, decked out in his feminine toilette and surrounded by only a handful of guards.

On his arrival, Yaour glanced about him, looking disconcerted by the absence of the warriors whom he expected to catch unawares. Talou walked before him, and the two monarchs exchanged greetings that Sirdah, who remained with us, translated in a murmur.

First, Yaour, ill concealing his discomfiture, asked if he wouldn't have the pleasure of seeing the handsome Ponukelean troops, reputed far and wide for their courage and proud bearing. Talou replied that his guest had come a little before the designated hour, and that his warriors, presently adjusting their finery, would assemble on the esplanade momentarily to enhance the splendor of the performance with their presence. Reassured, but fearing he'd roused the emperor's suspicions with his imprudent question, Yaour immediately feigned preoccupation with trifles. He began extravagantly admiring Talou's outfit and announcing his keen desire to own one just like it.

At these words, the emperor, who was seeking an occasion to gain time until the enemy army's arrival, abruptly turned toward our group and, through Sirdah, ordered us to find in our trunks an outfit similar to his.

Accustomed to playing Goethe's *Faust* on all her tours, Adinolfa ran off and returned after a moment, cradling in her arms the gown and wig she wore as Gretchen.

At the sight of the gift he was being offered, Yaour emitted yelps of joy. He laid his weapons on the ground and, thanks to his extremely svelte build, easily donned the gown, which fastened above his loincloth; then, putting on the blonde wig with its two thick braids, he took several majestic steps, evidently thrilled by the effect his bizarre get-up produced.

Suddenly there came the sound of an immense clamor outside the square, and Yaour, sensing a betrayal, quickly leapt to his weapons and tried to flee with his entourage. Only Gaiz-duh, switching to the ranks of his enemies, joined with the Ponukelean warriors who flew off in pursuit of the king, following Talou and Rao. Immediately attracted by the exciting spectacle taking place before our eyes, all of us ran in the same direction and soon reached the southern border of Ejur.

We could easily piece together what had just occurred. The Drelchkaffian army, following the royal directive, had crossed the Tez on a bridge of canoes; just as the last man set foot on the right

Raymond Roussel

bank, Talou's forces, with a rallying cry, had surged simultaneously
from the huts of Ejur and the bushes of the Behuliphruen to encircle
the foe on all sides, profiting from the very tactic Yaour had envisioned. Already the ground was littered with Drelchkaffian casual-
ties, and victory for the emperor's men seemed assured.

Yaour, still decked out in his gown and wig, had bravely thrown
himself into the fray and fought alongside his men. Armed with a
lance, Talou rushed him, carrying his train on his left arm, and a
strange duel was fought by these two monarchs of carnavalesque
appearance. At first the king managed to parry several thrusts, but
soon the emperor, after a clever feint, drove his shaft into his oppo-
nent's breast.

Disheartened by the killing of their chief, the decimated Drelch-
kaffians lost little time in surrendering and were brought to Ejur as
captives.

All the corpses except Yaour's were thrown into the Tez, which
dutifully washed them out to sea.

XIX

Shortly before talou's victory, an astonishing piece of news had spread as far as Ejur: people were talking of a European couple at Yaour's side, a young woman and her brother whose meanderings had led them across the Tez.

The brother seemed to keep a discreet profile, but the beautiful and captivating female traveler was openly conducting an affair with Yaour, on whom her powerful charms had produced a deep and lasting effect.

After the battle, Talou had the two strangers brought to him, leaving them free to circulate unguarded while he decided their fate.

The attractive explorer, a Frenchwoman named Louise Montalescot, quickly struck up a friendship with us and, delighted to find herself among compatriots, related the many twists of fate that had led her and her brother to this distant African land.

Of humble origins, Louise was born in the outskirts of Paris. Her father, who worked in a ceramics factory, earned a steady living by making various models of vases and containers; this work required a true sculptor's talent, but the good man remained the soul of modesty.

Louise had a younger brother, the object of her most ardent affections. Norbert—that was the boy's name—had trained under his father since early childhood and could easily model fine statuettes in the guise of flasks and candlestick holders.

Sent to school at an early age, Louise demonstrated a remarkable aptitude for work; thanks to her excellent grades, she was awarded a scholarship to attend a private girls' school and could thus pursue her studies more seriously. At twenty, having earned her diplomas, she lived comfortably off the lessons she gave, and meanwhile spent her days developing her knowledge of the arts and sciences. Consumed by a passion for hard work, she lamented the time she had to waste sleeping and eating.

She was especially fanatical about chemistry, and during her long nights of study she grimly pursued a certain grand discovery that had been germinating in her mind. She was trying to obtain, by a purely photographic process, a mechanism precise enough to guide a pencil or paintbrush with absolute steadiness. Already Louise was nearing her goal; but she was still lacking one essential oil, which thus far had eluded her. Every Sunday she went to collect samples in the woods around Paris, searching in vain for the as yet unknown plant that could perfect her mixture.

Reading in various explorers' memoirs many enchanting descriptions of tropical flora, the young woman dreamed of crossing the torrid lands of central Africa, convinced that its unparalleled vegetation would increase her slim chances for success a hundredfold.

To take her mind off her obsession, Louise devoted part of each day to writing a brief treatise on botany, an attractive, well-illustrated tome aimed at a general readership that highlighted the astounding marvels of the plant kingdom. She made short work of the volume, which went through a large printing and earned her a small fortune. Finding herself with this unexpected windfall, the young woman thought only of undertaking the great voyage she so ardently desired.

But for some time already, she had been experiencing a pain in her right lung—a kind of sharp, insistent pressure that felt like a supply of air she could not exhale. Wishing to get an authoritative opinion before setting off on her travels, she consulted Dr. Renesme, whose celebrated work on chest illnesses she had read and admired.

The great specialist was struck by the rarity of the case. An internal tumor had formed in Louise's lung, and the atony of the affected area interfered with the expulsion of inhaled air.

According to Renesme, the illness was surely caused by certain toxic gases that the young woman had absorbed while performing her chemical experiments.

It was now urgent to create an artificial outlet for the air, for without this precaution the tumor would continue to swell indefinitely. Moreover, the breathing tubes would produce a sound to let her monitor their good working order at all times—for the slightest obstruction of even one of her main organs would allow the tumescence to make irreversible progress.

Admirably endowed physically, Louise, despite her natural seriousness, was not above a certain coquetry. Perturbed by Renesme's diagnosis, she looked for a means of rendering as elegant and aesthetically pleasing as possible the surgical instrument that would henceforth be part of her body.

Taking as pretext her imminent departure for perilous horizons, she decided to wear men's clothing, which was better suited to the hardships of her intrepid journey.

She settled on an officer's uniform, which would allow her to disguise the sound-producing tubes as aiguillettes, much as one conceals a hearing horn in the armature of a fan or umbrella.

Renesme gamely accepted this whim and built his device according to the desired specifications.

The operation succeeded to perfection; the tumor, located at the base of the lung, could now escape through a narrow opening, to which the doctor fitted a stiff tube subdivided into several hollow, whistling aiguillettes.

Thanks to the beneficial effects of this safety valve, Louise could henceforth indulge in all sorts of strenuous activities without fear. Every evening she had to block the opening with a metal stopper after removing the device, which the calm, regular breathing of sleep made superfluous.

When she first saw herself in her officer's costume, the young woman felt somewhat consoled for her misfortune. Her new outfit

was in fact quite becoming, and Louise admired the effect produced by her magnificent blonde mane, which she let fall in natural ringlets beneath her thin policeman's kepi jauntily cocked over
one ear.

Even during her busiest periods of study, Louise had never neglected
her brother Norbert.

Her affection for him had grown only more attentive after the
disappearance of their parents, who had died at almost the same time
during a terrible winter that spawned several lethal epidemics.

Norbert now occupied his father's place at the ceramics factory,
where his marvelous dexterity allowed him to rapidly execute many
graceful, lifelike figurines. But apart from this genuine talent the
young man had little skill, and he was completely under the excellent influence of his sister.

Louise wanted to share her sudden wealth with Norbert and
resolved to bring him with her on her magnificent journey.

The young woman had recently taken an interest in a tame
magpie found under strange circumstances. The bird had appeared
to her for the first time one Sunday, in the middle of the Chaville
woods. Noon had just sounded in the distance, and Louise, after a
tiring morning of gathering plant samples, had sat down beneath a
tree to have her frugal lunch. Suddenly, a brazen and greedy magpie
came hopping toward her as if begging for breadcrumbs, which she
immediately tossed its way in abundance. The grateful bird hopped
still closer without any fear, letting itself be petted and picked up
by the generous benefactor, who, touched by this trusting sympathy,
took it back home with her and began training it. Soon the magpie came at the slightest call to perch on its mistress's shoulder and
pushed obedience to the point of fetching in its beak any light object
she pointed at.

Louise was now too attached to her winged pet to leave it in
someone else's care, and it was therefore with her on the day when,

full of hopeful exuberance, she and her brother boarded the express for Marseille.

Carried to Porto Novo by a rapid steamer, the siblings hastily recruited a small escort of whites and headed south. Louise's plan was to reach the Vorrh, which several explorers' accounts had mentioned; it was especially there that she imagined she'd discover all sorts of marvelous plants.

Her hopes were not disappointed when, after a long and wearying trek, she entered the imposing forest primeval. She began her research straightaway, feeling immense joy upon seeing, at virtually every step, some flower or plant that constituted a new and unknown treasure.

Before embarking on her trip, Louise had concocted a corrosive liquid to facilitate her chore. A droplet of this acid, poured onto the right kind of plant, would reveal the indubitable presence of the desired essence by causing a small combustion and some light smoke.

But despite the infinite variety of specimens that crowded the Vorrh, her persistent trials remained fruitless. For many days Louise pursued her task with courage, advancing ever forward beneath the remarkable foliage. Sometimes, spotting some strange and attractive leafage on a tree, she pointed it out to the magpie, which plucked it and brought it to her in its beak.

In this way they crossed the entire Vorrh from north to south without result. Louise, in despair, had reached the point of conducting her experiment only mechanically, when all of a sudden a droplet of her concoction, dribbled onto a new kind of plant simply out of habit, provoked the brief combustion she'd vainly awaited for so long.

The young woman experienced a moment of exhilaration that made up for all her past disappointments. She gathered up a copious amount of the precious delicate, red-colored plant, whose seeds, cultivated in a hothouse, should ensure her future provision.

It was at nightfall that the explorer had made her momentous discovery; they set up camp where they'd halted and everyone lay down to sleep, after a decent meal during which they made plans for an immediate return to Porto Novo.

But the next morning, Louise and Norbert awoke to find themselves alone. Their companions had betrayed them, making away, after cutting its strap, with a certain bag that the young woman always wore slung across her shoulder, whose various compartments contained a weighty supply of gold and banknotes. To avoid capture, the scoundrels had waited until they reached the farthest point of their journey, so as to leave the two abandoned siblings with no provisions and no hope of getting back.

Louise had no desire to tempt fate by trying to reach Porto Novo; instead she continued south, in hopes of encountering a native village where she could get repatriated against the promise of a ransom. She gathered an ample provision of fruits and soon emerged from the Vorrh, having crossed the whole of the vast forest without seeing a trace of Velbar or Sirdah, whom the fire would soon evict from their retreat.

After several hours of walking, Louise reached the Tez, whose course, at a certain distance from Ejur, veered distinctly northward. A tree trunk was drifting randomly down the rapids. At a sign from his sister, Norbert grabbed onto the long flotsam and, pushed by a strong branch that acted as a scull, the two exiles could ford the river, straddling the wet bark as best they could. The young woman was glad to put this barrier between her and her former guides, who might have second thoughts about leaving their victims alive and return with villainous intent.

From this point on, the two siblings invariably followed the left bank of the Tez and thus fell under the sway of Yaour, who was profoundly moved by Louise's beauty.

During her studies, the girl had circulated in a world of students whose very advanced attitudes had rubbed off on her; she openly displayed her disdain for certain social conventions and sometimes went so far as to advocate free love. Yaour, who was young and had a striking face, had a powerful effect on her imagination, with its love of the unexpected. As she saw it, two individuals drawn to each other by mutual attraction should let no prejudice hinder them. Happy and proud of the romantic side of the adventure, she gave herself unreservedly to this strange king whose passion had been ignited at first glance.

All plans for returning home were postponed by this unplanned denouement.

During their treacherous flight in the heart of the Vorrh, the guides had left behind a certain bag, whose contents, worthless to them but invaluable to Louise, included a host of objects and ingredients related to her great photographic discovery, as yet unfinished.

The young woman resumed her labors with renewed purpose, sure of her success now that she had the unobtainable essence furnished by the red plants from the virgin forest.

Still, her task demanded many more long and painstaking efforts, and she had not yet reached her goal when the Battle of the Tez broke out.

Concluding her story, Louise confessed her violent grief over the death of the unfortunate Yaour, whose glorious memory would forever hover above her entire existence.

XX

THE DAY AFTER HIS VICTORY, the emperor sent Sirdah over with a complicated mission.

Talou, who combined the functions of religious leader and sovereign, was to crown himself king of Drelchkaff, a privilege to which his latest triumph entitled him.

The monarch thought he might heighten the prestige of his eminent decree by having it coincide with the Incomparables' gala.

Seeking to impress his subjects, he also asked after some grandiose tradition that was customary among whites.

Juillard immediately thought of the Holy Ampulla and offered to provide all the relevant details on how to administer the sacred unction. Meanwhile, Chènevillot volunteered to build a small altar on the north side of Trophy Square.

This first question settled, Sirdah continued her list of demands.

As Yaour IX had no relatives directly descended from Yaour I, his death marked the definitive extinction of his bloodline.

To embellish the coronation ceremony and affirm the incontestable rights of the Talous, the emperor wished to exhibit a kind of genealogical record which, taking Suann as starting point, would underscore once and for all the annihilation of the rival branch.

Very proud of his European origins, the emperor expected the document to showcase the ancient portrait, piously handed down from father to son in the Talou lineage, that depicted the two Spanish sisters who had married Suann.

Juillard gladly assumed the task of drawing up this proclamation, which would decorate the altar that Chènevillot had already built in his mind.

Alongside these various details, a curious minor role was to be played by the actual body of the unfortunate Yaour.

The tip of the lance on which the emperor had impaled the late king was, like many Ponukelean weapons, coated with a virulent poison that not only caused certain death but also possessed the strange property of retarding putrefaction of the bodily tissues.

The corpse of the illustrious nemesis could therefore, even after an extended delay, be displayed for the ceremony beneath the wilted rubber tree formerly dedicated to the race of Yaours.

As the emperor saw it, this humiliation imposed on the cursed plant demanded, by contrast, a glorious decoration for the palm tree that Talou IV had later planted.

The painter Toresse was chosen to create a commemorative sign recalling the now-distant restoration, which fell on exactly the same date as the tree's original planting.

Sirdah further informed us that the day of the coronation would also see the deaths of all the convicts, with Rao as executioner.

Gaiz-duh, whose request for a sumptuous reward had been met only by this reply from the emperor: "You are a traitor, and you shall be punished as a traitor," was to be beheaded with an axe; its blade, made of a special wood as hard as steel, could prevent blood from spattering.

The soles of Mossem's feet would be seared with a red-hot poker, which would etch one by one the mendacious characters that he himself had inscribed on Sirdah's death certificate.

Rul would perish speared by the long golden needles that for so many years had ornamented her hair; their tips would pierce her flesh through the eyelets in the red corset, now reduced to rags by excess wear.

For Jizme, the emperor, whose imagination had run dry, asked us to suggest some torture common in our country. Chènevillot then had a thought that both spared the condemned woman any suffering and had the added advantage of possibly staying the execution for a very long time. Among his supplies, the architect had a late-model lightning rod, which he'd intended for the castle of Baron Ballesteros. It would be a simple matter, at the next severe electrical storm, to connect Jizme to the conducting wire of the apparatus and let her be electrocuted by the clouds. Now, since inclement weather was a rare occurrence in Ejur, it was not unlikely that some unforeseen event might deliver the poor unfortunate before the next bolt of lightning struck.

The industrious Nair's life would be spared because of the snares he constructed and their usefulness in killing mosquitoes. But, for the author of the illuminated love note addressed to Jizme, simple imprisonment without torture apparently constituted too gentle a punishment. Talou wanted to build at the edge of Trophy Square a kind of pedestal to which they'd attach the snare Seil-kor had set one certain evening. Condemned to perpetual immobility and barely allowed room to stretch out for sleep, Nair, his foot collared by the noose that had already proven fatal to him once before, would labor without respite to fashion his delicate traps. To add emotional torment to the exasperating physical constraint, the bowler hat, suede glove, and illustrated letter, the true instruments of his ridiculous misadventure, would be placed forever within his sight.

To round out the roster of those attending the coronation, Talou demanded that a prison be built, from which the convicts, the living proof of his absolute power, might witness his triumph.

After delivering this sinister news, Sirdah related a happier event scheduled for the day of the gala. This was her own cure by the sorcerer Bashkou, who was now under Talou's authority. In his impatience, the emperor had wanted to bring his daughter to the skillful healer immediately following the Battle of the Tez. But Sirdah had refused to regain her sight on a day stained by so much bloodshed. She preferred to keep this additional joy for the coronation day, already blessed by her father's dazzling glorification.

A few words concerning the Montalescots concluded Sirdah's mandate.

In the emperor's eyes, Louise deserved the supreme punishment merely because of her amorous liaison with his mortal enemy, every trace of whom had to be eradicated. Talou went so far as to include the inoffensive Norbert in the hatred inspired by everything that, directly or indirectly, had enjoyed Yaour's favor. But Sirdah had adroitly piqued her father's curiosity by describing the great discovery that haunted the young woman; eager to see the planned apparatus function, Talou had decided to suspend judgment of the student, who remained free to pursue her labors.

A week was all Chènevillot needed to complete his new projects.

At the north of Trophy Square rose a small altar with several steps preceding it; opposite, on the south side, stretched a prison intended for the convicts and, not far from the Incomparables' theater, rose a wooden pedestal, furnished with all the requisite accessories, on which Nair was immediately placed.

Especially taken with the idea of having Jizme die by celestial fire, Talou had fully approved Chènevillot's plan. Learning the nature of the execution awaiting her, the unfortunate had obtained two supreme favors from the emperor: to die on the decorated white mattress that her lover had once given her, and to wear around her neck, at the fatal instant, a chart showing three lunar phases; a remnant of the days when she held her dazzling receptions, it would relieve her hour of distress with memories of her once-omnipotent splendor.

Chènevillot lined the mattress in question with an electrocution device that lightning alone would activate.

XXI

THE MONTALESCOTS HAD SOON grown accustomed to their new residence. Louise delved passionately into her amazing discovery, while curious Norbert explored the Behuliphruen or the right bank of the Tez.

The ever faithful pet magpie won everyone's admiration through its marvelous affection and intelligence; the bird, making new progress every day, reliably performed its mistress's most varied commands.

One day, walking along the Tez, Norbert was attracted by the extreme malleability of a vaguely damp, yellowish earth, of which he promptly gathered a supply. The young man could from then on occupy his time modeling, with his usual facility, delightfully fashioned statuettes, which once dried in the sun acquired the look and consistency of terracotta. Talou, clearly intrigued by these artistic pursuits, seemed to be hatching some plan, which a chance occurrence soon brought to full maturity.

Since our arrival in Ejur, various animals, loaded onto the *Lynceus* to be slaughtered during the voyage, had contributed one by one to our board. Thanks to our parsimonious ship's steward, who was exceedingly thrifty with the precious reserves, several calves still remained to share their companions' fate. The provident cook finally started in on these survivors and one evening served us at dinner, alongside the appetizing slices of the first victim, a platter of finely seasoned calves' lungs. Talou, who by instinctive curiosity had always been partial to our European fare, carefully tasted this dish, whose provenance and appearance when uncooked he immediately wanted to know.

The next day, a sad and anxious Sirdah came to see us on her father's behalf, bearing his laborious directives that she annotated with numerous personal commentaries.

In her opinion, Talou loathed Louise, whose image was still linked in his mind with that of King Yaour. Brother and sister had been mixed up in the same fierce dislike, and the emperor offered them a double exeat only on condition that they perform impossible marvels, whose every detail he had meticulously elaborated in advance with cruel and malicious refinement.

Among the crates and bundles smashed open during the wreck of the *Lynceus* was a huge shipment of toys addressed to a dealer in Buenos Aires. Talou had ordered a demonstration of all these items, which were new to him, and took particular interest in the wind-up toys, whose key he turned himself. He had been especially delighted by a certain railroad that, due to its complex network of easily detachable tracks, rolled with remarkable ease. It was partly this amusing invention that engendered the plan Sirdah had come to detail. Inspired by his last dinner, Talou demanded that poor Norbert create a life-sized statue, fascinating to look at and light enough to roll over two tracks made of that same raw, inconsistent matter the steward had prepared for us the night before, without damaging them in the slightest. In addition, without this time setting any weight requirements, the emperor demanded three articulated sculptures, whose mechanism only the trained magpie would activate, with its beak or claws.

If these conditions were fulfilled—in addition to a successful demonstration of the device Louise was working to complete—the siblings would win their freedom and could join our detachment when we left for Porto Novo.

Despite the harshness of this ultimatum, Louise, rather than giving in to despair, understood that her duty was to encourage and guide Norbert.

The first thing was to find a material light, pliable, and resistant enough to be used to erect an almost weightless statue. We rummaged haphazardly through the luggage taken from the ship, and Louise suddenly let out a cry of joy on discovering several large parcels stuffed with uniformly black whalebone corset stays. Reading the labels, we saw that the shipment had been sent by a liquidation firm, which had probably sold off part of its excess inventory at a discount to some American manufacturer.

The stakes being too important to stand on ceremony, Louise made away with the merchandise, prepared to reimburse the addressee later on if need be.

To choose the fascinating subject the emperor demanded, the young woman had only to search her memory, copiously enriched by her countless readings. She recalled an anecdote related by Thucydides in his *History of the Peloponnesian War*, in a brief preamble in which the illustrious chronicler seeks to compare the Athenian character with the Spartan mentality.

Here is the substance of the classical tale translated by so many generations of schoolboys:

A rich Lacedemonian named Ktenas had in his service a large number of helots.

Instead of despising these slaves, whom his compatriots considered mere beasts of burden, Ktenas wanted to raise their moral and intellectual level by educating them. His noble, humanitarian goal was to make them his equals, and in order to force the laziest among them to study he resorted to severe punishments, not hesitating at times to use his power over life and death.

Without a doubt, the most recalcitrant of the group was a certain Saridakis, who, as ungifted as he was apathetic, shamelessly let himself be overtaken by all his comrades.

Despite the harshest reprimands, Saridakis made no progress, vainly devoting hours on end to the simple conjugation of auxiliary verbs.

Ktenas saw in this manifestation of utter inability the chance to strike fear into the minds of his pupils.

He gave Saridakis three days to memorize once and for all the verb εἰμί. After that, the helot would recite his lesson before all his fellow students and in front of Ktenas, whose hand, clutching a stiletto, would run through the laggard's heart at the first sign of error.

Knowing that the master meant what he said, Saridakis cudgeled his brains and made heroic efforts to prepare for the supreme test.

On the appointed day, Ktenas, assembling his slaves, placed himself near Saridakis, aiming the tip of his blade at the unfortunate's chest. The scene was brief: the pupil made a stupid mistake in the dual of the aorist, and a muffled thud was suddenly heard in the midst of an anxious silence. The helot, pierced to the heart, spun a moment before falling dead at the feet of his inexorable judge.

Louise unhesitatingly adopted this stirring model. Aided by his sister's directions, Norbert managed to erect a lightweight statue on wheels, using the flexible stays. The nails and tools he needed for the task were supplied by Chènevillot, who himself built a well-calibrated bascule, made to receive the delicate and fragile train tracks at the last minute. To complete the work, so full of impressive vigor, Louise traced in white letters on the black plinth a large explanatory title, preceding the famous dual conjugation on the helot's dying lips.

The emperor's other order, effigies with moving parts, demanded three new subjects.

Louise was an enthusiastic admirer of Kant, portraits of whom vividly crowded her mind. Under her supervision, Norbert executed a bust of the famous philosopher, carefully hollowing out the inside of the block to leave only a wafer-thin layer of clay at the top of the skull. Chènevillot fitted the cranial cavity with a system of powerful reflector lamps, whose brightness was meant to symbolize the ingenious flames of some luminous thought.

Next, Louise took inspiration from an old Breton legend that touchingly related the heroic and celebrated subterfuge of the nun Perpetua, who preferred to risk her own life rather than betray two fugitives hiding in her convent to the thugs pursuing them.

This time it was an entire group of figures that Norbert had to model with skill and patience.

Finally, the young man, his sister's docile instrument, portrayed the regent bowing before Louis XV; Louise, a student of history, liked the paradox contained in this humble sign of respect shown to a child by the most powerful man in the kingdom.

Each sculpture was provided with a very simple mechanism, specially adapted to the beak or claws of the magpie, whose training demanded far more effort than they ever would have expected.

Indeed, this new task was much more complex than the insignificant tours de force the bird had performed up until then. Its movements had to be executed in the correct order without guidance or prompting, and it was hard for the creature to retain such a long series of varied and precise instructions. Norbert helped his sister with the laborious instruction, which they had to get just right.

Meanwhile, Louise actively pursued her chemical endeavors, whose final adjustments demanded a workplace built with very particular lighting conditions in mind.

At her request, Chènevillot constructed a kind of very narrow cabin, whose walls, prudently devoid of openings, would let no sunshine through.

Only a very attenuated yellowish light was to be allowed into the confines of the laboratory; but a tinted window, even with the densest coating, would surely have produced disastrous glimmers on the strange photosensitive plate Louise was preparing.

The solution to the problem was found by Juillard, who had sat in on Louise's conversations with the architect.

The scholar's crate of books contained a precious copy of *The Fair Maid of Perth*, from the first edition of the celebrated work. The pages, more than a century old, were completely yellowed and could serve to filter and muffle the blinding brightness of the African sun.

Despite the incalculable price of this extremely rare item, Juillard unhesitatingly offered it to the student, who, finding it perfectly suited to her designs, thanked the kind donor warmly.

Chènevillot trimmed the pages into tiles, which, laid down in multiple layers and held in place by a fine framework, composed the top of the cabin. A skylight cut in the middle of this light roofing allowed the prisoner to emerge once in a while for some fresh air, after having scrupulously covered her various utensils and ingredients. Prudence winning out over comfort in such a serious matter, it was through this one opening, the sole egress by design, that Louise would enter and exit, using two small folding ladders with flat steps that the architect fashioned for this purpose. The slightest infiltration of light could in fact compromise the success of the entire project, and a roof skylight was more likely than any side door to form a hermetic seal, aided by its own weight.

The cabin stood on Trophy Square, not far from the Stock Exchange, from which Norbert's precisely aligned statues separated it. Before installing the roof, Chènevillot had arranged the interior, which contained one of the folding ladders, a portable chair, and a worktable laden with the equipment necessary for the marvelous discovery.

From then on, Louise spent the better part of her days shut up in the laboratory, among her concoctions, vials, and plants; she used the rest of her time to finish training the magpie, which faithfully kept her company inside the fragile hideaway.

When people asked the young woman about the success of her chemical mixtures, she seemed cheerful and optimistic.

XXII

I<small>T WAS DURING THESE</small> events that Seil-kor reappeared at the head of his band of black porters, who were buckling under the weight of copious goods bought with the ransom money. Each contributor had paid to the best of his means, and the families of the poorest sailors, pooling their savings, had resigned themselves to adding their share as a group.

After a long conference with the emperor, Seil-kor came to deliver the news. The letters we'd drafted had returned a sufficient sum, and on that score our freedom was guaranteed. But one unexpected condition remained to be fulfilled.

Ever since the bloody battle against the Drelchkaffian troops, Talou, seeking solitude beneath the tall trees of the Behuliphruen, had spent many hours composing a number of resounding stanzas which, taking as their subject the victory over Yaour, were to enrich the "Jeroukka" with a supplementary canto entitled "The Battle of the Tez."

Upon his coronation, the emperor would have his troops sing the entire epic; but the new canto, which he'd finished only that morning, was still unfamiliar to the Negro warriors, and long hours of study would be needed to teach it to so large a group.

Consequently, Talou assigned Carmichael the task of performing on the appointed day, in his resplendent falsetto, the most recent portion of the opus. Such a choice would have the further advantage of highlighting the unknown stanzas of the vast poem and underscoring this *premiere*, making it truly sensational.

To sing "The Battle of the Tez," the young Marseillais would wear his normal male garb, for Talou wished to be crowned king of Drelchkaff in the same costume he'd worn on the day of his victory, a striking outfit whose shape struck him as particularly majestic. The emperor, moreover, intended to figure in the program himself by singing Dariccelli's *Aubade*.

His explanation finished, Seil-kor handed Carmichael a large sheet of paper that he'd covered with strange but perfectly legible words, their perilous pronunciation faithfully indicated in French characters; it was "The Battle of the Tez," transcribed only moments before by the young Negro under the emperor's dictation.

The tune was supplied by a single, brief aria, which Seil-kor easily taught Carmichael.

Counting on fear to obtain a perfect rendition, Talou threatened that the slightest lapse in memory would be punished by three long hours of detention. During that time, Carmichael would practice the canto for a new recital subject to the same conditions, while standing perfectly still and facing the sycamores of Trophy Square under a Negro guard's strict surveillance.

Having obtained the young singer's reluctant consent, Seil-kor, still relaying Talou's mandate, demanded from us some simple advice on the role that Sirdah's thirty-six brothers might play in the coronation ceremony.

It seemed to us that children of that age, all designated as pages, could add to the picturesqueness of the scene by carrying the long train of their father's gown at the moment when the latter strode majestically toward the altar. But only six at most could fit around the long hem, and so it was necessary to draw lots. Chènevillot therefore agreed to fashion a large gaming die that would serve to elect the winners from among the boys, split into six rows.

As for the emperor's ten wives, they were to perform the Luenn'chetuz, a hieratic dance intimately linked with certain rare and notable rites.

To finish, Seil-kor showed us a long strip of tightly rolled parchment, covered with Talou's rudimentary drawings of warring forces.

During his campaigns, the emperor took daily notes using only images instead of words, setting down in sketches, while his memory was still fresh and precise, the various operations his troops had accomplished.

Once back in the capital, he used this strategic guide to compose his verses; in short, we had before our eyes the true canvas of the "Jeroukka."

Having discovered in our baggage a recording barometer whose workings he'd had explained to him, Talou dreamed of seeing his drawings parade by automatically on the spindles of the precious instrument.

La Billaudière-Maisonnial, accustomed to delicate work, volunteered to fulfill the imperial desire; he removed the fragile mechanism from the barometer casing and accelerated its movement, and soon an ingenious device, carrying the roll of parchment, was set to work near the Incomparables' stage.

XXIII

SEVERAL MORE DAYS PASSED, during which Carmichael learned to parrot the barbaric text of "The Battle of the Tez." Guided by Seilkor, he had easily retained the strange tune adapted to the stanzas and felt confident that he was up to the task of singing this new fragment of the "Jeroukka."

At the Stock Exchange, *the Carmichael* had not stopped climbing in value ever since a Ponukelean song, with its prodigiously bizarre words and music, had replaced the young Marseillais's standard repertoire.

As the great day approached, the speculations picked up momentum, and a final session, which promised to be intense, was scheduled for just before the start of the performances.

Eager to contribute to the magnificence of the gala by weaving the emperor a rich sacramental cloak, Bedu assembled his famous loom, which had suffered no damage in the shipwreck, astride the Tez.

He drew up a map of Africa surrounded by a vast area of ocean and marked all the territories now under Talou's scepter in glaring red.

The fact that the southern border of Drelchkaff was not clearly defined left the artist free license, and out of flattery he extended the kingdom all the way to the Cape of Good Hope, whose name he spelled out in capitals.

Once the paddles were adjusted, the machine was set in motion, and soon a heavy ceremonial garment was ready to be placed over the sovereign's shoulders at the solemn moment.

Encouraged by this success, Bedu decided to prepare a surprise for Sirdah, who had always shown us such kindness and devotion.

He designed a sumptuous pattern for a cape, to be decorated with many arresting scenes from the biblical Flood.

The inventor intended to fine-tune the device on the very morning of the coronation and have it operate in Sirdah's presence, for after her cure the girl would surely enjoy watching the vision provided by the magical workings of the miraculous machine.

As Bashkou's operation was to take place at nightfall, an acetylene beacon, found among the *Lynceus*'s gear and installed at water's edge, would project onto the machine the dazzling beams emitted by its reflector.

To enhance the portion of the spectacle involving the river, Fluxier decided to create several blue lozenges, which, when tossed into the currents, would create a variety of distinct and fleeting images on the water's surface.

Before setting to work, he consulted us collectively on the choice of subjects to treat and received a plethora of suggestions, from which he retained only the following:

1. Perseus brandishing the head of Medusa.

2. A Spanish feast accompanied by frenetic dancing.

3. The legend of the poet Giapalù, who, having come to seek inspiration at the picturesque site where the Var sprang from the ground, let his secrets be discovered by the old river, leaning forward in curiosity to read over his shoulder. The next day, the babbling currents recited his new verses from the source all the way to the river's mouth; bearing the stamp of genius, they immediately spread throughout the land unattributed. The dumbfounded Giapalù tried in vain to establish his authorship but was treated as a fraud, and the poor poet died of grief without ever having known fame.

4. A peculiarity of the Land of Cockaigne concerning the regu-

larity of the wind, which provided inhabitants with the exact time without having to wind up or maintain a clock.

5. A piquant tale involving the Prince of Conti, which he himself had discreetly related in his correspondence:

In the spring of 1695, François-Louis de Bourbon, the Prince of Conti, was the guest of an octogenarian, the Marquis of ***, whose château stood in the middle of a vast, shaded park.

The previous year, the marquis had married a young woman of whom he was keenly jealous, even though the love he showed her was purely paternal.

Every night, the Prince of Conti went to join the marquise, whose twenty years could not make do with such incessant solitude.

These visits required infinite precautions. To contrive a pretext for his sudden absence in case of discovery, the prince let loose in the park, before each rendezvous, a certain trained jay, which had long been used to accompanying him on all his travels.

One night, having grown suspicious, the marquis went to knock on the door of his guest's chamber; obtaining no reply, he entered the empty room and saw the missing man's clothes lying on a chest.

The octogenarian went straight to his wife's room and demanded she let him in immediately. The marquise silently opened and closed her window, allowing her lover to let himself drop gently to the ground. This maneuver having taken but a few seconds, the bolt of her door could be pulled back in time.

The jealous old man barged in without a word and vainly checked every corner of the room. After which, the possibility of escape through the window having occurred to him, he stalked out of the château and began hunting through the park.

Soon he discovered the half-dressed Conti, who said he was searching for his escaped jay.

The marquis decided to accompany his guest to see if he was telling the truth. After several steps, the prince cried, "There he is!"—

pointing at the trained bird sitting on a branch, who at the first call came to perch on his finger.

The old man's doubts were immediately allayed, and the marquise's honor remained intact.

Armed with these five subjects, Fuxier applied to his block of blue material the meticulous process he'd already completed for the internal modeling of the red lozenges used in the Shakespearean scene.

XXIV

ONE MORNING, SEIL-KOR'S DEVOTION to the emperor nearly proved fatal. At around ten o'clock, the young man was carried to Trophy Square, covered in blood, and put in the care of Dr. Leflaive.

His injury had been caused by a sudden and unexpected event.

Just minutes earlier, the traitor Gaiz-duh had managed to escape. Seil-kor, witnessing this bold move, had run after the fugitive, whom he'd soon caught and seized by the left arm.

Gaiz-duh, whose right hand clasped a knife, had twisted around in fury and struck Seil-kor in the head; the slight delay caused by this brief struggle had given the guards time to secure the prisoner and bring back the wounded man.

Dr. Leflaive bandaged the wound and promised to save the patient's life.

By the next day, he was out of mortal danger, but soon began showing signs of mental disturbance owing to a serious lesion in the brain. Indeed, Seil-kor had lost his memory and could not recognize anyone's face.

Darriand, visiting the patient, saw a marvelous opportunity to effect a miracle using his hypnotic plants. Possessing several rolls of blank celluloid, he asked Bedu to paint on one of those long, supple, transparent strips a certain number of scenes taken from the period of Seil-kor's life he recalled most vividly.

The idyll with Nina was the clear choice. Transported back to his time with his soulmate, whom he'd believe truly present before his eyes, the young Negro might experience a salutary emotion liable to restore his faculties in a single stroke.

Among the relics preserved by the poor lunatic, they found a large photograph of Nina in frontal view, which provided Bedu with precious details.

Having finished the preparation of his lozenges, Fuxier, yielding to our entreaties, gladly agreed to complete his series of experiments by ripening a cluster of grapes, each of which would contain a different subject.

We cast about for new inspirations. Free to set the size of the bunch as he wished, Fuxier fixed the number of grapes at ten and chose the following themes:

1. A glimpse of Celtic Gaul.

2. The famous vision of Count Valtguire, who in a dream saw a demon sawing at the body of his mortal enemy, Eudes, son of Robert the Strong. Encouraged by this sign, which seemed to promise him the support of Heaven by dooming his adversary to death and damnation, Valtguire, throwing caution to the winds, redoubled the intensity of the bloody battle he was waging against Eudes and his partisans. This rashness proved fatal and led to his capture followed by immediate beheading.

3. An evocation of ancient Rome in the time of its greatest splendor, symbolized by the games of the Circus.

4. Napoleon, victorious in Spain, but cursed by a populace seething with revolt.

5. A gospel of Saint Luke relating three miracles performed by Jesus on the children of the Guedaliels, whose humble hut, illuminated by the presence of the divine Master, was suddenly filled with joyous echoes after having witnessed the bitterest grief. Two days before the celestial visit, the oldest child, a boy of fifteen, pale and weak, had suddenly succumbed while plying his trade as a basket weaver. Stretched out on his pallet, he still held in his fingers the long wicker strand he'd been braiding at the fatal instant. Of the two

sisters the deceased had cherished, the first had fallen mute from her distress at the sight of the corpse, while the youngest, a poor invalid, ugly and hunchbacked, was no consolation to her parents for their dual misfortune. Upon entering, Jesus stretched his hand toward the comely aphonic, who, the moment she was cured, sang a long, full-throated trill that seemed to announce the return of joy and hope. A second gesture of the all-powerful hand, this time directed toward the deathbed, restored life to the dead boy, who, taking up his interrupted task, bent and knotted in his practiced fingers the supple and docile wicker strand. At the same moment, a new miracle was revealed to the dazzled parents' eyes: Jesus had just brushed his finger over the gentle invalid, now left beautiful and standing erect.

6. The Ballad of Hans the Robust, a legendary woodsman from the Black Forest, who despite his advanced age could carry more tree trunks and bundles on his shoulders than his six sons put together.

7. A passage from *Emile*, in which Jean-Jacques Rousseau lengthily describes the first stirrings of desire felt by his hero upon seeing a young stranger in a poppy-colored dress seated in her doorway.

8. A reproduction of Raphael's painting *St. Michael Vanquishing Satan*.

Armed with these materials, Fuxier set to work, offering us the captivating sight of his weird and patient method.

Sitting before his vine-stock, he burrowed into the buds of the future cluster with the help of extremely fine steel instruments—the very same ones he'd used to fashion the interior of his lozenges.

Sometimes he pulled from a minuscule box various coloring agents that would infuse the figures as they developed.

For hours he pursued his miraculous labors, focusing exclusively on the precise spot from which the grapes would emerge, deprived in advance of their seeds by this terrible trituration.

XXV

WHEN EVERYONE HAD DECLARED himself ready, Talou set the date of the coronation and chose in the Ponukelean calendar the day equivalent to June 25th.

On the 24th, the ichthyologist Martignon, who had never ceased his excursions along the coastlines, returned highly agitated by a surprising discovery he'd just made after a deep dive.

He was gingerly carrying in both arms an aquarium entirely concealed by a light plaid blanket, and refused to show us its contents so as not to spoil the effect the next day.

This event caused a notable volatility in *the Martignon* during the last session of speculation.

On June 25th, at two o'clock in the afternoon, everyone made final preparations for the grand ceremony.

A cruet, standing in for the Holy Ampulla, was borrowed from one of the *Lynceus*'s salad services and placed on the altar for Talou, whom Juillard had shown how to anoint his forehead.

Next to the flask hung a wide sheet of parchment, a kind of bull, dictated by the emperor to Rao, that contained a solemn proclamation.

Balbet, planning an extraordinary test of marksmanship, drove a long stake trimmed by one of Chènevillot's workmen into the ground, just to the right of the altar; behind it, standing in the desired axis, a sycamore trunk planed vertically to the architect's specifications provided a backstop to halt the bullets, thus avoiding troublesome ricochets.

On the upper tip of the stake the celebrated marksman placed a soft-boiled egg, which the ship's steward, on his instructions, had cooked so as to solidify the white while scrupulously preserving the runniness of the yolk.

The perfectly fresh egg had just been laid by one of the hens loaded onto the *Lynceus* in Marseille.

Olga Chervonenkhov, her hair and bust decorated with foliage gathered in the Behuliphruen, had decked herself out in a painstakingly improvised dancer's costume. Hector Boucharessas had given her one of his spare leotards, which, patiently cut open and restitched, now imprisoned the legs and thighs of the imposing matron; several window curtains, chosen from the stock of the upholsterer Beaucreau, had furnished the tulle for her tutu, and the whole was completed by a deeply plunging sky-blue corsage, originally from a formal gown the Livonian had brought to wear at evening balls in the great theaters of Buenos Aires.

In earlier days, when performing The Nymph's Dance, the then lithe and light Olga would come onstage riding a fawn, amid a deep and untamed forest décor. Wishing to recreate her famous entrance, the ex-ballerina planned to ride in on Sladki; a trial run the previous day had proven that the good-natured animal was strong enough to support its mistress's enormous girth for a little while.

While awaiting showtime, the tame and faithful elk plodded calmly at the Livonian's side.

That very morning Bedu had completed the painted filmstrip intended to reawaken Seil-kor's slumbering memory. Wishing to obtain very clear projections, Darriand decided to try the experiment after nightfall, and to bring in the pillbox hat, mask, and ruff that Nina had once cut out of paper; contact with these three objects, religiously preserved by the precocious suitor, might greatly assist the sudden resurrection of his former faculties.

Thanks to her assiduous efforts, Louise Montalescot had found the solution to the problem she'd sought for so long. By spending the entire night in her laboratory, sufficiently lit by the moon that was now full and extremely bright, the young woman was certain of completing her device, which would be fully operational by daybreak. The poetic glow of dawn would lend itself perfectly to a first attempt at automatic reproduction, and Talou, filled with curiosity, gave his consent to Sirdah, who had been sent to request his permission for a morning experiment.

As for the magpie, it now played its part with infallible sureness, and the emperor had only to choose a time to put it to the test. The helot statue itself was to be moved by the bird over two train tracks that Norbert had just fashioned from a provision of calves' lungs requisitioned from the ship's steward.

As four o'clock neared, Mossem, Rul, Gaiz-duh, and Jizme were transferred to the prison that Chènevillot had built.

Rao, who held the key, went to recruit a handful of slaves to help him in his role as organizer, with which the emperor had earlier entrusted him.

Soon Talou appeared in full regalia.

Everyone was present for the performance, including the Ponukelean troops assigned to sing the "Jeroukka."

Sensing that the solemn moment was nigh, Juillard addressed our group, already gathered at the south of the esplanade.

In awarding the decorations, the historian intended to rely solely on the impressions of the Negro public, whose naïve instincts struck him as more liable to provide a sincere, unbiased judgment.

As our applause could influence the native audience and, more to the point, interfere with the prize giver's observational duties, we were asked to observe a strict silence after each exhibition.

This recommendation had the added advantage of curbing the self-interested enthusiasm that a given candidate for the great sash of the Delta might inspire in certain of his shareholders.

At the last moment, wishing to make a spectacular entrance, the emperor ordered Rao to organize a procession outside Trophy Square that would advance slowly in a predetermined order.

We all fell silent, and it is now known how the coronation ceremony and gala performances, which Louise Montalescot's experiment completed after a peaceful night's rest, were followed by the irritating detention that Carmichael was now serving in my company under the watchful eye of a native sentinel.

XXVI

FOR THREE LONG HOURS, the young Marseillais, dreading a second punishment, had been studiously practicing "The Battle of the Tez," which he now murmured impeccably without my being able to catch a single mistake in the script onto which the sycamore's branches cast their shade.

Talou suddenly appeared in the distance, striding toward us with Sirdah beside him.

The emperor had come in person to free the marvelous performer, whom he wished to subject to a second trial without further ado.

Delighted to be put to the test while his memory was fresh and his confidence high, Carmichael, still keeping to the soprano register, began singing his incomprehensible piece self-assuredly, articulating it right to the end this time without a hint of error.

Dazzled by this perfect execution, Talou headed back to the imperial hut, charging Sirdah to convey to the interested party his complete satisfaction.

Liberated by this welcome verdict, Carmichael grabbed from my hands the infernal text that was now a reminder of so much anxious and tedious labor, and gleefully ripped it to shreds.

Silently condoning his innocent gesture of revenge, I left Trophy Square with him to attend to various chores related to packing, which there was now no reason to put off.

Our departure took place that same day, at the beginning of the afternoon. The Montalescots joined our procession, which, led by a fully recovered Seil-kor, included all the castaways from the *Lynceus*.

Talou had put at our disposal a certain number of natives ordered to carry our provisions and the few bags that were left us.

A stretcher lifted by four Negroes was reserved for Olga Chervonenkhov, who was still suffering from her muscle cramp.

A ten-day walk brought us to Porto Novo; there, showered with well-deserved gratitude for his loyal services, Seil-kor bade us farewell so that he and his retinue could head back to Ejur.

The captain of a large vessel about to embark for Marseille agreed to repatriate us. We were indeed all eager to return to France, for after such harrowing adventures it was out of the question to go straight to South America.

The crossing was uneventful, and on July 19th we took leave of each other on Quai de la Joliette, after a cordial exchange of handshakes from which only Tancrède Boucharessas had to refrain.

RAYMOND ROUSSEL was born in Paris in 1877. His writings, including the novels *Impressions of Africa* and *Locus Solus*, as well as volumes of poetry and drama, were largely ignored in his lifetime, but have since been championed by the likes of Raymond Queneau, Alain Robbe-Grillet, Georges Perec, Harry Mathews, and John Ashbery. Roussel died under mysterious circumstances in 1933, decades before his work began receiving the popular acceptance he craved.

MARK POLIZZOTTI is the author of *Revolution of the Mind: The Life of André Breton* and monographs on Luis Buñuel and Bob Dylan. He has translated over three dozen books.

PETROS ABATZOGLOU, *What Does Mrs. Freeman Want?*
MICHAL AJVAZ, *The Golden Age.*
   The Other City.
PIERRE ALBERT-BIROT, *Grabinoulor.*
YUZ ALESHKOVSKY, *Kangaroo.*
FELIPE ALFAU, *Chromos.*
   Locos.
IVAN ÂNGELO, *The Celebration.*
   The Tower of Glass.
DAVID ANTIN, *Talking.*
ANTÓNIO LOBO ANTUNES, *Knowledge of Hell.*
ALAIN ARIAS-MISSON, *Theatre of Incest.*
IFTIKHAR ARIF AND WAQAS KHWAJA, EDS., *Modern Poetry of Pakistan.*
JOHN ASHBERY AND JAMES SCHUYLER, *A Nest of Ninnies.*
GABRIELA AVIGUR-ROTEM, *Heatwave and Crazy Birds.*
HEIMRAD BÄCKER, *transcript.*
DJUNA BARNES, *Ladies Almanack.*
   Ryder.
JOHN BARTH, *LETTERS.*
   Sabbatical.
DONALD BARTHELME, *The King.*
   Paradise.
SVETISLAV BASARA, *Chinese Letter.*
RENÉ BELLETTO, *Dying.*
MARK BINELLI, *Sacco and Vanzetti Must Die!*
ANDREI BITOV, *Pushkin House.*
ANDREJ BLATNIK, *You Do Understand.*
LOUIS PAUL BOON, *Chapel Road.*
   My Little War.
   Summer in Termuren.
ROGER BOYLAN, *Killoyle.*
IGNÁCIO DE LOYOLA BRANDÃO, *Anonymous Celebrity.*
   The Good-Bye Angel.
   Teeth under the Sun.
   Zero.
BONNIE BREMSER, *Troia: Mexican Memoirs.*
CHRISTINE BROOKE-ROSE, *Amalgamemnon.*
BRIGID BROPHY, *In Transit.*
MEREDITH BROSNAN, *Mr. Dynamite.*
GERALD L. BRUNS, *Modern Poetry and the Idea of Language.*
EVGENY BUNIMOVICH AND J. KATES, EDS., *Contemporary Russian Poetry: An Anthology.*
GABRIELLE BURTON, *Heartbreak Hotel.*
MICHEL BUTOR, *Degrees.*
   Mobile.
   Portrait of the Artist as a Young Ape.
G. CABRERA INFANTE, *Infante's Inferno.*
   Three Trapped Tigers.
JULIETA CAMPOS, *The Fear of Losing Eurydice.*
ANNE CARSON, *Eros the Bittersweet.*
ORLY CASTEL-BLOOM, *Dolly City.*
CAMILO JOSÉ CELA, *Christ versus Arizona.*
   The Family of Pascual Duarte.
   The Hive.
LOUIS-FERDINAND CÉLINE, *Castle to Castle.*
   Conversations with Professor Y.
   London Bridge.
   Normance.
   North.
   Rigadoon.
HUGO CHARTERIS, *The Tide Is Right.*
JEROME CHARYN, *The Tar Baby.*
ERIC CHEVILLARD, *Demolishing Nisard.*
MARC CHOLODENKO, *Mordechai Schamz.*
JOSHUA COHEN, *Witz.*
EMILY HOLMES COLEMAN, *The Shutter of Snow.*
ROBERT COOVER, *A Night at the Movies.*
STANLEY CRAWFORD, *Log of the S.S. The Mrs Unguentine.*
   Some Instructions to My Wife.
ROBERT CREELEY, *Collected Prose.*
RENÉ CREVEL, *Putting My Foot in It.*
RALPH CUSACK, *Cadenza.*
SUSAN DAITCH, *L.C.*
   Storytown.
NICHOLAS DELBANCO, *The Count of Concord.*
   Sherbrookes.
NIGEL DENNIS, *Cards of Identity.*
PETER DIMOCK, *A Short Rhetoric for Leaving the Family.*
ARIEL DORFMAN, *Konfidenz.*
COLEMAN DOWELL, *The Houses of Children.*
   Island People.
   Too Much Flesh and Jabez.
ARKADII DRAGOMOSHCHENKO, *Dust.*
RIKKI DUCORNET, *The Complete Butcher's Tales.*
   The Fountains of Neptune.
   The Jade Cabinet.
   The One Marvelous Thing.
   Phosphor in Dreamland.
   The Stain.
   The Word "Desire."
WILLIAM EASTLAKE, *The Bamboo Bed.*
   Castle Keep.
   Lyric of the Circle Heart.
JEAN ECHENOZ, *Chopin's Move.*
STANLEY ELKIN, *A Bad Man.*
   Boswell: A Modern Comedy.
   Criers and Kibitzers, Kibitzers and Criers.
   The Dick Gibson Show.
   The Franchiser.
   George Mills.
   The Living End.
   The MacGuffin.
   The Magic Kingdom.
   Mrs. Ted Bliss.
   The Rabbi of Lud.
   Van Gogh's Room at Arles.
ANNIE ERNAUX, *Cleaned Out.*
LAUREN FAIRBANKS, *Muzzle Thyself.*
   Sister Carrie.
LESLIE A. FIEDLER, *Love and Death in the American Novel.*
JUAN FILLOY, *Op Oloop.*
GUSTAVE FLAUBERT, *Bouvard and Pécuchet.*
KASS FLEISHER, *Talking out of School.*
FORD MADOX FORD, *The March of Literature.*
JON FOSSE, *Aliss at the Fire.*
   Melancholy.
MAX FRISCH, *I'm Not Stiller.*
   Man in the Holocene.

CARLOS FUENTES, *Christopher Unborn.*
  Distant Relations.
  Terra Nostra.
  Where the Air Is Clear.
JANICE GALLOWAY, *Foreign Parts.*
  The Trick Is to Keep Breathing.
WILLIAM H. GASS, *Cartesian Sonata*
  and Other Novellas.
  Finding a Form.
  A Temple of Texts.
  The Tunnel.
  Willie Masters' Lonesome Wife.
GÉRARD GAVARRY, *Hoppla! 1 2 3.*
  Making a Novel.
ETIENNE GILSON,
  The Arts of the Beautiful.
  Forms and Substances in the Arts.
C. S. GISCOMBE, *Giscome Road.*
  Here.
  Prairie Style.
DOUGLAS GLOVER, *Bad News of the Heart.*
  The Enamoured Knight.
WITOLD GOMBROWICZ,
  A Kind of Testament.
KAREN ELIZABETH GORDON,
  The Red Shoes.
GEORGI GOSPODINOV, *Natural Novel.*
JUAN GOYTISOLO, *Count Julian.*
  Exiled from Almost Everywhere.
  Juan the Landless.
  Makbara.
  Marks of Identity.
PATRICK GRAINVILLE, *The Cave of Heaven.*
HENRY GREEN, *Back.*
  Blindness.
  Concluding.
  Doting.
  Nothing.
JIŘÍ GRUŠA, *The Questionnaire.*
GABRIEL GUDDING,
  Rhode Island Notebook.
MELA HARTWIG, *Am I a Redundant*
  Human Being?
JOHN HAWKES, *The Passion Artist.*
  Whistlejacket.
ALEKSANDAR HEMON, ED.,
  Best European Fiction.
AIDAN HIGGINS, *A Bestiary.*
  Balcony of Europe.
  Bornholm Night-Ferry.
  Darkling Plain: Texts for the Air.
  Flotsam and Jetsam.
  Langrishe, Go Down.
  Scenes from a Receding Past.
  Windy Arbours.
KEIZO HINO, *Isle of Dreams.*
KAZUSHI HOSAKA, *Plainsong.*
ALDOUS HUXLEY, *Antic Hay.*
  Crome Yellow.
  Point Counter Point.
  Those Barren Leaves.
  Time Must Have a Stop.
NAOYUKI II, *The Shadow of a Blue Cat.*
MIKHAIL IOSSEL AND JEFF PARKER, EDS.,
  Amerika: Russian Writers View the
  United States.
GERT JONKE, *The Distant Sound.*
  Geometric Regional Novel.
  Homage to Czerny.
  The System of Vienna.

JACQUES JOUET, *Mountain R.*
  Savage.
  Upstaged.
CHARLES JULIET, *Conversations with*
  Samuel Beckett and Bram van
  Velde.
MIEKO KANAI, *The Word Book.*
YORAM KANIUK, *Life on Sandpaper.*
HUGH KENNER, *The Counterfeiters.*
  Flaubert, Joyce and Beckett:
  The Stoic Comedians.
  Joyce's Voices.
DANILO KIŠ, *Garden, Ashes.*
  A Tomb for Boris Davidovich.
ANITA KONKKA, *A Fool's Paradise.*
GEORGE KONRÁD, *The City Builder.*
TADEUSZ KONWICKI, *A Minor Apocalypse.*
  The Polish Complex.
MENIS KOUMANDAREAS, *Koula.*
ELAINE KRAF, *The Princess of 72nd Street.*
JIM KRUSOE, *Iceland.*
EWA KURYLUK, *Century 21.*
EMILIO LASCANO TEGUI, *On Elegance*
  While Sleeping.
ERIC LAURRENT, *Do Not Touch.*
HERVÉ LE TELLIER, *The Sextine Chapel.*
  A Thousand Pearls (for a Thousand
  Pennies)
VIOLETTE LEDUC, *La Bâtarde.*
EDOUARD LEVÉ, *Suicide.*
SUZANNE JILL LEVINE, *The Subversive*
  Scribe: Translating Latin
  American Fiction.
DEBORAH LEVY, *Billy and Girl.*
  Pillow Talk in Europe and Other
  Places.
JOSÉ LEZAMA LIMA, *Paradiso.*
ROSA LIKSOM, *Dark Paradise.*
OSMAN LINS, *Avalovara.*
  The Queen of the Prisons of Greece.
ALF MAC LOCHLAINN,
  The Corpus in the Library.
  Out of Focus.
RON LOEWINSOHN, *Magnetic Field(s).*
MINA LOY, *Stories and Essays of Mina Loy.*
BRIAN LYNCH, *The Winner of Sorrow.*
D. KEITH MANO, *Take Five.*
MICHELINE AHARONIAN MARCOM,
  The Mirror in the Well.
BEN MARCUS,
  The Age of Wire and String.
WALLACE MARKFIELD,
  Teitlebaum's Window.
  To an Early Grave.
DAVID MARKSON, *Reader's Block.*
  Springer's Progress.
  Wittgenstein's Mistress.
CAROLE MASO, *AVA.*
LADISLAV MATEJKA AND KRYSTYNA
  POMORSKA, EDS.,
  Readings in Russian Poetics:
  Formalist and Structuralist Views.
HARRY MATHEWS,
  The Case of the Persevering Maltese:
  Collected Essays.
  Cigarettes.
  The Conversions.
  The Human Country: New and
  Collected Stories.
  The Journalist.

My Life in CIA.
Singular Pleasures.
The Sinking of the Odradek
  Stadium.
Tlooth.
20 Lines a Day.
JOSEPH MCELROY,
  Night Soul and Other Stories.
THOMAS MCGONIGLE,
  Going to Patchogue.
ROBERT L. MCLAUGHLIN, ED., *Innovations:*
  An Anthology of
  Modern & Contemporary Fiction.
ABDELWAHAB MEDDEB, *Talismano.*
HERMAN MELVILLE, *The Confidence-Man.*
AMANDA MICHALOPOULOU, *I'd Like.*
STEVEN MILLHAUSER,
  The Barnum Museum.
  In the Penny Arcade.
RALPH J. MILLS, JR.,
  Essays on Poetry.
MOMUS, *The Book of Jokes.*
CHRISTINE MONTALBETTI, *Western.*
OLIVE MOORE, *Spleen.*
NICHOLAS MOSLEY, *Accident.*
  Assassins.
  Catastrophe Practice.
  Children of Darkness and Light.
  Experience and Religion.
  God's Hazard.
  The Hesperides Tree.
  Hopeful Monsters.
  Imago Bird.
  Impossible Object.
  Inventing God.
  Judith.
  Look at the Dark.
  Natalie Natalia.
  Paradoxes of Peace.
  Serpent.
  Time at War.
  The Uses of Slime Mould:
  Essays of Four Decades.
WARREN MOTTE,
  Fables of the Novel: French Fiction
  since 1990.
  Fiction Now: The French Novel in
  the 21st Century.
  Oulipo: A Primer of Potential
  Literature.
YVES NAVARRE, *Our Share of Time.*
  Sweet Tooth.
DOROTHY NELSON, *In Night's City.*
  Tar and Feathers.
ESHKOL NEVO, *Homesick.*
WILFRIDO D. NOLLEDO, *But for the Lovers.*
FLANN O'BRIEN,
  At Swim-Two-Birds.
  At War.
  The Best of Myles.
  The Dalkey Archive.
  Further Cuttings.
  The Hard Life.
  The Poor Mouth.
  The Third Policeman.
CLAUDE OLLIER, *The Mise-en-Scène.*
  Wert and the Life Without End.
PATRIK OUŘEDNÍK, *Europeana.*
  The Opportune Moment, 1855.
BORIS PAHOR, *Necropolis.*

FERNANDO DEL PASO,
  News from the Empire.
  Palinuro of Mexico.
ROBERT PINGET, *The Inquisitory.*
  Mahu or The Material.
  Trio.
MANUEL PUIG,
  Betrayed by Rita Hayworth.
  The Buenos Aires Affair.
  Heartbreak Tango.
RAYMOND QUENEAU, *The Last Days.*
  Odile.
  Pierrot Mon Ami.
  Saint Glinglin.
ANN QUIN, *Berg.*
  Passages.
  Three.
  Tripticks.
ISHMAEL REED,
  The Free-Lance Pallbearers.
  The Last Days of Louisiana Red.
  Ishmael Reed: The Plays.
  Juice!
  Reckless Eyeballing.
  The Terrible Threes.
  The Terrible Twos.
  Yellow Back Radio Broke-Down.
JOÃO UBALDO RIBEIRO, *House of the*
  Fortunate Buddhas.
JEAN RICARDOU, *Place Names.*
RAINER MARIA RILKE, *The Notebooks of*
  Malte Laurids Brigge.
JULIÁN RÍOS, *The House of Ulysses.*
  Larva: A Midsummer Night's Babel.
  Poundemonium.
  Procession of Shadows.
AUGUSTO ROA BASTOS, *I the Supreme.*
DANIÊL ROBBERECHTS,
  Arriving in Avignon.
JEAN ROLIN, *The Explosion of the*
  Radiator Hose.
OLIVIER ROLIN, *Hotel Crystal.*
ALIX CLEO ROUBAUD, *Alix's Journal.*
JACQUES ROUBAUD, *The Form of a*
  City Changes Faster, Alas, Than
  the Human Heart.
  The Great Fire of London.
  Hortense in Exile.
  Hortense Is Abducted.
  The Loop.
  The Plurality of Worlds of Lewis.
  The Princess Hoppy.
  Some Thing Black.
LEON S. ROUDIEZ, *French Fiction Revisited.*
RAYMOND ROUSSEL, *Impressions of Africa.*
VEDRANA RUDAN, *Night.*
STIG SÆTERBAKKEN, *Siamese.*
LYDIE SALVAYRE, *The Company of Ghosts.*
  Everyday Life.
  The Lecture.
  Portrait of the Writer as a
  Domesticated Animal.
  The Power of Flies.
LUIS RAFAEL SÁNCHEZ,
  Macho Camacho's Beat.
SEVERO SARDUY, *Cobra & Maitreya.*
NATHALIE SARRAUTE,
  Do You Hear Them?
  Martereau.
  The Planetarium.

FOR A FULL LIST OF PUBLICATIONS, VISIT:
www.dalkeyarchive.com

SELECTED DALKEY ARCHIVE PAPERBACKS

Printed in the USA
CPSIA information can be obtained
at www.ICGtesting.com
JSHW022210140824
68134JS00018B/978

9 781564 786241